STORM and STEEL

ALSO BY JON SPRUNK

Shadow's Son

Shadow's Lure

Shadow's Master

Blood and Iron

JON SPRUNK

STORM and STEEL

THE BOOK OF THE BLACK EARTH
—— PART TWO ——

an imprint of Prometheus Books
Amherst, NY

Published 2015 by Pyr®, an imprint of Prometheus Books

Cover illustration © Jason Chan
Cover design by Grace M. Conti-Zilsberger
Map by Rhys Davies

Inquiries should be addressed to
Pyr
59 John Glenn Drive
Amherst, New York 14228
VOICE: 716–691–0133
FAX: 716–691–0137
WWW.PYRSF.COM

19 18 17 16 15   5 4 3 2 1

Library of Congress Cataloging-in-Publication Data

Sprunk, Jon, 1970-
    Storm and steel / by Jon Sprunk.
        pages ; cm. — (The book of the black earth ; part 2)
    ISBN 978-1-63388-010-8 (pbk.) — ISBN 978-1-63388-011-5 (e-book)
    I. Title.

PS3619.P78S76 2015
813'.6—dc23
                                                                    2015000805

Printed in the United States of America

This book is lovingly dedicated to my wife, Jenny, and our son, Logan.
And also to Lou Anders, Eddie Schneider, and Rene Sears,
who have supported this project with such love and devotion. I am forever in your debt.

All men are slaves to the gods.

—Kuldean proverb

CHAPTER ONE

It was a night of bad omens.

The mutton they'd eaten for dinner had dripped blood even though it appeared fully cooked. Brother Kelkaus, the house's sergeant-at-arms, broke his foot when the yard bell fell from its yoke. And a black bird had gotten inside the rectory during the evening's vespers, making an awful racket with its cawing and flapping before it could be chased away. So when Captain Appan-Amur left the warm confines of the main keep to perform his first rounds of the night, he was not surprised to see the crimson orb hovering above the city.

A blood moon.

Bats carved through the swarms of nightflies hovering above the grounds of the Chapter House, their leathery wings flapping at the end of every dive to regain altitude. Torches along the compound walls held the night at bay as sentries walked their posts.

Captain Appan pulled his cloak tighter around his shoulders. Winter had arrived early this year, bringing a brittle crispness to the night air. Out in the yard, a squad of his soldier-priests huddled around a flaming brazier. He angled his path to meet them.

"Good evening, Captain," one of the soldiers called out.

"Be at ease, brothers," Appan answered. They made a space for him, and he held out his hands to the flames in a show of camaraderie. "How goes this night's watch?"

They answered in a muffled chorus. No trouble so far, but he could see the tension in their expressions, the wariness in their eyes. Appan took note of it, and then pushed it to the back of his mind where his worries resided. Many of these men were campaign veterans, and they knew how to weather a siege.

With a nod, he left to continue his rounds. His knees creaked as he climbed to the battlements. He would be forty-four this coming spring.

STORM AND STEEL

He stopped at the top to gaze out over the parapet fortifications. Fires flickered in braziers spaced along the streets surrounding the Chapter House where units of the Queen's Guard stood behind wooden mantlets. The siege was going into its third month. The Temple of the Sun destroyed, brought down like a child's sandcastle. Amur's cult evicted from the city by the queen's command. He had burned that decree in the courtyard in front of the entire cohort. He half-recalled a speech about never abandoning their post, and afterward he'd sent a report to Ceasa explaining the situation. His last report, as it turned out. An hour later the first royal troops had arrived outside the house, and the waiting began.

Appan went along the wall-walk, stopping to greet each man on watch with a few words. They were tired, but he was impressed by their morale. He tried to reflect it back to them, although he felt the fool. Their situation was dire. He'd lost more than half his roster when the Temple fell. He barely had enough full-rank brothers left to man the walls, and it was taking its toll. On top of the long shifts for everyone, they had another problem. The Chapter House hadn't been provisioned for an extended siege when the queen's fiat came down. Every morning he went over the inventory with Sergeant-Provost Urlunn. Even cutting back to half rations, as he'd ordered just days into the siege, they had less than a month left before they starved. He had faith they would be relieved before that happened. And if not . . . *then we will die like true soldiers of Amur.*

Appan paused at the northwest tower. Across the street stood the town home of Lord Nidintugal, which had been requisitioned as the headquarters for the queen's forces. Somewhere inside were the scheming lackeys who commanded the siege in Her Majesty's name. He stretched out with his *zoana*, allowing it to trickle through his senses. Through the Kishargal dominion, he could feel the solidity of the stone rampart under his feet and the deep flows of energy that passed under the streets, the hidden lifeblood of the city. He followed those currents to the foundation stones of the enemy headquarters, as he had done a hundred times over these past couple months. All it would take was a few nudges in the right places, and the house would come down like the wrath of the Sun God upon their heads. But he resisted the temptation as he had many times before.

Appan glanced northward out of habit and winced as his gaze searched the empty space in the city skyline where the temple had once stood. He still found it difficult to believe. The temple had been so sturdy and dependable, like the love of a parent. Yet it had been brought down in one night by the queen's pet devil, an evil spirit in human guise if there ever was one. He had never met this "Lord" Horace, though he'd heard enough from the late Menarch Rimesh to know the westerner was the tumor infecting Erugash.

"G'evening, Captain."

Appan nodded to the soldier passing by on his rounds. "Evening, Brother Lurrag. How goes the watch?"

"All's quiet, sir."

Lurrag coughed into the crook of his elbow. He was a big man. Built like an ox, and he possessed a strong gift for wind magic, one of the strongest they'd seen in this Chapter House since Appan took over seven years ago. Some of the brothers whispered that Lurrag might be almost as powerful in the Imuvar dominion as the queen herself. If he had a dozen more like Lurrag, they could scatter the curs skulking outside their gates and break this siege. *And then march on the palace to bring the Harlot Queen to heel.*

Appan nodded. They didn't use salutes during armed conflicts, especially where the enemy could see and pick out the officers. "Carry on."

As the soldier continued on, Appan headed over to the gatehouse. He checked on the brothers on duty before descending back down to the bailey. Everything looked to be in order, and yet an uneasy feeling turned in his stomach. The same sensation he usually felt when a fight was imminent. He glanced along the walls one last time as he walked toward the central keep, half-convinced his nerves were playing tricks on him. *No good allowing my imagination to run—*

He halted in mid-step as one of his sentries on the south wall disappeared. The moon shone down on the city, its screen of clouds temporarily lifted. But he had seen a shadow move to engulf his soldier as if it had come alive and eaten him. The hairs along the back of the captain's neck stood up, tickled by the subtle itch of sorcery in the air. For a brief instant, the urge to run toward the safety of the keep nearly overwhelmed and unmanned him. Then he drew the sword at his side and called upon the full might of his *zoana*. Its power bolstered his courage. But what was his target? Shadows dancing on the walls?

He shouted for lights over the south wall. A few seconds later, spheres of golden light appeared, throwing the house's fortifications into stark relief. The wall-walk was vacant, no sign of the soldier who had been standing there only seconds before. Searching the ramparts for his missing soldier as shouts called out across the compound, Appan ran toward the nearest stairway. He was about to shout the alarm-sign when he felt a burst of magical power. A rent in the immaterial fabric of the Other world, followed by a quaver in the air as if a vast presence had just arrived inside the house. He turned at a flicker of movement on the edge of his vision and watched in dread as the sentry atop the southeast tower vanished inside an undulating wall of shadow. Appan could not stop the curse that whispered from his lips. "Gods' blood . . ."

By Amur's holy name, what deviltry is this?

At his call, more light-orbs appeared all across the bailey. The repaired yard bell began to ring. While his men focused on banishing the darkness, he scanned the walls. The south and west wall were bare. Priest-soldiers emerged from the barracks, many of them only half-dressed, but every man carried a weapon. He directed them to take up the empty sentry positions as he climbed to the top of the wall. By the time he reached the top he was sweating under his armor despite the coolness of the night.

He spared a quick glance over the wall. In the street, the queen's troops were watching, but he was surprised to see they weren't massing in formation. He'd assumed this shadow-play was the prelude to an attack. *Don't be lulled. This could be the work of the foreign devil. The Gods only know what cursed sorcery he possesses.*

Mindful that the lights made him an inviting target to all the archers below, Appan kept his head down. He was calling out to his men to be vigilant when an icy chill ran down his back. A light-orb over the eastern wall fizzled out like a snuffed candlewick. Darkness rushed over that section of the wall. He started to run in that direction, pressing past his men who watched with uncertainty, when another ball of magical light disappeared over the southeast tower. The captain stopped as all the light-orbs between him and the tower vanished, plunging half the compound into darkness.

Sweat cooled on his forehead and down the back of his neck. The tide of fear he had beaten down began to rise again, inching up from his stomach. He reached down with his *zoana*, into the very bones of the stone ramparts beneath his feet, but he had nowhere to go with the energy. Nothing to fight. Then he noticed things in the darkness as his night vision returned. Gray figures shambled like hunchback wraiths along the battlements. They appeared in several places at once, and every priest-soldier they touched fell senseless at their feet. Appan focused his wrath. With a prayer to the Sun Lord on his lips, he unleashed his power.

The parapet shuddered as the shockwave ran along its length. The cracks of shattering stone nearly deafened him as the battlements of the southeastern tower exploded. A cloud of dust filled the sky. One of his soldiers summoned a new light-orb in the heart of the shadowed area. Its sudden luminance showed the extent of the devastation. The allure atop the wall had collapsed for twenty paces on either side of the tower. Tattered crimson uniforms were strewn amid the rubble below. Appan said a silent prayer for his fallen brothers and commended their souls to paradise as he looked for the gray ghosts. His chest tightened as he found no trace of them. They had vanished as quickly as they arrived. The earth groaned as the tower shifted.

A muffled cry made Appan turn. The brothers on the wall behind him lay slumped at their posts. He started to call out for reinforcements when his gaze swept across the grounds. Priest-soldiers littered the courtyard, sprawled and slumped over each other. None of them moved. Not a sound broke the silence over the Chapter House, except the whisper of the breeze. Appan swallowed. He was alone.

A rush of cold air blew over him. It smelled faintly of old rot like a moldering tomb. Shivering, he tried to extend his *zoana* around him in a tight cocoon of protection, but it was gone. He reached for the power that had been a part of him his entire life, which he had painstakingly cultivated under the tutelage of his superiors until he became a living weapon consecrated to Amur. There was nothing inside him, as if something had reached inside and hollowed him out. Only his decades of training and rigid self-discipline kept him from screaming in frustration. And then he saw it. A shadow in the courtyard. Not gray, but black like a spike of darkness fallen from the night sky. Then it moved, and Appan saw the ripple of fabric. A long robe, its hem brushing the ground. A deep cowl that obscured the face. No regalia or sigils on its clothing, nothing that reflected a sliver of light.

Appan pointed his sword. "Begone from this holy house, spirit of evil. In the name of Amur, I cast you out!"

The figure stepped forward. Its voice slithered across the yard in a whisper like silk sliding over bare steel. "The time for posturing is over, Captain. I have come with a message for your hierarchs."

Appan clenched his jaws until his teeth ached. At the critical hour, he had failed the men under his command. It was a shame he knew he would never forget or forgive, but he swore to himself that he would one day have vengeance. "Speak, and I shall deliver your message, demon-spawn."

"Yes, Captain. You will."

A sudden pain sliced through Appan's midsection like he had been cut open by a knife. He clutched his stomach but found only the unbroken bronze scales of his outer armor. There was no blood or sign of injury. With a grimace, he took a step toward the figure in black but halted as another line of agony ripped through his innards. He bent over, gasping for breath. *Lord of Light, shield your servant from this creature of darkness!*

The torment moved through his body in sudden, excruciating bursts. He felt like his guts were being shredded by some unseen torturer. Sticky wetness filled his throat, forcing him to cough, and he stared in shock as a stream of blood poured from his mouth. It spattered on the stones at his feet, as black as tar in the moonlight. His sword dropped from his hand, clattered on the parapet, and fell over the side. Then his balance vanished, and he followed the weapon, tumbling forward through the air. His head spun past his feet and around again.

He landed on his back. Multiple bones shattered on the impact from his ankles all the way up to a meaty crunch at the back of his head. He had no idea how he remained conscious. The pain flooded his brain, too vast to comprehend. He squeezed his eyes shut as he rode the tide. He wanted to scream, but a great weight pressed down on his chest. Blood trickled from his mouth, his nose, and drenched the padded tunic under his armor.

The agony forced his eyes open. The stars glittered above him. He longed to see the sun rise one last time.

Appan looked down past his toes to the figure standing a score of paces away. His killer said nothing. He made no gesture. He merely turned and walked away across the yard. With a last burst of strength, Appan gasped at the departing figure. He couldn't form a word, just a wheezy rattle, as the figure stepped inside a shadow and disappeared.

The locals called it *Labri-Abnu*. The Old Stone. Situated atop a low tor of bare rock, its limestone walls surrounded an elevated platform topped by a brick dome. Round towers protected each of the structure's six corners overlooking the dusty road that cut through the wasted landscape, worn into a knee-deep gully by the wheels of countless wagon trains. The road ran southward along the eastern edge of the Iron Desert until it eventually crawled eastward to the great city of Erugash.

The fortress was so old that no one could remember who had built it. Certainly centuries older than the Akeshian Empire that currently occupied it. Jirom studied the fort through a gap between two large boulders. A cool wind blew down from the north, kicking up dust devils on the lonely plain. The sun touched the horizon. It was almost time.

"Scouts will be back soon."

Jirom nodded as Emanon settled down beside him. The man's nearness was comforting. He wanted to lean closer to feel his lover's warmth but held back. They refrained from personal contact when out in the field.

Emanon was alert, his eyes always moving, across the rebel fighters scattered amid this cluster of rocks, to the fort, to the road. *The burden of command. Better him than me.*

Jirom didn't expect the scouts to bring back any new information. The fort was going to be a tough nut to crack. He tried to settle his nerves, but it was a useless pursuit. They would calm once the bloodletting began. "You sure about this, Em?"

STORM AND STEEL

"What do you mercenaries say," Emanon asked, "when you're about to rush into some damned fool situation? 'We'll eat and drink in hell tonight!'"

Jirom looked sideways at his paramour. "It was just a job, Em. Not some romantic brotherhood where we drank each other's blood and pledged our souls to the cause."

He didn't mention he'd often thought of his fellow mercenaries as brothers, or that he sometimes missed those old bonds. The rebels, for all their zeal, weren't as tightly knit. That was something he thought about often. He had certain skills that were valuable to these men, but they weren't his followers to mold. "If your plan doesn't work, we'll be caught out in the open. Those archers on the walls will cut us down by the score."

"Too late to worry about that, handsome," Emanon whispered in his ear. "It's time."

They crept back through the field of boulders to a gravel-filled depression where sixty fighters in makeshift desert kit—loose tunics and pants, bleached scarves wound around their faces to protect against the sun and wind—waited out of sight. They were hunkered around Yadz as he spun some tale.

"—as big as a packhorse—"

"That's donkey shit, Yadz, and you know it! Ain't no such thing as scorpion men."

"If my da said he saw it, then he did. It was big and black as night with six legs—"

"Now I know yer lying, Yadz! Scorpions got eight legs."

"My da weren't counting the arms, Kasha. So shut yer mouth!"

Jirom slapped the hilt of his sword as he squatted down among them. "Are you stupid fuckers trying to alert every soldier in the country?"

Sheepish glances were passed around as the fighters quieted down. They'd trickled into Emanon's net after the battle at Omikur, a few at a time until he and Jirom decided they had enough to form a decent-sized strike group. Then they started to put Emanon's "master plan" into motion.

It was classic hit-and-run tactics. Every few days they emerged from their desert hideout to attack a different target. They sacked merchant trains and supply convoys, took out small outposts on the edges of the wastes. Jirom devised the tactics, and Emanon led the operations. So far, it had proven to be a good partnership, both on the battlefield and during the rare quiet moments they'd stolen together. Jirom allowed himself to think about those moments, so few when examined from a distance, but each so blindingly precious. Then he pushed them away as the anticipation of combat pulled at him.

This was their most ambitious attack so far, and Jirom had wondered at several points over the past few days if they were pushing too hard. The fortress was well situated and manned with an ample garrison. Jirom had considered pushing Emanon to reconsider, to move the attack to a less formidable target. He believed in the rebels' cause, believed that all men should be free of the yoke of slavery. Yet a part of him wanted to avoid escalating this conflict. There had been something romantic about their paltry campaign for freedom, and he feared that a larger struggle would swallow up too many of the ideals for which these former slaves fought. In the end he'd held his peace. He had promised to trust his captain, and he would. Whatever the outcome.

The scouts arrived like silent ghosts and huddled around him, their heads bent low.

"Nothing unusual happening at the Stone," Mahir said. The scout leader was a big, stocky Isurani who moved with the grace of a dancer. His bushy eyebrows nearly touched as he spoke. "But Seng saw something interesting."

Jirom glanced over at the smallest member of the scout squad. Seng hailed from the east, from some country none of them had ever heard of before. He claimed to have been an explorer searching out new trade routes when the Akeshians captured him and put him in chains. Jirom had a hunch, based on the little man's clandestine abilities, that Seng had been a spy, but he allowed the man to keep to his story. They all had secrets in their past.

"Four wagons approach from the north," Seng said in his soft voice. "Coming fast."

Emanon muttered a long stream of inventive curses. "How did we miss this? Jirom, didn't our source say there weren't any caravans due to come through until next sennight?"

Jirom ignored the question. "What about the escort, Seng?"

"Akeshian medium cavalry. Twoscore."

Emanon's cursing continued. Jirom frowned at the small scout. "Cavalry regulars? Are you sure about that?"

Seng folded his hands over his chest and nodded. "They display the sigil of the yellow mare."

Emanon dismissed the scouts and hunkered down in front of Jirom. "That's the sign of the Golden Charge outfit. Tough bastards. How do you want to handle this?"

Jirom ran his fingers along the hilt of the sword strapped to his side. He had replaced the handle's cord-wrapping with oxhide for a better grip. The smooth leather was reassuring to his touch. "They must be heading for the fort. If they get inside, it almost doubles the size of the garrison. We can't handle that many. We'll have to postpone the assault. With luck, the wagons will move on in a day or two and take their escort with them."

Emanon's left eyebrow rose slightly. It was an expression Jirom found distracting because it made the man look so damned good. "Or . . ."

"Or what?"

"Or we could incorporate this new wrinkle into our plan."

The muscles along Jirom's jaw tightened as he frowned. "How?"

Emanon bent closer and explained his idea. Jirom had to fight not to shake his head as he listened. It was crazy. Foolhardy and reckless. Worst of all, it was completely unscripted. But Emanon made the call, and all Jirom could do was go along with it. They quickly passed the new plan to the squad leaders, adjusted assignments, and gave the signal.

The rebel fighters moved with quiet efficiency through the rocks and onto the plain. Jirom hurried ahead with the advance units. Timing would be critical. The gathering darkness would help, but any errors would alert the fort garrison and end all chance for success.

While Jirom oversaw the positions of the fighters, Seng relayed that the caravan would arrive in five or six minutes. *That's cutting it damned close.*

He could make out a blurry cloud on the road. He wished he had time to plan this better. Pikes and polearms would have been a great help against cavalry, but they had planned for a fort assault, and so he was stuck with the tools at hand.

Mahir came over beside him while the others set up. "This is a bold move, boss."

Jirom nodded as he scanned the array of forces. "Problem, soldier?"

The scout leader shrugged. "Changing plans at the last moment don't exactly make a body feel comfortable."

"Plans change."

"Sure. Only . . ."

"Only what?"

Mahir spat in the dry soil. "A couple of the new recruits have been grumbling."

Jirom turned and looked him in the eye. "Anything I need to worry about?"

"Nope. Not yet, anyways. I just wanted you to know." He winked. "Covering my ass, you know?"

Jirom motioned for him to rejoin his squad. As much as he appreciated the vote of confidence, he wished the rebels didn't place so much trust in him.

Once all the units were in place, Jirom could barely see them. He peered back in the direction of the fort. There was only one place an ambush could be sprung without any chance of alerting the garrison, and that was directly in line with the boulder cluster. Everything looked good. He waited until the last moment before he found himself some cover behind a stunted olive tree.

The ground trembled as the caravan approached. Ten soldiers on horseback rode out front. Seng hadn't been wrong. These were true Akeshian lancers, the flower of the empire's legions. Chain hauberks, round shields, and polished conical helmets rushing past in a storm of gleaming steel. Jirom wiped his forehead. It was too late to reconsider. He had to roll the dice and pray for the best. He didn't have to wait long.

The caravan's vanguard passed by his position just a dozen heartbeats after he found cover. They rode past without slowing or changing their demeanor. Both good signs. Jirom counted in his head. When he reached ten, the first war-cries erupted behind him. He didn't have to look back to know that Emanon and his squads had ambushed the vanguard. The clash of steel and animal screams told the tale.

STORM AND STEEL

Jirom drew his sword. The *assurana* blade gleamed like molten iron in the dim starlight as he ran to intercept the first wagon. A pair of cavalrymen flanked each vehicle. At the first sign of attack, the nearest horsemen couched their lances and put spurs to flanks. They galloped toward the front of the caravan, granting Jirom a clear path to his prize. The oxen bellowed as the driver yanked back on the reins. He reached for something behind his seat, possibly a weapon, but Jirom grabbed him before he could turn back around and hauled him down. A blow from the sword's pommel laid the man out. Jirom jumped up to the driver's bench and slammed home the hand-brake. Only then did he peer into the back of the covered wagon.

Twenty faces stared at him. An entire infantry platoon filled the back of the wagon. Fully armed and armored, they sat on benches on either side of the long bed. Jirom drew back and swung with both hands. The sword's blade chopped through one of the support poles, and the wagon's canvas covering dropped on the sitting soldiers. He stood up and looked around for the closest assistance. Mahir's scouts were engaging a pair of horsemen a dozen paces away. Within seconds, the cavalrymen were down on the ground. Narrow-bladed daggers found the gaps in their armor and helms.

Jirom whistled and motioned to the soldiers fighting free of the canvas. The first infantryman to emerge from the back of the wagon received a clip to the temple with the flat of his sword. Blood flew as the man fell over the side. Then the rest of the soldiers shoved the tarp aside, and Jirom found himself facing a hedge of spears. He dove off the wagon.

A twinge ran across his shoulders as he hit the ground and rolled away. A horse nearly stomped on his head before he could get back to his feet. The soldiers from the wagon jumped down to meet him. Jirom raised his sword as he faced them. Fear exited his mind, and a placid tranquility came over him. The soldiers spread out as they came toward him, their spears held low as if he were a rabid boar preparing to charge them. Jirom remained still, willing to grant them the first move. The faces confronting him were mostly young, lacking many scars. Then he noticed the iron collars around their necks.

Dog soldiers.

For a moment he was back in the queen's training camp, struggling to survive its brutal measures. He had shed his collar, but some part of him would never leave that camp. Inspiration struck him for the second time this night. He lowered his sword.

The dog soldiers glanced at each other. Two of them continued to advance, but the rest held back. Jirom held his ground. A heartbeat later, Mahir's squad rushed from behind the wagon and swarmed over the dog soldiers, knocking them down. Within seconds the soldiers were disarmed and bound in heavy ropes.

Jirom surveyed the rest of the operation. The fighting was all but over now. Most of the cavalrymen had been dragged off their mounts, which evened the odds dramatically. A few soldiers had thrown down their weapons and run off. Jirom gave the signal not to pursue. Far to the north beyond the profile of the fortress, the sky was dark purple verging on black.

He helped the scouts secure the dog soldiers and then moved down the line. The third wagon had also contained an infantry platoon, which the rebels had uncovered and dealt with, albeit with more bloodshed than Mahir's team. The second wagon remained intact, its driver slumped on the front bench with a javelin through his stomach. Jirom didn't see any movement within, but still he was wary as he stepped up to the bench. A quick look revealed there was no one inside. He pulled back the canvas. Three long rectangular boxes sat end to end down the center of the bed. They had been anchored to the floor with steel chains.

Jirom spotted Emanon talking to some of the sergeants near the first wagon. He whistled. Emanon waved back and headed in his direction. "Are you all right?"

Jirom fought the urge to kiss the man on the lips. "Take a look at this."

Emanon hopped inside the wagon to examine the boxes. They were wooden, reinforced at the seams and corners with iron, with two key locks each. Emanon took a war-axe from his belt and attacked the chains securing the middle box. They parted after several blows, and he tossed them aside. The rebel captain raised his axe to smash the locks next, but Jirom held out a hand.

"Wait. What if they're enspelled?"

Emanon lowered the axe to his side. "I don't know much about Akeshian witchery. You think they could be cursed?"

"Perhaps. But they went through a lot of trouble to protect these chests. They must be important."

"Aye. Important."

"What if we—?"

Before Jirom finished his question, Emanon chopped down on one of the locks. The blade of the war-axe lodged in the iron sheathing. Jirom froze in expectation, but nothing happened. "Em, someday that luck of yours is going to fail."

"Probably so." Emanon hacked again, and splinters of wood flew from the box. "But that's why I have you. To pull my sorry ass out of the fire."

When the second lock had been shattered, Emanon heaved open the lid. Jirom clambered up beside him. Emanon's breath hissed between his teeth. "I don't fucking believe it."

Jirom leaned down and lifted an ingot from the box. He borrowed Emanon's axe and scratched the surface of the bar. The steel blade bit deep into the soft metal. He dropped it back in the box with a solid clank. Gold. And if the other two boxes were also filled with ingots, there had to be . . .

"A king's goat-fucking ransom," Emanon said with a laugh.

"Or a queen's."

"Aye. This must have been heading to Erugash. I wager it's tribute from the northern territories meant for Her Majesty's war chest." Emanon closed the lid and sat on it. "And that means we've just stuck a big old finger in her royal eye. She's going to want this back, and badly."

Jirom played out several scenarios in his head. Emanon was right. If this was intended for the royal treasury, the queen was going to be hot to get it back. Thus far the rebellion had survived by living in the shadows, striking at easy targets and fleeing before the empire's might could come down on them. Seizing this booty could change that. "If she wants it back," he said, "she'll have to come get it. And in the meantime, I have some ideas how we can put this to good use."

"Something in the way you say that makes me think you're going to get us in serious trouble."

"Is there any other kind?"

"And what about the Old Stone? If we don't strike now, we won't get the chance later. The gathering is almost upon us."

Emanon had been hearing rumors of a rebel gathering for the past few weeks. Finally, they'd gotten the official word: the captains of the various bands were convening. Ever since, Emanon had been on a tear to hit the Akeshians like never before.

"Leave it. We don't have time." Jirom indicated the storm clouds brewing to the north.

"Shit."

Emanon began shouting orders to depart. The captured lancers were put to death, quickly and without sympathy. The dog soldiers were freed and given the choice to join the rebels or flee on foot. Not surprisingly, most of them chose to stay once their collars were struck off. The rebels and new recruits climbed aboard the wagons and set off.

Sweat dripped down Horace's face, despite the cool breeze blowing across the long, narrow courtyard. It got in his eyes and ran in long rivulets down his naked torso. His skirt clung to his thighs as he circled around the patio's confines, sandals scuffing across the pavestones. His left hand was bunched into a fist, his other splayed open like a fan, both ready to react at the slightest provocation.

Across from him, his opponent circled as well in a long robe of black silk, face hidden under a deep hood. A slender tentacle of water snaked across the courtyard. Horace lowered his right hand to block. A burst of heat erupted from his palm, and the water jet evaporated in a sizzle of steam. He punched with his left fist while visualizing an image of a burning rope. He shaped the *zoana* inside him into a fiery lariat to hurl at his foe. At least, that's what he intended to do. The power refused to take the desired form. The flow sputtered and fought against his control. Before he could compel it to obey, a force seized his ankle. He fell hard on his back with a grunt.

STORM AND STEEL

Horace rolled onto his side and leapt back up, just in time to be struck square in the chest by a swarm of tiny white balls, shoving him back while they exploded against his bare skin in a shower of icy needles. He reacted out of instinct. A barrier of pure Shinar energy formed in front of him, deflecting the remaining cold spheres. Their impacts thudded against the invisible energy and spread webs of frost across its surface. Hissing from the sting of the icy splinters already lodged in his flesh, Horace tried to channel a flow of Imuvar into a sudden gust of wind. He felt the power pressing against his *qa*, building up inside, but again it refused to conform to his control. He grasped for it, and suddenly the *zoana* filled him. Instead of summoning a strong breeze, a streak of bright gold—almost like an impossibly long icicle carved to resemble a tongue of flame—sizzled across the courtyard.

His opponent darted sideways to avoid the evocation, and it struck the wall on the far side of the courtyard, drilling a hole as wide as a bread plate completely through the stone blocks. The edges of the hole were rimed in hoarfrost. Horace stopped and stared. *What in the world just happened?*

Before he got an answer, a sharp pain tore through the center of his chest. Then, not half a heartbeat later, a blast of frigid air swirled around him, freezing the sweat coating his body like he'd been dropped into a barrel of ice water. Bright light blinded his eyes as he felt himself falling. Horace tried to brace himself with his hands, but he fell on his back for a second time. All at once, the *zoana* drained out of him. For a moment, he was consumed by a terrible feeling of loss. Then a shadow loomed above him, blocking out the midday light.

"What say you, Lord Horace?"

Horace raised both hands. "I yield."

Lord Ubar pushed back his hood and squatted beside him. "Are you injured, *Inganaz*?"

He Who Does Not Bleed. The nickname the young lord had given him after the first time he used his power to deflect a chaos storm in the desert, because he did not display the immaculata.

Pinpricks of blood dotted his chest in crimson constellations. "I don't think so. Nothing more than my pride."

He groaned as he climbed to his feet with Ubar's assistance. A wave of dizziness took hold of him, but it passed quickly. For the past couple days they had taken to dueling in the private courtyards of this, the queen's villa in the small oasis town of Hikkak, two days' sail up a northern tributary of the Typhon River. It was Her Majesty's retreat from the city. They had arrived eight days ago—the queen and her private entourage, including some members of the court and a small army of guardsmen. As First Sword, Horace had been required to come along, and he was glad to be away from the city and his official duties for a while.

Lord Ubar had been assigned by the queen to take over his magical tutelage. The queen had decided to retain Ubar in her court, despite his father's treachery. Or perhaps because of it—Horace still did not understand the intricacies of Akeshian politics. In any case, the young lord was smart and capable, in addition to being good company.

Ubar peeled off his robe as he sat down on a tall stool at the edge of the courtyard. A court physician hurried to his side and began binding the several long gashes that covered the young lord's limbs and body. Horace felt a twinge of guilt at the sight. "I'm sorry you have to suffer for my training."

"My teachers used to say we suffer the immaculata because the body is too frail to contain the *zoana*. I don't know if that's true. It was all very metaphysical. Perhaps you are blessed, First Sword."

"I wish there was something I could do to repay you."

"Just learn well." Ubar smiled. "And swiftly."

"I'm trying, but I'm so . . . unsure of myself." He looked over at the hole in the wall. "What was that?"

Ubar nodded toward the newly made cavity. "A complex weaving. I believe it was Girru and Mordab blended together, but there was something else involved as well."

Horace suspected he knew what that extra component was. He could still feel the echo of the void in his chest, wanting to break free. "I can't control it sometimes. It's like the power wants to explode out of me all the time."

"The sage Mesanapuda said all *zoanii* begin as larvae, and it is only through rigorous study and self-examination that we emerge from the cocoon of our own ignorance."

"He sounds like the kind of guy who has an answer for everything."

Horace massaged the back of his head. Exploring his powers was an adventure in frustration. Sometimes he felt so strong, like he could move mountains, but again and again he failed at the simplest tasks. Exercises for young children such as lighting candles required all his concentration, and he still botched it half the time. Duels were the worst experience of all. Time and time again, Ubar bested him because he could not control that strength. At times, he felt like there was an entire world right before his eyes, but he couldn't see it. No wonder Lord Ubar called the Shinar dominion "the unseen realm."

"You are doing better," Ubar said.

Horace tried to laugh, but it came out as a grunt. "You're just being kind. You finished me with ease."

"Not so. I was forced to use every trick and tool in my arsenal to defeat you."

"That's the point. I'm so much stronger than you. I can feel it, sitting here next to you."

"This is true. Your aura shines like the sun. It's almost blinding."

"Exactly. No offense, but I should be able to win every time."

"Battling another *zoanii* requires more than pure strength. It takes control and experience. Much like swordplay, eh? Any brute can swing a sword, but a studied fencer knows how best to ply his blade, how to see an attack coming before it arrives." He darted his hands in front of him like two striking snakes. "How to feint in one direction so that his true offense slides past your guard to strike home."

Horace sighed, and Ubar slapped him on the back. "It will come to you. You must not be impatient. It was difficult for me, too. As a child, I wanted to know everything right away, always trying to run before I could stand. But to unlock the mysteries of the *zoana*, you must still your mind and open your *qa*. Only then will the path be revealed to you."

Horace was tempted to make a terse remark about wisdom being doled out in ambiguous nuggets, but Ubar was only trying to help. It wasn't his fault that no one alive knew how to control the Shinar dominion. In that endeavor, he was well and truly alone.

"Let's go find a cool drink."

They exited the courtyard through an arbor of vines with beautiful orange and pink blossoms that led into the villa's enormous gardens, surrounding them in a riot of colors and scents. Stone pathways wound among beds of well-pruned topiaries and burbling fountains. Birds twittered from hiding places within the foliage, and statues in alabaster, marble, and bronze decorated niches carved from the hedges.

Horace wiped the sweat from his forehead with the back of his arm. Lord Ubar smiled at the gesture. "I find it difficult to believe you are not cold."

"What? This?" Horace looked up at the clear blue sky. "This feels like a fine spring day back in Arnos. You don't know anything about real cold. Snow on the ground, all the streams and lakes frozen solid."

"It sounds dreadful."

"No. The change of the seasons is quite magical. You appreciate the warmer months, for sure, but there's something beautiful about a blanket of fresh snow covering everything, like the world has been reborn in virgin white."

"You miss it."

"I suppose, sometimes. But it's not as simple as being homesick. After my wife and son died, no place truly felt like home. I was happier at sea, to tell you the truth. Then, when I washed ashore here, it was like a new beginning. A fresh start."

On the other side of the garden was a gate leading back into the villa proper. Sunlight gleamed off its high walls and narrow minarets, built of white and red stone.

Ubar paused at the gate. He opened his mouth as if to say something but then closed it.

"Is something wrong?" Horace asked.

"I was not sure how to broach this subject with you, *Inganaz*. Forgive me. I have news that you might find disturbing."

"All right. Just spit it out."

"It concerns the town of Omikur."

An uneasy feeling gripped Horace's stomach. He hadn't heard much of anything about the town since the queen took him on a tour to see the siege firsthand. The memory of the massive storm that had ravaged the crusaders' defenses still haunted him.

"I have heard the royal legions conducted a new assault just days ago."

"Did the town fall?"

"Not yet, *Inganaz*. But it seems to be only a matter of time."

Horace felt the sudden urge to sit down. If Ubar's account was true, then hundreds—perhaps thousands—of soldiers were going to die. The Great Crusade was over, at least for the time being. *What does that mean for me? Should I be angry? Should I want revenge for men I've never met and didn't know? What does it mean if I don't? They were soldiers. They knew the risks when they signed up. But what soldier could understand the risk of Akeshian sorcery?*

As the moments piled up, Horace realized he wasn't angry. The feelings stirring inside him were a mélange of sorrow and disgust. Those lives were being wasted. Fathers, brothers, sons—all dying because their rulers could not find a peaceful way to resolve their disputes.

"*Kanadu*," he said. *Thank you.* "I'm glad you told me. It is . . . an unfortunate affair."

Horace reached for the handle, but the gate into the villa opened before him, and a man carrying a thick leather valise walked through. Mezim was his new secretary. Nearly a head shorter than Horace, with dark bronze skin, Mezim wore a long skirt of white linen with a straight red border, as befitted a member of the *khalata* caste of freed slaves.

After he was named First Sword, Horace soon realized how much responsibility the post entailed. He'd made inquiries and been furnished with someone to help him navigate his duties. Mezim understood the Akeshian system of government backward and forward. Every day Horace said a prayer of thanks for him.

The secretary bowed when he saw them. "Lord Horace, pardon my interruption. I have been searching for you."

Ubar nodded to Horace. "I will see you later, *Inganaz*."

"Tomorrow?" Horace asked. "At the third bell?"

"Very good."

They clasped forearms, and then Lord Ubar went inside.

Mezim handed Horace a bundle of flattened scrolls. "I have some dispatches from the city. As well as a petition from the royal armory requesting that your lordship approve the purchase of five tons of—"

Horace hadn't been listening. "What do you know about Omikur? It's an outpost town—"

"Sixteen leagues northwest of Erugash on the fringe of the Iron Desert," Mezim finished for him. "*Ai, Belum.* I am familiar with the location. I assume you are referring to the recent attack on said town?"

"What do you know about it?"

"Nothing was mentioned in today's reports. Shall I request a detailed update from Lord Dipatusu?"

"No, don't bother the High General."

"As you wish."

Horace entered the villa, and a chill touched him as he entered the huge house. The queen's villa covered a parcel of land the size of a city block with numerous abutting outbuildings.

"Her Majesty seems well pleased by the recent developments in the war effort," Mezim said, following behind him.

Yes. She would be.

Horace stopped in the middle of a broad corridor, flanked on both sides by caryatids of nude women. He wondered if this could be his opportunity to build a bridge between Akeshia and the West now that the invasion had been blunted. Both sides might be willing to come to the bargaining table, but he needed a lever, something to convince the queen of his good intentions.

Mezim juggled the documents in his arms until he came up with a particular scroll. "Your inquiry of Omikur reminds me. I have information about that other matter."

"Hmmm? Are you talking about Jirom?"

The first assignment he gave to Mezim when he hired him was to track down Jirom's whereabouts. They'd been able to confirm that Jirom was pressed into the royal military training camp, but the trail went cold after that. No one in the queen's court was able, or willing, to share the information. Horace had been told by various officials that the legions did not keep records for dog soldiers, the derogatory term they used for slaves drafted into the royal army, but he hadn't believed it for a minute. He'd seen firsthand how meticulous the Akeshians were about recording everything, from the most menial things like shopping lists and street repairs. Somewhere Jirom's name was on a list, and he intended to find it.

Horace didn't like how Mezim had prefaced his remark. "Don't tell me . . ."

"I have confirmation that a slave by that name was transferred to Omikur a little more than three months ago."

That would have been right before the Tammuris.

"Forgive me, *Belum*," Mezim said. "But I have found nothing after that point. The siege appears to have been a rather messy affair, with many dead and missing on both sides. The commanders of the Third Legion report they have no soldier named Jirom among their surviving forces. I'm afraid I must conclude that this man likely died in battle."

"No." Horace started walking again at a swift clip. "I do not accept that finding, Mezim. Keep digging. I want to know for sure. We will not give up until someone produces a body. Do you understand?"

"I will redouble my efforts."

"Good. What about the Chapter House attack?"

They'd heard about the killings at the fortress-temple of the Order of the Crimson Flame just a few days ago. Details had been sketchy, so Horace had ordered Mezim to find out what he could.

"I'm sorry to say the latest reports don't convey much more than before. The soldiers surrounding the House have testified they heard noises coming from inside. Screaming and such. It only lasted a short time, but the commander in charge decided to break down the gates and investigate in any case. They found everyone dead. The injuries are supposedly quite brutal. Decapitations and disembowelments. Yet no signs of who or what killed them."

Horace frowned, as the description reminded him of a night some months ago when he and Alyra had been attacked by *idimmu*—demons—at the royal palace. It was a night he preferred to forget. *I'm gathering quite a collection of those. Nights I'd rather not remember. It's almost like a curse hanging around my neck.*

"Come find me if anything new turns up," Horace said as he turned to a flight of stairs leading downward into the foundation of the villa's main building.

"One final matter," Mezim said. "Mistress Alyra has returned."

Horace froze on the step. Not long after the events at the Sun Temple, when he'd thought they had agreed to stay together and see where their relationship would lead, she had left. Vanished, with not much more than a cryptic note about having to track down some loose ends. That had been almost two months ago. Two months without a word, not knowing if she was alive or dead or in trouble.

"Thank you," he muttered, and started down the stairs.

Warm, humid air washed over Horace as he descended into a long, brick-lined chamber with a double-vaulted ceiling. One of this villa's most interesting features was the underground baths. At the far end, taking up most of the floor space, was a pool large enough to bathe the entire crew of a twin-masted schooner, all at the same time. Men and women lounged by its edge, eating and drinking while they soaked.

He went to a row of wooden stalls along the north wall to change out of his clothes and was intercepted by a young slave girl. She was entirely nude except for a silver collar around her neck. The collar and her pale skin, much lighter than most Akeshians, reminded him of the first time he met Alyra at the palace. The parallels to this moment made him uncomfortable, but he allowed the slave to lead him into a stall and stood while she undressed him. Horace tried to think of other things, but all his thoughts inevitably turned to Alyra, which only served to escalate the awkwardness. When he was disrobed, the slave escorted him down to a smaller pool of very hot, foamy water.

He couldn't hold back a quiet groan of pleasure as he stepped into the bath. The steaming water grasped his calves, washing away the tension from his muscles. The sensations became more intense with every step he descended. He had been looking forward to this all morning.

The slave girl lathered him in soap and rinsed him. Then she led him to the main pool. Horace didn't look any of the other bathers in the eye as he lowered himself into the water. Not quite as hot as the first pool, the main bath was the perfect temperature to relax.

The pool's edge was slick under his palms where his burn scars touched the polished stonework. Grief spun through him as he thought of his departed wife and child, but it was not as painful as it had once been. He lounged against the side of the pool with a long sigh.

Some of the other bathers looked over at him, but they kept to their private clusters. The slave brought him a pewter cup with chilled wine and offered him orange slices from a tray. Horace declined the fruit but sipped from the cup as he tried to unwind, while a multitude of problems jostled inside his brain. Jirom's disappearance, Alyra's absences, the duties of his position, not to mention his problem with controlling his powers. And now the new campaign against the crusaders at Omikur. He'd been hopeful his life would become easier after the *Tammuris*, but if anything it had gotten more complex. He wanted to run away to someplace quiet and peaceful. *I could always go back to sea.*

It was a tempting idea. Life aboard a ship was filled with routines and hard work. No women to distract him, no politics to muddle his head, no sense of impending doom. Just the wind and the water. But he couldn't go back. He'd witnessed too much to be content as a ship's carpenter ever again. As much as it frustrated him with its elusiveness, the *zoana* was part of him now. It was the salt in his blood, as the sailors were like to say.

"May I join you?"

Horace nearly spilled his cup when Alyra came up behind him. For a moment he couldn't say anything, could only stare at her in mute wonder. He'd almost forgotten how beautiful she was, especially unclothed with the water lapping about her hips. Her long blonde hair was down, curling around her shoulders down to the upper slopes of her breasts. Horace blinked and forced his gaze back to her face.

"I heard you were back," he said.

"Yes. I just returned."

He wanted to ask where she had been but held his tongue. There was something about the way she regarded him, a wariness he'd noticed before she left, that put him at a loss for words, afraid to say the wrong thing. The slave girl brought more wine, and Alyra accepted a cup. Horace allowed his to be refilled while he watched Alyra, trying to read her expression, to garner some hint of how she felt about him.

"So," he said after the slave had left them. "Did you accomplish your mission?"

Horace kicked himself mentally. If anything was sure to drive her away again, it would be prying into her affairs. She'd made that much clear.

"It's difficult to say," she replied after a long pause.

Sweating now, Horace cleared his throat. "Will you be staying long?"

"I don't know yet."

"I'd like . . . it would be nice if you . . . I mean . . ." He took a breath to steady himself. "I'm trying to say I missed you."

That brought a smile to her lips. "I missed you, too."

Horace breathed easier. Then he remembered they were both naked, sitting just a couple feet apart, and his awkwardness returned in force.

"How have you been getting along while I was away?" she asked.

"Well, I haven't received any challenges since . . . that night. So that's been good."

Alyra turned to watch a pair of noble ladies wading nearby. "Do you think they like you better, now that you've saved their queen's life? Or are they just too afraid to confront you directly?"

"That's tough to say. No one at the palace speaks to me except for the queen and Lord Ubar."

"Yes. I've heard that he was recalled to court. An odd development."

"I thought so, too. But I'm glad Byleth brought him back. He's a good man. Nothing at all like his father."

Alyra switched to the Arnossi tongue. "Be careful, Horace. He's still Akeshian and *zoanii*. Backbiting and deception are bred into them."

He frowned at her depiction but nodded so as not to start an argument. "I'll keep that in mind."

"While you're at it, keep both eyes on Byleth as well," she said. "The queen is no blushing ingenue."

"Point taken. While you're here, you can help me avoid making any disastrous mistakes."

"You're the First Sword, Horace. Any mistake can be disastrous. However, I'm not as adept at court politics as Lord Mulcibar. You'll need to find your own way."

The mention of Mulcibar's name sobered Horace and doused his mood. He missed the old nobleman. Part of him still felt responsible for his death.

Horace finished his wine and set the empty cup on the ledge of the pool as Queen Byleth entered the bath chamber with a small entourage. The queen strode to the hot pool where her handmaidens removed her clothing and jewelry. Lord Xantu, as ominous as ever in his black robe, stood nearby as the queen was washed. He had taken to growing out his hair, which now hung down to his collar.

"Beautiful. Isn't she?" Alyra asked, gazing at the queen.

Horace cleared his throat. "I, uh . . . sure. Yes, I suppose."

"She still hasn't selected a new bodyguard to replace Lord Gilgar?"

"Not yet. She's been genuinely upset since . . . well, you know."

"I bet she has."

The vicious tone in her voice irritated him for no good reason. He had expected she would be happier to see him, but everything felt disjointed, as if they'd reverted back to being strangers again.

Horace tensed as the queen was rinsed, the water sluicing down her body. Her eyes locked onto him from across the chamber, and he felt her terrible magnetism working on him. *Keep your mind on Alyra, fool!*

"I've missed you," he repeated.

"You look like you haven't been getting enough sleep."

The way she tilted her head gave him hope that she was inviting him to speak more intimately, so he plunged ahead. "I worry about you when you're gone."

"I've told you before, Horace. You don't need to worry."

And just like that, the invitation vanished. Horace didn't know what to say next.

Blanket-sized towels were brought to dry the queen. Then she departed the chamber without coming to the large pool, taking her retinue with her. Horace couldn't stop the sigh of relief from escaping his lips. Being in the presence of both Alyra and the queen was beyond uncomfortable. In fact, he'd prefer to continue this conversation somewhere more private. He turned to Alyra, but the slave girl interrupted before he could ask her.

"Pardon me, *Belum*," she said with a bowed head. "Her Majesty invites you to sup with her this evening. At the eighth bell, if it pleases you."

"Ah, of course," he replied.

The slave backed away, and Horace swallowed, wondering how Alyra would react. Yet nothing in her demeanor changed. If anything, she appeared amused by the situation. He decided to take a chance. "Can I see you tonight?"

"I'll be in my chambers, if you can get away from the queen."

Before Horace could think of a witty reply, she left the pool. He watched her climb out, enjoying every curve and line of her body. He settled back into the water as she entered a dressing stall. His heart thumped loud in his chest, and his thoughts were scattered. There were problems that required his immediate attention, but they seemed insignificant all of a sudden. Alyra was back, but now he had to go prepare to meet the queen.

He shivered as he left the warm water. A few of the nobles turned to watch him go, but he ignored them. A slave girl, a different one this time, approached to help him dress, but he waved her away.

CHAPTER TWO

The landscape of his mind extended like a vast sheet of leaden glass, devoid of features or landmarks. Pale light filtered down from the hazy sky where the sun, a distant orb of deeper gray, pulsed with fierce energy. It was his *qa*, the gateway to his power.

Horace focused on the endless plain. This was his hidden inner world, which he had constructed with Lord Ubar's help. Here he had solace from the pressures of the outside world, though they never left him completely alone. His *zoana*, for one, was something he couldn't escape, not even here. He felt it throbbing behind his *qa*, calling to him like a siren's lure. Early in his training he had often accessed it from this relaxed state of mind, but lately that had become problematic.

He realized he was focused on the gateway to his power again and tried pulling his attention away, but the orb pulsed faster. A moment too late, he noticed it had opened. Just a crack, but that was enough. A rush of Shinar uncoiled across the ethereal sky of his hidden world in streaks of violet so deep they were almost black. Horace did nothing for a little while except observe the display. It was beautiful and terrifying at the same time. He reached out to the bands of energy. He didn't force it back through his *qa*, instead aiming to coax it. This was something he'd been working on. He'd been told the power would react to how it was handled. A harsh grip caused the *zoana* to gush like a bursting dam, but a softer approach yielded a more measured flow. So far, he hadn't been able to make it work, and this time wasn't any different. The *zoana* refused to return of its own accord, as if it was playing coy.

Horace pushed back against the frustration building inside him, threatening to unravel his concentration. At this pace he would die of old age before he mastered his powers. Ubar was a dutiful instructor, but there was little he could tell Horace about the void. The Shinar dominion was a mystery to most sorcerers. Not even Lord Mulcibar had been able to deliver much insight about its workings. Horace had been hoping to find his own path through trial and error, but the way continued to elude him. The feeling that there was something wrong stayed with him, but he couldn't pinpoint what it was, and so it grew.

After a time—he could never be sure of how long he had been inside this meditative retreat—Horace gave up on coaxing the flow of Shinar and went straight to the gateway. With a firm shove, he slammed it closed. The purple bands evaporated, leaving the sky a hazy gray once again. The uniform blankness calmed him once again, soothing away his qualms. His head buzzed with a pleasant euphoria. It was almost like floating. Absently, he noticed that the muscles in his physical body had begun to unkink themselves. And he allowed himself to drift along on these sensations, not pushing his thoughts in any one direction, content to simply exist in this tranquil moment.

A face shimmered in his consciousness. Its soft edges surrounded in golden hair. Delicate eyebrows pinched together as her lips arched in a delicious frown. The blue of her eyes dazzling like a clear midsummer sky. Passing underneath this vision, Horace gazed up at the woman he loved. Or thought he loved. Things had become . . . complicated. With his first wife, Sari, he remembered they had just fallen in together like two old friends, as comfortable with each other as if they shared one mind. But it was different with Alyra. She tested and goaded him, challenging his every decision. Being with her was intoxicating, but also demanding.

Points of bright light flickered on the edges of his awareness, disturbing his calm. Alyra's face shuddered like a leaf caught in a stiff wind and gently faded from view. Horace fixed his gaze on the disturbance. A bank of dark gray clouds billowed far out on the plain, moving toward his position. Every so often, light would twinkle inside the inky mass. Ghoulish green like the lightning from a chaos storm. His calm evaporated.

The gray fog bordering his hidden world no longer felt soothing. Instead, it had taken on a disturbing aspect. He sensed hostility within the approaching darkness, although he couldn't say from what. He felt compelled to investigate, even though the part of him still connected to the conscious world wanted to break free. There was something about the phenomenon that drew him onward. He felt himself moving forward. Distant noises echoed. Faint crackles. They were almost familiar, but not quite. Then an invisible force took hold of him. He struggled against the unseen grasp, even as it pulled him deeper into the murky clouds. His mental vision vanished in the haze. Panicked, he reached for his physical body. The grasp gave another hard yank, and then the world exploded in a rush of gray and white.

Horace blinked as the vision faded, to be slowly replaced by the contours of a familiar room. White plaster walls surrounded him. The ceiling was sapphire blue. The wooden floor was reassuringly solid beneath his crossed legs. He placed both hands on the floor, palms down, and took comfort in its solidity.

Lord Mulcibar's *ganzir* mat laid spread out before him. As always when looking upon it, his gaze was drawn along the geometric shapes that seemed to move and pulse as if the mat were a living thing. He followed the pattern through each of the four elemental quadrants to the central circle, inside which sat the figure of a tiny man stitched in bright platinum thread. When he had first started meditating with the *ganzir*, the pattern had served to calm his mind as well as focus it. But lately that tranquility had become more and more elusive. Rather than moving forward, it felt like his study of the *zoana* was regressing, which only made him feel less confident, feeding a cycle of uncertainty and apprehension. Lord Ubar tried to help, but it seemed no one could diagnose this particular problem, which made it all the more infuriating.

Each day he expected a revelation, a sudden epiphany that would make sense of this power dwelling inside him. Yet day after day, week upon week, he fought and struggled for the barest scraps, failing far more often than he succeeded.

He'd learned that the power was often passed down from parent to child, which explained the structure of Akeshian society. However, nothing in the texts he'd read said anything about outlander magic. His parents, for certain, had possessed no special gifts of mysticism, or anyone else in his family. His entire life before the crusade had been mundane, with neither great sorrows nor extravagant bliss. Until he'd lost Sari and Josef. And since that day, nothing had been the same. Some part of him had driven him to the sea after their deaths to seek his own obliteration. Suicide hadn't been a conscious decision, but looking back he could see how he had been on a path to self-destruction.

Then he'd wrecked on the shores of this new, ancient, bloodthirsty land, and everything had changed. Battered and floundering, he clung to the only lifeline within reach—his power—and prayed it would someday carry him to a safe haven. Each night he went to sleep exhausted and disappointed.

He let out a deep breath and stood up, his joints aching as if he'd been sitting for hours. The image of the dark clouds lingered. *It's gone now. Just a figment of my imagination.*

The words did nothing to ease his anxiety as he crossed the room. Large and beautifully decorated, with marble accents and fine hardwood furniture that reminded him of the great palaces of Avice, this borrowed suite was on the same floor as the queen's apartments. But in a different wing, for which he was especially grateful. It wasn't easy living in the royal presence for a ship-builder of modest birth.

He left the parlor to enter the bedchamber. Horace took off his sleeping robe and tossed it on the bed as he went to one of the two large wardrobes. Selecting a lightweight tunic and skirt, he put them on with a pair of comfortable sandals. When he had finished lacing the footwear, he looked himself over in the tall cheval glass in the corner. The white silk tunic was embroidered with gold thread in interconnected squares along the high collar and down the neck. The same pattern was repeated down the side of the long skirt and around the bottom. The broad leather belt had rings to hold a scabbard, but he didn't have a weapon here. He'd decided to leave the blade of the First Sword at home. After all, this was supposed to be a vacation.

His hair was getting long. He pulled it back in a queue like the young Akeshian men wore but then decided to let it hang free. *No use pretending to be something I'm not. Not that anyone would let me forget I'm a foreign savage, even if I shaved it all off.*

He was heading back out to the parlor when the suite door opened and a young male slave entered. He bowed from the waist and said, "The queen is ready for your arrival."

He was the first to arrive.

Twelve red leather couches surrounded the long dining table. Goblets of beaten gold and crystal were arrayed on the polished surface along with a variety of porcelain bowls and cups. At first glance Horace took the utensils to be gold, too. Then he looked closer at the pale hue and decided they must be an alloy, possibly electrum. A centerpiece of four candles surrounded by fresh lotuses completed the elegant tableau.

Horace walked around the chamber. Tapestries imported from the West covered the walls from floor to ceiling. In them, men and women in classical garb were depicted at a grand feast, eating and drinking as they made merry. A sideboard had been set up with several sealed jars, presumably wine or spirits, as well as an array of cutlery knives and long forks.

Another door opened, and two men walked in. By the cut and design of their robes, they both belonged to the *zoanii* class. Lord Temuni was older and exceedingly slim with a long, narrow chin to match his sharp nose, while Lord Oriathu was short and stout, his clothes straining to contain his round paunch. Both men were shaved bald in the custom of the ruling class. Horace resisted the urge to reach up and touch his hair.

The *zoanii* looked to Horace in unison, and they both strolled to the opposite side of the table in a not-so-subtle gesture. Horace did his best to ignore them. He was already sweating under his tunic, despite the cool breeze blowing in through the open shutters.

More guests arrived—eleven in all, including him. All nobility of various ranks, the cream of the royal court. Horace had seen most them several times at the palace, either at official events or in passing. He knew their names and even a little about the cliques into which they aligned themselves, mostly thanks to Mezim. They all watched him. Not openly—that was not the Akeshian way. Instead, they glanced at him with sideways looks and expansive sweeps that were meant to appear to take in the entire room, but he noticed their eyes lingered on him a little longer than the artwork or the place settings. They mingled and chatted, their voices light and full of mirth. At least, so it seemed on the surface. Already in his short time at court Horace had learned enough about Akeshian politics to understand a smidgen of the game they played. The lesser players circled their superiors, but not just those with which they were allied. No, they circled their foes as well in an intricate dance that somewhat resembled the movement of fish schools, flowing in and among each other, sometimes matching their movements before breaking apart for no outward reason. Meanwhile, the two largest "fish" in the room, Lord Temuni and *Sarleskar* Balashi, who was the acting commander of the queen's military since Prince Zazil's mysterious disappearance. An incident, by the way, which no one—in typical court fashion—ever talked about, as if there were an unspoken rule that members vanished every so often, and it was best not to discuss it. The whole thing made his head hurt.

Fortunately, servants orbited the room with carafes of wine and liquor. Horace gulped down the first cup of red wine and sipped at the second, feeling somewhat better.

A door opened at the far end of the room. Lord Xantu came in, wearing his customary robe of deep black, head freshly shaved. Four handmaidens entered behind him, all of them wearing identical purple gowns cut to expose their left breasts. Each bare nipple was painted gold. The handmaidens formed an aisle from the door, through which arrived Byleth. Never one to allow herself to be outshone, the queen wore a sheath gown of indigo silk so sheer it was virtually transparent. A heavy necklace of gold and sapphires did nothing to distract from her sensuality as she sauntered to the table.

"My lords and ladies," Byleth said, holding up her arm as if inviting an embrace. "Please, be welcome." She looked to him and held out her hand. "Lord Horace, come take your place beside me."

He took the couch beside her. The upholstery was so supple that lying on it was a sensual experience. Byleth had told him she designed these couches especially for him, presumably to make him feel more at home. She had been so excited to show him that he hadn't had the heart to tell her they were an affection of the elite class of the fallen Nimean Empire, not something modern Arnossi used in their homes. Although their padded tops were comfortable to lie on, the odd position made it difficult to eat or drink without making a mess or choking.

Byleth smiled as her guests got settled. "My cooks have been busy with a special surprise for tonight."

"That's very kind, Your Excellency," Horace said. "I have the latest reports from Erugash. There aren't any new developments on the Chapter House attack, but I've ordered a complete inquiry."

Byleth placed a hand on his arm. "I've seen the reports, Horace. Please, be at ease tonight. Our duties can wait until tomorrow, yes?"

She clapped her hands once, and a dozen servants in fine dress entered carrying covered silver platters. These platters were set down on the table and the covers removed all at once to reveal an exotic selection of foods. Horace leaned forward for a better look. One dish was lined with rows of quail, stuffed and roasted in a glaze. Another was piled with slabs of grilled meat that looked like Arnossi beef, but he found it hard to believe. There were also two soup bowls, fresh bread slathered in melted butter and honey, and other wonderful foods. The smells were divine. Before Horace said anything, the servants began loading his plate with choice selections from each platter.

"I hope you like it," Byleth said as she accepted a filled wine glass from a handmaiden. "I went to great lengths to obtain the finest delicacies of your homeland."

"This is . . . extraordinary."

He smiled and made a show of trying everything, even the tortoise eggs, which he really didn't care for. The other guests ate more selectively. As they picked at the unfamiliar food, it reminded Horace of when he had first arrived in this country and how alien everything had seemed.

The queen raised her glass. "To our continued friendship. May it ever grow closer."

Everyone drank to the toast. Horace hesitated a moment before he sipped from his cup. While his closeness with Alyra had entered a strange, uncertain place since the *Tammuris*, his relationship with the queen had flourished. *Not too hard to guess why. I saved her life, twice, and brought down her enemies.*

As a slave girl passed, the queen reached out to stop her. "Lord Horace, I believe you've already met my newest acquisition."

She pulled the girl by the wrist to stand before them, and Horace realized he had met her. She was the slave who had bathed him down in the hot springs. Her pale skin glowed almost translucent in the candlelight, contrasting sharply with her long chestnut hair. "This is Kelcia. She's from Hestria, which borders Arnos, if I'm not mistaken."

Horace dried his lips with a cloth napkin. "You are correct, Excellence."

STORM AND STEEL

He kept his face impassive, as if they were discussing the weather instead of a person made into property. He also avoided looking directly into the slave's eyes, even as the queen stroked the girl like a prized pet.

"Well, I had to replace Alyra," Byleth said, gazing up at the slave with a smile. "And this one is quite talented."

With a wink, she dismissed the girl. "I adore the hot baths at this house. Especially when the weather turns cold. I wish I could spend all winter here. Tell me, have your rooms been warm enough . . . at night?"

"Quite warm enough, Excellence."

She reached out and touched his wrist. Just a light touch, but it sent a jolt up his arm and set his heart to beating faster. "I forget that you are accustomed to the cold. You must find us hot-blooded, eh?"

"Well, I certainly understand why your people wear less clothing than us. And I've come to appreciate the balmy climate, I must admit."

"I've heard that the women of Arnos cover their entire bodies when they go out in public," Lady Ishmi said. "Even their hair is bound under caps. Is that true?"

As eyes shifted toward him, Horace put down his cup. "Well, Arnossi ladies certainly dress with more . . . ah, modesty. As for their hats, there are many fashions. I'm not exactly an authority."

Lord Oriathu cleared his throat with a cough. "We saw plenty of local natives on the island of Thym. Their manner of dress was odd, but from what I recall the womenfolk were no more demure than most peasants."

Byleth signaled, and a servant came over to refill Horace's cup, this time with a wine with a deep amber color. "Try this," Byleth said. "It's a rare vintage from the Jade Kingdoms. I cannot pronounce the name, but I find it entrancing."

While their cups were filled, the rest of the lords and ladies conversed. More platters were brought in with dishes from different parts of the western world. It began with a spicy red soup that made Horace's eyes water, and then onto a course of tiny fish served in a chilled sweet sauce. After that came an entrée of roasted fowl coated with slivers of orange.

Byleth insisted Horace be served first for each course. He tried to protest, but she wouldn't take no for an answer. Several times he found her watching him eat, almost like a doting mother. However, there was something predatory in her gaze.

"I never tire of hearing about your homeland," she said. "What else is different?"

He wiped his mouth before answering. "Almost everything, Excellence. Our customs are almost completely unalike."

"Such as?"

"Well . . ." He searched for an example, and his gaze settled on the tabletop. "You prefer to eat sitting on the floor, while we sit in chairs or sometimes on tall stools."

"Stools?" she asked with a laugh. "Are you teasing me?"

"Not at all, Excellence."

"You must call me Byleth. I command it."

Horace cleared his throat. "As you wish. The foods we eat are very different. Yours are so hot they burn my tongue. Even your native fruits have a sharper taste."

She leaned closer. "And do you find that all this heat makes for hotter passions as well?"

"Perhaps in some cases, Excel—Byleth. But overall I find most of your subjects to be rather even-keeled, as we mariners might say. Perhaps more so than many of my countrymen, who you might consider ill-mannered in comparison if you were to meet them."

"Horace, I am constantly amazed at your candor. If all the men of Arnos are like you, I think it must be a very honest realm."

He felt the eyes of the nobles upon him and wanted to slide down under the table. "Uh, I don't know about that. We have our flaws, certainly."

"Indeed. One of them seems to be a desire to invade my territory."

The sudden turn in the conversation sobered him like a slap across the face. He didn't know how to respond. Should he apologize? Or change the subject?

The queen laughed. "Forgive me, Horace. That was impolite. I do not blame you for the actions of your government. Indeed, you have acted with as much honor as any member of my court. You understand this concept of honor, yes?"

"Uh, well, I'm trying to, Excel—Byleth. In any case, I thought the crusade had been halted."

"For now. Yet, I know something of the ways of your military, Horace. They will regroup and try again. They are nothing if not persistent."

In that, we surely agree.

"I only heard about Omikur today." He cleared his throat. "I was disheartened that the situation is coming to such a grim end."

She speared a slice of orange and put it in her mouth. After she swallowed, she took a sip from her glass. "We feel no empathy for those who would try to steal our lands."

One noblewoman whispered in Lord Oriathu's ear, and they both chuckled as they looked in Horace's direction.

He focused his attention on the queen. "Of course not. However, if there was a way to avoid future war, that would be a good thing. Don't you agree?"

The conversation around the table died down, until the only sounds came from the servants as they moved about the room.

The queen popped an olive into her mouth. "Of course, if the circumstances could be decided in a way that favored Erugash. But your leaders are not inclined to negotiate in good faith, Horace. Furthermore, the consensus of the imperial court seems to be to crush the savages—pardon me, the *crusaders*—and push them back into the ocean."

"It's actually a sea," Horace murmured.

"Pardon," she said. "What do you mean, it is a sea?"

"The ocean. Technically, it's a sea. We call it the Midland Sea."

The ire vanished from the queen's face, replaced by a look of intense curiosity. "Truly?"

Horace pushed his platter aside. Dipping his finger in his wine, he drew a rough outline of the Akeshian coastline on the table's surface, from the shores of Arnos, Altaia, and Etonia in the north down to the headlands of the southern continent.

"This." He tapped the open space between Akeshia and the western nations. "Is the Midland Sea. Farther west past a few other countries is where you'd find the Ergard Ocean, which stretches on for . . . well, to the edge of the world, as far as we know."

Everyone was straining to see the crude map.

"Fascinating," Byleth said. "We know so little about the West beyond our own colonies. Tell me, are these things universally known among your people?"

"Well, it's common knowledge among sailors. I was friends with the pilot of the *Bantu Ray*—the ship I sailed on before I crashed here. His name was Belais Reymeiger, and he knew more about the seas and coasts than anyone I ever met."

"May I ask a favor, Lord Horace? Would you meet with our royal cartographers and help them produce a more accurate map?"

Horace hesitated before answering. He remembered how paranoid Belais had been about his precious charts and logbook falling into enemy hands. Apparently, navigation material was considered a national secret. However a gesture of goodwill might convince the queen he was really on her side or at least a trusted neutral arbiter. He believed the Akeshians wanted peace as much as he did. They just needed to know they could trust him. "Of course. However I can be of service."

Byleth caressed the back of his hand. "I'm glad to hear you say that, Horace. I've been thinking about your role as my First Sword. Now that the thorn of Omikur has been removed from our side, we intend to devote our attention to crushing the slave rebellion once and for all time. I wish you to undertake this duty."

"Me? Excellence, I'm not sure I am the right choice."

"I am," she said, and smiled at him in a way that made his heart beat faster.

Horace struggled for a suitable reason to turn down this "honor." He had no intention of harming the slaves fighting for their freedom. In fact, he'd rather help them achieve their final goal. "Excellence, I wouldn't know the first thing about ending a rebellion. I could help more by bringing our two nations together in peace. Perhaps I could act as an ambassa—"

STORM AND STEEL

The queen clapped her hands. Horace shifted on his couch as everyone else filed out of the room. Lord Xantu was the last to depart, casting a stern gaze around the room before he closed the door behind him.

Once they were alone, Byleth squeezed his hand. "Horace, you are the only one I can trust with this. Too many in court wish to topple me from the throne so they can fight over the scraps. I need you. I need your *strength*, now more than ever before. I finally have a chance to rule my city in truth, and I will not allow it to fail."

He put his hand over hers. Her bones were so tiny and slender he felt he could crush her fingers if he squeezed too hard. "What if you reached out to them? These fugitive slaves are your subjects, too. They only want to be free, the same as any other man or woman."

She pulled her hand away. "No. They have revolted against their lawful queen, and in so doing they have damned themselves in the eyes of the gods. They must be stamped out, or else my reign will collapse."

"What if you approached the problem in a different way?"

The queen held out her glass to him. It was empty. "I'm listening."

He refilled it to the brim. "We could take a two-pronged attack, so to speak. Use the military to suppress the violence and protect your citizens, but also change the laws to improve the lives of your subjects, especially the slaves. If they didn't feel backed into a corner, they might be willing to find a peaceful solution. And it wouldn't hurt to offer clemency to those who vow to give up their revolt."

"You never fail to surprise me, Horace of Tines. Most of my *zoanii* would leap at this chance to garner my favor and increase their own authority, and yet you remained focused on your ideals. As unchangeable as a stone. I will consider your ideas."

She traced her fingertips down the side of his face. "You are a remarkable man, unlike any I've ever met. Stay with me tonight."

Horace's stomach dropped. Sweat broke out across his forehead and down the back of his neck. "Excellence, I—uh, I'm not sure what to say."

She leaned into him and brushed her lips across his chin. "Say you will make me yours this night."

"I can't. I'm sorry, but I have feelings for another."

Her laughter surprised him. "Why should that matter?" She studied his face and then clucked her tongue. "*Zoanii* are free to love whomever they desire, with no attachments. Is it my former handmaiden? Bring her along if you like. My bed is large enough for all of us. Your relationship with that little freed slave you keep has nothing to do with what I want."

He pulled back from her hands. "Excellence, it has everything to do with me and who I am."

Her eyes narrowed. "And if I should insist?"

A blunt pressure pressed against the back of his head. Just a light touch, but he realized she was questing at the edges of his mind. He envisioned a steel helmet clamping down on his head. Their eyes locked in a silent contest of wills. In the recesses of his mind, a soft voice whispered. *You want her so just take her. Right here. Show her what kind of a man you are.*

The door opened, and one of the queen's handmaidens entered. Byleth glared at the slave, but the probing touch vanished. Horace remained on guard as the girl knelt beside the queen and handed her a small roll of papyrus. His concern for his own safety vanished as the blood drained from the queen's face. Even on the terrace of the Sun Temple, as she was about to be wed to the prince of Nisus and possibly murdered thereafter, he hadn't seen her so shaken.

"What is it?" he asked.

Byleth banished the handmaiden with a curt gesture and then crumpled up the scroll, throwing it on the table. "A caravan was attacked by a band of rebel slaves. They seized the gold that was intended for our royal coffers." She glared at him. "Gold we need to fend off our enemies."

"I am truly sorry. Was anyone hurt in the attack?"

"Hurt?" she yelled. "The soldiers guarding that convoy had better be dead, or they'll wish they were when I flay the skin from their backs and nail them to stakes along that road as a reminder of what happens to those who fail!"

Horace let out a silent breath, not sure what he could say that wouldn't fuel her rage. But she didn't give him the chance. "First Sword, you will issue an order in our name at once, pronouncing death for anyone who harbors or aids the rebellion."

Horace frowned. Such an order would be a death sentence for Alyra and her associates, as well as, he suspected, thousands of Akeshian commoners. It would begin a persecution that could last months or years. *Not unlike what the Great Crusade intends for this empire. She doesn't understand what she's asking me to do.*

Byleth stood up. "If you are going to remain in Erugash, you will obey our commands. Or you will face our displeasure."

Defeated, he bowed his head. "As you wish, Excellence."

As she left the room, Byleth called over her shoulder. "Rest well, Lord Horace. We depart for home in the morning."

The beauty of the villa gardens was haunting by night, when the darkness blurred the outlines of blossom and leaf, and their lush fragrances rode the cool breezes. Alyra walked the narrow paths between the bowers with quick steps, down to the western edge where many secluded nooks and niches could be found. Her ears strained at every turn, half-expecting to stumble upon illicit lovers in fierce embrace or, worse, cloaked conspirators hatching nefarious schemes. But the luck of the Silver Lady was with her, delivering her without incident to the spot of her own secret assignation.

She found Sefkahet standing by a pond. Moonlight reflected off the still waters, bathing the woman in silver luminance. Alyra cleared her throat, and Sefkahet turned. Then she smiled. "I'm glad you reached out to me."

Alyra came over and stood beside her, both of them looking down into the brilliant surface. "I'm sorry we haven't spoken in so long."

"Don't worry, Alyra." Sef bent down closer. "I'm the one who knows you best. Now, are you going to kiss me, or do I have to beg?"

Alyra was too distracted to really want it, but she hadn't seen her friend and confidant in weeks. So she allowed Sef to lean in for a kiss. After a few seconds, she pulled back. Sef ran her fingers up and down Alyra's arm. "I've missed you. I won't ask where you've been, but I'm glad you're back. Please say you can stay for a bit."

"For a short while. I needed to see you."

"I like how you say that."

Alyra moved sideways to avoid another kiss. "Not for that, Sef. I need to talk."

The other woman stepped back and composed herself in a flash. "All right. You got my attention, Alyra. What's wrong?"

"I've been investigating the massacre at the Chapter House."

Sef's eyes widened. "In Erugash? Alyra, you shouldn't be poking around in that. The queen was livid when the news reached us. If she ever found out—"

"I've been careful. Trust me on that. But have you heard any details on the murders of the Order brethren?"

"Just a few things through the network. Every member of the house was killed in a single night. Sentries outside heard strange noises, but nothing to suggest a battle was being fought within the fortress until the Queen's Guard forced an entry and found the bodies."

"I've seen the bodies."

The revelation poured out of her, unleashed by the mountain of anxiety that had been weighing her down for the past fortnight. "They were ripped apart as if a pack of wild beasts had torn into them. But not with teeth or claws."

"Weapons," Sef said. "Knives and pinchers, perhaps."

Alyra shook her head and looked back down at the pond. "No. Nothing made by human hands could've caused the wounds I saw."

"You mean it was sorcery. But Alyra, most of the queen's court was here with us when the attack happened."

"Indeed. And outside the court, what other group in Erugash has the power to slaughter dozens of men, most of them sorcerers to boot, without the neighbors noticing?"

Sef shook her head slowly, her recently won composure falling away to reveal deep concern. "If you're right, you realize what it means. Outsiders must have infiltrated the city. How is that possible? The wards on the wall and gates—"

"I know. It's crazy to even consider. But it's the only theory I can come up with. That's why I needed to talk to you. To get advice on how to proceed."

Sef frowned as her head tilted to the side, allowing her hair to fall down from her face in a lustrous black wave. "You mean you wanted to talk to the network."

"Before, I would have taken this directly to Cipher," Alyra said. "But after what happened . . ."

"No, it's all right. I understand. But I can't pretend this came from me. My superiors are going to know someone supplied it, and I'll have to tell them the truth."

"I accept that."

"Does this information come with the price? Shall I tell them it's a peace offering?"

"No. Just say I thought you needed to know."

Sef stepped closer again and caressed her arms. The touch was exhilarating, but Alyra fought it. She knew what Sef wanted, and some part of her wanted it, too. But things had gotten messy between them, mixing the mission and their personal feelings for each other. Alyra had tried to break it off, but every time she saw Sef, the feelings returned in full force.

"Stay with me tonight," Sef breathed into her ear.

"I can't. You know the other handmaidens would talk, and it would mean a mess of trouble for both of us if the queen found out."

"Then I'll come to you. After the queen retires for the night, I can slip out and—"

Alyra took a long step backward, breaking free of Sef's touch. "No."

Sefkahet looked as if she wanted to keep pursuing, but she held back. "Why not? You said you missed me."

"I do. But this can't go on, Sef. You're still with the network, and I'm outside."

"But it's not that, is it? It's him. Night was right. You've fallen for him. Alyra, he doesn't know you like I do. He can't love you the way I do."

Alyra turned away to hide the tears forming in her eyes. "It doesn't matter. I know what I have to do, and I'm doing it. I can't have you in here." She touched her chest. "It's too painful trying to juggle everything. Please. This isn't easy for me, but it's what has to happen."

She waited for a response, but there was nothing except the stirring of the leaves in the wind. Alyra turned back to find Sefkahet was gone. The darkness closed in tighter around her as if a blanket had fallen over the moon. Standing by the pond, she let the tears fall.

Horace looked both ways down the corridor as he knocked on the door again. It was late—almost midnight—but he needed to see her. His head was awhirl, and he needed to make sense of it all. And it started with her. He knocked a third time, but still no answer. He placed his hand on the latch. After a moment's hesitation, he opened it.

"Alyra?"

He pitched his voice low so it wouldn't echo out into the hallway. Her room was dark and small with only a narrow bed against the far wall. A bag with a carrying strap sat at the foot of the bed, clothes spilling out. Horace went over to the bronze lamp fashioned in the shape of a dolphin hanging by a chain and felt it. It was warm, but not hot. She'd been gone for a little while.

He left and started down the hallway in the direction of the stairs. Down the east wing corridor he saw a cluster of guardsmen outside the queen's suite, including the commander and his tall lieutenant. Horace went over to them. The soldiers saluted as he approached.

"Good evening, *Belum*," Captain Dyvim said. The leader of the Queen's Guard was an older gentleman of the *hekatatum* warrior caste. Horace found him a bit stiff but a likeable fellow nonetheless.

"How goes the watch?" Horace asked.

"All quiet. If you're here to see Her Majesty, I would suggest waiting until morning."

"No, no. I'm just prowling around. Have you happened to see Lady Alyra recently?"

"I have not. Lieutenant Orthen?"

"No, sir," the lieutenant said in a surprisingly soft voice. "I could send out a detachment to locate her, if my lord wishes."

"No. That's not necessary. Have a good night, Captain."

Dyvim bowed again and was imitated by his men. "And you, as well, *Belum*."

With a friendly nod, Horace resumed his search. He went downstairs and reached the villa's atrium without seeing anyone except a pair of guards walking patrol. He almost ran into a young woman in a short dress hurrying in the front entrance. Then he saw her gold collar and recognized her as one of the queen's handmaidens.

"Pardon me," he said.

She kept her eyes on the floor as she moved out of his way. "Please forgive me, Great Lord." Her words were pitched almost too low to hear.

"It was my fault. I'm trying to find someone. You know Alyra, right? She's not in her room."

"She is in the gardens," the woman said, almost whispering. She looked upset. "Down by the meditation pool."

"*Kanadu.* Have a good evening."

As he continued out the door, Horace looked back over his shoulder. The handmaiden was climbing the stairs. Her head was bent down, her shoulders shaking, as if she were crying. *I hope it's not something I said. Poor girl.*

Outside, the night was cool with a fresh breeze. The drooping trees surrounding the villa's estate swayed to the rhythm of the wind. The gardens spread out on all sides of the main house, divided by stone paths and leafy hedges, broken by the rooftops of small pavilions like wooden islands in the greenery. It was quiet, except for the buzzing of locusts and the occasional birdcall.

Horace made his way through the winding paths. A few minutes later, he found Alyra standing beside a scenic pond. He held back for a moment to watch her, standing in the pale moonlight. She bent down to smell the petals of a broad, white bloom, and he wished time would freeze in that instant. She was the purest thing in his life. *She's a spy. Dealing in duplicity, and yet she's never false to herself. Why can't I be that way?*

But he was torn between two worlds and two desires. He shifted his feet, the leather of his sandals scraping across the stone underfoot, and she turned. She kept her hands at her sides as she spotted him. Her eyes were hidden in deep shadows. "How long have you been there?"

All my life?

"I needed to find you." He spoke in Arnossi.

She stepped forward, flower petals brushing against her legs. "Here I am."

"I was hoping you'd be back soon. I have something for you."

Horace reached into his sash and pulled out a small object. She took it in her hand. The carving was done in a light wood, polished to an amber sheen. "A sea turtle?" she asked.

"It's from Thym. You told me you and your family lived there when you were young."

She held the carving in both hands, examining the detail. "That was thoughtful of you."

"Things haven't been the same since you left. The job is . . . well, it's a lot more work than I anticipated."

"It's an important position. You've come a long way since I first met you."

"I'm still the same man. At least, I hope I am."

"It's not so easy to tell."

"You've been gone. I've had to hold things together here without you. Without Mulcibar. I tell you, Alyra, I feel like a fraud most of the time. People are making all these demands of me, and I don't know what to do anymore."

"The queen wants you to do something?"

He didn't want to get into this with her, but it was pointless to hide it. She'd find out soon enough. "She wants me to oversee the halt of the slave uprising."

"She wants you to crush them. Kill them all and make an example of them."

It wasn't a question. "Yes. Something like that."

"And you didn't refuse."

"I tried to refuse. It's not as easy as it sounds when royalty is staring you in the face. She expects to be obeyed."

Her head was bowed so he couldn't see her face in the gloom. "I'm sure you tried your best."

"I did. What about you? What have you been doing all this time?"

"The same thing I was doing when you met me."

"Of course. Your mission. It must be nice to have only one worry."

"I worry. But the threat is not ended. If anything, it's worse now."

"How could it be worse? The Sun Temple is destroyed. The queen is safe now, and I'm a member of her court. I wouldn't let anything threaten you."

She looked up. Her eyes, shining, pierced through him. "Because you're so vital, she couldn't deny you anything. Right? She could never make you betray your ideals."

"It's not like that. I don't intend to let anyone be hurt. I'm in a position to help the rebels, to bring about a peaceful solution."

Her laugh was short and painful, cutting through his emotional barricades. "Then you don't know anything, Horace. The rebels aren't interested in a peaceful resolution. They will fight until they get what they want."

He hadn't considered that. All these things he wanted to do, everything he wanted to be, perhaps they weren't as compatible as he'd believed. Could he serve the queen faithfully and still hold true to his values? Did he have any choice at this point? "Then I guess I'll have to convince them."

"Like the way you convinced the queen to be merciful?"

"She's considering my plan."

Alyra shook her head. "No, she's goading you into doing something you don't want. She's in your head, Horace. She owns you."

"Sounds like you're the one trying to control me. And you're angry someone else has my attention."

She turned away so her profile was facing him. The moonlight cascaded down her long hair, turning it to white gold. "Then I feel sorry for you. You don't even know how lost you are."

"If I don't handle this problem, Byleth will find someone else. And you can bet that person won't have any problem with killing as many rebels as it takes to put the matter to rest. Is that what you want?"

"It's not about what I want, Horace. I'm not the one making the decision."

"Dammit, I'm trying to make this work! I'm trying to bridge the gap, but you aren't making it any easier."

"I know and I'm sorry, but I can't help you with this."

"No? Then maybe you're the one who's lost, Alyra. Or maybe you never cared in the first place."

He flinched even as the words came out of his mouth, but he was too angry to take them back. She had cut him deep and then twisted the knife for good measure.

Instead, he stalked away. The *zoana* stirred inside him as he left the gardens, like a caged beast that wanted to be free. He kept it on a tight leash, though it would have felt good to lash out, to destroy something and watch it fall to pieces, to feel the power surging through him.

He threw open the door to his suite, not caring at the noise as it slammed against the interior wall, then slammed it shut behind him. His nerves were frayed. His cheeks hurt from clenching his jaws so hard. *Relax. Exploding isn't going to help.*

He glanced down at the floor and considered meditating, but he wasn't in the mood. Instead, he went to the spirits cabinet and fished out a bottle of plum wine. The pale violet liquid sloshed inside as he held it up. He twisted off the top and took a deep gulp as he went out onto his private balcony. Sitting in a chair, drinking from the bottle, he looked out through the arched branches of the trees and caught a glimpse of the river's faint shimmer. The wind picked up, shaking the leaves.

He told himself he wouldn't think about Alyra, but his thoughts crept back to her like a beaten dog slinking back home. This wasn't how he had imagined her homecoming. Now everything was ruined. Shattered.

Perhaps he couldn't have everything he wanted, but he refused to quit just because things were becoming more complicated. He had his title and his power. And he also had the queen's trust, for now. They would be enough. *And if not, then I'll cross those waters when I come to them.*

The alcohol spread through his body in a warm wave that washed away the hurt. He sat and rode that wave as the stars wheeled above the villa, thinking of all the endless possibilities before him.

CHAPTER THREE

He soared high above the shadow-dappled ground. Stars sparkled in the deep-black sky above him. Scattered moonbeams stabbed through him yet left no mark in his ethereal flesh. With a gusty laugh, Horace shot into a bank of gathering thunderheads.

His vision dimmed for a few seconds, and then he was flying over a rippling desert plain. A powerful energy burgeoned inside him, growing as the clouds stirred around him. They moved in a circle with him at the epicenter, slowly at first but with increasing velocity. The air cooled. The power inside him flared, building in waves until it exploded in a satisfying crackle of thunder.

He was the storm. The driving wind. The pouring rain. His voice was a hurricane.

Far below among the dunes and barren rocks, a town huddled behind scarred stone walls. Lights shone within, waving feebly in the rising wind. More lights twinkled outside the walls, but his wrath was focused on the stone towers and slanted rooftops inside. He did not know where this ire for the town came from, nor did he care. All that mattered was the power inside him, surging to be unleashed.

With a thrust of his hand, a jagged bolt of lightning flashed down at the town. Its green glow illuminated a maze of streets and hovels huddled around the larger structures. Flames erupted from inside the building he'd struck. Thunder boomed in his ears, drowning out every sound except the howling winds. Again and again his incandescent fury rained down, and with each attack he felt his strength flowing through him like a burning river, scorching away the tribulations of a mundane life that had haunted him for too long. Tired of being weak and at the mercy of others, he reveled in this newfound supremacy. But a voice in the back of his mind whispered it wasn't new. No, he'd always had this potential, buried so deep it might never have come to light if not for . . .

STORM AND STEEL

Lightning flashed, blinding him, and in that moment he was back aboard the *Bantu Ray* as the converted merchant carrack struggled in the grip of a nightmare storm. Verdant light flashed in the sky, and something opened inside him, like a hidden inner doorway opening for the first time. Dark energy seethed within. Then a wave of cold water crashed over him, carrying him away, and the moment was lost.

He watched the fires roar below and the tiny figures scurrying to escape the destruction he had wrought. He wanted to be free from the restraints that bound him, free to roam the earth, doing as he pleased, destroying all that stood in his way. Yet some force held him in this place. He strained against it, ceasing his rampage on the town to direct his strength in this new direction, to breaking free. Yet the power holding him resisted. He struggled harder, until something started to change inside him. Bits of energy drifted away from him, charging the air with their power, while at the same time a weird sensation akin to vertigo twisted his core. His view of the vista below grew dim and distant, as if the entire world were fading from his sight. Or perhaps he was the one who was fading. The last sound he heard was a peal of thunder, growing louder.

Coming closer.

Horace bolted upright with a sharp pain in his chest. For a heartbeat he didn't know where he was. Was he the storm soaring over the desert? Or was he the man?

He sat in a padded chair on the balcony of his room at the villa where he'd fallen asleep. The trees below swayed, their leaves thrashing in the wind. Something thrummed in the air, like a host of vibrations, invisible and inaudible, faintly palpitating across his skin. Rubbing his chest through his tunic, he started to stand up when the floor rumbled beneath his feet. *Am I still dreaming?*

The floor bucked, sending him stumbling into the stone balustrade surrounding the balcony. A grinding rumble like stone being ripped apart resounded through the villa, punctuated by a staccato of distant *thumps*. The balcony shuddered with each impact. When it started to tear away from the villa, Horace jumped through the doorway back into his room. A piece of bronze sculpture tumbled over from the bedside table onto the floor. Horace scrambled for the door. He heard the first detonation as he reached for the latch handle.

The windows in his room exploded, spraying glass everywhere. Shards nicked his arms and hands as he covered his face. Through his fingers he saw a growing light outside the windows, pulsating orange and yellow. Raw heat washed across his back as he threw himself to the floor. He grabbed for his power and tried the first thing that came to mind, conjuring a cloud of cool mist around himself. The *zoana* stuttered inside him, present but not obeying his will. He pulled harder, and suddenly he couldn't breathe. He was inside a solid bubble of water. It filled his mouth and nose, suffocating him as the inferno washed over him. He thrashed on the floor and tried to spit it out, but the liquid just kept coming. He was on the verge of passing out when he finally managed to sever his connection to the power. With a choking cough, he vomited up the last of the water.

Horace coughed as he got on his hands and knees. The flames had retreated, leaving the room clogged with smoke. He crawled to the nearer window and peeked over the scorched sill. A stand of trees stood far back from the east side of the villa. A party of men stood on the grassy sward between the villa and the woods. Eight men in dark robes. Their gleaming masks stared in his direction, the bronze features fashioned into the likenesses of strange beasts. Three of the masked men raised their hands, fingers together like a salute. Prickles ran down Horace's spine a heartbeat before a barrage of bright lights rushed toward him.

Terrified that he might kill himself with his own magic, Horace didn't dare reach for it as he ducked under the window. The walls rocked as hostile magic struck the side of the villa. Fire seared the outer brick facing, and ice froze the mortar solid. A windstorm battered the manor while the ground shook. Crawling back from the window under a storm of frozen hail, Horace could feel the structure of the villa shaking around him.

A jet of flame flashed in his peripheral vision. Biting back his fear, Horace reacted as he'd learned from Ubar, using his feel of the *zoana* to follow the tether of power back to its source on the lawn. Before he could talk himself out it, he seized a thread of Shinar and severed that ethereal connection with a quick slash. The fire evaporated in an instant, leaving behind a haze of smoke and soot. Horace was starting to stand up when a gale of bitter wind surged through the window and threw him backward. His arms spun as he tried to catch his balance, but the wind held him captive until it smashed him against the opposite wall. Eyes squeezed shut, he struggled to free himself, but the winds buffeted him without relent. After three tries, he found the connection to the Imuvar dominion fueling the winds and sliced it apart. Suddenly unsuspended, he fell to his knees. A blinding light shone through the window. Something was building outside the villa, over the figures on the lawn. Horace felt its power coalescing, a combination of at least two dominions. It was time to abandon ship. Staying on his hands and knees, he scurried toward the door. He opened it just in time.

The concussion lifted Horace across the threshold and into the hallway. He landed on his side, jamming his elbow hard against the floor. Gasping through clenched teeth, he fumbled his way to his feet. The hallway was dark. The floor, he noticed, was slightly askew. *This whole damned house is coming down.*

He glanced in the direction of the queen's suite but then ran in the other direction, toward the south wing. To Alyra's room.

The floor shook again, and he almost ran over Mezim before a flash of light illuminated the secretary running in the opposite direction.

"Mezim!"

"My lord!"

"This way!"

They ran to Alyra's room. The door was closed. Praying she was inside, Horace shoved it open with his shoulder. Though the oil lamps were unlit, the window shutters were open, allowing stilettos of moonlight to stab inside. He approached the bed, where a long lump lay under the sheets.

"Al—," he started to call to her when a silvery streak flashed toward him from the shadows behind the door.

Horace flinched away, almost tripping on the loose rug, as the point of a narrow blade hovered in front of his face.

"Horace?" Alyra lowered the knife.

He let out a deep breath and tried to still his thumping heart. Then he saw a slender woman standing behind Alyra. It was the handmaiden he had seen earlier.

Alyra gestured to the slave woman. "This is Sefkahet. We were just talking. What's happening?"

Horace held out a hand. "It's an attack. We need to get out of here."

"Just a moment."

He waited anxiously as Alyra knelt down and reached under the small bed. She retrieved a leather satchel and slung it over her shoulder. Then she nodded to him as she stood up. "Where are we going?"

"To find the queen."

Horace led the women out to the hallway where Mezim waited, glancing anxiously all around. Distant lights through the windows cast flickering shadows across the walls. Horace started down the hallway in the direction of the royal apartment, but Alyra jerked him to a halt by grabbing his arm. "Wait! Stop!"

All at once, Horace felt the overwhelming urge to shake her. Here he was, risking his life to save her, and she couldn't help herself from questioning him. "What?"

"What's the plan?"

"We find the queen and get her away from here. Hopefully, to someplace safe."

"And where is that?"

"I don't have a damned clue! All right? Let's just try to get of this alive."

She released his arm. "All right."

He spun around and hurried down the hall, trusting the others to keep up. Some of the floorboards had sprung loose, making for treacherous footing. As they got to the main body of the villa, the sound of quick footsteps made Horace stop short. He peered around a corner as Ubar appeared, hustling toward them.

Horace stepped out into the open. "Lord Ubar, it's me."

"Lord Horace!" The *zoanii* slowed his gait. "I was coming to find you. Please hurry. We must get to Her Majesty."

"That's where we were heading," Alyra said, coming to stand behind Horace. "Are you all right?"

"Quite fine," Ubar replied, pausing to take in Mezim and the hand-maiden. "But we must hurry. The energies surrounding the house are growing in magnitude."

Horace could feel it, too. A gathering sense of dread from outside the villa's walls, like a great wave about to break over the gunwales.

They found the first body at the mouth of the corridor leading to the queen's private suite. A member of the Queen's Guard. Three more lay behind him. The stench of blood and shit filled the hallway. Ubar held a sleeve to his mouth as he stepped past the soldiers. Horace forced himself to look down at them. *They were my responsibility. And I failed them.*

Horace thought to look for signs of sorcery on the bodies—burns or bizarre fractures—but instead he saw blood from long slashes, the lethal strikes delivered to their throats and across their torsos. He saw a shadow move in his peripheral vision a heartbeat before he thought to call out a warning.

A figure cloaked in black from head to foot emerged from the darkness of the hallway. His garb looked like leather, but it fit his body like a second skin. A knife, its blade blackened as well, leapt out at Lord Ubar. Horace tried to focus his *zoana* to strike the assassin, but the power refused to answer his call.

"No!" he shouted.

The point of the knife stopped six inches from Ubar's turned back as if it had run into a stone wall. The attacker struggled as a faint shimmer of frost rimed his blade. Then the ice flowed up his hand and arm. He pulled back as if for another thrust, but Ubar raised a hand. The assassin stumbled backward, his blade dropped, clutching at his chest. He sank to his knees and then fell over, unmoving. A stream of clear water dribbled from his open mouth.

"A Blood Knife," Ubar said. "Assassin from Scavia. Legendary in their prowess."

Horace shook his head. "I'm sorry. I tried to—"

A second shadow in the same black skin-suit detached from the opposite side of the corridor, coming up behind Ubar on silent steps. Ubar started to turn, and Horace lunged forward, hoping to grab the knife before it struck.

The assassin stopped suddenly and turned, reaching back, but crumpled before he could complete the action.

Alyra knelt behind him. She withdrew a slim knife from his back and wiped the blade on the dead assassin's clothes before she stood up. Horace noticed her hands were shaking ever so slightly. He wanted to say something supportive, but instead he just nodded.

Lord Ubar's face had turned a pale shade of bronze, his eyes slightly glassy. Horace took him by the elbow. "You all right?"

Ubar nodded twice, his lips pressed tight together. "We should continue."

The door to the queen's apartments was closed. Ubar reached for the latch, but Horace stopped him. Motioning the young lord aside, Horace opened an inner pathway to the Mordab dominion. At least he tried to. His *qa* remained closed. He actually felt embarrassed as the seconds passed and he was still fumbling to access his power. *Why is this happening now?*

"Hurry," Alyra whispered behind them.

Horace finally gave up and motioned to Ubar. "Freeze the door frame."

Ubar nodded and stared at the doorway. Frost formed along the wooden frame. Horace could sense the presence of the *zoana*, could feel the tiny pockets of moisture hidden inside the wood begin to freeze and swell, making the wood crackle. When Ubar was done, Horace backed up a step and kicked the door.

The latch handle mechanism flew apart, and the door swung inward to reveal a battlefield. A massive hole loomed in the northern wall, opening out into night. The edges of the hole were singed black like the inside of a kiln. Two more dead guardsmen lay on the floor. One was frozen stiff, and the other had been bent backward until his spine snapped. One armored man remained standing, the big lieutenant of the Queen's Guard. Horace couldn't recall his name, but there was no sign of Captain Dyvim.

The queen stood in front of the bedchamber in a gauzy nightdress. Fiery eruptions outside the villa highlighted her features—her wide eyes, her lips pulled back in a snarl, nostrils flared. Streams of semisolid air projected from her hands, one after another, too fast for Horace to follow, and the windstorm surrounding the manor shrieked with every release. Lord Xantu stood beside her, hurling jets of raging fire at their foes. While they battled, attacks from the outside continued to rain upon the villa.

Now that he was here, Horace didn't know what to do. But Ubar didn't hesitate. He ran over to join the queen's defense, and Horace saw a translucent barrier of what looked like water vapor form around Byleth. Before he could decide how to handle the situation, Xantu glanced over. "Man the east windows! They'll try there again any moment!"

Horace turned to obey, but Alyra pulled him to a stop. He looked at her and saw the anxiety in her eyes. "We need to leave, Horace."

The fires outside reflected in Byleth's eyes as she turned her head. Blood dripped in a steady stream from a cut along her left cheek. "No! We stand against these traitors who would dare attack their queen!"

With a long look to Alyra to show the tight spot he was in, and a quick glance at the handmaiden, Horace entrusted them to Mezim and crossed to the other side of the room. He stepped over a mess of cushions, pillows, and clothing strewn over the floor. The windows had been busted out. Their shutters had broken loose, and glass fragments were scattered everywhere. Horace peered out but couldn't see anything more than the darkness. He considered conjuring a ball of light but decided against it. For one thing, there no sense drawing attention to himself. Also, his recent failures to connect with the *zoana* weighed on his mind. He felt out of control. Lord Mulcibar had warned him that he might someday become a danger to himself and those around him. It seemed that day had come.

A shout from behind made him turn. Alyra stood just inside the doorway with the slave woman by her side. The way they stood together, so close, made him wonder. Almost as if they were sisters. He mentally flogged himself. *Of course she still has close friends in the queen's service. She spent so long in the palace. I should have made the effort to free them as well.*

Byleth still stood before the hole in the wall. Lord Xantu had fallen to his knees, bloodied hands pressed to his face. Ubar stepped to take the lord's place beside the queen, but a hail of tiny stones ripped through his watery barrier. Horace hissed as a small flat stone tore through his thin tunic and sliced into his side. He pulled the ripped fabric away with a grimace. A quick look assured him that it wasn't bleeding much, though he couldn't see whether the stone had exited the wound or was still lodged inside.

However, Ubar had collapsed in a heap beside Xantu. Byleth held her ground alone, her sheer dress ripped to bloody shreds. Horace was about to go to her when he felt something outside the villa. Building up, like the explosion at his suite, but this was far more powerful. There was nowhere to go. Nowhere to escape what was coming.

He rushed across the room, pausing only to grab Alyra by the wrist and haul her over toward the hole, trusting the handmaiden and Mezim to come along. Horace let go when they reached Ubar. As Alyra knelt down beside the youth, Horace grabbed the queen around her waist. He dropped to his knees, dragging them both down to the floor. The villa shuddered.

Horace pointed at Xantu, unconscious on the floor. "Get him over here!"

The tall guard lieutenant seized Lord Xantu by an ankle and pulled him over to the group. Meanwhile, Horace was bracing himself. This was his best idea, and he had no way of knowing if it would work. The force gathering outside the villa continued to grow. It felt like a mountain teetering over their heads. The queen's face was ashen, her lips pressed into a tight frown.

He reached for his *qa*. He felt the energy pulsing behind it, but the fear that it would elude his grasp almost overwhelmed him. Then he felt a firm grip on his arm. Alyra was looking at him intently. She nodded.

I can do this.

Taking a deep breath, he delved into the pathway to his power. The pain in his chest returned at once, an icy heat suffusing his lungs and making him gasp, but all physical sensations were pushed to the back of his mind as the *zoana* came to life within him. It filled him up, allowing him to feel every muscle and sinew, every bone and organ. He wanted to shout, but he clamped down on his exuberance and channeled the Shinar dominion into the strongest, widest barrier he was able. His nerves burned as the power expanded into an invisible sphere around them. Just as it solidified, a sound like thunder filled the room, and a titanic force slammed against the shield. Horace was crushed down on top of Byleth. She yelped as they were both pressed against the bare floorboards. Wood splintered as the weight increased on top of them.

STORM AND STEEL

Horace felt the power fueling the shield starting to slip from his mental grasp. The ache in his chest was getting too painful to ignore. He started to think of contingency plans, but nothing came to mind.

And then the floor gave way beneath them.

His stomach dropped in a sickening rush as he fell. He glimpsed a stark light as they plunged to the floor below. Then he landed on his knees on the ground floor between two forms he thought might be Byleth and Alyra, hard enough to send shivers up through to his hips. His startled lungs sucked in a mouthful of dusty air as he collapsed on his stomach. He lay still, concentrating on just breathing. His heart was racing. The blood thrummed in his ears. Yet, he was alive. He peered over at Alyra, and saw her blinking in the gloom. Blood welled from a cut on her chin, but otherwise she appeared all right. He started to turn toward the queen when he heard a groan from above. He looked up, and his heart almost stopped as a shower of plaster and wooden beams rained down on them.

Horace struggled to reinforce his Shinar barrier before the villa's roof crashed down on them. Someone shrieked as all light was extinguished from view. Pressure built up inside Horace as he fought to hold up the massive load. He imagined he could feel his internal organs mashing flat, imagined his blood trying to escape through his eyes and eardrums. He held onto his *zoana* with every ounce of control he could summon, but it was unraveling fast. *Not now. Not now. Focus!*

He redoubled his effort to hold onto the power keeping them alive. Just as he thought he had it under control, the floor underneath opened up, and he was falling again. Falling into darkness.

Horace shifted away from the stone digging into his side, but there was precious little space, and so he was reduced to wriggling back and forth until the nuisance got pushed aside. His foot touched someone's leg.

"Sorry," he whispered.

"Don't speak," Byleth said in a tired voice. "You're using up the air."

There was some shifting as the others adjusted their positions inside this, their rocky prison. Horace settled back in the dark. His head was pounding, but that pain was nothing compared to the agony cutting through his chest, as if a sharp knife were trying to split open his breastbone from the inside. Somehow he had remained conscious when they landed in one of the villa's many sub-cellars. That had been an hour ago, or maybe two, and the strain of maintaining his protective shield for so long was taking its toll. But it was the only thing standing between them and the mountain of debris threatening to crush them. *This is how I die? After surviving the desert and slavery, a duel to the death in the Grand Arena, and the enmity of an entire priesthood, I'm going to die trapped under a house like a roach.*

He could almost hear his mother's voice. *But he had so much potential!*

Potential. Aye, that and a copper bit will buy you a bowl of gruel in any dockside slophouse in Avice.

"Get your elbow out of my back, Sefkahet!"

Someone moved hastily at the queen's outburst. Horace couldn't help from smiling.

"Oh," Byleth muttered. "Enough of this sitting in the dark!"

A globe of pale blue light appeared above them near the top of his shield. The seven of them—himself, Byleth, Xantu, the tall lieutenant, Mezim, Alyra's friend, and Alyra—lay around a concave bowl of impacted debris. *At least I'll die in good company. A queen, a lord, a soldier, my secretary, a slave, and. . . .*

He didn't know how to describe Alyra, and that was part of their problem. He didn't know where the spy ended and the woman began, and every time they spoke he went immediately on the defensive, so afraid that she—the person who knew him best—couldn't stand what she saw when she looked at him. *Is that guilt speaking? Or am I protecting myself from getting hurt again? I almost didn't recover when Sari died. I don't know if I could survive another abandonment.*

"I thought I saw you in my chambers before our precipitous fall," Byleth said to Alyra. "It's curious, my dear, how often you turn up after having left my service *and* gained your liberty."

Alyra lowered her eyes. "If my presence offends, Majesty, I will remove myself."

Byleth waved her hand. "Well, it seems we are all stuck here together for the time being. So I suppose we shall have to put aside propriety for the time being, eh?"

Stones clattered as Lord Ubar sat up. "Majesty, did you know the identity of the attackers? I believe I saw six of them, in all."

"Eight." Horace coughed into his hand to clear away the dust. "I counted eight people outside my chamber window. They wore masks."

No one said anything, though Horace could hear them breathing. He had his own ideas about those robed figures. He'd been expecting some form of retribution from the Sun Cult. It wouldn't have surprised him to discover those dark robes were blood-red, the distinguishing hue of the Order of the Crimson Flame. Killing him and the queen had to be high on their list of priorities. *And they might still succeed if we don't find a way out of here.*

He didn't have many ideas about that, unfortunately. All his power was dedicated to keeping the shield intact, and it was flagging.

"Perhaps—"

Ubar started to say something, but Mezim cut him off. "What was that?"

"What?" Horace asked.

"I heard something."

"I did, too," Alyra said.

Then Horace heard it. A crunching noise from somewhere above them, like metal biting into loose earth. *Rescue? Or is it our killers come to finish the job?*

No one spoke. Even the sounds of breathing abated as the digging got closer. It seemed to take forever, and every second Horace's head felt ready to burst. The flows of *zoana* inside him fluctuated until he clamped down on them again. Sweat dripped down his forehead, and his tongue felt swollen.

Finally, a shaft of pale sunlight pierced the earthen shell above them. Horace blinked and shaded his eyes. Alyra lay beside him, looking mostly unharmed. The cut on her chin had stopped bleeding. Everyone in the pit was covered in dust. The queen and her bodyguards sported some minor wounds, but Ubar's appearance shocked him. The youth's face was a mask of dried blood. He moved slowly as the others gathered around the opening. Horace crawled over to him.

"Take it easy," he said, and put a hand on the young lord's shoulder. "We're not even sure what's up there."

"I don't sense any *zoanii* above."

Horace took a moment to extend his own senses up through the debris. He didn't feel anyone accessing the *zoana* above either, but it was difficult to be sure because the queen and both her bodyguards had called upon their power. Their auras were almost blinding to his inner senses. "Just to be on the safe side, stay put."

Ubar settled back against the stony bed as the hole above them widened. Horace made out iron tools, spades, and picks, digging away the mass of earth and stone covering them. A loud *clunk* echoed inside the pit as a tool struck the invisible barrier. Excited voices chattered above, and a brown face appeared in the open space, peering down at them. Horace let out a sigh as he recognized Eannatum, the villa's chief steward.

"Horace," the queen said. "Lower your protection and let them inside."

That was easier said than done. Horace eyed the concave ceiling above them. If he released the barrier, he had every reason to believe the debris would bury them alive.

Ubar touched his elbow. "First Sword, I do not have my father's skill with the Kishargal dominion. But if you were to fuse the soil over our heads together, I believe it might hold long enough for us to escape."

Horace considered the problem. He wasn't a master of the earth dominion either, but he understood what Ubar was saying. The question was whether he possessed the strength to accomplish it while maintaining the shield. He took a deep breath and prepared to split his attention between two separate flows of *zoana*.

Byleth crawled over to him. Her hair was caked with dirt, her face smudged and bleeding, and yet she remained exquisite. She took his right hand. "We will lend you our strength, First Sword. Xantu, attend us."

Alyra had to shift out of the way to make room as Xantu crawled past her. The sorcerer took Horace's other hand. The *zoanii*'s dark eyes gleamed faintly in the gloom, and Horace thought he detected a hint of a smile. He cleared his throat. "All right. What do I do?"

Without warning, raw power surged into him from both directions. For a moment, Horace felt like it was going to rip him apart. Yet, the power joined the flow of *zoana* already operating inside him and reinforced it. The added power shored up his weakening protective barrier immediately, and he felt he had plenty to spare, though the pain in his chest also became more intense at the same time. Wanting to get this over as fast as possible, he opened himself to the Kishargal dominion. His borrowed strength made it ridiculously easy to call upon the second channel. He sent it straight up into the rock and dirt packed above them and saw the solution. Feeling confident, he called upon a third channel, this time from the dominion of fire, and joined it to the flow of earth. The mingled skeins entered the loose earth and spread out. Each piece of stone fused to the debris around it. The artificial ceiling crackled like roasting oats as the effect spread outward and upward. Horace kept it up until a broad shell had coagulated above them. Then he backed off. The ceiling was now a solid curve of mottled stone.

"Ready?" he asked.

Everyone nodded. Holding his breath, Horace drew back on the power holding up the shield. Cracks appeared in the rocky shell, and bits of dirt rained down, but the shell held. Horace released the last bit of his *zoana* with a long sigh. Byleth and Xantu let go of him. Hands reached down from the open hole.

The queen was the first one out. Horace started to indicate for Alyra to take her turn, but Xantu pushed ahead, grabbing the edge of the hole and pulling himself out.

"Lord Ubar," Alyra said. "You're injured. You should go next."

Horace and the big lieutenant helped Ubar to stand. The young lord limped, favoring one leg. The posture reminded Horace at once of Lord Mulcibar.

Ubar clapped a hand on his shoulder. "You saved us, Lord Horace. I will forever be in your debt."

"Nonsense. I was just saving my own skin."

Ubar smiled through the blood. "The texts of Sippa say that humility is the highest virtue. If that is true, you are a most virtuous man, my friend."

Ubar was lifted out, and the women went after him, leaving Horace and his secretary as the last ones in the pit. When the rescuers reached down, Mezim insisted that Horace go next. Too tired to care, Horace grasped their stringy wrists and allowed himself to be pulled up, only then remarking to himself that Ubar had called him friend. *I've got precious few of them these days.*

His first breath of the air outside the pit was so rich he got dizzy and almost lost his grip on the hands pulling him out. As the group of men helped him stand beside the pit, Horace noticed their iron collars. He felt a twinge of sadness as he thanked them. The men, all of them covered in grime and sweat, bowed low before him, and that only made him feel worse. They deserved to be freed for their heroic service. He looked toward the queen, sitting on a low end table nearby, the slave woman kneeling beside her. "Excellence, I—"

The words died in his throat as he gazed upon the devastation. Half the villa had collapsed, including the entire northern face. Huge piles of rubble, with jagged timbers jutting from the brick and stonework, spilled into the surrounding gardens. Much of the wreckage was scorched, some of it melted into black slag. A haze of dust hung above the grounds, catching in the early morning light. A handful of soldiers stood around the periphery, wide-eyed, with bared weapons in their hands. Yet there was no sign of the enemy who had caused this destruction.

"First Sword."

Horace looked over to Byleth, who was now standing as a squad of guardsmen approached, carrying a dust-shrouded body. It was Captain Dyvim. His open eyes stared up at the night sky as he was brought forward.

"And we found this, Majesty," one of the guards said.

He held up what appeared to be a long strip of black cloth. It was a piece from the skin-tight leather armor the two assassins in the corridor had been wearing. In the bright light, Horace could see the mottled scales, like the skin of a black snake.

"Scavian," Lord Xantu said in a disgusted tone.

"Yes," the queen said. "No doubt hired with Sun Cult gold."

She dismissed the soldiers with a flick of her fingers. "First Sword, my guard requires a new leader." She pointed to the lieutenant. "He will do for the time being."

Horace bowed his head as the queen stalked away, with Lord Xantu and the new captain of her guard in tow. Then he went over to Alyra, who stood off by herself, surveying the damage. "Hey," he said, not sure what else to say to her.

"It's horrible. It's just . . . beyond words."

"I know. I can't believe we survived. But don't worry. We'll find the people responsible for this."

Her eyes were moist as she turned toward him. "Find them? *You're* responsible, Horace. You and the queen, both."

Shocked, Horace glanced over at Byleth, but the queen was talking to Lord Xantu. No one was paying attention to Alyra and him. "Are you insane?" he hissed. "You saw what happened. We were attacked in the middle of the night. How is that my fault?"

"You push people, Horace. You started causing trouble the moment you stepped foot in this country, and you haven't once stopped long enough to consider how you're affecting the people around you."

"I don't think that's fair." He tried to offer some proof that she was wrong, but all his excuses fell apart before they reached his lips. Was this his doing? He'd certainly managed to rack up a hefty list of enemies in his short time here, but he didn't believe that was entirely his fault. Some people, especially the *zoanii* in the queen's court and the priests of the Sun Cult, had decided to hate him from the start.

He was about to ask if he could find her something to drink, but she walked away, picking her way through the rubble. He longed to call her back, to say something crucial that could convince her of his good intentions, but there was nothing he could do. The gulf between them had grown too wide to cross with just a few words. *And growing wider every day.*

Byleth was giving orders as servants scurried about, trying to save what they could from the wreckage. Horace found a burnt cushion and sat down. He felt like if he closed his eyes, he could sleep for a hundred years.

Then Mezim was beside him, helping him up. "Come along. We'll have that injury looked at and then find something presentable to wear."

Horace looked down at the cut in his side. Blood soaked his ragged tunic, and he'd hardly noticed it. He could only shake his head as Mezim led him away.

CHAPTER FOUR

G ray dunes rolled across the plains below like waves of sooty ice on a frozen sea. Eight days aboard this flying boat, and most of it had offered no better view than this barren ocean seemingly devoid of life. The dunes continued south to become the Great Desert. Or, as some Akeshian scholars called it, the Southern Bulwark. For centuries it had kept the empire safe from invasion. And, like the ocean, it possessed a lure for certain intrepid souls. The empire's history was littered with noble attempts to tame the desert, to build great cities amid its shifting sands, each eventually succumbing to the inevitable.

Or so Abdiel had heard. He had never felt any great desire to see a desert, much less live in one. He wasn't overly fond of sand, and there was the oppressive heat to consider. He imagined himself lying atop a sand mound, dying of thirst, and then banished the image from his mind.

He had seen the ocean once, the real ocean, many years ago on a tour of the western empire. Abdiel looked up to the front of the flying ship where his master, Lord Mebishnu, spoke with the vessel's captain. His master's rise through the ranks of the Order of the Crimson Flame had been swift and certain. Oh, yes. Lord Mebishnu was a man who took what he wanted. *Now, if only he would set his eyes on a proper wife, things would be so much better.*

That was the reason Abdiel had visited the Temple of Amur to make a special donation when he learned of this trip. The women of the imperial court at Ceasa, for all their impeccable breeding, were a clutch of asps, in his opinion. He was hoping his master would find a better selection of good, upstanding ladies out here. Nisus, he'd heard, was a center of piety and forthrightness, exactly the kind of place to find his master a bride.

Abdiel approached to see if his master had need of him.

"The desert is beautiful from this height, isn't it?" the ship's captain asked. Abdiel hadn't bothered to learn the man's name. Why bother? What was a sailor but just another servant?

STORM AND STEEL

Mebishnu glanced over the railing before returning his gaze to the far horizon. "How long before we reach Nisus?"

"Within the hour, your lordship."

"Your *Eminence*," Abdiel hissed under his breath. How dare the man not use the proper title when addressing an official envoy of the Greater Temple?

"Pardon me, Your Eminence!" the captain hurried to say and added a short bow. "I meant no offense."

Mebishnu passed it off with a wave of his hand. "I'm sure you have duties to attend to, Captain. I'll take up no more of your valuable time."

The captain bowed again as he backed away. "Thank you, Your Eminence. It is a pleasure to have you aboard."

Abdiel gave a small sigh to show his disapproval at such meaningless flatteries. The captain's face turned dark in a scowl, but Abdiel turned his back on the man. "Master, would you like a cool drink? Lemon juice, perhaps?"

"No, Abdiel. I'm not thirsty."

Not thirsty for drink, but for something else, eh?

"Of course, Master."

The deck tilted as the flying barge turned in a wide arc, descending slowly over the swollen waters of the Typhon River. High walls appeared on the horizon, growing swiftly as they approached. The city walls were built from yellow stone, but its square towers were black like iron teeth protruding from a jaundiced jaw. The city sat in an oxbow of the river so that it was surrounded on three sides by water. A magnificent yellow-stone bridge spanned to the southern bank, its long arch supported by massive piers. A multitude of tents were pitched along that far shore.

As the barge descended nearer, Abdiel could make out men moving among the makeshift shelters. Soldiers in armor and bright helms. Chariots performed maneuvers across hard-packed drilling grounds. This, then, must be the army of three kings.

He placed one hand on the deck's broad railing as the ground slowly rose up to meet them. Taking off in this flying contraption had been bad enough, but he liked descending even worse. A man his age shouldn't be taxing his heart with such things.

The barge landed on the river. Its wide hull churned up the sluggish waters as the great vessel slowed. Abdiel let go of the railing just as the rest of their party emerged from their accommodations below. Eleven brothers of the Crimson Flame, each of them a little green around the ears. Their long robes fluttered in the breeze like the wings of great red birds, and Abdiel forgave them for their lapse of fortitude. For these birds were fierce predators, the most powerful and loyal sorcerers of the Order, hand-selected by the Primarch to accompany his master on this vital mission. Abdiel had been present during his master's audience with His Grand Luminance the night before they departed the capital.

"You must not fail in this matter, my son," the Primarch had said from the raised chair in the High Council's chamber. The tattoos on his bare scalp gleamed like red gold in the light of a hundred lamps. Abdiel had sighed with reverence to see them with his own eyes.

"I understand, Great Father," Mebishnu replied, his voice strong and confident. "I pledge my life to this task."

"Failure would mean not merely the loss of a single city to the growing darkness, but perhaps the entire empire. The queen of Erugash must be punished for her wickedness, and that punishment must come by our hand, my son. You understand that. And that same hand must eradicate the foreign devil in her bosom. That is the cancer *you* must cut away."

The Primarch had rubbed his forehead with both hands as if trying to scrub away a stubborn stain, and Abdiel had felt such sweet sorrow at the gesture. So beauteous, yet so human. "If we lose Erugash, then we are open to attack from the foreign invaders. Just as our forebears conquered the tribes who had settled these lands before us, the invaders will gobble up the empire one town at a time."

"Amur—his name be praised," Mebishnu said, "would never allow that to happen, Great Father."

"No? Think not that we are a special race, my son. The Sun Lord is eternal. Should we fall, He would shine His blessed glory on another people. The destiny of our race rests in your hands. I can trust no one else with this matter."

"I will not fail, Great Father."

Abdiel had taken one last glimpse of the Primarch as they were ushered out of His divine presence. It had been the second-greatest day of his life, outshined only by the birth of his master. And as they were taken away, he'd been struck by the realization that those two miraculous events—the birth and the audience—might alter the course of history.

As Mebishnu returned the genuflections of his brethren with a solemn nod, the barge drifted gently against the shore. Sailors scurried about at their duties. Abdiel waited as they set up the wooden bridge to the shore and made sure he was the first one off the vessel. He almost wept as his feet touched down on solid ground again. The flying barges were a wonderful innovation, much faster than traveling by water or caravan, yet one could not rest easily when soaring thousands of feet above the earth. He shaded his eyes and looked up at the sun, just a few fingerbreadths from high noon. *Yet, we were closer to you, Holy Lord, when we rode upon the winds beneath Your radiant light.*

He turned as his master came down the bridge, speaking again to the ship's captain. "Your orders are to remain here until further notice."

"Of course, Your Eminence. Would you like an escort?"

"No, Captain. Just make sure the ship is ready to fly at any time, day or night."

Mebishnu joined Abdiel on the shore. The rest of the Order brothers had already disembarked, looking a little better now that they were off the boat. They stood along the riverbank, taking in the massive city of tents spread out before them. *This is my master's moment to make his mark. People will look upon this day as the beginning of a glorious new era. Praise be to the Sun Lord.*

"What say you, Abdiel?" Mebishnu asked. "Shall we go forth to find our hosts?"

Abdiel patted the official diplomatic satchel hanging from his shoulder. "Of course, Master. Of course. It's not polite to keep a king waiting, much less three of them, eh?"

"Quite right. Come along."

With a surge of pride, Abdiel walked two steps behind his master toward the camp, with the rest of their delegation following behind. He felt a twinge of indignation to notice there was no reception waiting for them. An envoy from the Temple deserved the proper recognition. At the very least, their hosts could have come out to greet them. But all he saw were tents and pavilions and soldiers, lots of soldiers, sitting around on the ground, eating and conversing as if they had no cares in the world.

Then a man in a golden robe rushed toward them, weaving his way through the soldiery. He was a short man, a trifle wide around the middle with his belly hanging over the sash that kept his robe closed. Abdiel was shocked to see the handful of scarlet tattoos dotting his bald head. *This man is a priest of the Light? Holy Amur, forfend!*

"Lord Mebishnu!" the priest called out. He arrived to meet them, huffing for breath, beads of perspiration gathering on his forehead and cheeks.

Mebishnu introduced himself and his brethren.

The little, fat priest folded his hands across his midsection and made a deep bow. "Greetings, Your Eminence. I am Shabra-Amur, advisor to King Moloch. His Gracious Majesty greets you with all honor and requests that you come with me to his outer palace so that he might have the pleasure of your counsel."

Mebishnu gave his consent with a brief nod, and the priest scurried away almost as swiftly as he had arrived. A few of the nearby soldiers had listened to the brief conversation, but none of them showed any additional respect. Abdiel mumbled a curse on their genitals and spat on the ground as he followed his master through the sea of tents.

It was evident that this army had been stationed here for some time by the nauseating collection of smells and the complacent demeanor of the soldiers. *If they remain here much longer, this tent-city will sprout taverns and brothels if it hasn't already, and then it risks becoming a permanent encampment.*

Off in the distance two flying ships floated above the desert plain, one to the south and the other eastward. Though it was difficult to tell at this distance, each appeared to be gigantic and lavishly decorated, recalling the classic style of imperial war barges.

Finally, the priest led them to a sprawling pavilion at the center of the vast camp. The "outer palace" was not as grand as its name, although it was quite large. The canvas rooftop sagged in several places, and the walls were spattered with mud. A pole holding up a limp flag was planted near the entrance, sporting the colors of three cities: Nisus, Chiresh, and Hirak.

The structure was surrounded by a cordon of Nisusi White Sphinxes, standing at strict attention as befitted the proudest cadre in the western empire. Their armor and weapons gleamed with polish. Abdiel nodded with appreciation for their devotion as the procession was escorted inside.

They were brought into a large room that was decorated like a feast hall. A variety of people sat on cushions around a massive round table. Some looked to be military officers, but most of them wore civilian clothing. And very rich garb at that.

Three large thrones stood at the far side of the table. The chair on the left was occupied by an old man wrapped in a robe of pale-green silk. Abdiel guessed this was King Sumuel of Chiresh. Despite the king's apparent frailty, it was said he ruled his city with a firm hand. In the right-hand throne sat a monarch with a roguish cast to his gaze. Young and handsome with a full head of lustrous black hair, this could only be King Ramsu of Hirak. Apparently he had a roving eye, despite having just married his sixth wife. Abdiel took an instant dislike to the young king, but his attention was pulled to the center seat occupied by a large man with a ponderous belly. His robe, so vast it looked like a tent itself, was deep burgundy with gold trim at the collar and cuffs. His receding hair was pulled back into an oiled queue. Abdiel remembered him from that long-ago tour. King Moloch of Nisus hadn't changed much in the intervening years, except to grow fatter and balder.

Shabra-Amur stopped halfway to the table and bowed low. "Great Rulers, I bring before you Lord Mebishnu of Ceasa, ambassador from the Greater Temple of Amur."

Mebishnu stepped past the priest and bowed. Abdiel noted that it was not a full obeisance as was customary when a subject met a monarch, much less three kings all together, but instead the less formal genuflection required when meeting persons of slightly higher rank.

"Emissary!" King Moloch shouted. The piper in the corner ceased his play, and every head in the room turned as the obese king of Nisus raised a golden cup. "You are a most welcome sight! Enter and join our table."

Abdiel followed Mebishnu and stood behind him as he was offered a stool at the king's left hand. Slaves appeared with wine and food. Abdiel took each plate and decanter from their hands to inspect its contents before personally serving it to his master, though he knew Mebishnu would eat none of it.

The rest of the delegation remained at the doorway, stiff-backed with arms by their sides as if they were standing for review on a parade ground.

King Moloch put a pheasant leg in his mouth and slurped as he pulled the bone out, stripped of all its meat and gristle. Then he chewed on the denuded bone. "What about your brother priests? We have enough food and wine for all, unless they find our company distasteful?"

"Not at all, Majesty," Mebishnu said. "But they are sworn to holy oaths. Neither food nor drink shall pass their lips until after evening vespers, in the privacy of their quarters."

With a sharp crack, the king split open the bone and proceeded to suck out the marrow. "As they will. Never let it be said that we impugned upon the customs of the Sun Temple."

"Your hospitality is legendary, Majesty. I thank you."

"So, what news do you bring from Ceasa, Lord Mebishnu? Has the emperor decided to join our righteous cause and drag that upstart bitch Byleth from her throne?"

Fists thumped the table as the other guests showed their agreement. King Sumuel watched the assembly with a wary eye as he sipped from a small cup, carefully tended by his own body-slave. King Ramsu was too busy eating dates from the hands of a comely slave girl to pay attention.

"I'm afraid not, Majesty," Mebishnu answered. "Though the emperor sends His regards to all His faithful servants."

King Moloch's eyes narrowed to mere slits in his corpulent face. *And now we see a glimmer of that renowned irritability.*

Abdiel knew his master saw it as well. A ruler who could not control his temper, especially in front of his peers and subjects, was a dangerous creature. Such a trait also made him too volatile to trust.

"However," Mebishnu continued, "I was not sent to carry messages but to hear answers."

"Answers? To what?"

"The first question concerns this army's lack of progress. By our reports, you have been camped here outside the walls of your city for the better part of a month. Why the delay?"

King Moloch's cup rang with a dull clank as it bounced off the table and rolled to the far side. "Does the Primarch think we are dragging our feet? Is that it, eh? Does he not believe that we want that bitch's head for the murder of our dear son? What proof can we give, Emissary? What proof would satisfy the Temple of our sincerity? Is it blood he desires?"

"If your slave sins against you, better to slay him and lose a single servant than to stay your hand and lose them all," Mebishnu quoted. It was one of Abdiel's favorite lines from the holy scripts.

A man stood up from the table. Younger than most of the assembled nobles, yet he exuded an aura of authority. His silk robe was parted to reveal a heavy gold amulet on his hairless chest. "I do not like the tone you use, Emissary. I think you ought to apologize to our royal hosts before something unfortunate happens to you and your acolytes."

The others sat still, their gazes darting back and forth between the two men. Mebishnu lifted a single finger. The young man's left hand, wrapped in a fiery nimbus, shot forward to attack. But the flames sputtered and died before they could fly forth. Mebishnu hardly looked over as the young noble toppled to the carpeted floor, his body pierced by a dozen long spears of solid stone.

Mebishnu wiped a trickle of blood from his left nostril. "His Divine Radiance only desires faithful obedience, as any father wishes from his sons."

The three kings shifted in their wooden thrones but said nothing. King Moloch grunted and called for another goblet. "Of course, as it should be."

Abdiel poured his master some wine and didn't spill a drop despite the slight shaking of his hands.

"The Primarch," Mebishnu said, "still awaits an answer. Why has this army not marched for Erugash?"

King Moloch leaned forward on his throne. "I will tell you why we wait. My brother kings prefer to remain under the shadow of my walls, feasting and drinking in safety instead of marching to seek vengeance for my murdered son!"

"Preposterous," King Ramsu said with a mouth full of date. "Because you insisted on merging our forces here at Nisus, my soldiers only arrived three days ago after a long and dusty trek. They require rest before we start for Erugash."

"Why didn't you send them by river then?" King Moloch demanded.

"In winter?" Ramsu asked. "Don't be daft. I would have lost half my ships in the flooding water."

King Sumuel wagged a finger at Moloch. "Your vengeance is your own affair. Hirak and Chiresh only agreed to join your little war for our share of the spoils. But so far Nisus has refused to agree to a fair division of the captured territories." He shrugged to Mebishnu. "And so we wait until our demands are met. It matters little to me whether we leave tomorrow or a month from now. Erugash will fall to us in time, and we shall have our due rewards."

Mebishnu took a sip from his cup. "Those matters will be finalized this very day, under my authority as the Temple representative. Does anyone challenge my right?"

When no one spoke, Mebishnu nodded. "Good. My second question concerns a disturbing tale we heard during our journey. It seems an attempt was made on Queen Byleth's life. Very messy and ill-advised. Worst of all, it failed."

Of the three kings, only Moloch could meet Mebishnu's gaze, and his royal face was flushed with blood. "You may be the legate of the Holy Sun, Lord Mebishnu. But take care not to rise too high, lest you get burned."

Abdiel stepped back as his master stood up. This was the delicate moment. *Remain calm, Master. Use prudence.*

"You still do not understand," Mebishnu said. "I am not here to advise you but to take command."

Abdiel retrieved the scrolls from the satchel he wore, and Mebishnu presented them to King Moloch. "These are signed by the hands of the emperor and the Primarch. They grant me authority over this army and all persons attached to it. Your Royal Persons may, of course, retire to your home cities for the duration of the campaign, but you will have to trust us to make the proper distributions of any assets seized."

Abdiel watched King Moloch's ruddy face, waiting for the explosion. Yet the Nisusi king remained in control of his emotions, for once.

"We leave tomorrow, my kings," Mebishnu said. Then, looking at Sumuel, he added, "Because when Erugash falls *does* matter to the Primarch."

"By all means." King Moloch accepted another gold cup from a slave. "Let us toast to our assured success!"

Abdiel clucked his tongue silently. *Nothing is assured, King. A bloated pig like you should know that. Do not tempt the gods. See my master, standing so calm before you. So commanding. That is the model you should seek to emulate. Alas, there are far too few good men in this empire and far too many slovenly leeches.*

As Mebishnu toasted with them, a lady near the head of the table spoke up. She was young and quite beautiful, but Abdiel thought she might be related to King Ramsu, as they had similar features. "Emissary, we've heard stories here, too. Most terrible news coming out of Erugash. First, the queen tore down the sacred temple, and now she has slain all the members of the Order stationed there. Is this really true?"

All eyes turned to Mebishnu. He coughed into his fist and took a slow, deep breath. "I'm afraid the rumors are true. Her Majesty's forces seized the Chapter House and put everyone inside to the sword. Not a single life was spared." He thumped the knuckles of his left hand on the table as his gaze swept around the chamber. "But know that this is why I have been sent. To exact justice on this most unrighteous queen. Blood will be answered with blood. This I swear to you all."

"And I as well!" King Moloch roared, raising his goblet. "We shall have vengeance on the whore-queen of Erugash!"

Mebishnu left the table, heading for the door. Abdiel spared a glance for the young noble on the floor. His blood had created a wide pool on the carpet. *The folly of youth, that they do not appreciate the gifts they have been given until it is too late.*

"Eminence!" King Moloch called after him. "Will you not stay and take your ease with us after such a long journey?"

"Forgive me, Majesty. The day wanes and I must find my peace in medita-tion, to prepare for the great task we undertake. Fear not. I shall attend you all—" Mebishnu glanced at each of the three kings in turn. "—tomorrow."

The three kings all nodded as if dismissing a common petitioner, but Abdiel kept his ire to himself as he followed his master out of the feasting hall and then out of the tent palace. *The fools should be cleaning his sandals with their royal tongues. Ah, well. Perhaps some fortunate arrows or spears will find their necks during the battle to come and put us out of our misery.*

They made their way back through the camp. The waning afternoon sun threw long shadows across the rows of tents. Abdiel crossed his arms over his chest as a cool zephyr ruffled his robe and wished he'd brought a cloak.

When they reached the river, the ship was tied down with two sailors standing at the bottom of the landing ramp. Abdiel hurried ahead. His master would want complete privacy for his meditation, followed by a light supper once the sun had gone down. He had almost reached the ramp when a slave boy, no older than thirteen or fourteen, darted out from the nearest tents toward their party. Fearing some kind of attack, Abdiel moved to intercept but was too slow.

The slave knelt directly in front of Mebishnu with his forehead pressed to the ground.

"What is it, boy?" Mebishnu asked.

"Greetings, Great Lord of the Sun."

His accent was terrible. Thick and tongue-heavy. That and his sun-browned skin made Abdiel guess he was from one of the southern kingdoms beyond the Great Desert.

"Lord Mebishnu," the slave continued. "My master invites you to dine with him this evening."

Abdiel was moving forward to shoe the slave away when Mebishnu halted him with a gesture. "Who is your master?"

"Lord Pumash of House Luradessus, Great Lord."

The name stoked something in the back of Abdiel's mind. The House of Luradessus was a minor one, but he had heard of this Lord Pumash. The man was supposedly well-connected in mercantile interests across the empire, which lent him influence in many circles. Not a man to ignore, for certain.

Fortunately, Mebishnu recognized this without his servant's advice. "Tell your master I will be happy to dine with him."

"He said to tell you he will expect you at sunset, if it please you."

"That will do."

STORM AND STEEL

The slave bowed, and Mebishnu continued onward to the ship. Abdiel hurried ahead, irritated by the interruption, to prepare his master's private room with the proper candles and incense and the rug situated before the portable fane of the Sun Lord. When all was ready, he left his master alone.

An hour later, Abdiel entered with a jug of water and a clean glass. He found his master seated at the cabin's small table in a fresh robe, this one vibrant scarlet with white borders, looking refreshed as he read a scroll by candlelight. He looked up as Abdiel filled the glass and set it on the table. "Did you eat something, Abdiel?"

"No, Master. You know me. I don't have much of an appetite."

"Still, you should eat to keep up your strength."

Abdiel nodded his head. "It is time for your meeting with Lord Pumash. The brothers of your Order are prepared to escort you."

"Not all of them, Abdiel." There was a sparkle in his master's eyes that hadn't been there before his mediation. A twinkle that bespoke, perhaps, of renewed conviction. "I'll just be bringing Brother Opiru. The rest shall remain onboard until I return."

Abdiel was tempted to question this decision, but he held his tongue. "Yes, Master. We shall await you on the deck."

When Mebishnu exited the cabin, Abdiel and Brother Opiru followed him off the ship. Brother Opiru spoke seldom, and when he did it was with a soft voice that nevertheless possessed the strength of conviction. As such, Abdiel treated the warrior-priest with a large measure of respect, even beyond what he was due because of his rank.

Their search for Lord Pumash's dwelling did not take as long as Abdiel had feared. Lord Pumash was a well-known figure in camp. Following the directions given by a corporal in King Sumuel's army, they found a small pavilion of plain cloth amid a cluster of more colorful tents. No sentries or attendants stood at the door flap, which hung down over the entrance.

Abdiel rushed forward to scratch on the cloth door. A moment later, the same slave boy who had extended the invitation poked his head out. With a deep bow, he stepped aside and held open the flap. Abdiel followed his master inside while Brother Opiru remained without.

The large tent consisted of only a single chamber, which evidently served as reception chamber, dining room, kitchen, and bedchamber, all in one. A second slave, a pretty girl barely out of her teen years, stood near the far wall next to a tall, broad-shouldered man with his back to the entrance. As Mebishnu entered, the man turned around. Abdiel was impressed by his first sight of Lord Pumash. The nobleman was powerfully built with the light-bronze complexion of the upper castes. His short beard was combed and oiled. By his appearance, he could fit into any royal court in the empire.

"Please enter and be welcome!" Lord Pumash said, holding out his hands in greeting. "I apologize for the meanness of my home."

Mebishnu met him at the center of the room. "No need to apologize. I'm sure it is not easy to maintain a lavish lifestyle when traveling with an army."

"Most true. Please sit. May I offer you wine? It is an Altaian vintage. Quite good for relaxing the palate."

Mebishnu took the seat offered to him at a small table. Only two places had been set. Although the tent's furnishings were sparse, the dinnerware was fine porcelain and crystal glass. The female slave poured wine for them both, and this time Abdiel did not interfere.

Lord Pumash raised his glass in a toast. "To new acquaintances and the opportunities they bring."

"An interesting toast," Mebishnu said after he had tried the wine.

"I'm always keen on meeting new people. After all, mutual advantage is the lifeblood of a vibrant trade practice."

"I would be interested in hearing more about your practice, Lord Pumash. I admit I know very little about you save your reputation for honest dealings."

The nobleman placed a hand on his chest and dropped his chin in a deep nod. "Your words honor me. In my line of trade, a man's good name is more precious than gold. I deal mainly in exotic goods, such as precious metals, expert crafts, rare spices, and specialty slaves."

"Specialty slaves?"

"Yes. Such as Lena here, for instance." Lord Pumash looked to the slave woman. "She was brought from Etonia."

"She's a crusader's woman?"

"Precisely. That alone lends her a special value. But she has also been trained to be a court companion. She's an exquisite dancer. She sings and plays several instruments. She even composes poetry in three languages."

"Remarkable."

"Yes, quite. She has a keen mind, which allows for the highest level of training. Thus, she is worth much, much more. You would not believe some of the offers I've received for her, just in this camp alone."

Mebishnu nodded as he took a drink. Talk of money and trade bored him, as was only proper. Abdiel did not approve of *zoanii* sullying themselves with such matters. That's what accounting slaves were for.

Lena served a first course of honeyed figs with a white wine. Mebishnu took a bite out of courtesy.

Lord Pumash gestured to Mebishnu's plate, "Is the food not to your liking? I can have something else prepared. Bring the oranges for Lord Mebishnu."

His master wiped his mouth with a linen napkin. "No. Please, forgive me. It's just that I am eager to hear why you requested this meeting. As you mentioned, we are not acquainted. Our families, as far as I know, have not done business together. What can I do for you?"

"Ah, it's not what you can do for me, Eminence. But rather what we can do for each other. You came here on a specific mission, did you not? To goad these kings into action against the queen of Erugash."

"I've made no secret of my mission, Lord Pumash. Your sources are correct, as far as that goes."

"And," Lord Pumash said as he speared a fig with his fork, "you have no doubt already ascertained the source of the resistance to this plan, eh? No need to answer. You, too, are preceded by your reputation. Each of our royal hosts blames the other for the delay. Ramsu blames Moloch for gathering the armies here so far from his lands. Sumuel blames Moloch for attempting to take the lion's share of the anticipated spoils. And Moloch blames them both for feeding off his largesse."

Impressive. He must have well-placed spies in the households of all three monarchs.

"Let us assume for the sake of debate that what you've said is true." Mebishnu leaned back, holding his wine cup. "What is it to you? You've still not told me what you want."

"To help you. To be more precise, I wish to help your mission succeed in the removal of Queen Byleth from power."

"If your sources have told you that I need or want outside interference, then they missed the mark."

Lord Pumash leaned back as well, mirroring Mebishnu's posture. "But you do, my lord. Need assistance, that is. Because no matter what these kings have told you, it is all a sham."

Mebishnu's eyebrows came together in a line. Abdiel knew well that expression and he prayed that Lord Pumash would not further antagonize his master. "Explain what you mean," Mebishnu said.

"Whatever the kings say, the true reason they do not move from this spot is fear."

The two slaves cleared the first course and set down a platter of roasted lamb on a bed of wild rice and lentils. Lena cut generous portions for both of them, serving Mebishnu first and her master second. Only after they had each taken a bite and exchanged appreciative nods did Mebishnu speak. "Fear of what?"

"Queen Byleth has a new *zoanii* in her court. A foreigner with extraordinary power. Some say he was responsible for the destruction of your temple in Erugash. It is also said this man may have the power to control the chaos storms."

Mebishnu sipped from his glass and then wiped his mouth with the cloth again. "Rumors are a dangerous thing to trust. One must always consider the source."

Lord Pumash smiled, revealing his white teeth. "I agree completely. Believe me when I say I would not have mentioned these things if my sources were not impeccable."

Yes, this is all very interesting and mysterious, Lord Pumash, but enough with the games. Time to put your tiles on the table.

"In this case, your rumors are accurate. This savage comes from the West beyond the ocean. He is known to possess the *zoana*, although reports of his prowess vary. One of our envoys was attempting to neutralize this threat—"

"You speak of Menarch Rimesh."

Mebishnu's jaws clenched at the interruption. "Yes. The same. The menarch was attempting to neutralize—"

"I'm afraid he is dead."

Abdiel almost gasped aloud. That information was a carefully guarded secret. Few outside the Temple hierarchy even suspected it.

Mebishnu, to his credit, recovered with grace. "I cannot confirm that."

"No need, Your Eminence. You have my condolences. Were you close to Menarch Rimesh?"

"No. I only met him once, years ago."

Abdiel remembered that meeting as well. It had been at the high holy festival of *Shamaz* almost a decade ago, when Mebishnu was still enrolled at the Order's academy. Rimesh et'Caliphane had been a well-known personage within the school. Some had believed he might one day ascend to the Primarchy.

"He was a most devout servant of our Lord," Mebishnu said. "And will be sorely missed. But we were talking about something else."

"The queen's foreigner," Lord Pumash said.

"Whatever power he might possess, no man can withstand the might of Amur. You and our hosts must have faith."

"Faith is fine and good, but these kings will want assurances that the cult of the Sun God is focused on this problem."

Ah, and now we come to meat of the matter.

"I am here, am I not?" Mebishnu asked. "What greater assurance could they ask for?"

"Your Eminence, I'm afraid these three rulers are more moved by matters of flesh and coin than holy writs, if you'll excuse my candor."

"And that's where your assistance comes into play?"

"Exactly."

Both slaves came to clear the table. A pitcher of plum-colored wine was placed in the center, and then the slaves withdrew to a corner of the tent. Lord Pumash offered more drink, but Mebishnu placed a hand over his cup. "My lord?"

"King Ramsu owes my cartel a significant sum of money. His Majesty has a penchant for gambling—chariot races in particular—but abysmal luck. In exchange for a more lenient return rate, I believe he would be agreeable to making good on his commitment to this campaign. Likewise, King Sumuel's youngest son was born with poor lungs and relies on a rare pollen from the Far East to live, a substance which only my company can provide. I think you understand where this is going, eh?"

"I think I do. So, speaking in the hypothetical, how soon do you believe you can convince the leaders of this army to begin moving on Erugash?"

"That depends on you."

And now we come to real topic of this meeting. Lord Pumash's compensation.

Mebishnu tapped his left hand on the edge of the table, indicating his host should continue. Lord Pumash set down his glass. "In addition to goading these kings into action, my cartel will assist with provisioning and transportation for the army. In exchange, when Erugash is back under the control of your cult, we will be granted complete control of all trade within the city. In perpetuity."

Abdiel held his breath as he waited for his master's reaction. Yet Mebishnu sat still, showing nothing on his face. After several breaths, he said, "Agreed. Do you require documentation from the hierarchy endorsing my decision?"

"Not at all. We are both men of our word. What we have forged here tonight will remain ironclad."

Mebishnu got up from his seat. "When can I expect to see results, Lord Pumash?"

"I have already sent messages to begin the process, Your Eminence. I was reasonably confident we could reach an understanding. By tomorrow morning, this army will begin its march into history."

I wager you were. And what if my master had not taken the bait? Would you be pulling strings to ensure that his mission was doomed?

With a nod of his head, Mebishnu departed. Abdiel bowed to their host before trailing back out into the night. He and Brother Opiru had to hurry to keep up as his master strode through the encampment.

CHAPTER FIVE

"**I** don't like the look of it."

Jirom nodded, shading his eyes against the late afternoon sun. The village sat in a vast dustbowl in the southern flats of the Iron Desert. Mud-brick buildings huddled around a dusty stretch of road, their backs turned to the desert wastes. Cool winds scoured it, filling the spaces between the buildings with grit and sand. The windows were covered with wooden shutters, sand-blasted like the brick faces around them.

He and Emanon lay side by side at the top of a dune overlooking the settlement. They had ridden across the wastes like all the demons of hell were on their tail, sleeping in brief snatches, eating as they traveled. The men were exhausted, and the animals were in worse shape. They needed someplace to rest.

"It looks like it was hit by a storm not long ago," Jirom said. "But I think it'll be safe if just a few of us enter and try not to attract attention."

Emanon crawled back down from the summit and rolled over onto his back. "I'd rather just keep moving. We can't be more than a day or two from the river."

"More like four. You care to tell me about this gathering we're heading toward?"

"I don't know much about it myself. You were there when I got word of it."

"But you have an idea what we'll find there."

Emanon grunted. "You don't want to hear my suspicions."

"Fine. In that case the men need a break before they fall apart. Two of the horses have thrown shoes, and it's only a matter of time before one or both of them pull up lame. Then we either ditch the gold or pull the wagon ourselves."

"We're not leaving the gold."

"Then we need to stop. And we could also use some information. We've been marching blind out here for a while now."

Emanon spat into the sand and wiped his mouth with the back of a gauntleted hand. "You think this little shit hole is going to have any information worth hearing?"

"You never know. Traders make their way out this far. I passed through here once, years ago. We were making our way up to Nemedia. Or trying to, at least. We got this far before our captain decided to turn around."

"He got cold feet?"

"Our previous commander had died from an arrow through the spleen just a month before, and we elected one of the sergeants to take his place. It wasn't a good fit. Taeblor was a good squad leader, but he didn't have the chops for the head job. He took us back to Bylos, where we settled in as an arm of the local garrison."

"Guarding grocers and sheep all day doesn't sound like you."

"I didn't stick around for long. Signed on with another company and marched the hell away from there."

"You don't talk about your past much."

"It was a long time ago, Em. What's done is done. Anyway, if I'm right, then we'll find what we need here."

Emanon scratched his stubbly chin. "I still don't know about this idea of yours. That gold could supply us for . . . well, for fucking ever. Wasting it on mercs just doesn't seem wise."

Jirom glanced over his shoulder to the wagon sitting at the bottom of the dune. Their team sprawled out around the vehicle like a pack of beaten dogs. "These men have courage, but they aren't ready to stand toe-to-toe with Akeshian soldiers. If you want this rebellion to do more than just hit supply depots and undermanned border stations, we need professional fighters."

"And this is the place? It doesn't look big enough to even have a name."

"It's called Inshem. If you want to hire unattached sellswords, this is the place."

Emanon sighed. "All right. This is your world. Let's do it."

They climbed down to the others. Emanon selected Jerkul's squad to accompany them, left orders for the rest to dig in, and then they set off. They took the two horses that needed shoeing and left the rest behind.

The road leading into the town was more of a trough, scoured by wind and sand. The town's appearance didn't improve as they got closer. Jirom might have taken it for abandoned if not for a handful of people he'd seen walking about. He was fairly certain this was the right place, but he'd seen hundreds of dusty villages during his travels, and after a while they all started to look alike.

"Why does the empire allow such a place to survive?" Emanon asked. "Why not just wipe them out?"

"The Akeshians use mercenaries, too." The noises of a cheering crowd came from a cluster of shanties arranged in a loose circle on the town's western edge. Jirom paused for a few seconds, listening. "Erugash used to supplement its legions with sellswords. Then they started pressing slaves into the armies."

He broke off from the squad and headed in the direction of the noise.

"Jirom!" Emanon called after him.

Jirom nodded toward the circle of shacks. "Look for a hostel on the main street. It's the only three-story building in town. I'll meet you there."

"Main street? This hog sty only has one street!"

Jirom left the road and made his way across the uneven ground. This was probably a bad idea, but he couldn't help himself.

The collection of small buildings off from the main village formed a shoddy arena. Gladiator games were popular entertainment with mercs. He himself had watched them in his past life, and the irony hadn't escaped him during his own enslavement into the sport.

Wooden stands were set up inside the circle of buildings, surrounding a deep pit carved out of the rocky soil. It was tiny, maybe ten paces across. Down in the hole, two men fought with clubs. The brutal smacks as their weapons struck home resounded around the cheap arena. The audience of about fifty people—mostly men—shouted encouragement as the two fighters brawled for their pleasure. It reminded him of some of the worst places he'd fought in.

As the people watched the fight, Jirom found himself scanning the crowd. He wondered how he'd feel if he saw Thraxes in the stands. He couldn't make up his mind whether he would kill him or buy him a drink. For better or worse, there was no sign of his former owner. Nothing except the memories of painful times, that is.

STORM AND STEEL

"Two coppers."

Jirom turned to the man who'd come up to him. He was probably in his late twenties, tall and lean, with a deep tan complexion. He held out a tin cup. "It's two coppers to watch the fights. Everyone has to pa—"

The man glanced at the brands on Jirom's cheek and stepped away. Then he turned and disappeared behind the stands.

Not wanting to attract any more notice, Jirom left the arena and headed into the village proper. As the shouts and groans faded behind him, he considered his plan to find suitable fighters for Emanon's cause. They had to be of high quality with a good reputation, but those kinds of mercenaries were rare and demanded the highest fees. Maybe more than he could offer. *Especially to help a bunch of ragtag slaves go up against the most powerful empire in the world. They'd have to be more than a little crazy to sign up for that.*

He passed between the outer buildings into the middle of town. Emanon hadn't been exaggerating. This town only had one real artery that passed through its center. The buildings on either side varied from small shacks made from odds and ends to the three-story hostelry that dominated the center square. Surrounding the hostel were three brothels, five taverns, and a smattering of flophouses.

There weren't many people out on the street. As he walked to the hostel, Jirom spotted a pair of men in the doorway of the nearest and largest brothel. By the flashes of steel under their cloaks and the way they stood, relaxed but alert, hands near their belts, he took them for mercenaries. One of them was young with a chubby face. The other was older and missing an eye.

Trying not to stare at them, Jirom resisted the compulsion to reach down and make sure his sword was loose in its scabbard as he went into the hostel.

The sunlight penetrated a few feet into the interior before it was swallowed by the room's natural gloom. The floor was covered in sawdust. Tables sat along the unadorned walls, leaving the center area vacant. A doorway separated the front room from the back of house, and a set of steps climbed to the second floor. An army of eyes turned toward him.

Less than half of the tables were occupied. A few patrons stood rather than sit in the low-backed chairs and benches scattered about. Everyone was armed, and almost everyone wore some kind of armor over grubby clothing. Jirom spotted Emanon and his crew sitting around a pair of tables against the left-side wall and went over to join them.

Emanon pushed out a chair for Jirom with his foot. "Friendly crowd in here. What's the plan? You *do* have a plan for this, right?"

Jirom glanced around the dark room, trying to make out faces. He didn't remember much about the last time he was here. He'd been inebriated most of the time. He vaguely recalled having to leave town in a hurry, though he couldn't remember why. "Just try to blend in. The interested parties will come to us."

That's what he hoped. He'd always been on the other side of these kinds of transactions, selling his sword instead of buying. But he'd seen it done enough times to know what to look for. The desperate crews would approach first, the companies that needed a fast infusion of gold to pay off debtors, and the sorts who would take any job because their skills didn't allow them to be picky about their employers. The rebels needed to be patient until the bigger fish came out to look them over.

It also didn't pay to be too obvious about what they were looking for. The men who gathered in places like this were often short-tempered and suspicious. They had to be in order to survive in a profession where only the strongest and most dangerous prevailed.

There are no old mercs, one of his former captains had told him. *Only empty purses and broken promises.*

"What about them?" Emanon jerked his chin toward a crowded table across the room.

The men seated there were involved in a quiet conversation, their heads huddled together. They looked the part—dirty, ragged, a little desperate—but Jirom shook his head. He was looking for a specific sort of hired sword. Those who said there was no honor among mercenaries were liars, but it wasn't a common attribute either. He wouldn't trust Emanon's cause to the sort of sellsword who would take their coin and turn tail at the first sign of trouble. Nor to the kind that would sell them out to a higher bidder. They needed men who knew the value of loyalty. *Maybe I'm fooling myself. Or maybe I've been out of the life so long I can't tell the good from the bad anymore.*

Jirom was about to suggest they order something to eat when a rough voice spoke behind him in the argot used by southern mercenaries.

"I saw you."

Jirom turned to the man standing at his shoulder. He was of average height but built like a bullock with a broad chest and bulging shoulders. His skin was dark ebony, and he had ritualistic white scars across his cheeks. Weapons hung from his body—two swords, several knives, an obsidian war-axe tucked into his belt.

Just as Jirom was about to say they'd never met before, the man repeated, "I saw you. In Takharet."

Takharet? That name rings true, though I can't place it.

"You killed three men that day."

Now he remembered. Takharet was a shitty little town like this one, just another on the long chain of places where he'd been forced to fight in the pits. So what was this man's problem? Had one of those dead men been his brother or a friend? Jirom's left hand drifted down to his sword. "I've killed a lot of men. What's that to you?"

The wide man stared for a few seconds, and then smiled, his thumbs stuffed into the expanse of his broad belt. "I never forget a good fighter. I made a lot of money on you that day. Hey, are you still fighting?" He gestured over in the general direction of the outdoor arena.

Jirom shook his head. "No. Not anymore."

"Too bad, eh? You were truly magnificent."

The big man clapped Jirom on the shoulder. "These men drink on me!"

Then he walked away, his heavy strides shaking the floorboards. Jirom waited quietly, avoiding Emanon's pointed glances.

"I think he liked you," the rebel captain whispered with his famous wolfish grin.

"Shut up," Jirom grumbled back.

Footsteps on the stairs made them both look around. A lean man stood on the bottom step, looking in their direction. He didn't wear armor, but a pair of long knives rested on his belt. They looked well-used. Then Jirom noticed his face. *O holy of holies. Can it be?*

"What?" Emanon asked. He gazed at the man on the stairs. "You know him?"

I did. Once upon a time. And I never thought to see him again on this side of the grave.

The man gestured. It was subtle, but the message was clear. *Follow me.*

Jirom got up. "Stay here. I'll be back soon."

"The hell I will." Emanon stood to join him. "I go where you go."

Jirom clenched his teeth but decided not to argue. "All right. But let me do the talking."

Emanon nodded. "The rest of you ugly mutts stay here and try not to piss yourselves while we're gone."

"Will do, Captain," Jerkul said with a one-finger salute.

Jirom and Emanon crossed over to the stairs. The man had gone up before them, his boots hardly making a sound. The stairs shook when Jirom when stepped on the bottom tread. With a silent prayer on his lips, he carefully ascended the rickety steps.

The second floor of the building was vaguely familiar. A short hall led off the stairs, studded by three doors. The man stood by the door at the end of the hall with his hand on the latch. Beckoning them to follow, he ducked inside.

"This feels like an ambush waiting to happen," Emanon whispered, half-drawing his sword. "I'd feel better if you told me who this guy is."

"An old friend. I think."

"Huh. Well, that's reassuring. We could get a couple more bodies from camp."

"No. The fewer, the better. If you want to leave, I would under—"

"Suggest that again, and I'll do what my pappy used to do to me when I did something bad." Emanon frowned. "Then again, you'd probably like that too much."

Jirom nudged him in the ribs. "We'll discuss it later. Stick close."

"Like a bee to honey."

The door opened at a touch. Jirom kept one hand on the hilt of his sword as he peeked inside. A short hallway opened into a room. There were two windows, but both shutters were closed. The only light came from the seams around the lowered shades. Jirom stepped inside and immediately moved to the side to give Emanon room to enter. There was movement inside the room, beside what appeared to be a low settee. Someone whispered.

"Yes," a voice said out loud. "It's him."

Bright light filled the room. Jirom blinked and drew his sword halfway from its scabbard before he recognized the face peering at him. "Three Moons?"

A coarse laugh echoed as two men stepped forward to meet them. Jirom recognized them at once. The man they had followed upstairs was Longar, and the other man, short and stooped with weathered mahogany skin and a gleaming pate, was called Three Moons. He had served with them both before his capture by the Akeshians.

"I never thought we'd see you again," Longar said. "I should've known you would come back someday. And more popular than ever. Men downstairs are saying the best gladiator in the empire is here."

"So much for avoiding notice," Emanon whispered.

Longar cracked a small smile. He had been one of the best infiltrators and long-range recon men Jirom had ever served with back in their company days. He looked healthy enough, for a man who was supposedly dead.

Three Moons, on the other hand, looked more than dead. Then again, the shaman-for-hire was ancient and had a bad habit of ingesting any hallucinogenic substance he could get his hands on. Jirom couldn't easily count the number of times he'd had to fish Three Moons out of some dead-end drug den or underground hooch kitchen. He couldn't believe it was really them. "The last I saw of you two was—"

"Pardisha," Longar said.

Three Moons hawked and spat on the floor, which was covered in grime and stains. The light seemed to be emanating from the ceiling, but there was no lamp or lantern to be seen. "A cursed place," the hedge wizard said. "Would that the Company had never stepped foot inside its devilish gates. We lost much there."

"The Company?" Emanon asked.

Three Moons squinted at him. "Who's this? You start up a new unit, Sergeant?"

Emanon glanced at Jirom. "Sergeant?"

"Another life," Jirom replied, hoping Emanon would shut up and let him get to the bottom of this. "I thought you were both dead."

Pardisha was a border town in Isuran far to the south beyond the Great Desert. Jirom's old mercenary unit had been employed to defend it from hostile neighbors. All had gone well until an Akeshian legion arrived at the town's doorstep demanding a full surrender. The Company had stayed and fought. And lost. Most of his brothers had paid with their lives. Those who survived had been offered their lives in exchange for an iron collar. He'd taken it, and thus his career as a gladiator slave had begun. However, neither Longar nor Three Moons had been among the handful of surviving mercs.

"We bugged out," Longar said.

He looked away as he said it, as if not proud to admit it. Jirom could sympathize. That had been a tough decision for all of them, whether to stay and likely die, or slip away if the chance presented itself. He couldn't blame them. Much.

Three Moons's gaze was steadier. "After the Akeshians broke through the city gates, I used a glamor to hide myself from their eyes. It was a close thing. There were four wizards attached to that legion. Lucky for me, they were having too much fun pulverizing the town to notice a mouse like me scurrying past."

"I found him a couple miles outside town," Longar added.

"Aye, I nearly pissed myself when he come sneaking up behind me like a gods-damned wraith."

"What happened to you?" Longar asked.

"Captured," Jirom answered. "I've been living in the empire ever since."

Three Moons leaned forward. "I see the collar scars. But you got away from them eventually, huh?"

Jirom nodded to Emanon. "He got me out. Now I fight with him."

Three Moons grinned, revealing rows of brown-stained teeth. "Fight? Against the Akeshians? You never were the shiniest coin in the purse, Sergeant. It's good to see some things never change."

"What about you two? After Pardisha, I would've thought the empire was the last place you'd run to."

STORM AND STEEL

Three Moons beckoned as he sat down on the low couch. Jirom joined him as Longar pulled up a footstool for himself. Emanon declined and leaned against the wall, his arms crossed. Three Moons pulled out a curved pipe from between the cushions and put it to his lips. There was a flicker of flame from his thumb, and he sat back, pulling at the stem. After a couple puffs, he sighed, and Jirom caught the distinctive scent of kafir.

"We spent some time down south," Longar said. "But word about what happened got around. Weren't too many units in the market for a couple of deserters."

"You didn't desert. We lost, and you escaped capture. Wasn't anything else you could do."

Longar shrugged, a gesture so familiar it filled Jirom with nostalgia. "We could've come back to find you."

"There wasn't anything for you to find except a pair of collars for yourselves, or worse. But that's in the past. Did anyone else survive?"

"A corporal from the Third Platoon. Farelph. But he went off on his own months ago, and we haven't seen him since."

"So have you thought about starting your own company? Pardisha or not, you both have enough seniority with the guild to hoist your own banner."

Three Moons exhaled a long stream of purple smoke. "Too much work. But you sound like a man with a proposition, Sergeant. Care to fill us in?"

"We're looking to hire some dependable men."

Three Moons laughed, which turned into a coughing fit. Once he could breathe again, he said, "In this ass pit? You must be desperate."

"We found you, didn't we?"

The minor wizard waved his hand as if clearing the air. "Mere happenstance. Does this have anything to do with that slave revolt we've been hearing about?"

"Maybe it does," Emanon said.

Jirom shot his lover a hard glance, and Emanon shrugged. Jirom turned his attention back to his old comrades-in-arms. "What have you heard?"

"Nothing good. It seems that some dog soldiers from the empire broke free and started a little rebellion instead of doing the smart thing and disappearing. We heard about this place called— what was it, Longar?"

"Omikur."

Three Moons took another puff. His eyelids were drooping. "Aye. That's where these rebel slaves made a stand and got royally fucked. Least, that's what we heard. Now you show up here looking to hire some swords."

"We won at Omikur," Emanon growled. "Destroyed almost the entire Third Legion and more than one of those Akeshian wizards that made you piss your skirts."

"That so, freeman?" Three Moons asked with a lopsided grin. "Well, then, we apologize. We didn't realize we were in the presence of genuine war heroes."

"We have the money to pay," Jirom said before Emanon could retort. "What we need are veteran soldiers, especially squad leaders."

"There's not much selection here, Sergeant. I know because we've been looking to add some swords to our ranks, too. But since the Isuran campaign most of the free companies have moved on, either north to sign with the crusaders or south to greener pastures. So what you have left are the dregs and hangers-on. Not near enough to conquer an empire, if that's what you're asking. And after Omikur—no offense—I doubt you'll find any fighters willing to join your war of vengeance. It's a death wish."

"You may be right about that." Emanon cleared his throat. "I told you this would be a waste of time, Jirom. These two have lost their nerve, and I wouldn't pay a week-old shit for all the rest of the fleas in this place put together. Let's get out of here."

Longar had shifted the way he sat. Just a little, but Jirom noticed how the scout's posture had gathered like a coiled spring, his hands resting on his lap but ready to seize any of the several knives on his person. Three Moons didn't move at all, but then again he was a wizard.

"Settle down, brother." Jirom looked from Longar to Emanon. "Wait for me downstairs."

Emanon just stood there for a moment, but then he shrugged and left the room.

"What are you caught up in, Sarge?" Three Moons asked. His eyes were bloodshot, though he seemed lucid. "I've never seen you like this. What hold does that one have over you?"

Jirom ran a hand over his scalp. He was tired of being coy, of always deflecting questions. "He's my lover. And my captain."

Longar stared at him for a long moment.

Three Moons smiled with his head tilted to the side. "Well, I'm happy for you. But what's that got to do with throwing away your life on a fool's crusade? You and I both know your ragtag troupe of slaves don't stand a chance against the empire."

"Emanon has a plan, and so far it's worked out. We hit hard and fast. The Akeshians have to hold ground, but we're free to attack at will and disappear afterward. But with every attack, we attract more and more slaves who want to fight back."

Three Moons scratched his nose. "But you need vets to lead them."

"Precisely."

"Tell him, Three Moons," Longar said.

"I was getting to it, lad."

"Tell me what?" Jirom asked.

"We signed on with an outfit," Longar said. "The Bronze Blades, out of Isuran."

Jirom had never heard of them, but his hopes were rekindled. "How many fighters?"

"Round about eighty," Three Moons answered, and then he smiled. "But it's an elite unit. All long-timers like us. Platoon sergeants and specialists. Even got us a couple sappers."

"Any chance your elite unit is looking for work?"

Three Moons stood up. "Well, you'll have to talk to the captain about that."

Jirom almost didn't believe his ears. Three Moons had never, in all their years together, deferred to his superiors on anything. Maybe Pardisha had changed him. *Gods know it changed me.*

"Fair warning, Sergeant. We don't come cheap. The captain also insists on first payment up front, and you pay the guild's percentage, too. I hope your war chest is deep."

Jirom got up. "Don't worry. It is."

Longar opened the door and nodded to someone on the other side. "He's ready."

Three Moons smiled as he tapped out his pipe. "It's good to see you, Sergeant. But I don't know if going up against Akeshian legionnaires is the best idea. We were hoping to sign on with a larger company heading away from the empire. Far away."

"I wouldn't blame your captain if he wants to turn us down."

"That's just it. This captain isn't the sort to turn down a challenge. I just hope this isn't another Pardisha. I wonder whatever happened to our old boss, the Amir, after the Akeshians took over his city."

Jirom shrugged. "He sold us out and tried to make a separate peace with the Akeshians. So I put a knife through his heart."

Downstairs, Emanon stood with Jerkul and his squad, all of them shooting wary looks around as if they expected an ambush at any moment. As Longar and Three Moons headed to the door to the back room, Jirom gestured for Emanon to join them.

The hostel's back room was like another world. Instead of stained furniture and sawdust on the floor, it was immaculate. Red walls and bronze accents gave it a garish atmosphere. There was only one table, but it was large enough to seat twenty people. One man sat alone, who stood up as they entered.

He was a few years older than Jirom and had a nut-brown complexion. His receding hair was shorn almost down to the scalp and glistened with some kind of oil. He wore faded leathers without insignia or devices.

Longar made introductions. "Sir, this is Jirom and his captain, Emanon. Gentlemen, this is Captain Ovar of the Bronze Blades."

The captain indicated the cushioned seats before them. "Please be seated, sirs."

Emanon leaned over and whispered, "Why do I feel like a lamb walking into the slaughterhouse?"

"Relax," Jirom whispered back. "We can trust them."

Hoping that was true, Jirom nevertheless made sure he had clear access to his sword as they sat down. Longar and Three Moons took chairs on either side of their commander. Three Moons took his pipe back out and filled it with leaf from a pouch while beer and plates of olives were set out.

Captain Ovar nodded to Jirom as he took a tankard. "I've heard a lot of stories about you from these two. They say you were a top-notch sergeant back in your old outfit."

"I served as best I could."

"Well, that's in the past. We're here to talk about the future. I've heard the basics, but I want to know the details. What do you need and how much are you willing to pay?"

At Emanon's nod, Jirom addressed the mercenary leader. "The guild's premium wage is ten silver ounces per month, right?"

"It is. That's five Akeshian moons, if you're using local coin. Squad leaders draw double pay, and officers get triple."

"We'll pay twice the premium rate."

Captain Ovar's gaze didn't waver a hair, which was intriguing. "I'll be honest with you. Fighting against the empire isn't exactly a sound wager. We're not a big outfit, after all. We were looking for garrison duty in one of the smaller towns around these parts."

Jirom shifted in his seat, not liking what he was hearing. Three Moons had said this captain liked a challenge. "Garrison duty is a job for crews that don't like to get their hands dirty, not new companies looking to make a name for themselves."

The captain didn't blink, but he nodded. "Go on."

"The rebels of the western territories are gathering." Jirom ignored a sharp look from Emanon. "Something big is brewing, so that's where we're heading. The uprising isn't going away, Captain. It's just getting started. These slaves don't have the training, yet, but they're fighting for something more important than money or property. And they won't stop until they get it."

Large, white teeth showed through parted lips. "I can see why your old comrades think so highly of you. You are persuasive."

"And don't forget about the money," Emanon grumbled.

"Aye. The money is certainly tempting. But before I sign a contract with a new employer, I must know something."

Jirom braced himself. "What's that, Captain?"

"What happens when the war is won?"

Jirom pushed back his seat and stood up. Longar and Three Moons watched him but didn't move. Emanon stood as well.

"When we win this war," Jirom said, "every slave in this empire will be freed. Every king and queen of Akeshia will come in person to bow at our feet. And you, Captain, will collect the biggest bonus in history."

Captain Ovar climbed to his feet. "Well, then, gentlemen. I believe we have a deal. When do we march out?"

Emanon took a long drink from his cup and slammed it down. "Why wait?"

Ismail glanced over as Yadz dropped his shovel and kicked it across the ground. "This is bullshit! Why the hell are we even doing this?"

"Because those are our orders?" Kasha answered from the hip-deep trench he'd been digging for the past hour. The ditch bent at a right angle near the middle for no reason.

Ismail went back to work. His ears, however, remained open as he listened to the others complain.

Yadz snatched up his canteen. After a long, gulping pull, he let out a deep groan. "I'm so sick of all this marching and digging shit. Why can't we go into town, too? I'd like to see the sights. Maybe find a girl to tickle. Or have something better to drink than dirty water."

Kasha straightened up. "Yeah, Corporal. Why can't we? I could go for a tall drink in a cool saloon."

Corporal Idris raised his voice as some of the other troopers chimed in. "Quiet down! You're not going because the captain don't want you mucking things up. So shut up and keep digging. Yadz, I swear if you don't have that trench dug by nightfall I'm going to bury you in it."

Those words compelled Ismail to dig with renewed conviction. The corporal was big and mean and covered in scars. Ismail had whip scars of his own, but the corporal had knife wounds and punctures and one long gray slash down the side of his face that crumpled his cheek into a permanent crater. The corporal didn't talk about that one, but the other men said he'd gotten it at Omikur. Ismail had heard a whole lot about that battle. Enough to make him damned glad he hadn't been there. The survivors walked differently than everybody else. They looked different, too. There was something in their eyes, like they'd been to the other side of the grave and Death had sent them back. Still, Ismail couldn't help but agree with Yadz. He'd only been with these rebels a few days, and already he was tired of marching and digging trenches, too.

He had been born a slave on a large plantation east of Nisus, where he'd worked in the fields until he was full-grown. He fell in love with another slave, Peira, and in defiance of the rules they lived together as husband and wife in secret. When Peira got pregnant, their master sold Ismail to the army. As he was put in chains and loaded onto a wagon, Ismail had looked back at his wife, heavy with their child, sobbing on her mother's shoulder.

He'd been on his way to the training camps when the rebels struck their caravan. At first he thought they were just bandits, hardly more than fifty of them wearing scraps of mismatched armor and no uniforms. Of course, he'd heard of the slave rebellion. Stories of their exploits passed among the plantations from slave to slave. In his imagination they had been a vast horde of angry faces eager to spill blood. The reality was sobering. Still, they fought like evil spirits. When they had given him the choice of either walking away or joining them, he agreed without hesitation. At last, to be free.

But freedom was a strange thing. Before his rescue, he'd only known it as an idea, as distant from his reality as the moon above the earth. Now that he possessed it, he felt almost drunk with the possibilities, and also more than a little terrified. The world suddenly seemed so much bigger than it had before, able to swallow up a man if he wasn't careful.

He'd thought the rebels were going to ride off to another country with the gold they'd stolen. He wasn't exactly pleased when he found out they were heading deeper into the desert. Apparently, this unit had some kind of hideout among the dunes and cacti. That's when the doubts had started creeping into his head. *This was a mistake. But I'm stuck again, just as much a slave as when I was wearing a collar.*

He looked over at the town, half a mile from their campsite. It wasn't much. Just a clump of buildings along a dusty desert road. He didn't know how they survived out here. He didn't see any fields, just barren ground as hard as clay and too dry to support anything but scrub grass and pricker-bushes. What did the people eat? Rocks?

An hour later, his trench was dug to the corporal's satisfaction, and Ismail lay down inside, hands resting across his stomach, waiting for the mess call. The sun's rays couldn't reach him at the bottom of the hole, and tonight promised to be as cold as last night. From beyond the confines of his little nook, Corporal Idris was threatening Yadz with physical violence, but it seemed distant, like the yelling was coming from miles away. Ismail was tempted to close his eyes and complete the feeling of seclusion, but a thought had lodged in the back of his mind and refused to leave him in peace.

Sitting up, he peeked over the top of his trench in the direction of the town again. So close, and yet it seemed like another world. He'd never get there without being seen, at least not until nightfall. And if he was caught leaving, he'd have to face the corporal's wrath. Maybe the sergeant's, too.

And don't even think about the lieutenant. He's the biggest, meanest one of them all, with that big red sword and mountains of muscles. He looks like he could twist off a man's head if he got the notion. If half the stories they tell about him are true, then he's done a lot worse than that. No, sir. I'll just stay nice and comfy in my little—

"Greetings, brother."

Ismail jumped back as a rebel from another squad knelt beside his trench. He was a small man with a delicate face, almost feminine. His skin looked gold in the waning sunlight. He wore the same sand-colored garb as the other veterans, though his clothes were cleaner than most and well mended.

The rebel touched his chest. "I am Seng. One of Sergeant Mahir's scouts. You are thinking about the village there, yes?"

Ismail shook his head. "No, not at all. I was just watching for danger, you know? Never know when danger will appear right in front of your nose."

"There is no need to obfuscate, brother. I, too, would like to see what lies within. Alas, our commanders have not sanctioned it. What are we to do?"

"Not much, I suppose. It ain't worth getting our heads thumped by the corporal."

"Yes, dereliction of duty is a heinous thing." Seng leaned down a little closer and lowered his voice. "But surely a little look around would not harm anyone, eh?"

"Sure. Just stretch the legs and have a little peek. But how do we—?"

"Leave that to me, brother."

Seng got up and walked over to Mahir, the sergeant in charge of the scouts. They talked for a few minutes, until Ismail began to get nervous. Then Seng headed back toward him.

"The matter is taken care of," Seng said.

"What do you mean, taken care of?"

"I asked my commander to consider you as a recruit for the scouts. He has graciously authorized me to take you on a short training operation this evening."

"What training operation? Oh! You mean—"

"Yes, brother. We are free to reconnoiter the town."

Ismail suspected he was being pranked, but the small man seemed genuine. "Really?"

"It is a certainty, brother. Shall we go?"

He didn't wait to be asked twice. Leaving his shovel and field kit behind, he scrambled out of the hole. Then, on second thought, he reached down to fish out his sword and buckled the belt around his waist.

"I do not believe we will need that," Seng said, indicating the weapon.

"Better to have it and not need it, right?"

"As you wish."

Seng led the way past the maze of trenches to the outer pickets where bored sentries amused themselves by tossing stones out into the scrub. The small scout nodded to the nearest watchmen, and they nodded back. And just like that he and Ismail left the camp.

Ismail kept looking over his shoulder, fully expecting to hear shouts of alarm, but everything remained quiet. He spent so much time looking back he almost lost Seng in the gathering twilight. The small man's clothing blended seamlessly with the landscape. Ismail spotted a hint of movement, and quickly followed it until he saw the back of Seng's head in front of him. He kept close thereafter.

Seng was amazing. Not just good at melting into the terrain; he also moved as quiet as a field mouse. Ismail tried to emulate him, but his efforts weren't so graceful. His every footfall sounded like a stomping wildebeest in comparison. He lost count of how many times he tripped over a rock or brush root. Through it all, Seng remained patient, as if this really was some kind of training exercise. As the minutes passed, Ismail found himself taking it more and more seriously, going as far as trying to walk in the scout's footsteps. Suddenly, Seng stopped, and Ismail almost ran into him. The sun had sunk behind the western plains, leaving the sky streaked in shades of blue and purple.

Seng pulled him down into a crouch.

"What's wrong?" he asked in a hushed whisper.

The scout pointed to a cluster of flat roofs. They had reached the town already. Lights shone in several windows, looking awfully inviting to Ismail. He thought back to his old master's plantation and his wife.

As they watched, a small party of men left the town. Squinting, Ismail realized it was the captain's gang, heading back to camp. He felt a sudden urge to race back to his trench.

"Be calm," Seng whispered.

Then he pressed something into Ismail's hand. It was small pouch. Inside he felt the unmistakable discs of money. It felt like a tidy sum. Certainly more than he'd ever held before. "What's this?"

"You are not happy joining the insurrection, yes?"

Was this part of the test? "'Course I am. I don't want to be a slave no more."

"No need to be slave or soldier. Take the money and find a new life."

Ismail looked down at the pouch. All at once, a tremendous weight settled in his chest. No one had ever given him such a personal gift. No one except Peira. "I . . . I can't, okay? The captain freed me. I don't know how, but I got to pay him back. And I want to fight. I do! It's just . . . no one's ever looked out for me before. You know?"

A soft hand touched his shoulder. "We walk a difficult path, brother. No one would blame if you wished to depart."

"Thanks. I just wish I knew what the captain was planning. Then maybe it would set things right in my head."

STORM AND STEEL

The sounds of crunching boot steps and jingling gear caught his ear. A few seconds later, a second group of men left the town. Six dozen or maybe more. They carried lanterns as they trod in loose rows, and by their light Ismail could see the gleam of weapons and armor, shields and helms. No uniforms though. *Mercenaries by the look of them. But why are they heading toward the camp?*

"I believe," Seng whispered, "the captain has found a use for the gold shipment."

Ismail imagined how that would change things. *Holy Mother Kishar, we just doubled our numbers. Even if they ain't worth a damn in a fight, we might scare the masters to death showing up with such an army.*

He handed the pouch back. "Here, keep the money. I'm staying for now. With these new recruits, things are going to get easier. I'm sure of it."

Seng tucked the money into his sand-colored tunic. "As you say, brother. Shall we investigate this hamlet?"

"Nah. I'm for heading back. I want a better look at those mercs."

"As you say, brother."

CHAPTER SIX

Leaning on the rail of the royal pleasure barge, Horace stared across the river. Gentle breezes created ripples across its silty brown waters. Long-legged ibises strutted along the shore hunting for fish. Dragonflies as long as his hand flittered above the forest of reeds and water blossoms.

The river's power brushed against the bottom of the boat, sluggish yet powerful. That quiet strength reminded him of the dream he'd been dreaming just before the attack. He'd been flying above the earth in the midst of a chaos storm, immune to the mundane problems of the people below. He couldn't get it out of his head.

Yet now he was back in his own body, surrounded by his troubles. The last two days had passed slowly as they traveled along the river. Not that the barge was a poor mode of travel. On the contrary, it was a grand vessel. Almost two hundred feet long with graceful lines, it was propelled through the river by forty oarsmen in the ship's waist. All slaves, unfortunately, but Horace tried not to think about that. Some other time, he might have enjoyed this trip, with the smells and the sounds of water all around him. Yet the attack had left him feeling edgy and tense, as if an invisible noose were slowly tightening around his neck. Lord Mulcibar, before his disappearance, had told him that Akeshian politics were a cutthroat business. Horace only wished the old man was still here to advise him. *Lord knows I could use some advice these days.*

The queen's command that he crush the slave rebellion was paramount in his thoughts. He didn't know if he could do it, not the way she wanted. He needed to find a way to make her see they were people. Better yet, he wished he could convince her to free them all. That was the crux of her problem, but she would never accept it. Nor would the nobles or the merchants or the owners of the vast farms outside Erugash. Their entire way of life relied upon the existence of slaves. How could one man change an entire society? It was impossible. Yet if he couldn't, then he feared he would lose Alyra forever. Just a short while ago, he'd thought they were meant to be together, a second chance at love.

Maybe we're too different to make it work. We want different things, although most of the time I can't understand what she truly wants. For me to leave the court and abandon this new life I've made? Then what? She can't believe the queen, or any of the empire's rulers, would just let me walk away. Without the queen's protection, we'd be swamped under endless waves of assassins. And now, with my powers proving unpredictable, how long before one of those attempts succeeds?

He pressed his temples with the heels of both hands, wishing he could squeeze away his stress.

"By the gods, I'm ready to be off this boat."

Horace glanced over at Lord Ubar, who had come to join him at the larboard railing. A bandage was wrapped around his forehead. The young nobleman had not had a relaxing voyage, spending most of his time in his bunk belowdecks or leaning over the sides, throwing back up what little food he could get down. His copper skin had taken on a greenish tinge. Though Horace thought the weather was pleasant, Lord Ubar looked like he was freezing, wrapped up in a long cloak with a fur collar.

"It shouldn't be long now," Horace replied.

"Does the Typhon call to you?"

Horace gazed back down into the murky waters. He considered telling Ubar about his failure to control his *zoana* during the attack on the villa, and how he'd been too afraid to attempt summoning the power ever since. *No, I don't think you want to hear that. Much better to continue to see me as your secret weapon, defender of your queen and city. Better, that is, until I fail at the wrong time and someone pays for it with their life. You're a good man, Ubar, but you don't have the answers I need. And I'm starting to doubt anyone does.*

"I don't see anything except water and silt," he lied.

Ubar nodded toward the rear of the vessel. "I suppose you must be eager to be away from these *siku masaku*, too. Eh?"

"*Siku masu . . . ?*"

"It means a tight place."

"Ah, close quarters. Yes, I am."

He looked past the noble to the pavilion set up on the aft deck. Brass poles held aloft a sheet of purple silk to shade Her Majesty and a few others, sitting in chairs and couches as they sipped chilled wine from golden cups. To Horace, it looked like a scene out of a painting about the decadence of the old world. The queen sat amid her courtiers, laughing and gesturing as if she were having the time of her life instead of running from the latest attempt to end her existence. They had spoken only briefly since leaving the villa. The queen had insulated herself within a cocoon of bodyguards and sycophants—scions from the noble houses of Erugash. He got the feeling she blamed him for the attack and wondered if she was waiting for him to fall on his sword.

Not me, Your Excellence. If you want me dead, you'll have to do it the old-fashioned way. Although I doubt you'd do it yourself. Am I going to wake up some night to find Xantu standing over me? Perhaps I should hire some additional guards for the house.

Looking around, Horace noticed the person absent from the deck. Although he didn't know for sure what was behind the queen's diffidence, it didn't bother him nearly as much as Alyra's behavior. Since the attack, she had gone out of her way to avoid him, too. Without the queen's ability to keep him at bay with a wall of soldiers and *zoanii*, Alyra simply disappeared whenever he tried to speak with her, which was an impressive feat on a ship. After a few tries to find out what was wrong with her, he'd stopped altogether and spent the majority of the voyage alone, eating or reading by himself, and watching the scenery pass by. Like Ubar, he was ready to make landfall, if only to escape the pervasive tension that hung over the barge. "I'm just wondering if it's ever going to end."

When Ubar patted his stomach and made a face in sympathy, Horace pushed back from the rail. "Not the trip. I mean the assassination attempts. The feeling I get whenever I walk into a dark room that there's someone waiting to kill me. Things were bad before, but it seems worse now. I'm hardly sleeping. I worry that the food has been poisoned."

"Life is a one continuous race we will never win. We can only persevere to the finish."

"Another nugget of wisdom from your dead philosopher?"

Ubar smiled and shrugged. "I had excellent tutors."

"We're all going to die anyway, so why worry about it?"

"Something like that."

"That's the worst advice I ever heard."

Ubar glanced at him, and they both started laughing. Horace looked over the youth's shoulder and saw the queen watching them. Then she held out her cup to a slave to refill and looked away.

"No, my biggest problem," Horace said, "is that I've been placed in charge of quelling the slave rebellion. But I don't know the first thing about it. Even if I did, the queen's council won't listen to anything I say. Well, that's not quite true. They listen. . . ."

"But they find ways to circumvent your intentions?"

"Exactly. None of my commands are followed, but I can never prove who was responsible afterward. I tried telling the queen, but she didn't seem to hear me."

"You still have much to learn about politics, *Inganaz*."

Horace grunted, wishing he had a drink. The wound in his side was starting to bother him again, and the afternoon heat was parching his throat. Yet all the servants were aft with the queen, and he didn't want to go back there. "That isn't news to me."

"The queen will not directly intervene in a conflict between the members of her court. To do so would lessen her esteem in the eyes of the *zoanii*. So those desiring her royal munificence must seek a way that is not obvious. It is a shadow game where one pretends not to care about those things which are the most important, and thus conceal one's true intentions."

"All I want is to please the queen while not making any new enemies. I've got more than enough already."

"That is the trick of it."

Horace rubbed his forehead. "Wait a moment. Ubar, you could be the answer to my prayers."

"I'm sorry. I don't under—"

"I need someone who can speak the language, as it were. Someone who has the pedigree to get people to stand up and listen."

"But you are the First Sword."

"And most of the court wants me gone. I need help, and you're the only person who seems to be talking to me right now."

"That should be a warning for both of us. However, I am of a mind to help you."

Horace almost wept with relief. "*Kanadu!* It means a great deal to me. There's a lot of rebel activity in the western part of the realm, but I can't be everywhere at once. So I need you to go to Sekhatun as my official envoy."

"Sekhatun?" Ubar frowned. "Lord Horace, I'm not sure I would be the most effective choice to represent you there."

"Why not? That's your home, isn't it? You probably know every important person in the town."

"That is precisely the problem. I do know everyone in Sekhatun, and they know me quite well also. Since my father's disgrace and loss of title, my family is in poor repute. My mother and sister had to move to Erugash to escape the stain of dishonor. Two of my cousins died by their own hand, unable to face it. The new leaders of Sekhatun would have no reason to treat with me."

"Yes, they will. Because you'll be carrying a written order from the queen giving you the power to act in her behalf. If the governor gives you any problems, you can have him executed."

"That is . . . I'm unsure how to react. What exactly do you want me to do there? I don't have any military experience."

"That's all right. You possess the most important trait for this mission: my trust. I need someone who is willing to take a . . . *lighter* touch in regards to this problem."

"Lighter? In what way?"

"I want you to try to make contact with the rebels."

"To what end?"

"To de-escalate the situation, for one thing. And also, I'm hoping we can come to some kind of agreement with the slaves."

Lord Ubar's eyebrows shot up. "An armistice? I was not aware Her Majesty was seeking a peaceful resolution to this matter."

Horace gave his most sincere smile, feeling horrible that he had to mislead this young man who had quickly become a good friend to him. "The queen wishes this insurrection to end as soon as possible. She and I have every faith you are the right person for this job."

Ubar looked down, his expression suddenly pensive. "I am happy to serve in whatever manner Her Majesty desires. Perhaps, if it is my destiny, this may allow me to restore the honor of my family's name."

Horace gritted his teeth, hating himself as he clapped the young man on the shoulder. "I hope so. You're doing me a great service, which I won't forget."

"Of course. If you will excuse me. . . ."

Looking pale all of a sudden, Ubar rushed to the other side of the deck and leaned over the side. Trying to ignore the sounds of vomiting, Horace resumed his study of the river. He didn't enjoy manipulating people, especially someone like Ubar, but he didn't see that he had much choice if he wanted to survive. Now he could turn his mind to other issues, like finding out who had tried to kill him and the entire royal court.

The barge slowed as it turned out of the main channel. Erugash rose from the shore, shining in the midday sun. Vines clung to the massive limestone blocks of the river wall. Built at the water's edge upon the bones of older versions of the city stretching back hundreds and perhaps thousands of years, the wall stood as a bulwark against both waterborne invasion and the ever-advancing tide of the Typhon. Great domes and arching bridges peeked above the battlements alongside the step-terraced summits of vast palaces.

As the barge neared the docks, servants arrived from below decks, carrying what little remained of the royal baggage after the attack. Alyra arrived with them. Watching her, Horace felt a knot in his throat. He still didn't know what to do about her. Part of him wanted to forget everything that had passed between them and go his separate way, but each time he saw her, his heart ached. He just wished things could be simpler between them.

The queen's retinue assembled on the deck in fine regalia. Byleth had retired inside her shaded pavilion at the rear of the barge with the drapes pulled shut. As the barge bumped gently against the side of the dock, the curtains were pulled back and she emerged, looking magnificent as usual in a gown of white silk. Her hair was done up in a tower wrapped with gold chains and pearls as large as pigeon eggs. Lord Xantu followed a pace behind her.

Disturbing shouts filled the air, and Horace noticed for the first time that a crowd had gathered around the dock. A cordon of royal guardsmen held the people back as they surged toward the barge.

Lord Ubar came to stand by Horace again. He looked better, as if their imminent landfall had cleared up his seasickness. "I feared this would happen. News of the Chapter House has spread."

The people in the crowd were mainly men. Common folk, judging by their plain garments. None appeared armed, although the sheer number of them—at least a couple hundred—was intimidating. Since he'd arrived in Erugash, Horace had never seen such a demonstration before.

"The people still revere the cult of Amur." Ubar glanced over at the queen as she made her way to the gunnels where sailors were preparing the gangplank. "Despite Her Majesty's long-standing conflict with the priesthood."

Horace would have liked to say he felt bad for what had happened to the priests of the Chapter House. He still recalled the terror that had closed around him the night of the villa attack, the certainty that he was going to die, horribly and viciously. He wouldn't wish that on his worst enemy. Yet the Order would have killed him for his role in their temple's destruction. It was simply a matter of when. And now he could breathe a little easier.

Preceded by her bodyguards, the queen departed the barge and entered a palanquin waiting for her. Lord Xantu strode ahead of the car with a wedge of soldiers, clearing the way as the royal entourage got underway. The rest of the court followed behind in rented litters.

Making his way down the gangplank, Horace hoped to slip away. Back at the palace there would be a welcoming ceremony followed by a formal audience with speeches and presentations, and most of the court would be expected to join in the frivolity lasting late into the night. He just wanted to go home, away from the pomp.

Gurita, the commander of his house guard, waited at the bottom of the ramp with two more guards and a string of horses.

Horace beckoned to Mezim. "There's a change of plan," he told the secretary. "I'm going back to the manor."

"With your permission, I will go to the palace to check on the latest news."

"Yes, do that."

Horace walked down to his guards. "I'm glad to see you men. How has everything been since I left?"

Captain Gurita saluted. He was a big, burly man whose nose looked as if it had been broken at least twice, and as a result he spoke with a deep nasal tone. "Good to see you, your lordship. Things have been interesting. As you can see, some of the citizens are not too happy. There have been some riots in the poorer areas, but nothing serious."

I wonder if those riots had anything to do with the rebellion?

They provided Horace with a tall gelding, already saddled and ready. As he climbed into the saddle, he looked around for Alyra, but she was lost in the crowd. Sighing to himself, he joined the procession.

The chain of litter cars crawled at a turtle's pace until they were past the throng of protesters. After that, they sped along the wide boulevard leading into the city center. A few blocks from the palace, Horace gestured to his guards and turned down a side street. Giving his steed a kick, he found himself smiling as he trotted away, as if he were leaving his problems behind him. Then he came to the wide round plaza known as the Wheel. On most days it was filled with merchants and traders dealing their wares, but today Horace found it almost empty. He saw the reason soon enough. A gallows had been erected at the center of the plaza. Eleven iron cages hung from the crossbeam. Inside each cage was a person. Ten men and one woman. Some bore signs of beating and whipping. All of them wore an iron collar, their only garment. Clouds of flies buzzed around the cages, crawling on the inmates, in their hair, on their faces. Most of them didn't move, and Horace thought they might be dead. Until he saw an eye blink or a hand twitch. They were all alive, although barely. A wooden sign hung atop the gallows.

Treacherous slaves who dared to raise their hands against their lawful masters.

Horace gritted his teeth as he rode past the sickening display. He'd been told that Akeshian owners were cracking down hard on their slaves because of the growing insurrection, but this was the first he'd seen it for himself. *Lord, help Ubar in his mission. He might be our only chance to end this with minimal bloodshed.*

Taking the avenue on the north end of the Wheel, he entered the Cattle

Quarter, home to the city's wealthiest families. And his home, too, for the last three months. When he'd first moved into the estate, he had been confused by the district's name until Alyra explained to him that wealth in Akeshia had once been measured by how many cows a man owned.

The sight of the peach-colored walls relieved him after the long journey. The manor house was like a miniature palace, its grounds surrounded by a high stone wall.

A variety of objects cluttered the street outside his gate. Bowls and boxes and bundles of flowers. He even saw a goat staked by the wall, gnawing on what appeared to be a sculpture of a man's head carved out of wood. Half a dozen people stood in the street, facing his home. *Oh, no. I thought these lunatics would have given up by now.*

In the days following the fall of the Sun Temple, gifts had begun appearing outside his home. They were inconsequential at first—cheap trinkets, a loaf of bread, the occasional jar of wine, and such. But with each day, the gifts had become more numerous and extravagant. His staff hadn't known who was leaving them until the first admirers showed up, singing songs and chanting *"Belzama!"* with the zeal of true believers, although he didn't have a clue what they thought they believed in. For the next week, Horace had ordered his servants to provide the gathering with water and food and ask them kindly to leave. But the people refused the sustenance and ignored the request. After that, Horace had left orders for these people to be left alone with the hopes they would disperse on their own. That did not appear to be the case.

"What do they want?" Horace said as he approached his home.

"Well, that's hard to say," Captain Gurita said, looking over. "But if I had to venture a guess, I'd say they believe you were sent by . . ." He glanced up toward the heavens.

"They think I come from the sky?"

"So to say, your lordship. To be more precise, they think you were sent by the gods."

"That's insane!"

"Pardon me, but you may want to go easy on these, uh, admirers. Times are hard, and people need something to believe in."

"I'm not going to pose as some kind of demigod just to appease their superstitions."

"Not saying you would, your lordship. Just don't discount their need for hope."

Horace swallowed the retort on his tongue. Half the city viewed him as a gift from the gods, and the other half as a curse. "I'm not discounting it, but I'm not the one they should put their faith in."

The house gates opened as they got close. Harxes, his new house steward, rushed out holding a staff across his body as if he expected to fend off a host of attackers. The people in the street did not move, but they stopped chanting as they spotted Horace and his guards. Then they lowered their faces to the ground in genuflection.

"This is a nightmare," Horace muttered.

"*Belzama!*" the people shouted, and resumed their chant, which now included a drawn-out blessing "on the Lord of Storms and his house for all time."

Harxes came over, waving his staff around, though he didn't actually hit anyone. "Forgive me, *Belum*," he said, huffing as he bowed before Horace. "I've tried to clear them away each day, but they come right back. Shall I call for the Watch?"

"No, don't bother. They aren't hurting anyone. But send all that food to the nearest poorhouse before it spoils."

"As you command. May I escort you inside?"

They filed through the gate. The house's southern wings enclosed an outer courtyard that was paved in red brick and featured a central fountain of three sphinxes spitting water.

Horace winced as he dismounted, surprised at how sore such a short ride could make him. More evidence that he was getting soft. He rubbed his hands together, remembering the feel of calluses on his fingers. Now all he could feel were the waxy burn scars seared into his palms. He resolved to get more physical activity. As he walked to the front door of his home, he hit upon an idea. He would take a boat out on the river. No servants, no guards. Just him and a dinghy. *When am I going to find time for that? I'm already up to my eyebrows in work, and I'm sure there's a mountain of correspondence waiting in my office. But it would be nice. . . .*

The door was held open by Mekkano, one of his newer servants he'd hired after Menarch Rimesh and his cultists had killed most of his staff when they kidnapped him. Horace forced himself to smile as he walked past, but every time he saw one of the new hires, it reminded him of that hellish experience. Captured, put in chains, and thrown into a pit. If not for Alyra, he might still be there right now. *Don't forget Lord Astaptah. Without him, you and the queen might both be dead.*

The cook waited in the foyer with a large clay cup. Horace accepted it and took a sip. The brown beer was thick and rich. Sighing with relief, he performed the ritual spilling on the floor to thank the gods for his safe arrival. It was a ridiculous custom, of course, but he did it to make his servants feel better. Another thing Alyra had told him, that Akeshian servants expected their employer to follow the traditions of their culture, even if he was a foreigner. It seemed to work, as the servants all smiled at his attempts to emulate their ways, from speaking their language to observing their religious idiosyncrasies, of which there were many. Akeshians took their gods and myths very seriously.

Thinking of Alyra, Horace wanted to ask if she had come home yet, but he held his tongue. If she wanted space, he could give it to her. *She knows where to find me if she wants to talk. And if she doesn't, well, then I guess I'll have to deal with it. Best to keep busy to take my mind off her.*

As he handed the cup back, Horace allowed himself to relax. He was home again. Safe. Or as safe as he could be. No place in Akeshia was truly safe. *Not even a royal villa in the country.*

Harxes withdrew a scroll from his robe and held it out. "This arrived for you two days ago. From Lord Mulcibar's estate."

The name jarred Horace out of his musing. He took the scroll and inspected the imprint rolled across the wax seal. It was from Lord Mulcibar's house, but with a different personal signature. With a nod, Horace went upstairs to change out of his traveling clothes. His room was laid out just as he had left it. The bed was of Akeshian construction, low to the ground with a firm reed mattress, but Horace had introduced western-style sheets of fine linen that were cooler than woolen blankets and didn't make him sweat, like silk did. He also insisted on real pillows stuffed with feathers rather than the stiff bolsters used by the locals.

A vase of fresh lilies sat by the open window. A robe—silver silk with black trim at the cuffs and collar—and clean sandals had been set out, as well as the copper bathtub, filled and ready for him. He stripped down and slipped into the lukewarm water with a sigh. Although he missed the hot springs under the queen's villa, this was just the thing on a hot day. He closed his eyes and tried to forget his troubles for a little while.

After a few minutes, his curiosity got the better of him, and he picked the scroll up off the floor. He broke the seal and unrolled the papyrus sheet. The letter within was written in a fine, precise hand, close enough to Lord Mulcibar's script that Horace had to peer closely to see the differences.

> *First Sword of Erugash, Protector of the City, Horace of Arnos,*
> *I greet you. Since learning of my great-uncle's passing, I have recently returned to Erugash to take possession of my inheritance.*
> *It has come to my attention that certain items of property have been bequeathed to your lordship. I invite you to visit at your convenience so that I may make your acquaintance and enjoy the pleasure of knowing one who was counted as a friend of my late uncle, who now dwells among the stars above forever and ever.*
> *—Lady Anshara of the House Alulu*

The style of the writing was so stilted that Horace had to read it through twice to make sure he had the full meaning. Lord Mulcibar had never mentioned any family, certainly not a niece. Horace wondered where she had come from. *Probably a rural estate where she was kept away from the troubles at court. But now she's here. I should talk to her. Tell her what became of her uncle.*

It wasn't a conversation he looked forward to, but it was the right thing to do. He was also curious what "items of property" Mulcibar had left to him. *That old man was always full of surprises.*

Setting the letter aside, Horace closed his eyes and allowed the outside world to drift away. His problems could wait until he finished his bath.

Long shadows stretched across the city, cast from a hundred roofs and spires. The moon had risen in the east while the sun was setting in the west. A good omen, as Lady Sippa chased her brother from the sky. This was a night for deciding important matters and making pacts. In the long-ago antiquity of the empire, nights like these were host to great orgies of flesh, and sometimes blood, as the Kuldeans who had come before the empire slaked their primitive thirsts. Or so she had been taught.

Byleth shivered in the cool embrace of the night breezes. She had gone without a cloak, for her rooms were stifling with many braziers and incense burners, and she yearned for the chill, the cool touch on her skin that drove away the lethargy that wanted to claim her. She'd returned to find her city in the grip of chaos. Demonstrations occurred daily, of which the display at the docks had only been the latest example. Though the city prisons were full, the protests continued. The commander of the city militia reported the people were angry about the attack on the Chapter House. *As if that was my fault!*

Though, truth be told, the anger had really begun before that when Horace brought down the Sun Temple. Her people wanted him removed from his post and banished, if not worse. They didn't understand she needed him. *At least for a little while longer.*

She wondered what the rulers of the other nine imperial cities were doing at this moment. Of course, she didn't have to wonder about some of them. Her spies had reported that King Moloch of Nisus had joined with the monarchs of Chiresh and Hirak, combining their legions into a single army. Their objective was simple: to drag her down from her throne, and thereafter they would likely install some puppet chosen by the Sun Cult. She supposed she should be frightened, and some part of her was, but overriding the fear was a feeling of intense rage. Rage that they, her fellow kings, should dare to band together against her. For what? She'd only defended her reign the same as any of them would do. Yet the other monarchs of the empire had never truly accepted her as their equal, and so they continually plotted against her. All with the covert blessing of the emperor, no doubt.

STORM AND STEEL

It was because she was a woman, the first queen in over a hundred years. The last one before her had been Queen Pur-Adimun of Thuum. The histories called her the Tigress Queen for her ferocity. A woman had to be a tigress in this world if she didn't want to be used and discarded. Was it any wonder she longed for independence? In many ways, that idea had been the primary motivation of her life. Her father had never coddled her, and she took her strength from his memory. *Father, I wish I could talk to you now. I need some wisdom if I'm going to survive this path I've chosen to walk. Some wisdom and a great deal of luck.*

"I am here."

Byleth turned to see Lord Astaptah standing at the room's entrance. He wore his customary garb, a long robe of black cloth. No symbol of his status. It was an odd thing, Byleth realized as she faced him. When she hadn't seen Astaptah in a while, she thought of him as a quiet, decent man. Yet each time she was confronted with his person, her skin crawled as if she had turned over a rock and found a serpent slithering underneath. It wasn't his outward appearance, although his foreign features—too narrow and angular to be Akeshian, the complexion too golden—and deep amber eyes could be disconcerting. No, it was the way he looked at her, the probing glances that held no shred of humility or decorum. She could almost believe he thought of her as just another person, a tool to be used. *Used and discarded.*

"I sent for you over an hour ago," she said.

"And I have come. What do you want?"

"I'm still cross with you." Byleth reclined on a divan, deciding to be playful with her vizier if only to watch him fume. "You did not dismantle the Storm Engine as I commanded the night I was supposed to marry."

"A good thing, too. Else we would have suffered months of delay when you commanded me to rebuild it after you survived."

Survived with your help, you mean. Oh Astaptah, you are not as inscrutable as you would like to believe. You are, after all, still just a man. Clever and valuable, but just a man.

For a moment, she found herself longing for Zazil. For all his faults, her brother had been a man of action. She might have forgiven him for his betrayals if not for his utter incompetence. "Never mind that. The next time you disobey my command, you will suffer for it. Do I make myself clear?"

Lord Astaptah bowed, perhaps a trifle deeper than his usual obeisance. "I am ever your faithful partner."

Yes, but I wish you were more of a loyal servant.

"All right then," Byleth said. "Tell me what you know about the incident at the Chapter House."

"Only what is common knowledge. The royal guard continued to invest the Order's position after you departed from the city. There was little activity to be seen from the outside until eight nights ago when a disturbance was heard by one of your officers. The soldiers eventually entered to find the priests dead."

"What could have happened?"

"I have not had reason to conjecture. Have you been to the site?"

"No. I've ordered an investigation, although I doubt we shall discover anything about the identity of the killers. The culprits apparently had the ability to get in and out of the compound without being detected by my soldiers or my *zoanii*. Still, I intend to know the truth about this attack. I don't give a damn about the lives of those Order zealots, but I don't enjoy the idea of a nest of murderers—possibly with political motives—lurking inside my city."

She stood up and paced across the white carpet. Her eyes alighted on the mural of the gods and focused briefly on the figure of Erimu. The goddess's pitch-black eyes glittered as if they were real, peering into this room from the fathomless Abyss. "Of course, the people are unhappy about it, though only the Silver Lady knows why. The Cult of Amur had been no friend to the commons while they were in power, but to see the protests in my streets you would think the Sun-whores had been loved more than myself."

She paused, waiting for Lord Astaptah to deny that observation as the other members of her court had been so quick to do. Yet he merely stood in silence, watching her. "Did you know there was a public burning today?" She resumed pacing. "An outlaw priest of the Sun Cult set himself on fire at the palace gates. A crowd of people watched."

"I have heard," he said, "that three cities, including Nisus, have declared war on you."

"Yes. I received the formal declaration while I was away. A punishment for the death of the prince of Nisus, naturally. But I don't know what is motivating the other kings to join in, beyond the natural desire for more lands. My agents tell me the armies are gathering at Nisus. Strangely, though, they already have enough troops to lay siege to this city, but they have not yet marched."

Astaptah was quiet for a few seconds, staring at the window on the other side of the room. Then he said, "What if these two incidents, the Chapter House and the impending war, are related in some way."

Byleth stopped pacing and looked at him. "How so?"

"I cannot say with authority, but the king of Nisus is firmly under the thumb of the Sun Cult. Who would profit from inciting the followers of Amur here in Erugash if not the armies preparing to seize your throne?"

"And that would also explain why those armies haven't marched yet. Damn them. This couldn't have happened at a worse time. I will *not* allow the Sun Cult to reestablish its power in my city. That's why I need you to stop this army before it reaches Erugash."

Lord Astaptah's eyebrows lifted a hair. "Thus we return to the subject of the Storm Engine."

"Yes, yes. Spare me your righteous indignation. Your decision to disobey me does have some benefit. Can you do it?"

"Isn't that why you have an army?"

"The legions are needed elsewhere. At Omikur, for one, since you failed to destroy it once again."

"The engine operated within acceptable margins during the charging phase. A storm was generated and was underway when a malfunction occurred."

"I don't care about malfunctions! The town still stands. I commanded you to destroy it down to the last stone."

"Complications are bound to happen," he replied, a touch too smoothly. "They can be corrected, but it takes time and . . ."

Her ire grew as his words drifted away, knowing where this was going. "What kind of complications? The desert take you, Astaptah. Just say what you want and be done with it."

"The machine requires additional calibration since the last demonstration. And for that I require—"

"More victims for your experiments."

"Test subjects."

"I've given you scores of *victims*, including my most trusted adviser and my own brother!" Her *zoana* surged through her veins, almost begging her to smash him into the floor. "But it's never enough. You won't be satisfied until you've bled this city dry."

Byleth expected a response to her outburst, if only a denial of her fears. Yet Lord Astaptah remained perfectly still, as if he were watching a performance in the park. "Fine," she said. "I will get you more test subjects, but you must do what you can in the meantime. I don't need to remind you of what will happen to you should I be overthrown. The Cult of Amur would like nothing better than to send your soul to the underworld in a blaze of fire."

"No doubt. I will do what can be done, though it may all be in vain. For I fear the imperial court will surely censor you and demand that you present yourself in Ceasa to answer for your actions."

Byleth harbored the same fear, though she was wise enough to keep it from reflecting in her expression. "I will do no such thing, as you well know. I have done nothing to deserve this antagonism from my peers. What happened to Prince Tatannu was none of my doing, and I explained as much in my letter to his father. And the Sun Cult struck at me first, without provocation."

"Which makes no difference to the Primarch, and it is he who has the ear of the emperor."

"You think I don't know that?" Byleth didn't realize she had resumed pacing until she almost ran into the wall. "I have escaped one trap only to find myself in another."

"Then it might be time to reevaluate."

She turned back at him, her arms crossed over her breasts. "Go on."

"Are you prepared to contest for the empire, as your father attempted before you?"

Attempted and failed. The disgrace that stains my blood to this day and may forever more unless I do something to cleanse it.

STORM AND STEEL

Yet one lesson she had learned from her father's failure was that she needed powerful allies if she wanted to capture the Chalcedony Throne. The politics of the empire was a mercurial thing, always in flux. The ten cities tended to balance themselves between various factions that played off each other. Urim, Semira, and Yuldir usually aligned themselves with Ceasa, creating an imperialistic bloc in the east. As Epur and Thuum vied frequently with Yuldir for dominance of the central Typhon valley, they opposed the imperialists on most matters. Chiresh and Hirak usually switched between the two factions, depending on which side offered them the most to gain.

Even before the prince's death, Nisus had traditionally aligned itself against Erugash because of their long-standing rivalry over the trade routes to the west. Because of this, their support was rarely sought by either faction, which contented Byleth. Like her father, she tried to remain out of imperial politics unless it was vital to her personal well-being. But no matter what scenario she imagined, she could not see a way to sway enough cities to support her bid for empress to make it even a remote possibility. Ceasa, with the backing of the Sun Cult, was too powerful to challenge. *Not without the Storm Engine. That's the key. But I need to know I can count on it. If I can cow the other cities into getting out of my way, I might have a chance.*

Astaptah intruded upon her thoughts. "What do you intend to do about the slave uprising?"

"The First Sword has been charged with putting it down." Astaptah's expression—a slight downward twist of his thin lips—made her ask, "Why?"

"He may not be the best man for the job. His loyalties are no doubt conflicted. The First Sword was, after all, once a slave himself."

Byleth knew that, but Horace had come to mean so much to her, and to her plans for the future, that she'd quite forgotten about his past travails. "I've made my decision. You need to concern yourself with the task at hand. Find a way to stop that army before it crosses the Typhon."

He bowed from the waist. "As you command."

She went back to the window, not bothering to watch him leave. It was a small gesture, but it spoke of the trust she granted him, against all reason. He had proven himself on the night of the *Tammuris* when her life hung in the balance. Yet, more than that, he was her final opportunity. *A woman must be a tigress to prosper in this world, and tigresses know no fear.*

Down below, her city prepared for nightfall. Light poured from the windows of homes as families gathered for the evening meal. From festhalls and pleasure houses where men and women slaked their lusts, to the temples where priests and priestesses chanted the evening vespers, they were all her people. And they were oblivious to the doom poised above their heads.

Silver Lady of the Moon, watch over us all.

CHAPTER SEVEN

The Muharet Hills rose from the central salt marshes of the river delta. Covered in thick forest and surrounded by leagues of treacherous wetlands, they were difficult to approach from any direction, and thus they had been left uninhabited since the dawn of antiquity. Branches of the mighty Typhon meandered through the moss-covered trees, carving out islands of dry ground. In the morning, white mist cloaked their hoary slopes, obscuring all but the tip of the central hilltop.

Jirom blinked away a trickle of sweat as he kept an eye out for predators. Even a medium-sized crocodile could snap a man's leg in its powerful jaws or with a tail swipe.

He marched at the middle of the column as they headed toward the large hill. There, according to the messages they had received at various rebel hideouts, was where the gathering would take place. Emanon had said little more than that about it, which didn't seem to bother anyone else. Jirom supposed the longtime rebels were accustomed to Emanon's detachment, but he couldn't shake the feeling that Emanon was angry at him for some reason.

The farther they traveled, away from the merchant roads and towns of the empire, the more uneasy Jirom became. It was the same feeling he'd felt at the Old Stone before they attacked the caravan. He trusted Emanon with his life but wondered privately if this wasn't a bad idea.

They had left the wagon behind two days ago when they reached the edge of the delta, its wheels being unsuited to this wet terrain. The rebels took turns pulling the sled they'd built from wagon parts, on which rested the treasure boxes from the raid under a heap of leather hides.

The Bronze Blades traveled alongside the rebels. Seventy-seven men-at-arms, they ranged from pikemen and heavy infantry to crossbowmen and specialists. Their leader, Captain Ovar, rode the ugliest horse Jirom had ever seen, a creature covered in patches of yellow and red with a shit-brown mane.

"I see you're admiring my Lessa," the mercenary captain said, riding over closer. *Actually, I can't decide whether to steal it so I can get off my feet or cook and eat it.*

"A fine animal," Jirom forced himself to say. No use insulting the hired swords. He half-remembered something his mother used to say about attracting more bees with honey, but it had sounded like a bunch of horseshit to him. Most people responded to strength. Sweet words were best left for pillow talk.

"So this meeting we're headed toward. Your captain hasn't been very forthcoming about it. I don't expect you to betray his confidence, but I'd like to know if my men are going to be in danger."

Jirom looked at him out of the sides of his eyes. "Captain Ovar, you know as much as I do. From past experience I can tell you to keep your men on a tight leash, because trouble usually follows us."

"That's good advice, Lieutenant. By the way, how do you like being an officer? You never made it past sergeant before, right?"

"It's just like any other rank. The shit runs downhill and the complaints run in the opposite direction. Being an officer just means more responsibility and less people to listen to your bitching." He glanced back at the man. "So who do you complain to, Captain?"

Ovar smiled up at the sky. "To the only ones who will listen without talking back."

Jirom couldn't help chuckling at that. However, he remained vigilant around the mercenary leader. Longar and Three Moons had spoken highly of him, but there was no telling how far his loyalty really ran. When the fighting started—and Jirom had no doubt there would be more battles in their future—would these sellswords stand or flee?

A whistle called out from ahead. Emanon was huddled with a group of scouts. Longar was among them. He had taken command of the pathfinders, as smoothly as if they were back in the old Company. Jirom quickened his pace to catch up. Captain Ovar came along, invited or not.

"They find something?" Jirom asked when they got nearer.

"An outer marker." Emanon swatted at a flying insect buzzing around his head. "We're almost there."

Jirom looked ahead. The slopes of the hills, about a mile away, were visible through the gaps in the forest canopy. "So are you going to tell us what you've got planned at this big meeting?"

"Nothing. Honestly, Jirom. I wish I could take credit, but the other captains must have put it together. Hell, I would've picked someplace more hospitable."

"Like a cave in the desert?"

Emanon clapped his hands and then peeled them apart. The annoying insect was smashed into a green pulp. Two more flew past his face. "Maybe."

Jirom sighed. He was tired of this game. He took Emanon by the arm and pulled him aside. He didn't care who saw. "What the fuck is your problem?"

"I don't know what you're talking about."

"You keep saying you don't know anything, but this meeting—or whatever it is—sounds like what you've been wanting all along. Getting these small groups to band together to fight the Akeshians."

"Sounds like a good idea, doesn't it?"

"So tell me what's wrong."

"I guess I'm not good at sharing." He waved his hand at the fighters marching past. "For a long time, I was all these men had, and they were all I had. Now things are changing. The way you took charge in that merc haven, it showed me I'm expendable."

"That's insane. Every one of these men would lay down their life for you. Me included. You built this movement, and you're still in command. But you need to learn to delegate. The bigger this rebellion gets, the less control you're going to have unless you learn to trust your officers."

"See. You know more about command structure than I do."

Jirom lowered his head until their gazes were level and stared into Emanon's deep-green eyes. "I might have more experience, but I'm not the leader you are. I could never do what you do."

"So you're saying I should just quit complaining and get back to running this crew."

"You got it, Captain." Jirom winked. "And if you have something to say, then just spit it out. Or next time you try keeping things from me, I'll knock your head against a tree."

Emanon smiled. Just a little. "Sounds like something you'd do."

With that, Emanon marched ahead.

"He has an interesting command style," Captain Ovar said.

Jirom watched the back of his departing partner, wondering what the man had planned this time. Only the gods knew. "No, he's just an asshole sometimes."

They crossed through another swampy valley before they reached the tall hill at the center of the delta. Stony ridges curved around its base to form a huge natural basin. A narrow creek meandered through the center, out into the marsh beyond, but otherwise the ground was dry and firm. Hundreds of tents and crude shelters crowded the basin. Numerous campfires twinkled under the trees, filling the air with a haze of wood smoke. People congregated around the fires. Not just men, but plenty of women and children, too. In all, Jirom estimated there were between two and three thousand people camped here.

Emanon set up his band on the southern edge of the gathering site and told them to dig in for an extended stay. Then he left before Jirom could talk to him.

Left in charge, Jirom supervised the construction of crude shelters for the band. Then he helped move the treasure boxes inside one of the lodgings and put Jerkul in charge of guarding them. The sergeant selected one of his fighters to stand the first watch.

"Guard them," Jerkul instructed. "But don't look like you're guarding them."

"How the shit can I guard them without looking like I am?" the rebel asked.

Jerkul growled under his breath. "Just don't draw attention to yourself. Or them. We don't want anyone sniffing around. Got it?"

"Sure, sure. I got it, for shit's sake."

Jirom left them to figure it out. He noticed the mercenaries making their camp a stone's throw away. It was a true military camp, squared up with lines as straight as an arrow's flight. He grabbed one of the rebel corporals, Lappu, and told him he wanted their camp fortified the same way. "And line the ditch with a double row of sharpened stakes, one cubit high."

"Double row. One cubit. Got it."

Taking a pull from his waterskin, Jirom went back to surveying the basin. Whoever set up this encampment had at least possessed enough sense to post pickets all around the ridge. A regular procession of observers moved up and down the wooded slopes. Much like Emanon's band, the rebel fighters gathered were a motley collection. They wore a wide variety of armor, most of it looking like bits and pieces of gear collected from battlefields. Their weapons were equally eclectic, although most carried some form of spear, long or short. To Jirom's eye they looked undisciplined, little more than a mob.

"Ain't much to look at, eh?"

Three Moons spat into a pool of brackish water and scratched his nose. He looked even more ancient in the fading light. His face gleamed with sweat, making every line and crack stand out.

"No, but they've noticed your crew's arrival." Jirom hadn't missed all the curious glances toward the mercenary camp. Captain Ovar's men didn't look or act like freed slaves. "It's not too late to back out, old-timer."

The sorcerer clucked his tongue and grinned. "And miss all the fun? No, sir. I want to be there when this band of fools butts heads with a full Akeshian legion."

"Be careful what you wish for."

"Yep." Three Moons spat again into the dingy water. "The gods just might hear and give you a bellyful of attention. That's why we signed on."

"What's that supposed to mean?"

"We're old men. All of us. And that's a curse for soldiers like us, to outlive all your friends and find yourself without anything left to fight for. The boys and I are here because we want to go out on our feet, so to speak."

Jirom swallowed as the cold realization sank in. "You think we're all going to die."

"Victory or death. One is about the same as the other."

Is that what I sound like to these young fighters? Gods, strike me mute if I do.

"Come with me, old man."

"Where we going?"

"I'm tired of waiting around for something interesting to happen."

STORM AND STEEL

"About fucking time, Sergeant. Oh, sorry. *Lieutenant*."

"Funny. Call your captain to tag along, too. He'll probably want to see this."

As Jirom suspected, Ovar was quite interested in a look around. The three of them made their way through the large encampment. Rebels sat around smoky fires, cooking and eating, pissing and shitting in holes dug under the trees, screwing under blankets. There were a lot of dogs nosing around. Not the wild kind; these animals had the look of domesticated pets, though they roamed the camp in small packs.

Jirom wanted to find Emanon, but more importantly he wanted to discover who had called this convocation. The bulk of the camp formed a vast semicircle around the base of the hill. If there was a command center, he was guessing it would be at the middle, so that's the direction he headed. He had to wade through throngs of people several times. Some of them called out, asking questions about where they had come from and what they knew about the "war against imperial aggression." That was a common phrase he heard from several mouths. *As if calling a rebellion something else is going to make it any easier to win.*

He wondered what these people were thinking. Then he looked closer and saw the fear. The preternatural brightness in their eyes as if they were on the verge of tears even as they smiled and laughed. He heard the strained tightness in their voices. He'd seen it before in the gladiator arena. Mainly from the newer slave-fighters as they prepared for their first—and usually last—bout, right before the gate opened and they were thrust into the fray. Seeing it, he felt ashamed for judging them. They were holding together as best they could in the face of an enemy so vast and powerful that just the act of defiance was a measure of courage. *If they all die tomorrow, they would still die as heroes. Because they dare to seize freedom with both hands, no matter how terrible the cost.*

It was easier for him. He'd been fighting all his life. This was just another campaign, except that this might be the first time he'd fought for something he believed in, instead of fighting for pay or mere survival. *Damn you, Emanon. Where in the hells did you go?*

Three Moons pointed to a group of wooden posts driven upright into the ground near the foot of the hill. They had been painted bright red, and objects hung from them on long spikes. Feathers, strings of beads, even small bones.

Totems.

He hadn't seen their like since he left his homeland. His people vener-
ated the gods of the earth and sky, appeased them with offerings, and warded
off unwanted spirits with fetishes like these posts. But what were they to the
rebels? Then he heard the drums. A low rumble like distant thunder, sending
vibrations through the earth. He felt them through his feet, reminding him of
his childhood when he would join his family and neighbors in the traditional
dances. The sounds quickened his pulse. He hurried ahead, trusting Three
Moons to keep up.

They were stopped outside the posts by a cordon of sentries. Beyond
them, a bonfire burned in a hollow recess gouged out of the hill. Its rear wall
was sheer, forming a natural concave wall three man-lengths high. A dozen
men sat around the fire, and Emanon was among them.

As Jirom made to join his captain, a pair of guards moved to block him.
"Only the chosen can pass here," said a guard with a bristly, black beard down
to his round stomach.

Jirom pointed to Emanon. "I've come to see my warleader."

The bearded sentry ground the butt of his spear in the soil. "Go back to
your tent and wait like the rest."

Jirom was considering a violent response when Three Moons stepped
forward. "Pardon us," he said.

The totem posts on either side began to shake, causing the fetishes nailed
to them to rattle. Heads turns as the rattling grew louder, until even the
council of captains stopped debating and stood up to look in their direction.
The sentries stepped back, hands lifted in surrender. Jirom grimaced at Three
Moons, and the sorcerer winked. Behind them, Captain Ovar just watched.
They walked up to the bonfire.

The rebel commanders were a mixed bunch, both old and young. Most
had the sun-bronzed complexion and nondescript garb of desert warriors, but
one stood out from the rest. Jirom noted him immediately. He was bigger
than anyone else sitting at the fire, both tall and powerfully built, wearing
little more than a few scraps of rawhide like he was still a slave. His skin
was lighter than most of his comrades, and he wore his night-black hair in

long braids down to his shoulders. His eyes were deep and dark, hiding his thoughts. A huge war-mace lay by his side.

"What was that display about?" Emanon hissed under his breath as he stalked over to intercept them.

"What display?" Three Moons asked with a mottled brown grin. "The spirits of this land are strong. Sometimes they speak through the whisper of the wind and the quaking of stone."

Jirom redirected Emanon's attention to the big man with the dark eyes. "Who's that?"

"Ramagesh. He was once a body-slave to the prince of Chiresh, or so I've heard. The rumor is that he killed his royal master on a hunting trip. Snapped his neck. Then he ran away to join the rebellion. He's been tearing up the countryside between Hirak and Epur ever since, and making quite a name for himself."

"Did he call this assembly?"

"No." Emanon pointed to a skinny, bare-chested man who stood on the far side of the bonfire. His hair was pulled back in a knot at the top of his head. "That would be Neskarig. They call him the General. Watch out for him. He's a black-hearted bastard."

"You know him?"

Emanon's mouth turned down in a sour grimace. "Aye. He was the man who freed me."

Jirom waited for Emanon to keep going. There was obviously more to that story. But his lover headed back to the fire. Jirom followed. A few of the other commanders looked over as Jirom, Captain Ovar, and Three Moons sat down with Emanon, but no one tried to stop them.

"You didn't miss much," Emanon said. "These old warthogs were just swapping stories about how many enemies they've killed. If you believe half of what they say, the Akeshians have already been wiped out several times over."

One of the commanders, a stout veteran with a jagged scar around his neck, pointed at Jirom. "This is the one we've heard about, Emanon? Jirom the Red-Blade Wielder?"

"It is. I found him in one of Byleth's army camps. He was a gladiator before that. He took that sword from Hazael et'Tanunak's corpse." He nodded to Jirom. "Show them the blade."

Jirom frowned. He didn't like the idea of people talking about him when he wasn't around. But he grabbed the hilt of the *assurana* sword and drew it halfway. The blade gleamed scarlet in the firelight. Murmurs passed around the bonfire. They died down as Neskarig lifted a hand. The drums fell silent.

"Jirom Red-Blade, we welcome your voice to this council." He spoke slowly and softly, yet everyone listened. "Brothers, I have called you together to discuss our great enemy. As most of you already know, a battle was fought at the city of Omikur. With the aid of the soldiers of Etonia, we crushed the legions assembled against us. However, the queen of Erugash returned with fell sorcery. The town remains under siege, and many brave warriors lost their lives."

Heads nodded as the commanders passed around sober glances.

Neskarig pointed toward Jirom's party. "Emanon was there. He knows of what I speak."

Emanon grunted. It was the sound he made when he didn't want to talk. Yet he said, "Aye, we were at Omikur. We ambushed the queen's soldiers and won the day. But we left before the bitch struck back. Of what followed after, we're as ignorant as the rest of you."

The commanders next talked in low voices about the great army gathering at Nisus. Evidently, some of the kings of Akeshia were about to march on Erugash. Jirom found that hard to believe, but reminded himself that these Akeshians were crazy, so nothing should surprise him. No one bothered to include him or Emanon, who sat and stared into the fire, though many cautious glances were thrown in Captain Ovar's direction.

Jirom watched Ramagesh, who had not spoken to anyone yet. He merely sat and watched the others. *He's waiting for something. What is it? Perhaps he is the General's pet.*

"We should return to Omikur!" one of the commanders said, striking the ground with his fist as he spoke. "And crush the queen's legions again. We dealt them a hard blow before. Now we should finish the job!"

His words received many nods of agreement, and another commander said, "Exactly! The foreigners trapped inside would be valuable allies."

STORM AND STEEL

Then a short, squat commander with a bald head and shaggy eyebrows grumbled, "Fuck those foreign bastards! They invade our lands, seeking to steal our gold. Rape our women! No, let them rot inside that tomb they call Omikur."

Many fists pounded the ground.

"Then let us attack Nisus!" the first commander spoke. When a chorus of hisses rained down on him, he held up both hands. "Listen! Once that army leaves, the city will be guarded by only old men and boys. While the Nisusi and Erugashi grind themselves to dust, we shall live like kings!"

"Shut up, Lorchis!" the short commander barked. "You're always going on about Nisus. It's too big of a target for us, even guarded by old geezers."

"So what do we do?"

Glances moved around the campfire as the rebels mumbled and shrugged. Jirom was waiting for the General to speak up when a voice rose up beside him.

"Now is the time."

Everyone looked over as Emanon stood up. Jirom saw Neskarig begin to rise as well, but Ramagesh shook his head. The General sat back down, a sour frown on his face. *So, the big one is not the pet. He holds the leash.*

Emanon hitched his thumbs in his leather belt as he looked around at the other captains. Jirom had to force himself not to smile. He loved how Emanon looked when he was giving a speech, so confident and in control. He himself had never felt comfortable speaking in front of groups. He didn't like so many eyes upon him.

"Now is the time," Emanon repeated, "to push harder. To be more aggressive and take the fight to our enemy. The queen is beset by enemies on all sides. My men and I have struck inside her city. We have attacked her outposts and holdings. All this with just a handful of fighters. Yet, if we banded together—"

"We heard about your mission in Erugash," the stout captain said. "All you did was kick the wasps' nest and draw attention to the rest of us!"

Several captains added their voices to this charge.

"Some of us," another leader said, "like working in the shadows. We've been gaining support with the locals. They feed us and hide us when the Akeshians come looking."

"But we'll never be free hiding in the shadows." Emanon took a deep breath and let it out. "Not without a fight. The empire won't relent until it has crushed us. This is a fight to the death."

All the captains were shouting now. Jirom couldn't tell if Emanon had swayed enough of them to matter as they argued among themselves. He didn't see how it could be resolved with words. These men were, at heart, little different from the tribal elders of his homeland. Each seeking to retain power over his personal fiefdom. Emanon was the only one here who saw how this tribalism would lead to eventual defeat.

"He is right."

The council quieted as a deep voice rose above their chatter. A strange feeling lodged behind Jirom's breastbone as Ramagesh stood up. He rose above the others like a giant. The firelight painted him in bloody tones and cast angular shadows across the rock wall behind him. A bone-hilted kukri was sheathed at his hip.

"Emanon speaks the truth of it," Ramagesh said. He pounded his fists together with a solid thump. "We must band together if we want to be victorious. The time for quiet action is over. The empire knows of our cause, and even now the kings of Akeshia are moving to crush us. But if we stand together, my brothers, nothing can defeat us. We shall be as the whirlwind that flattens homes and scatters armies. We shall not stop until all men are freed from bondage, even if it means shedding the last drop of our blood."

There was power in his words. Jirom felt it coursing through him. Before he knew it, he was standing with the rest of the captains. Many of them cheered Ramagesh's words. Rebels from beyond the totem posts watched. Some joined the cheering, even though they did not know what they were celebrating. Emanon, however, stood silently. Jirom touched his hand, but Emanon stepped away. He approached Ramagesh, who now conferred quietly with Neskarig.

"Where then?" Emanon asked, loud enough to be heard above the din. "Where will we focus our combined might?"

The cheering died down as the captains, and then the people gathered beyond the posts, stopped to listen. Jirom knew what Emanon wanted, but it didn't seem feasible. Not yet. These fighters were drunk on eloquent oratory, but he could lose them with the wrong word.

"What do you suggest?" Neskarig asked.

Don't say it, Em. Defer to the future, until these men have learned to respect you as I do.

"Erugash."

Jirom held his breath as his fear became reality. He looked around the council fire and saw the call to action die in the eyes of the assembled captains.

"Shit on a stick," Three Moons muttered.

Jirom was forced to agree. Emanon had bitten off too much, and now he'd lost them. Neskarig looked as if he wanted to say something, but he held his tongue. *Aye, you're a cagey jackal, aren't you?*

After a moment, Ramagesh broke the silence that had descended over the gathering. His gaze swept across the assembly, eventually landing on Jirom. The intensity of his stare was a palpable thing. "Red-Blade, what do you say about this?"

Jirom shifted his feet at the sudden attention. This was the last thing he wanted. He felt the pressure of the gazes upon him, especially from Ramagesh. He knew what he should say, but he also knew it wouldn't make a difference. At best, he could cause a rift among the rebels, and this was a time when they needed to stand united if they were to have any hope of survival. However, his true loyalty lay not with the rebellion but with one man.

"I stand with my warleader."

Shouts echoed around the bonfire as the captains vented their opposition.

"We can't stand against the *zoanii*!"

"Erugash has never been taken! Not even by the combined armies of the other nine cities!"

"We'll all be crucified!"

Jirom weathered their condemnation. He felt a touch and looked down to see Emanon's fingers brushing his hand. It was all the consolation he needed. For now.

Finally, Ramagesh lifted his mace to the night sky. His voice battered down the rest of the council. "No, my brothers. We are not ready to face the queen. One day we shall be, but today is not that day. Yet we will strike and let the empire know the strength of our conviction, and we shall keep hitting them until the crowned heads of Akeshia fall at our feet. But enough talk for tonight. My throat is dry and my spirit longs for the salve of brotherhood. Let us talk more tomorrow, when we've had time to consider our words with care."

Feet stamped on the hard ground, a sound that spread through the basin. The drums joined in, matching the beat with their deep booms, until it seemed as if the hills were bouncing to the rhythm. *This is a leader that men would follow to the very gates of the lowest hell.*

Jirom turned to Emanon, trying to gauge his lover's reaction, but Emanon's face was like granite. "Now what?"

The rebel captain sighed. "Now I have to go twist some arms, or else this is all for nothing."

"Is that going to help matters? Ramagesh and the General hold the others in the palms of their hands. They aren't going to budge without a good reason."

"I'm still going to try."

You risk driving them further away. The campaign against the empire will be long and bloody. Bide your time. Wait until the other commanders are looking for a new direction, when they'll be more open to your suggestions.

Instead, he said, "What do you want us to do?"

"Get back to camp and sit tight on those coin boxes."

Emanon turned to go, and Jirom put a hand on his forearm. "Be careful."

With a wink, his captain strode away toward the haphazard array of tents north of the council area. Jirom watched him, wondering why he felt a lump in his stomach. It was the same feeling he used to get before a battle.

"He's quite a jackass," Three Moons said. He had scavenged a skin from somewhere. By the purple color to his lips, it was wine. He passed the skin to Jirom. "I can see why you like him."

"He makes me insane sometimes." Jirom took a sip. He'd guessed wrong; it was brandy, and surprisingly strong at that. The liquor burned as it ran down his throat. "But I love him. I make no apology for that."

STORM AND STEEL

"I wouldn't think so, though I must admit it's difficult to understand this new . . . you. The Sergeant Jirom I remember once almost beat a man to death with his fists for disobeying an order."

Jirom looked him in the eyes. "You think I've changed? Disobey me and find out."

Jirom smiled to take the sting out the words. "Come on, old man. Let's go see what trouble our boys are getting into. Captain, care to join us?"

Captain Ovar shook his head. He'd been standing back during the entire conversation, just watching and listening. "No, gentlemen. I'm going to find my blanket. I have a feeling tomorrow is going to be a busy day."

As the mercenary captain strode off, Jirom and Three Moons walked back through the camp on their own, passing the skin back and forth.

"I've seen you do a lot of tricks," Jirom said. "Like rattling those totems back there. But you don't bleed when working your magic. Why not?"

Three Moons picked something out of his teeth, held it up, and then put whatever it was back into his mouth. "You've been spending time around those 'Keshii sorcerers, eh?"

"Aye. The blood runs down their arms and faces when they work their spells."

"We're just different," Three Moons answered with another pull from the skin. "The 'Keshii feed their power from within, so it rips them up when it comes out. But me, well, I'm just a backwoods warlock. I talk to the spirits, and sometimes they show up to play."

Jirom shook his head at Three Moons' idea of "play." Then again, having witnessed the awesome power at the disposal of those Akeshii sorcerers, he suddenly saw his former company-mate in a different light.

By the time they reached their band, pleasant warmth had spread through Jirom's insides, and his thoughts were cushioned in a gentle haze. They returned to find supper was being served. A fighter brought them each a bowl containing some kind of soupy stew that smelled of mutton. They ate around the bonfire. All save Emanon, who had not returned.

Jirom set his bowl aside when he was done. The stars had come out, a net of diamonds shining over the valley basin. The air was sticky, but a breeze kept the worst of the heat at bay.

Three Moons lay sprawled beside the fire with the empty wineskin tucked under his arm. His snores rivaled a cat being skinned alive. Every so often, one of the fighters would look over as if contemplating shoving something in the wizard's mouth to shut him up, but none of them were dumb enough to try it. Longar had spent the last couple days scaring them half to death with tales of Three Moons' legendary outbursts, usually when drunk, many of which had resulted in extensive property damage.

After a while, Jirom stood up. Most of his men had gone to sleep. Sentries were stationed at the four cardinal points around their unit's small plot of ground, with another man sitting outside the tent with the treasure boxes. He left orders for them to be relieved at midnight and then went to find his own bed. He discovered that someone had taken the time to erect a crude shelter of stripped tree branches over his blankets. His kit bag was inside, too.

He took off his sword-belt and propped the weapon against the lean-to. He was unlacing his boiled leather jerkin when a pair of familiar hands appeared from behind to help. The deft fingers dipped inside the armor to caress his stomach. "Did you have any luck convincing them?"

Emanon's lips pressed against the back of his right ear. "Not much. You were right. None of them wanted to speak out against Ramagesh."

Jirom leaned back into his lover's arms. "It might be for the best. I've seen what the empire can do when provoked. And an attack on Erugash would incite the rest of the cities to exact revenge."

Emanon released him, drawing his arms away. "So what are you saying? That we're beaten already?"

Jirom turned around and reached out, but Emanon batted his hands aside. Jirom felt his hands clench into tight fists, almost as if it were happening to someone else. His blood pumped hot and fierce through his chest. He had to make an effort to keep control of his temper. "That's not what I'm saying. You know this army can't match up to a pitched battle against even a single legion. With the crusaders driven back to the coast, we're on our own. We need a smart campaign. Continue hitting them and running before they can strike back."

"I'm sick of hitting and running. We aren't going to defeat an empire with pinpricks."

Jirom stepped closer so he could look down at his captain. "Not all at once, but we can bleed them. At the same time we can use some of that gold to buy help on the inside. What was the name of that agent in the queen's boudoir?"

"I'm not backing down, Jirom."

He could see the ferocity turning his lover's eyes a deeper shade of green until they became almost black. The huskiness in his voice caused Jirom's blood to boil, but this time for a different reason. "All right. Then we don't back down."

Emanon kissed the underside of his chin while his hands peeled Jirom's jerkin back. "I just need you to have faith."

Jirom pulled his captain down on the soft bedroll and started stripping away his clothes. He kissed every inch of skin that he bared. He got to Emanon's stomach before he halted. "You never told me. What is Ramagesh's plan? Where does he want to attack?"

"Some town up north on the Typhon main artery. Oh, do that again."

"What's it called?"

Emanon made a pleased noise in the back of his throat. "Um? Sekhatun. Just a little trading town near, uh . . . yes, right there."

Why does that name sound familiar?

Then he remembered. That's where he and Horace had met. Coincidence? He was combing through his memories of the place, which were a little vague since he'd been kept in a dark cell most of his stay there, when Emanon took his hand and guided it lower. Then Jirom stopped thinking about the rebellion for a time.

The streets of the Dredge twisted and crooked like the tunnels of a serpent's warren, turning back on themselves and leading to dead ends as often as not. This district had once been the home of craftsmen—sandal makers, dyers, hemp weavers, and papyrus presses—but over time the better-off citizens had moved to nicer neighborhoods, leaving behind those who could not afford to escape. And so the neighborhood fell into a cycle of squalor, with each successive generation poorer and more desperate than their forebears.

Alyra stepped around a puddle that may or may not have been mud on her way down what passed for the "main street" of the Dredge. She kept one hand on the handle of her knife under her cloak. The city had become less hospitable over the past few months, especially at night. The people were riled. Previously, that would have given her hope, as it must surely encourage the network of agents for which she had worked for several years in its plan to destabilize the empire. Now she wasn't so sure. Things had become complicated.

Eyes followed her as she passed through a narrow court surrounded by tall buildings, beer shops, and smoking dens pressed between rows of family homes. She could feel them searching her, watching for signs of weakness or wealth, anything that might trigger their predatory instincts. Alyra usually brought someone else when she came here, but she hadn't asked Sefkahet because of the tension between them. Not to mention that the queen's return would have the palace in a minor uproar for the next few days.

Alyra remembered when she had been a handmaiden, the constant sense of excitement and fear haunting her every waking moment, and most of the sleeping ones, too. Now that she was free, she appreciated having more control over her life, but she still missed the access into the hidden affairs of the palace that she'd once possessed. *Horace, you came into my life and turned everything upside down. Most days I don't know whether to bless you or curse you for that.*

After the *Tammuris* debacle, the network safehouse in the Dredge had closed down. Alyra had left several messages in drop locations but received no replies. As near as she could tell, she'd been exiled from the spy ring. It wasn't a mystery why. She'd been ordered to leave Horace to his fate as he wallowed in the dungeons under the Sun Temple, and she had refused. Had it been out of love? She didn't know, but since then she'd continued the mission on her own, using the assets she had cultivated to assist the local rebels.

She'd been shocked this morning to find an encrypted message on her bedside table. With trembling hands, she had locked the door to her room and sat down to decipher it. As the words hidden within the message emerged, she'd thought her heart would stop.

Come to the lily house at the fourth hour. All is forgiven.

With anxiety weighing in her stomach like a ball of lead, she had dressed and left the manor, pausing only to leave word with the servants that she would be gone for most of the day.

She knew right away what the message had meant by the "lily house." When she'd first come to Erugash as part of a slaver caravan, she'd been kept at a secret location until her handlers could arrange for her to be "bought" by the palace. It had been a quaint house at the southern tail of the Dredge, unremarkable in any way among the other poor homes except for a picture of a gorgeous white lily painted on the front door. She'd never been back to the place since entering the queen's service, but it made sense.

She followed the directions in her head, trying to find the right street. This part of the city was only partially familiar to her, and everything looked different in the dark. After getting turned around a couple of times, she finally sighted a pale candle at the end of a crooked street, packed between two homes that appeared abandoned.

Alyra stopped a few doors away and dipped into the shadow of a small alley. The door beside the candle was painted with a white lily. Watching the house, she considered what she was going to say to whoever had invited her here. She assumed that the line "all is forgiven" meant she was being welcomed back to the network, but she couldn't be sure. After serving the Nemedia government for years, she'd come to understand the way they operated. Her choice to save Horace had been, to them, a betrayal of the worst kind. So, was this a setup to lure her to a remote place so the network could punish her for the transgression? If so, why now? What did they want?

Making sure her knife was loose in its sheath, Alyra stepped out of the alley. Just as she stepped up to the door, it opened before her, the painted panels giving way to the darkness within. Then a familiar figure appeared. The old woman Alyra had seen so many times before at the old safehouse.

The front room was just the way she remembered it, except older and dustier. Two small oil lamps showed plaster walls covered in cracks and a scuffed wood floor. Stairs led up to the second floor. A wooden bench sat against the far wall under the alcoves for the hearth gods, all empty.

A hallway led back to the kitchen and eating area, but at a gesture from the old woman, Alyra took the stairs. Nostalgia nibbled at her heart as she saw the frescoes on the walls of the upstairs hallway. A pastoral scene of three young shepherds watching over their flock in a valley between two towering mountains. She and Sefkahet had drawn it over several days while they waited for their positions at the palace to be secured. Alyra ran her fingers over the smooth plaster, up to the rough spots at the top that they hadn't had time to finish. She remembered they had planned to paint a starry sky overhead, but they'd been called away to start their new lives as slaves to the queen. It seemed like another lifetime, as if this picture had been painted by another girl. A girl who didn't understand the trials she would one day face, the heartaches she would have to endure.

"I wasn't sure you'd remember this place."

Cipher stood in the doorway to the bedroom where she'd once stayed. His face was leaner than she remembered. He'd lost weight, and silver hairs gleamed at his temples.

"Of course," she replied. "This is where I first met you. I recall you always had a worried look on your face. That much, at least, hadn't changed."

"Pardon all the secrecy, but the old safehouse wasn't . . . well, safe anymore. Since the night of the Fall, we've been driven deeper underground."

"The Fall. That's an interesting way to put it. Yes, a lot of things fell on that night. One of them was my esteem for the network."

"You know that wasn't my decision, Alyra. I had my orders."

"Your orders were unconscionable, to let a good man die because the network saw some slight advantage in his death. And how did that work out?"

"We want you back. This comes from Night himself."

Alyra wanted to laugh in his face. Instead, she only allowed herself to smile. "Why should I consider it? You turned against me. I have my own assets now and more influence than ever before. I know why you need me, but what do I need with you?"

He actually looked pained as he said, "Things are happening, and we don't have enough eyes in the right places. More than that, we have a mission that needs done. The rebels are gaining ground, and the network sees an opportunity to capitalize on their success. But our relationship with their leadership hasn't been on good terms since you left."

"I didn't leave. You left me."

"And I apologize for that mistake. Trust me when I tell you it won't happen again."

Trust is a funny thing, Cipher. Once it's lost, you can't easily get it back again. I think we're both going to learn that the hard way.

"Assuming I'm willing to return," she said, "what do you want me to do?"

He held out a slip of papyrus. "Go to this address and retrieve a series of letters. They're from various *zoanii* houses, pledging their support to the man listed if the queen should be deposed."

"A coup? What does that have to do with the rebellion?"

"That's what we want to find out. We need to know who's involved and what they are planning."

"That's it? Just get these letters?"

"That's it."

"You still haven't said what's in it for me."

Cipher's thin brows came together over the bridge of his nose. "Alyra, you were never a mercenary in the past."

"Things change. My life is different now. I'm going to need a few things from the network."

"Such as?"

"I need someone inside the Civil Planning Office."

"City planning? Whatever for?"

"That's my business. Second, I need to see everything the network knows about the killings at the Chapter House."

"Alyra, I can't—"

"Don't argue, just get it."

"I have to check a few sources, but you'll have the information by the end of the week."

"Perfect. Oh, and one more thing. Find another place to meet. Somewhere outside the Dredge."

As she left, Alyra felt his eyes follow her down the stairs. The old woman had vanished, so she let herself out.

Pulling the door shut behind her, Alyra let out a long breath. She released the hilt of her knife hidden under her cloak for the first time since she'd entered the house. The skin of her palm stuck to the handle for a moment before it came loose. What would have happened if she'd refused the offer? Would they have allowed her to leave alive? Somehow, despite Cipher's conciliatory tone, she doubted it.

She took one last look at the white lily on the door. So delicate and lovely. She wondered who had painted it. She turned away, eager to put this place behind her. She still didn't understand why she had accepted the mission. Just as she was getting free of the network's machinations, they had succeeded in pulling her back in.

She's fetching. Not exactly gorgeous, but she's striking to look at. And so tall! I wonder why she dresses so conservatively.

Byleth cleared her throat and nodded as Lady Anshara spoke. They sat in one of the palace's smaller audience chambers, the queen on an ancient wooden throne and the lady on a settee a few feet away. Lady Anshara was twenty-five years of age, with her silky black hair wrapped into a long braid. She wore a dress of green silk with short sleeves and a divided skirt. Interesting tattoos covered both her exposed arms, of lotus blossoms and various animals along swirls of pale-blue water. Her eyes were a bit too small, her mouth a trifle too narrow, yet there was something about her that reminded Byleth of an old painting.

"Thank you, Majesty, for inviting me. It is good to get out of my late uncle's home for a little while."

"That place is a maze," Byleth said. "I spent many summers roaming its halls and alcoves. Lord Mulcibar, may his memory shine forever, was a great man and a great friend to the throne."

"That is most kind of you to say, Majesty."

"You were most recently living in Ceasa, were you not?"

"Yes, Majesty. I've been studying under Mistress Udina for the past year."

STORM AND STEEL

Byleth glanced to the side where Xantu stood. Lady Udina of House Purimu had a reputation as one of the most demanding and sought-after teachers of the art in all the empire. She tutored only the most promising *zoanii*. Byleth herself had wanted to apply, once upon a time, but fate had intervened when her father was killed and she became queen.

"Majesty, I was hoping to be allowed to join your court."

"Of course I would be delighted, my dear. Although I must say I'm surprised. I assumed you would be returning to the capital after you put your uncle's affairs in order." She gave the woman a coy smile. "I'm sure nothing here could compare to the legendary entertainments of the imperial court."

Lady Anshara made a tiny, rigid shake of her head. "If it pleases Your Majesty, I am committed to remaining here in Erugash. For many generations, my family has served this city and its monarchs."

The lady slipped off her chair and went down on both knees. Xantu started to make a defensive warding, but Byleth stopped him from interfering with an upraised finger.

"Majesty, my queen," Lady Anshara said, "Forgive my presumption, but I seek to take up my late uncle's mantle. To advise you and serve you, if you will have me."

Byleth gazed deep into Anshara's eyes. They gave open invitation for a mind-sift, and Byleth was tempted, but she liked this young woman's poise and confidence. She placed a hand on her head. "I accept your service, Lady Anshara. You are hereby made a member of our personal guard, charged with protecting our person from all threats, with all the rights and privileges of that rank."

The lady's eyes held a faint glisten of moisture as she nodded. "Thank you, Majesty. It will be my sincerest honor and pleasure."

"All right then. Get off your knees. Lord Xantu will explain your duties."

Lady Anshara bowed low and backed away. "Yes, Majesty."

Then, without being told, she went to stand against the wall opposite from Xantu.

Byleth exchanged glances with Xantu, both of them indicating surprise at this turn of events, and then she nodded to the nuncio by the chamber doors. The man left to fetch the next audience.

Her day was packed with meetings as she tried to manage several crises from the palace at once. She needed to assure her loyal *zoanii* that all was well in the realm, and also confer with those nobles who had been reticent toward her since the fall of the Sun Temple, hoping to sway them to her cause. Lastly, as much as she detested it, she had to meet with members of the lesser castes—the merchants and bankers and guildsmen, those who dealt with the other cities on a regular basis—to convince them to invest their funds in Erugash's future.

While she waited, Byleth daydreamed about escaping the palace for a walk in the gardens. It seemed impossible that she had only just returned from hiatus. *Of course, that could be because someone tried to kill me, so it wasn't much of a vacation.*

She came back to reality as Hetta entered from the door hidden behind a tapestry and hurried over. Byleth allowed herself to ravage the girl with her eyes. Hetta was quickly maturing into a delicious morsel, so meek and demure and possessing an incredible threshold for pain, or pleasure.

"Mistress," the handmaiden whispered, holding out a tiny scroll. She looked ready to cry any moment. "From the Temple of the Moon."

Byleth frowned as she took the message. The seal had been broken and the message inspected by her guard before delivering it to her. Inside was a brief message from the Eldest Daughter, the second-ranking priestess at the temple. The contents stabbed at her heart, but Byleth kept the emotion from showing on her face. She gave the scroll back to Hetta and dismissed her.

Just then, the main door opened to admit a portly man in a fine suit of silk and ermine.

"Master Brukanar," Byleth said with a forced smile. "Please enter and be welcome. We have much to discuss."

CHAPTER EIGHT

Nostalgia engulfed Horace as he stepped out of the carriage. He hadn't been back to Lord Mulcibar's estate since his visit, as a prisoner of the queen's court.

The place looked the same from the outside, imposing in its hugeness, like a castle masquerading as a private home. Three footmen in uniform showed him to the door and ushered him inside with such deference it made him a little nervous. More servants waited inside the massive atrium. Within seconds Horace had been offered wine, fresh fruit, a hot bath, and a change of footwear. Refusing it all with as much good grace as he could summon, he asked to see the mistress of the house. He was shown into a parlor room large enough to hold the entire royal stables—only a slight exaggeration—and left alone.

He strolled around the room, looking at the beautiful décor. Several of the paintings on the walls were taller than him. Each showed what he assumed were famous moments in Akeshian history, though he didn't know enough to identify them. He mentally labeled them as "serious men sitting around a long table," "gloomy men talking in an arbor," and "angry men shouting and waving their fists at a stone monument."

There was a glass case containing tiny porcelain figurines that were incredibly lifelike. Another case displayed weapons. Mounted between two bronze busts was a large document in a handsome frame. Horace had just begun translating it, and probably butchering the intended meaning, when a door opened.

He turned to see a tall woman enter. She wore a dress, but there was something militant about her. Perhaps it was the way she stood, or how she examined him, sizing him up from across the room. Oddly, he didn't notice any family resemblance to Mulcibar.

"Lady Anshara? I'm Horace. I received your letter and wanted to pay my respects."

She crossed over to him and gestured to a pair of stiff couches. "Please sit. I will call for refreshment."

STORM AND STEEL

Horace took the seat closer to the window. He tried to hide a grimace as he sat down; the couch was every bit as uncomfortable as it looked. When the lady raised her eyebrows, he touched his side. "My injury. It's still healing."

"*Ai.* The attack at the queen's winter palace. I've read your report. How fortunate that Her Majesty survived."

Horace forced a smile. "Indeed. It seems there is always some danger in the queen's vicinity."

"Until now, perhaps. I intend to change that. You see, I've just joined Her Majesty's personal guard."

A chill ran down Horace's back. He hadn't even considered that she would be a sorceress. *That's stupid of me. Her uncle was one of the most respected* zoanii *in the city. Of course there was every chance she had inherited his talent.*

"Then I feel better knowing the queen is in such good hands."

He smiled again, but it faltered on his face. Her expression never changed. She was as stoic as an abbot, which made him think of Gilgar. "I, uh, knew the former occupant of that post. Lord Xantu's brother—"

He hadn't finished his thought before she winced in disgust. "May his name never be spoken again. Of all the crimes of humanity, First Sword, betrayal of one's liege is the most heinous."

"I, uh . . . agree, my lady."

She clapped her hands together, almost making him jump. Two burly men entered carrying a large trunk between them.

"My late uncle left this for your lordship. Per his final instructions, I am delivering it to you."

"Thank you," he murmured as he studied the container. It was twice as big as a typical seaman's footlocker and made from a deep black wood with bronze fittings. Seals of red wax covered the three latches on the front face. What would Mulcibar leave him? Then he remembered he had something for her. "Oh, here."

Horace reached into a pocket and drew out Mulcibar's amulet, which he'd kept since the old man's disappearance. He didn't really want to give it away, but it belonged here with the old man's heir.

Lady Anshara took the amulet and held it up. "I remember this. I saw my uncle wearing it on occasion." She traced the sigils on the mirrored face. "Its purpose is to harness the power of the moon to ward off hostile influences. Sadly, it's been exposed to sunlight."

"What? Why is that bad?"

"The sun and moon represent opposite forces in the mystical arts. Once the device was touched by sunlight, it became impotent."

A feeling of deep sorrow overtook Horace at the news. He felt as if he had soiled Mulcibar's memory by ruining the talisman. "I'm very sorry. I don't know much about the *zoana* yet. Your uncle was tutoring me for a time. Unfortunately, he passed too early to give me a proper education."

She held the amulet out to him. "Here. Keep it as a memento. I insist."

He took it back gingerly, as if it were a holy relic. "I'll treasure it."

Lady Anshara stood up without warning. "I have many new duties to attend to."

A little startled, he got to his feet. "Of course. As do I. Thank you again. If you need anything, please let me know."

"That is very kind. Good day, Lord Horace."

Still holding the amulet, he followed a servant out to the courtyard. He blinked against the bright sunlight before hastily tucking the amulet back into his pocket. Then he hurried to his carriage.

A hundred paces. No more than a bowshot was all that separated the two shores of the Typhon at this point on the northern edge of the delta, fifty leagues from where it flowed into the sea. The lights of Sekhatun twinkled on the other side of the dark waters. The stars had only come out within the past hour, and the moon had yet to make an appearance this night. The only sounds were the lulling trill of the river, the faint buzz of insects, and the occasional call of a hunting *reket*.

Jirom looked over his shoulder for the tenth time since they'd arrived. The southern shore of the river was overgrown with tall swamp grass and stunted mangrove trees. Fireflies swarmed over the water like tiny will-o'-the-wisps.

Emanon stood beside him underneath the low canopy. Ramagesh, his two-handed mace slung over his shoulder, stood a few yards away with Neskarig and two other rebel captains who had accompanied them. Smerdis was a tall man with unusually thick arms and shoulders, as if he'd been a metalsmith before he joined the cause. Rurtimo Lom was a full head shorter but stockier in build; he wore a leather patch over his right eye. Both had been chosen because of their close ties to Ramagesh, which surprised no one.

The only question Jirom had was why he and Emanon had been selected to join this party. *Perhaps to keep eyes on us.*

From here, Sekhatun looked peaceful. No sign of the cruelty that went on inside its walls. The town was a hub for the slave trade in this province. Jirom had been glad to hear that its former lord, Isiratu, had been killed in the collapse of the temple of Amur in Erugash. He touched the brand on his cheek, a gift from the late nobleman.

But it wasn't old memories that troubled him about this operation. Sekhatun was the seat of the queen's power in this part of the empire. The trade passing through its gates and docks had made Erugash wealthy. He feared the rebels weren't ready for an attack of this magnitude. So far, he and Emanon had been able to select targets where they had the advantage in numbers. This time, they would be rolling the bones and praying for fortune's favor. He disliked gambling, especially with men's lives.

Emanon squeezed his arm. "I think they're here."

The morning after the council meeting, Ramagesh had announced that he and a select few captains would be meeting with a local sympathizer who had information about the target. Jirom had expected he and Emanon would be excluded, but he was surprised when Ramagesh personally invited them both. On the two-day journey through the marshy delta, Ramagesh had shown them every hospitality. He marched beside them during the day, regaling them with stories about his life. He had been born a slave in the house of a minor lord in Semira, on the eastern side of the empire. He had served as a bodyguard in his master's house, until he killed his master and his master's eldest son while on a trading trip in Ceasa. He escaped in the capital's vast populace, eventually meeting the nascent rebellion there and joining their ranks. He'd been fighting the empire from the shadows ever since.

Both nights, Ramagesh had shared his fire with them as well, although Emanon hadn't been overly polite about it. Jirom understood his lover's frustration with being relegated to a subordinate status after being his own man for so long, but he hoped Emanon would come to realize they needed a stable command structure if the rebellion was ever going to pose a serious threat to the Akeshian military. For his part, he was accustomed to taking orders. Although he had enjoyed the months when Emanon's band roamed free, it was comforting to belong to a larger organization. It reminded him of the old days when he had been a squad leader, responsible only for the men directly under his care.

Ramagesh and Neskarig moved out of the shadows of the trees, and Emanon followed with the other captains. Jirom remained a couple paces behind, watching Emanon's back. Before they'd left, Three Moons had told Jirom to be careful, but he didn't need to be told. Even if Jirom wasn't suspicious by nature, Ramagesh and the General behaved as if this entire operation were just for show. *But who is the audience?*

The captains went down to the water's edge. Jirom was unsure what they were waiting for, until he saw the tiny light bobbing over the river. Then the prow of a boat appeared. Jirom dropped a hand to the hilt of his sword as the vessel landed. It was a river barge, one of the smaller types used by merchants to ferry their goods. Several men stood on the wide single deck. The light came from a shuttered lantern hanging by a hook from the vessel's aft, where a lone helmsman plied the sweep.

The barge landed on the bank with a soft crunch, and the passengers got off. Three men wrapped in dark cloaks. As they stepped onto the shore, they lowered their hoods. All three were young, barely in their twenties. One stood ahead of the others. He was a handsome youth, with short-cropped black hair and a fair copper complexion. He spoke first. "Which of you is Ramagesh?"

Ramagesh stepped forward. "Durlang."

The two gripped forearms, and then Ramagesh introduced the captains. Durlang greeted everyone cordially while his two companions remained where they stood, silent and observant.

Once the introductions were done, the youth held out a leather satchel to

Ramagesh. "I have the information you want. Garrison numbers, duty schedules, patrol sweeps. Even fortification assessments by the royal engineers. Everything you'll need to plan your attack."

"Very good." Ramagesh handed the satchel to Neskarig. He took a bulging sack in return and passed it to the youth. "And here is your payment, as we agreed."

Durlang made the bag disappear under his cloak. "I also bring some news, which I'm happy to pass along for free. A new envoy from Erugash arrived yesterday."

Smerdis harrumphed. "A royal envoy could bring a fine ransom, if we get him alive."

"And if not," Rurtimo Lom said, "we can plop his head on a spike to show the queen what happens if she crosses us."

What are these idiots thinking? A head on a spike isn't going to cow a queen like Byleth. It'll only encourage her to come back at us harder, like Omikur. Ramagesh better talk some sense into his new lieutenants.

"Who is this envoy?" Ramagesh asked.

"Lord Ubar of House Nipthuras."

Jirom almost choked on his tongue. He remembered Lord Ubar from the trek to Erugash. Why was he back in Sekhatun? What did that mean?

"His father died not long ago," Neskarig said. "When the temple fell, right?"

Durlang confirmed it. "Indeed. Lord Ubar hasn't been back to town since that event. We assumed he was being held prisoner by the queen."

"And what word does this son of Isiratu bring?" Ramagesh asked.

Good. At least someone here is thinking ahead.

"He says he wishes to meet with the rebel slaves on behalf of the First Sword."

A warm rush spread through Jirom's body. So Horace was not the enemy, as he'd feared for months now. *He's reaching out to us. This is a good sign.*

Neskarig scowled. "Meet? To what end?"

"To discuss a peaceful resolution. Or so he says."

Smerdis laughed, short and harsh. "It's a trap. The queen thinks we're stupid enough to fall prey to her ruse."

"Perhaps not—" Ramagesh started to say.

"No, Smerdis is right," Emanon interjected. "It smells like a trick. The empire believes the movement will crumble if it can kill our leadership."

Jirom stared at his lover's back, not believing his ears. He'd told Emanon several times he didn't think Horace would betray them to the Akeshians.

"I agree," Neskarig said. "We shouldn't trust anything coming from Erugash."

Ramagesh turned to look at Jirom. "What do you say, Red-Blade? Is this offer a trick?"

Jirom glanced at Emanon, who had turned along with the rest of the party to observe him. He chose his words carefully. "I know this First Sword. Horace Delrosa. We were slaves together for a time." He paused for a moment. "He is a good man. If this envoy truly speaks for him, then I would trust him."

Ramagesh nodded. "Jirom and I think alike. I will meet with this man."

Smerdis and Rurtimo Lom began to argue, but Neskarig silenced them with a downward slash of his hand. Ramagesh pulled Durlang aside to speak privately.

Jirom avoided looking at Emanon, afraid of what he would see on his face. Emanon said nothing, standing with the other captains.

After a few minutes, Ramagesh and the agent shook hands, and the three men from Sekhatun climbed back aboard the barge as it pushed off from shore. "Durlang will set up the meeting for tomorrow night," Ramagesh said. "Jirom, if you don't mind, I'd like your help going over this information on the town's defenses."

The captains filed through the trees, back toward the temporary camp they'd set up a mile to the south. Jirom fell in beside Emanon. As they walked, he stole a glance at his lover, but Emanon stared straight ahead, giving no indication how he felt. Jirom opened his mouth to say something but closed it when he couldn't decide what to say.

I know I hurt him, but I won't apologize for being truthful.

"I'm fine," Emanon said, low enough that no one else would hear.

"You sure?"

"Yep. I just hope you're right about your old friend."

Jirom nodded and kept walking. *I hope so, too.*

They returned to the campsite to find a pot of lamb and curry bubbling over the fire. The ground had been cleared to make room for a dozen men to sleep. They'd brought no tents or materials to build shelter, only blankets. The half-dozen rebel fighters they'd left behind stirred as they arrived.

Jirom went over to Three Moons, who sat with his back against the trunk of an ancient tree. As Jirom sat down, Three Moons took a sip from the wine-skin in his hand and offered it to him. Jirom shook his head. He looked for Emanon, but the captain had disappeared. Everyone else assembled around the campfire to eat.

"What happened at the secret meeting?" Three Moons asked.

Jirom related the events on the riverbank while Three Moons enjoyed his libations. Afterward, the warlock belched and murmured, "It seems our new leader is quite resourceful."

Ramagesh sat by the fire, talking with the others while they ate. He looked the part of a freedom fighter. Carrying only his tools of war, able to survive off the land, commanding the respect of his men.

"Aye," Jirom said. "I wish Emanon could see it. We have enough problems without fighting among ourselves."

"He'll come around. You remember Corporal Vargi?"

"How could I forget? He crowed like a rooster in front of the barracks every morning. Everyone wanted to kill him."

"Except no one did. Sergeant Fazzu made sure of that."

"He was a mean son of a goat. I always wondered why he took such a shine to Vargi."

"Because they were bunkmates, if you take my meaning."

Three Moons glanced down at Jirom's crotch, and then back up to his face.

Jirom wanted to smack himself in the head for not seeing it. "That explains a lot. I should have guessed. So you're saying I'm Vargi and Emanon is my Fazzu?"

"Doesn't matter who is who. What matters is they accepted each other, right or wrong. Everything else worked itself out."

"I'll keep that in mind. I just wish I knew how this attack was going to play out. It could either be a masterstroke or an epic disaster."

"Want me to throw the bones? I think I'm still sober enough to read our weird."

"Don't bother. The gods never tell you anything with a straight answer."

Jirom accepted a bowl of stew and a hunk of bread from one of the cooks. The stew was hot, but it was so good after a long day of marching that he couldn't resist shoveling it into his mouth right away. After a few bites, he grabbed the skin from Three Moons and took a drink to quench the heat. And nearly choked as the sharp bite of alcohol flooded his mouth. He spat what he hadn't inadvertently swallowed on the ground. "What the hells is that?"

Three Moons took back the skin. "It's my own recipe. Equal parts of plum brandy, northern firewater, and millet wine."

"It tastes like fermented horse piss."

"I hesitate to ask how you know that," Smerdis said as he came over and plopped down beside them.

Jirom looked sideways at Three Moons, who shrugged and held out the skin.

The rebel captain took a swig and winced, his eyes almost closing in pain as he swallowed. "Uh, that's a . . . that's . . . I don't know what to call that."

"Horse piss," Jirom said.

"Well, I've tasted worse." Smerdis scooped some stew from his bowl with a pair of fingers, which he sucked clean before taking them out of his mouth. "Damn, I swear Laris can make anything into a fine meal."

"Which one is Laris?"

Smerdis pointed out a young rebel by the fire. He was skinny with bronze-colored hair that came down to his shoulders. "He was a stablehand before he ran away to join the good fight. Can you believe that?"

"We all have a past," Jirom said.

"That's the honest truth. Especially you two, eh? One a wizard and the other . . . I heard about how you got that red sword. Killed one of Her Highness's commanders. That's nice work."

Not sure how to respond, Jirom only nodded. Three Moons had closed his eyes and rested his head back against the tree. Longar had entered the camp, his boots covered in mud. Leaves and twigs stuck in his hair. The scout leader took a bowl and turned toward them. He looked like he was going to come over, until he spotted Smerdis. With a neutral expression, he found an empty rock on the edge of the camp.

Smerdis dug into his bowl and pulled out a gnarled root. He bit into it with a crunch. "Hmm. Not bad. Anyway, I don't mean to pry, but some of the boys have been wondering why you follow Emanon in the first place. From what we hear, you're the muscle *and* the brains of that operation."

"Emanon is the reason we're free today. He is our leader, the only leader some of us will ever follow."

Smerdis spat a piece of gristle in the direction of the fire, but it landed a couple feet shy. "Don't get me wrong, but your captain has always been something of a wild hair. That's why he was forced to operate out of that training camp."

"What do you mean? Who forced him?"

"The movement did. We mostly recruit from the outer towns and villages, places where the empire doesn't keep a large presence. Emanon started plucking slaves from the big plantations along the Typhon, right from the belly of the bitch. Stirred up a mess of trouble that had all of us looking over our shoulders. Patrols were increased. Akeshians started crucifying anyone who stepped out of line. The captains called a big meeting, and Emanon got put straight."

Apparently, the rebellion didn't know Emanon had returned to sacking rural homesteads after Omikur. That was something to think about. "So he started recruiting from the legions' camps? Isn't that even riskier, for him and you?"

Smerdis tossed his empty bowl on the ground. "Yep. Most of the captains thought he'd be caught and impaled on a pole. Some were even praying for it. But that bastard has more luck than a three-headed calf."

And that threatens you. Because you can't control him.

"And you believe I would help you?"

The rebel captain grinned and winked. "Nah, not really. I just wanted to get a sense of you. It's no secret that most of us don't trust your boss, but it's a small comfort knowing his second-in-command has a sensible head on his shoulders."

"Glad I could ease your mind."

Jirom stood up. Three Moons opened an eye to watch him but then closed it, not moving. Jirom started in the direction of his bedroll, but he passed by it and kept walking, out of the camp altogether. He was too irritated to think about sleep. These rebels were like a pack of cats trapped in a bag together, all clawing at each other instead of focused on finding a way out. All except for Ramagesh. It wasn't until he was fifty paces away from camp that Jirom remembered the rebel leader had asked to meet with him to talk strategy.

He'll find me tomorrow. Unless I keep walking. Just keep going and disappear. Gods above, how many times has that thought crossed my mind? Always before it was Emanon who kept me here. Now he's angry at me. To hells with him. To hells with them all.

Yet, despite his ire, he stopped at a fallen tree beside a narrow creek. Sitting on the mossy trunk, he listened to the sounds of marshy wilds. It was peaceful here, certainly more peaceful than the conversations around camp. Even worse, he didn't know who he could trust among these new allies, and that made him nervous.

A bird cawed in the darkness, over and over, but was never answered.

Laughter floated through the camp as Ismail sliced a long strip of bark from the stick in his hand. A pile of damp shavings rested between his feet.

Half of his unit was gathered around a bonfire, including Kasha, Cambys, Yadz, and Corporal Idris, drinking and swapping the same old stories he'd heard before. The other half was out trying to find dry firewood.

They'd been in this swampy forest for two days, and he was sick of the place already. The bugs, the smells, and all the people. Hundreds of rebels from across the region with legions of camp followers and hangers-on, all mingling and living in one place. He was starting to have dreams about stabbing people in their sleep. And now the captain and lieutenant had gone off with the other commanders on some secret mission. Wondering why he didn't get out when he had the chance, Ismail cut another strip of bark from the stick.

"Where's Partha?"

Ismail shrugged without bothering to look up at the questioner. "Dunno. Out for a walk, I guess."

The other man—Ismail thought his name was Theom, but he wasn't sure and didn't care enough to ask—muttered a reasonably inventive curse. "We got trouble, Ishy. We need to find the sergeant fast."

Ismail stopped whittling and glanced up with one eye. Theom, or whatever his name was, loomed over him, big and blocky like a tree trunk. The two diamond brands on his left cheek made him even uglier. "I told you. I don't like that."

"What? Calling you Ishy? Fine. Whatever. Help me find the sergeant."

"Go find him yourself."

The rebel soldier cursed again and stomped off into the woods. Ismail was glad to be left alone again. He'd thought things were looking up after the mercs signed on, but he soon learned otherwise. Over in their adjoining camp, just twenty paces away under a canopy of tree limbs, the mercenaries sat around their own fires. They were a strange crew, even stranger than the rebel slaves the captain had collected. For one thing, they hardly talked. At least, not to anyone outside their band. They had weird habits, too, like the way they set up their camp. Instead of a circle of shelters surrounding a common area, they set up their tents in rows. And every time they got a spare minute, they were always working on something. Sharpening blades, rewrapping handles, repairing armor, fiddling with those sideways bows they carried. Just watching them made him angry, like they were trying to make everyone else look bad.

To make matters worse, the captain treated them like they were living gods. Like they were going to win this war all by themselves. But Ismail knew better. Grunts like him would still be the ones dying while the mercs got all the glory. Things didn't change, just the scenery.

Ismail had just about finished whittling his stick into a much thinner stick when he heard the sound of tromping boots. A big group of rebel fighters appeared, wearing their fighting gear and weapons bared. Ismail's unit reacted like a kicked beehive, all of them standing up and jabbering back and forth. Then Ismail recognized one of the new arrivals. He'd seen the man hanging out with the rebel's new leader, Ramagesh.

The group quickly surrounded his unit. Corporal Idris, who had been the last one still sitting, stood up and walked over to the arrivals. "What's all this?" he asked in his usual gruff tone.

The man Ismail had seen before pointed at the low, leaf-covered shelters the unit had made for sleeping. "We've come to get that gold you got hidden. Ramagesh says it belongs to the cause now."

"Ramagesh says, eh?" Corporal Idris leaned over and spat at the man's feet. "Well, Ramagesh don't command this unit, and our captain ain't here. So you boys just move along."

Ramagesh's man moved so fast Ismail didn't see it coming. One moment the corporal was standing up, looking ominous, and the next he was down on his back clutching his face.

"Get the gold!" the man shouted.

The rest of Emanon's band poured out of their tents and lean-tos, including Mahir's scouts with their bows in hand. Ismail spotted Seng moving through the trees like a flitting ghost. Sergeant Partha finally arrived with the other squad leaders, all them looking ready for a fight, but they were still heavily outnumbered. Ismail glanced over at the mercenaries' camp. A few of them were looking over, but none seemed inclined to lend a hand.

The sergeants started arguing with Ramagesh's men, but they were getting shoved around pretty badly. Some of the new arrivals started tossing the shelters, one by one.

Hell, no. I didn't pull that gold halfway across the swamp just to see someone else walk away with it.

Ismail stood up. "Stay the fuck back!"

Heads turned in his direction. Ismail strode forward, swinging his stick back and forth. He didn't know where this newfound courage was coming from, but he decided not to question it. He remembered too late that he wasn't wearing his sword. "No one is taking anything from us. Not Ramagesh. Not hoary old Endu himself! And if any of you motherless sons of goats tries, there's going to be blood spilled!"

The leader of the new arrivals pushed through the crowd toward him. "Is that so? Maybe we'll start with you then."

Ismail started to have second thoughts, but he didn't want to appear craven in front of everyone, so he continued to bluster. "Damned right you will."

He was trying to work out how he was going to fight off the entire group with just a shaved stick and a knife when an arrow struck a tree less than a pace away from the leader's head, causing him to halt in his tracks like a startled deer. Ismail felt his own heart lurch as he peeked over his shoulder and saw the mercs all looking his way. One of them lowered his bow with a nasty grin.

"You all stay out of this!" the leader called over to them. "This don't concern outsiders."

Captain Ovar strode out of the mercs' camp as casually as if he were taking an evening promenade. Tall and lean with big shoulders—what the veterans called *rangy*—he had a dark bronze complexion worn and weathered by years in his profession. "Ah, but it does," he said in an accented Akeshian. "That's our pay chest you're trying to lift, boy. And that don't sit right with us."

Ramagesh's men began to look uncomfortable with the odds as they sized up the mercenary crew. Their leader glowered, his lips pressed into a tight frown. "You'll regret this when the commander gets back."

"I'm sure you're right," Captain Ovar said. "But until then, make yourself scarce."

Feeling silly standing between the men with a stick in his hand, Ismail went back to the fallen log where he'd been sitting. "I've seen a lot of stupid things in my life," Captain Ovar said as he came over. "But that might have been the stupidest."

Ismail shrugged as he sat down. He considered the stick and decided perhaps he could whittle it down into something useful, like a spoon. "I just don't like seeing people take things that aren't theirs."

"A keen sense of justice, is that it? Well, I hope you show better sense in the future. There's no place in this world for idealists."

Ain't that the truth.

As the mercenary captain went back to his own camp, Ismail got to work on his spoon. Or maybe fork. *Yeah. Definitely a fork.*

Ramagesh's men didn't go all the way back to the center of the encampment. Their leader positioned the bulk of his men close enough to keep watch over Captain Emanon's unit. They found places to sit among the swamp's hillocks, and both sides settled down into what looked to become a very icy standoff.

Every so often Ismail glanced over at the arrow stuck in the tree.

There were times when being a freewoman had its benefits, Alyra thought as she passed from the city center, with its fine estates and temples, into the Garden Quarter. Freewomen could come and go as they pleased without worrying about whether their absence would be noticed by a prying owner. However, freewomen in Akeshia were almost always noticed, especially when they were alone, whereas a slave could blend into her surroundings.

She crossed the stone bridge over an artificial canal where the clay streets gave way to smooth cobbles made from river stones. Shade trees lined the boulevards here, blocking out the wan moonlight to create shadowy tunnels. This part of the city was home to older noble houses. Tall walls surrounded the palaces with their soaring minarets and marble domes. Lights occasionally moved behind the walls as armed guards walked the grounds.

Her destination was in the oldest section of the neighborhood at the end of a winding avenue. Ancient cypresses loomed beyond the estate's stone walls, covered in patches of gray and white lichens. The heavy bronze gates, wide enough to admit two carriages side by side, were black with age. The estate belonged to a former general. Lord Qaphanum et'Porranu. Alyra had done a little digging on him. Although he had retired from his official post not long after Byleth assumed the throne, the lord-general still maintained many of his political ties, including a personal connection to the Order of the Crimson Flame. Two of his nephews were members of the Order, both stationed in other cities. The more she'd learned about him, the more Alyra suspected Cipher was right. This was precisely the sort of man who would support a coup. Now, if she could just find the evidence.

She wasn't sure what game the network was playing here. She doubted the Nemedians wanted to aid Byleth—the fall of a major city-state could kick off a civil war that might conceivably expand to embroil the entire empire. That seemed like the best possible outcome for the spy ring. So what were they going to do with the information? It troubled her that she couldn't see their plan.

Looking around to be sure she wasn't being watched, Alyra ran to the north end of the wall and dipped around the corner. Back off the road, the walled estate was enclosed with private woods.

Moving among the trees, she approached the side gate where she was supposed to meet her contact. Alyra breathed easier when a small light gleamed through the bars. She darted toward it, her heart beating hard in her throat. "Katara?" she whispered.

She said it so fast she wasn't sure the other had heard her until the reply came back. "Yes."

The woman inside opened the gate with a slight squeak of rubbing metal. She held a lamp in one hand and a key in the other. She was tall, easily a hand taller than Alyra. Her willowy frame was wrapped in a long shawl that hung down to her knees. Under the shawl, Alyra could see a fine gown of undyed linen and an iron collar. Narrower than most collars and tightly fit around the woman's slender neck, it reminded Alyra of the golden one she had worn for years. She ducked inside the gate. "Sorry I'm late. It couldn't be helped."

If her tone was brusque, Katara did not comment on it. "Come. The slaves' entrance is this way."

The estate's main house sprawled across an acre of ground with many wings. The central portion reached up four stories including a pointed roof surrounded by eight minarets built in an antique style. The stonework was exquisite, even in the dark. Tall rows of hedges divided an intricate series of gardens. Like many homes of the wealthy, the manor had several entrances. The one for slaves was a small door hidden between two flowering bushes that rose almost of the height of the roof.

The door led into a small kitchen. From there, Alyra followed Katara down a narrow hallway of plain, unadorned plaster. The hallway branched out in several directions, all of the passages unlit.

Katara handed Alyra the lamp. The wick shook in the oil reservoir as it changed hands. "The master's study is the last door." She pointed down a hall leading to the south end of the manor. "It is not locked, but take care not to disturb anything. He notices when his private things are out of place."

That will make searching for his secrets more difficult.

"I must be back to bed before the master wakes," Katara said.

"Thank you. I know you're taking a risk."

The woman looked down her nose. "I'm the mistress of a wealthy lord who treats me kindly, which is a far cry from the midden where I grew up. I owed a debt, and now that debt is paid. Tell them I will not betray my master again."

Alyra was taken aback. Yet part of her understood what the woman was saying. "So you're happy?"

"I'm content, and that is enough. The luck of the Silver Lady be with you."

Left alone, Alyra headed down the corridor. Colorful frescoes covered the walls with scenes of fine living—a family lounging beside a tranquil pool, two men practicing archery in a green meadow, an equestrian hunt. The ceiling was sky-blue.

Guided by the lamp's feeble light, she strained her ears for any sounds. According to her information, the manor's owner tended to retire early. Alyra hoped he remained true to that habit tonight.

She found the study where Katara had said it would be. The door was unlocked, which made things easier. As she lifted the brass latch, the door beside the study rattled. Alyra glanced back the way she had come, but there was nowhere to hide in the hallway. Holding her breath, she shoved open the study door, darted inside, and closed it quickly. As the latch clicked, she pressed her ear to the wooden panels and listened. Too late, she realized the lamplight could probably be seen through the crack beneath the door. She felt for her knife but didn't draw it. She didn't want to have to use it on the owner of the house or his family. Fortunately, the person outside didn't seem to have spotted her, as footsteps sounded down the hallway away from the study.

Relieved, Alyra took a moment to look around. The room was large and square, about ten paces on a side. Heavy draperies covered the windows in the south wall, and a musty smell hung in the air. She expected a desk or table but instead saw only two chairs facing a hearth on the far side of the room. Three of the four walls were covered with wooden shelves from floor to ceiling. *This might take longer than I expected.*

She started searching. Setting the lamp on the back of a chair, Alyra tried to determine if the shelves were filed with some kind of system. But, after finding things as varied as plans for the estate's landscaping kept alongside warehouses inventories, she wasn't sure the order was based on any logic at all. She was going through the papers as fast as she could when footsteps sounded outside the study again.

She rushed over to the lamp and shielded its light with her cupped hands. Waiting in the dark, she tried to decide what to do if she was discovered. Fight or flee? She hadn't checked the covered window, but it was possible she could get out that way before an alarm was raised. A faint sound met her ears, and for a moment she thought the person outside was lifting the door's latch. A burst of anxiety set her heart to pounding. Then the sound of another door opening came from the hallway outside, and a couple seconds later it closed again.

With perspiration breaking out under her arms, Alyra carried the lamp to the next row of niches. She went through the writings as quickly as possible, cursing under her breath as her exasperation grew. After nearly half an hour of looking, she found some interesting things. Among them were the last instructions to the local Order Chapter House. According to the document, which had no names attached, the captain-curate was ordered to stay and defend the house at all costs. The interesting part was a confirmation that Order reinforcements were imminent. If the occupants of the Chapter House had survived until help arrived, Alyra wondered how that would have changed the balances of power in Erugash. How far would the queen have gone in her defiance of the Sun Cult?

She also found a copy of the captain-curate's final will. She skimmed through it but didn't see anything noteworthy. Clearly, the commander of the Chapter House had been prepared to meet his end. She put the document back in its place.

Tucked behind a roll of blank papyrus was a stack of letters between the lord-general and one of his nephews in Hirak. A quick perusal discovered nothing unusual. The text of the letters was uninteresting—mainly a dry accounting of the life of a temple priest—but there was something about them that raised her suspicions. They were *too* boring, as if the writers had wanted these letters to be passed off as meaningless by unwanted eyes. Thinking they might contain coded messages, she stuffed them into her bag.

Alyra glanced across the rows of shelves. She hadn't found any mention of a plan to attack the queen. In fact, it was just the opposite. The Order's last orders had clearly stated the captain-curate was not to provoke the queen in any way, to only defend themselves in extreme circumstances. She'd come up blank.

She was about to leave when she noticed an odd detail. A piece of the paneling behind one of the shelves on the east wall was slightly askew, so it didn't join properly with its mate. Alyra went over and tapped that section, and it swung inward to reveal a secret nook. A roll of papers was hidden inside. She took them over to the lamp and went through them quickly, her heart beating faster with every sheet she unrolled.

It was all here, just as Cipher had expected. Letters from noble families in other cities, including one from a prominent house with imperial blood ties, all promising their support for Lord Qaphanum if the queen were usurped. They were dissatisfied with Byleth's leadership and her friction with the Sun Cult. Alyra didn't see a response from Lord Qaphanum to any of these letters, but these were enough. She added them to her satchel. Then she blew out the lamp and went to the door.

The hallway outside was quiet, but she waited for a slow count of fifty to be sure. Then she left the study and stole down the hallway. She left the manor by the slaves' entrance, pausing only to be sure there were no guards in the area before she raced across the lawn. Slipping out the side gate, she closed it behind her as quietly as possible and then let out a long breath.

It was done. She'd found what she came for, but what now? Could she trust the network with this evidence? That was the question.

A cool wind picked up as she emerged from the tree cover and hurried down the street. Alyra pulled her cloak tighter around her shoulders. She wasn't sure she wanted to go back to Horace's house tonight. She felt cut off from him, like she needed room to breathe and clear her head. She considered spending the night with Sefkahet, but that would just bring on a different set of problems.

Trying to make herself small in the darkness, she headed back to the Cattle Quarter.

CHAPTER NINE

The battle lines were drawn. Horace stared across the gleaming battlefield at his adversaries. Their cool glances returned nothing but mocking challenge. When he placed a hand upon the hilt of his sword, his enemies looked back and forth among themselves, yet none of them faltered in their resolve. The silence stretched out for minutes that seemed like hours. Finally, he lowered his gaze and let out a long sigh. He was beaten.

Horace slumped back in his chair as the other ministers filed out of the council chamber, leaving him alone at the long polished table. A hot breeze played across the back of his neck from the open window behind him. Flames flickered in the half-dozen lamps hanging from the chamber ceiling, throwing shadows across the walls.

For the last three hours he'd tried with every ounce of persuasion he possessed to convince the council to ratify new orders concerning his prosecution of the rebellion. Things he thought were commonsense to deescalate the conflict, which was quickly growing out of control across the queen's province. Yet they had defied him on every single one, not budging an inch no matter what he tried. In fact, their proposals would only exacerbate the tension. Angered that the council had rebuffed his solutions, Horace refused to agree to their remedies as well, and so both sides were stymied. The final hour of the meeting had been spent in a contest of wills, with the entire council arrayed against him. Tempers flew and harsh words exchanged. One minister had called him a filthy *pukkarag*, whatever that was.

Horace reached for the cup in front of him, only to find it empty. He started to look for a pitcher to refill it but gave up. His head was already swimming with wine fumes, and his stomach threatened to rebel if he didn't eat something. He pushed himself to his feet and left. A pair of his personal guards joined him at the door.

Thankfully, none of the council members were waiting to confront him in the hallway, as had happened before. Since the *Tammuris* he hadn't received any personal challenges, either, but his detractors hadn't ceased in their efforts to bring him down. They just took different tacks to undermine his authority, like these council sessions. Formerly, the First Sword could act unilaterally in the queen's name, but the council had called a secret session just a few days after the holy day while he was still convalescing from his injuries and passed a special law that required all his orders to be approved by them. Horace had taken the matter to the queen, but Byleth told him she wouldn't interfere. All the while, he knew various members of the court were trying to convince the queen to take a harsher course in regards to the rebellion, erasing all his efforts.

Swaying a little, he made his way up a flight of marble stairs to his office on the second-highest tier of the palace. Mezim met him with a sheaf of scrolls.

"Master, I've put together a list of witnesses to the self-immolation yesterday morning. And the Tanners' Guild sent a request that they be allowed to increase the price of their wares."

Horace took the list of witnesses. "Why are they petitioning me? Isn't that something for the city minister to handle?"

"For most guilds, yes, but the tanners and leatherworkers fall under the purview of the First Sword because their industry has been deemed of utmost value in times of war.

"There's also a report from each legion detailing their current inventories and budgets for the rest of the year. Oh, and quotes from various grain suppliers for next season. Once you select one, I'll arrange for delivery of the first payment with the royal treasury."

Most of what Mezim said went over his head, but Horace nodded. "I don't have time to deal with that. Send the petitions to the High General's office. Is there any news from Lord Ubar's expedition?"

"Not as yet. But I will check with the palace messenger service right away."

"What about the search for Jirom?"

"I put a dispatch on your desk from an officer of the Third Legion who was at the battle of Omikur. He reports that almost all the dog soldiers were killed in action, either by the enemy or by the legionnaires themselves when the slaves tried to rebel. However he has no confirmation of your friend's demise.

Apparently, the dog soldiers were buried in mass graves in the desert, and finding evidence of a single man is exceedingly difficult."

"Of course," Horace muttered to himself. "Nothing can ever be easy, can it?"

"Pardon?"

"Nothing. Go find out about Lord Ubar."

"At once. There's just one last thing. The protests continue in various places around the city."

"*Ai*, I noticed a couple on my way in."

"The royal chancellor has voiced some concern about safety. . . ."

"Of course. We can't have Master Unagon wetting himself. Order additional guards at the palace gates and on the queen's personal detail. Anything else?"

"*Neh, Belum.*"

As his secretary scurried away, Horace walked to his office at the back of the suite. The guards took up positions outside.

His inner sanctum was bare, with the only furnishings being a desk and chair. The former was a gift from the queen. A handsome block of cedar, its front was carved with a relief image of the palace and the entire desk painted with the rich red varnish.

A yawn escaped him as he sat down and opened the first field report. After a quick scan, he opened another, and then a third. They weren't good. Over the past two months more than six separate attacks had occurred, including the one that so incensed the queen—the royal caravan sacked and its contents, listed only as "tribute from the northern estates," stolen. Clearly, the rebellion was gaining momentum. *And making my job nearly impossible with the same stroke.*

As he read more, a pattern emerged. The rebels seemed to attack at random, never hitting the same target twice and slipping away before reinforcements could arrive. Horace had sent the forces at his disposal to bolster important garrisons, but it was never enough. There were too many potential targets to cover them all.

Also included among the dispatches were reports of *zoanii* cracking down in their own fiefs with harsh penalties for just about any infraction. One lord in a town east of Erugash had allegedly boiled eighteen of his field slaves alive because he suspected them of collaborating with the rebels. No proof of their guilt was found. Horace pounded his fist on the desk. These draconian methods were only making the problem worse. But, just like with the council, the noble caste refused to hear reason.

Horace put down the scrolls and rubbed his eyes. He wasn't getting anywhere. His head hurt, and he was too tired to think straight. What he wanted more than anything was something to eat and a strong drink, and perhaps to look at the stars from his terrace until he fell asleep. He called for Mezim, but there was no answer. With a sigh, Horace pushed his chair away from the desk and got up. His guards stood outside the door. Beckoning them to follow, he left the suite.

They passed a few people Horace knew from court on the way out, but he didn't stop to talk. Not that they seemed eager to see him either. He'd always assumed a powerful title would attract all sorts of people, those seeking favors and wanting to form alliances, but in his case the elevation to First Sword had made him less popular with the other *zoanii*, if that was possible.

This entire country is insane. I must be mad to stay here with them. Or too damned stubborn to give up on a losing proposition. Only a few days back at the palace and I'm ready to slit my stomach. Let someone else deal with these headaches.

He left the palace by the west gate. Horace declined a palanquin when offered, deciding he wanted to walk instead. It was a nice evening. A pleasant breeze from off the canal kept the insects at bay. The moon was just rising above the skyline, limning the city's roofs and towers in a soft silver glow.

Most of the government buildings were closing. Street cleaners worked the avenues, cleaning up the day's accumulation of refuse and animal dung. Slave-borne litters navigated the boulevards like proud ships, led by linkboys with burning brands to ward off the night.

Horace passed by the site of the demolished Sun Temple. The gates were chained. Through the iron bars Horace could see the vast pile of stone and debris. It still boggled his mind that he was responsible for such devastation. He'd heard that sinkholes had opened in the temple courtyard as a result of the collapse. Work crews had been assigned to fill them, but according to the reports the larger ones kept opening up.

Horace was considering stopping at an eatery for supper when three men appeared at the end of the block, barring the way. Their crimson robes wavered in the evening breeze. Standing still, their faces hidden under deep hoods and hands pulled up into their sleeves, they nonetheless radiated an aura of malice.

The Order of the Crimson Flame.

Horace wondered how these three had gotten into the city. There was something strange in the way the sorcerer-priests stood, hunched over at the shoulders as if they were in pain.

His bodyguards drew their weapons and stepped ahead of him. Horace thought to stop them, but before he could a stinging wind reeking of ozone and burning metal rushed down the street. With one arm thrown over his face, Horace closed his eyes against the cloud of flying dust swirling around him and reached for his *zoana*. To his surprise, the power answered his call. It felt so good flowing through him, like a lover's embrace or the taste of mulled brandy on a cold day. He quickly formed a bubble of air around himself and his guards that blocked out the foul wind. Then he fashioned the first offensive attack that came to mind. He wove together strands of fire into a seething sphere. Its angry vermillion glow blinded his eyes. With a grunt, he hurled it through the swirling dust cloud in the direction of the priests.

A sudden spike of pain pierced his chest. Gasping, Horace squeezed his eyes shut just before the sphere exploded. A torrent of scalding heat engulfed the street, buffeting him with the blowback. The air howled one last time before it died away.

Rubbing the grit from his eyes, Horace peered down the street. The three robed men were gone. Vanished as if they had never existed, a circle of untouched clay pavement where they had been standing. The rest of the street, however, was awash in flames. Pangs of guilt stabbed Horace as he witnessed the damage he had wrought. The outer facings of the buildings on both sides—homes, shops, a winehall—were completely torn away, exposing the singed beams of their interiors. His only hope was that no one had been killed, but the guilt fed the fire of rage burning inside him. He reached for his *zoana* again to combat the fires before they burned out of control, and he had to battle with his *qa* to keep it open. Finally, he wrested away enough power from the Mordab dominion to summon a gentle mist. The flames sizzled as the water vapor dampened their ire, but it did nothing to cool Horace.

Then he noticed something inside the circle of pristine pavement where the priests had been standing. A person lying on the street, covered by a shimmering sheet of yellow silk.

His guards rushed ahead of him as Horace approached the figure. He caught the edge of the silk sheet with his toe and kicked it away. His stomach clenched in a painful spasm when he saw the face staring up at him. A face he knew well. *Mulcibar.*

A thousand questions crowded Horace's mind as he looked down at his friend's corpse, but they were battered down by a tide of rage. Ever since the night of the *Tammuris* he had struggled with Mulcibar's loss, fearing he may have buried his one-time mentor under the rubble of the fallen Sun Temple. Now to be faced with the proof that Mulcibar had not been inside the temple when it fell, that he must have been alive all this time, threatened to break down the walls of his self-control. The *zoana* surged inside him, wanting a release, but he held it in tight check as he beckoned to his guards. They rolled the corpse inside the yellow sheet and picked it up.

The street was empty as they marched toward his home, a silent funeral procession.

"Lock the doors! All of them!"

Horace barked orders as he strode into his home. Directing his guards to carry their burden to the dining room, he swept the dinner service off the table and commanded them to place Mulcibar on top. Lamps were lit around the room.

Harxes rushed in, holding his staff. "Master! What's happening?"

"Lock down the house and keep everyone inside. Where's Alyra?"

"I believe the mistress in her chambers, Master."

"Go make sure. And have two of the house guards stay with her at all times until you hear otherwise from me. Understood?"

"*Ai*, Master!"

As the steward ran off, Horace looked down at Mulcibar, still wrapped in the yellow sheet. He heard Alyra's voice coming down the stairs. Then she entered the room. "There you are. Horace, what did you say to . . . ?" Her voice trailed off. "Is that what I think it is?"

Horace pulled back the sheet. Alyra's sharp intake of breath summed up his feelings. He still balanced on the edge of his rage, but he had calmed down enough to feel the thread of sadness winding inside him, as taut as a harp's strings. He felt like his temper could snap with the wrong word. He imagined the Order priests coming here to punish him for his transgressions, and he welcomed the idea. Anything to assuage the guilt he felt for not continuing the search for his friend. If he hadn't gotten so involved with the queen's machinations, maybe Mulcibar would still be alive.

"What happened?"

Horace could only shake his head. "Three Red Robes stopped me on the way home. I thought they wanted a fight, but they just disappeared and left his body behind. I thought all the Sun priests were gone from the city, but these three were as brazen as dockside whores."

Alyra bent over the body, examining it with a meticulousness that both impressed Horace and made him uneasy, that she could be so clinical with a person they had both known.

Mulcibar's face was bruised with a nasty round cut in the center of his forehead. Dried blood stained his temples and down his cheeks. His body was naked beneath the silk, revealing battered arms and long welts across the rib cage. His wrists, so emaciated they almost looked like they could belong to a child, were black with bruises.

"It's obvious they tortured him," she said, touching the welts. "But I don't know how. None of this looks like other victims I've seen."

"Damn it!" Horace threw the sheet back over Mulcibar's face and turned. "Harxes!"

The steward appeared in the doorway. "Here, Master!"

"No one gets in or out until I return."

"Where are you going?" Alyra asked.

STORM AND STEEL

Horace stalked out of the room without answering, through the foyer to the front door. Flinging it open, he looked back to the guards behind him. "Stay here and protect her. No matter what happens."

They saluted and took up positions inside as he closed the door behind him. He heard the sound of the wooden bar settling into brackets on the other side, barring the entrance. Though it wouldn't stop a sorcerer, it made him feel a little better.

What was he doing? He hadn't answered Alyra because he didn't know. There was no plan, just an empty, helpless feeling that melded with his rage and demanded retribution. He needed a target.

Standing alone, separated from the buildings around it by a wide square, the fortress was deathly quiet. The moon's rays glinted off specks of mica in the dark gray stones of its walls. A murder of crows perched atop the ramparts, cawing softly in the night. They took off with tremulous flutters as Horace arrived.

The headache pounded behind his eyes as he stared at the Chapter House. His rage had brought him here. The fortress was largely vacant, with only a single guard post outside the main gate where four soldiers in royal livery stood around a brazier.

Before he gave the idea conscious thought, the *zoana* was there, filling him with its heady power. The Kishargal dominion opened, yawning in the pit of his stomach. He drew forth as much as he could hold, until the energy filled every ounce of his being and felt like it was pushing against his skin, wanting to be released.

The *zoana* flowed out of him of its own accord, following seams in the ground under the street, fissures he had never known existed. They reached far down into the earth like the roots of a bottomless pit beneath his feet, but he focused on the surface. In his mind he could see the magic penetrating the foundation of the Chapter House walls, the tendrils working into every pore and crack no matter how small, widening them as they pierced deeper into the stonework.

As he worked, a foreign sensation tickled the back of his mind, as if he were being watched. He tried not to think about it. Then he noticed that another thread of *zoana* had insinuated itself into his weaving, a thread of the void that had entered through his *qa* without being called. The discovery was chilling, but it also felt *right*. The Shinar combined easily with the Kishargal to create something new, a powerful dark energy that set his nerves to buzzing. The ground trembled beneath his feet. Horace just followed his instincts, and they told him the Order had to pay.

A deep rumble rose from the street, and with it returned the pain, drilling into his chest like a blunt awl. The guards at the fortress's front gate staggered and fell to the ground, their pikes clattering beside them. Horace almost jumped when the first stone fell, knocked loose from a crenellation atop the southern wall. The clay of the street shattered as it landed. Within a dozen heartbeats, stones were falling all along the fortress ramparts. A crackling sound ripped through the night, and then the entire western wall collapsed, spilling into the street.

Sweat poured down Horace's face as he exerted himself harder, pushing the *zoana* out. He reached through the ground for the central keep. He imagined cracks running up the sides of the stout tower of stone and brick, breaking off pieces of masonry. A distant growl clawed at the air, and then the keep's top floor crumbled, collapsing into the floor beneath it. The walls split open under the strain, and moments later the entire structure disintegrated in upon itself.

Horace reveled in the act of pure destruction. It was a balm easing the ache of losing Mulcibar. As the last walls collapsed, he observed that the damage wasn't contained to just the Chapter House. The streets surrounding the Order fortress were caught in the aftershock. Bricks and slate shingles crashed. Trees toppled over. The portico of a stately townhouse collapsed in a pile of broken stone. Horace pulled back on the power, seeking to cut it off. Yet the *zoana* fought back like a ten-stone swordfish on the line. Finally, he succeeding in slamming his *qa* shut, and the power evaporated as quickly as it had come.

The pains in his head and chest flared to the point where he couldn't see straight. Motes of silver and gray light danced in front of his eyes. He couldn't believe what he'd just done. He felt empty. The rage was gone, leaving only a vague sensation of loss in its place. He nearly swallowed his tongue as his vision cleared and he gazed upon the results. The entire neighborhood looked as if it had been struck by an earthquake. *Why can't I control this? What's wrong with me?*

He couldn't do this anymore. Sooner or later he was going to kill someone, and he wouldn't be able to live with himself.

Three robed figures appeared from the shadows before him, startling Horace out of his recriminations. He fumbled to reopen his *qa* again until the three men pulled back their hoods.

"First Sword," Lord Xantu said. A frown creased his brow. "I did not think to find you here this night."

Horace breathed a little easier. The other two were *zoanii* he had seen in Xantu's company, though he didn't know their names.

"I . . ." Horace took a breath. "I'm sorry. I had an encounter with the Order earlier and it left me. . . ."

"I heard of the appearance of three Crimson brothers on the Street of Stars," Lord Xantu said. "They attacked you?"

"Sort of. They vanished before anything happened, but they left behind the body of Lord Mulcibar."

"Has word of this been sent to Her Majesty?"

"No, not yet. I wasn't thinking straight." Horace looked past them to the mound of rubble filling the square where the fortress had stood only minutes ago. "I didn't even think it was possible to do so much damage. What are you doing out here?"

Xantu flicked two fingers, and his protégées departed, walking back toward the ruins. "We have been ordered to keep watch over the Chapter House."

"In case anyone returned to the scene, eh?"

Xantu didn't reply, but he tilted his head slightly to the side as if considering the question.

Horace ran his hands through his sweaty hair. The evening, which had seemed so balmy a couple hours ago, had turned cool. "I don't know how I'm going to explain this."

"I must send word of this to the queen, First Sword. Yet, if I may speak on Her Majesty's behalf, I do not believe she will be vexed by your actions. She is, after all, a most gracious mistress."

Horace let out a shallow sigh. "Indeed."

With a nod to Lord Xantu, Horace left the square with his head aching worse than before and a lump in his stomach. At least the feeling of being watched had faded.

They arrived at the rendezvous point before the sunrise. The growing light filtered through the canopy of leafy branches to illuminate the ruins of an ancient city. Mossy stones half-buried in the soft earth, forming a network of lumps amid the trees. Here and there, pieces of clean white stone broke through the carpet of marsh grass. Bases of colossal pillars. Broken statues, their features worn away by time and the elements. The shattered remains of walkways. Spider webs cloaked the fallen monuments, spun by black and brown spiders as wide across as a man's hand. The smells of damp earth and dead leaves clung to the place.

Jirom saw what he took at first to be a round hillock rising a score of feet above the riverbank, but the shape was too perfect to be natural. While the other captains waited by the water's edge, he went to investigate the hill, careful not to run into any webs. He pushed aside a curtain of snaking vines to find, to his surprise, a curving wall of pale dolomite rising before him. It was a dome, submerged in the muck and overgrown with vegetation. Despite its age, the surface of the stone was smooth to the touch. Had this city fallen to a calamity like famine or war, or had the marshland simply swallowed it, piece by piece, until nothing was left?

Captain Smerdis slapped his neck and pulled back his hand to reveal a bloody glob. "Fucking gnats and bloodsuckers. Why are we meeting him here?"

"It's far from prying eyes," Emanon answered. He made pointed glances to the east, west, and south. "With plenty of avenues for escape if things go wrong."

Rurtimo Lom picked up a piece of stone and turned it over in his hands. "What happened here?"

STORM AND STEEL

Ramagesh strode out from the tree line. "The same that happens to all things in time. They fall. Just like the Akeshians shall fall under our blades."

That brought smiles to the faces of the rebel captains. But not Emanon, who stood apart from the others, and apart from Jirom, too. He had not returned to camp until just before they were about to leave. When Jirom asked him where he'd been all night, he didn't answer, but it was clear by the dark circles under his eyes that he hadn't slept. Jirom worried that his lover would do something careless, if not at this meeting then later, perhaps back at the main encampment.

To take his mind off Emanon, Jirom studied the area. This section of the river bowed, protecting their entire northern flank. They would hear an approaching boat long before it landed. And while the trees obscured their vision, they also provided safe paths to exit if this meeting went badly. Ramagesh had brought him, Emanon, Smerdis, and Rurtimo Lom, but no one else.

"Why didn't the General come with us?" he asked.

"He's taking care of other business," Ramagesh answered.

Since no one else questioned that, Jirom let it go. Neskarig and Ramagesh obviously had formed an alliance, but he didn't know either man enough to gauge how deep that bond went. He was learning, however. He and Ramagesh had discussed the intelligence on Sekhatun on their way to the ruins, and Jirom discovered that the rebel leader possessed a keen mind for tactics. Together they fleshed out several possible plans of attack to exploit the town's weaknesses. Its walls, for example, though surrounding the entire town, had been allowed to decay over the years without adequate repair. The gates, too, were not as fortified as they needed to be to repel a concerted assault. They both agreed that if multiple breaches could be opened, their force could potentially overwhelm the garrison.

A sound drew Jirom's attention. The assembled captains turned at the swishing thwacks of people cutting their way through the foliage, coming from the east. Jirom loosened his sword in its scabbard but then dropped his hand from the hilt. Emanon merely glanced toward the noise as if hardly interested and then looked away to resume his study of the trees surrounding the ruins. Jirom longed to thaw the ice between them, but there was nothing to do or say. And now was not the time, in any case.

Five men emerged from the swamp. Four were soldiers in steel helms and armor. The two in front held broad-bladed short swords in their hands, which they used to clear a path through the underbrush. The pair in back held bows. They surrounded a young man.

Lord Ubar had changed a little since the last time Jirom had seen him. His hair, which had been long and usually pulled back in a queue, was cut short and flat on top in the style favored by Akeshian legionnaires. He wore a tunic and long skirt, both plain white. During the trek to Erugash, Jirom remembered the son of Isiratu being a quiet youth who did not draw attention to himself. But, as he entered the ruins of the fallen town, the young lord walked with the confidence of an older man.

Ramagesh strode forward to meet them. The soldiers started to draw in close around the young lord, but they backed away when Ubar gestured. Lord Ubar greeted Ramagesh with an extended hand, and they shook. Ramagesh introduced the captains, but Ubar's gaze settled on Jirom.

"I have seen you before," Ubar said. His light eyes shone in the early morning light.

Everyone turned to look at Jirom, which increased his apprehension. "Yes, my lord," he answered, adding the honorific at the last moment. It didn't hurt to be polite, and the young noble was quite handsome. "I'm Jirom, son of Khiren. I was the slave of your father, for a brief time."

Lord Ubar had the good grace not to feign embarrassment, which impressed Jirom. The young nobleman merely nodded as if they were discussing happier times.

"Lord Ubar," Ramagesh said. "We've gathered here at your request, though some of us are doubtful of your intentions."

Smerdis scowled. "You've got that right."

"Let me put your minds at ease," Ubar said. "I have come to negotiate on the authority vested in me by the First Sword of Erugash and Her Royal Highness, Queen Byleth of House Urdrammor."

"Negotiate what?"

STORM AND STEEL

"Your surrender, of course."

Rurtimo Lom hawked and spat at the young lord's feet. Captain Smerdis dropped a hand to the war-axe on his belt. Jirom tensed, waiting to see which side would break the peace first.

However, Ramagesh shoved Rurtimo Lom back to the rear of their party and shot a hard glance at Smerdis. Hard enough to convince the captain to move his hand away from his weapon. "Forgive my brothers," Ramagesh said. "But no one is considering surrender. Surrender means a return to slavery, and we would rather die than put on the collar again."

Jirom wondered about that for a moment. What would he do if he were back in Pardisha again, faced with the choice of execution or slavery? He honestly couldn't say.

Ubar said, "You must understand that your cause is doomed to fail. However, the First Sword is prepared to be lenient with those of our subjects who have offered violent rebellion against their divine sovereign. Although each of you deserves death, these sins may be forgiven if this situation comes to a peaceful conclusion."

"I'm not sure what all he said," Smerdis said, "but I don't think I like it."

Jirom agreed, though he was interested to hear more of what this envoy had to say.

"How can we trust your queen to honor this amnesty?" Ramagesh asked.

"Exactly," Emanon said, entering the conversation. "What's to say you won't execute every one of us the moment we put down our arms?"

"Damned straight!" Rurtimo Lom said. "The minute we give over, you'll round us up and take our heads. You think we're stupid?"

"Unless . . ."

Emanon came over to stand with the other captains.

"Unless what?" Ramagesh asked.

Emanon looked to the envoy. "We'll consider your queen's offer, if our demand is met."

"What demand is that?" Ubar asked.

"Freedom."

"I've already granted that you and your men will be pardoned—"

"No," Emanon said. "Freedom for every slave in Erugash and its territories."

"What?"

Jirom almost echoed the envoy's astonishment. The queen would never accept such a condition. It was insane to even ask for it. *But isn't that what we're fighting for? The liberty of every slave. And not just in Erugash. All across the empire.*

Ramagesh looked about to cut in, but Emanon kept talking. "We also demand a vow, sworn by the queen before her entire court, that she will not seek vengeance against any slave who rose up against her."

Ubar's face contorted in an array of emotions from shock to outrage. Yet the young envoy kept his composure as he said, "Why would Her Majesty accept such demands from the likes of you?"

Emanon opened his mouth, but it was Ramagesh who answered first. "Because we're winning the war, your lordship. We harry your trade routes and threaten your holdings, and each day our numbers grow as more and more slaves leak from your grasp to join our movement."

Both sides stared at each other for several long seconds. Then Lord Ubar said, "I am not empowered to discuss such matters. If you wish, I will deliver your demands to the First Sword."

Ramagesh agreed, and the two men reached out to clasp hands. Jirom was watching the exchange when he detected a slight movement behind Emanon. A face appeared from the foliage, followed by an arm, holding up a short throwing spear. Jirom reacted without thinking.

"Down!" he shouted as he leapt toward Emanon.

They collided chest-to-chest and fell to the ground. Shouts echoed through the ruins. He looked up to see Lord Ubar staring down at him, the spear jutting from his side, blood spreading across his white tunic. He collapsed with a slight gasp.

More spears flew through the air. Three of the envoy's guards fell before they could strike a single blow to avenge their lord. The fourth fell to Ramagesh's mace, the weapon caving in the side of the soldier's helmet. The other captains stood still as the last soldier fell to the marshy ground, his eyes as still as glass.

Jirom started to get up until the point of a spear jabbed him in the shoulder. One of Ramagesh's fighters, a bearded rebel in his thirties, stood over him with the weapon ready to stab. Jirom fell back to the earth beside Emanon, who likewise stayed where he was. "You all right?" Jirom asked.

"Not a scratch," Emanon replied. "Yet."

Other armed men had appeared from the surrounding forest. Jirom cursed under his breath when he saw Neskarig among them.

"Let them up," Ramagesh said, and the spearman backed away. The rebel leader came over to them. "Jirom, Emanon. I'm sorry I couldn't tell you about this beforehand, but I didn't know if I could trust you."

Ramagesh bent down beside the young envoy and pulled free the spear that had killed him. Even smeared in blood and dirt, the silvery point gleamed. "This metal is a gift from the gods. For all his power, this wizard never had a chance. You understand why it had to be this way?"

Jirom understood all too well. Now the rebels were fully committed. There could be no peace now. No surrender. They either won, or they all died. "You had no intention of treating fairly with them."

The rebel commander stood back up. "Of course not. Emanon convinced me."

Emanon burst out with a grunt. "Me? I never said anything about betraying a peace talk."

"You said we must be bold in our operations. No more fighting from the shadows. I agree, and this is how it begins. Victory lies before us."

Neskarig came over to Ubar's body with a sword. The General bent down and began hacking at the youth's neck.

"So what will it be?" Ramagesh asked. "Are you with us?"

Jirom exchanged glances with Emanon. "It doesn't look like we have much choice."

Ramagesh placed a hand on Jirom's shoulder. "Every man has a choice, son of Khiren. We want you with us, to share in our eventual triumph over the Akeshians. What say you?"

His words took Jirom back to another time, back to Pardisha when he'd been faced with the choice between slavery and death. In the end, it was no choice at all.

"We're with you," Emanon said.

Ramagesh smiled. Behind him, Neskarig held up Ubar's head.

CHAPTER TEN

Twilight had slipped into darkness by the time Horace returned home. The silver sickle of the moon hung above the eastern skyline on its path through the stars. Torches burned in the front gate where two of his house guard stood sentry. They saluted as he approached.

"Any trouble?"

"No, sir," one of the guards replied. "It's been quiet."

He saw a few objects sitting against the front wall. Bundles of cut flowers, bowls holding some kind of liquid, and even what he assumed was an honest-to-goodness sheaf of wheat. More donations from his adherents, but at least there weren't as many as before.

Horace went inside. Candles illuminated the foyer. He peeked into the dining room to check on things, and saw that Mulcibar's body had been removed.

"Good evening, Master," Harxes said as he stood up from a chair in the corner. He looked half-asleep.

"Where did the body go?" Horace asked.

"I had it taken down to the cold cellar, the better to preserve it."

"I want to send a message to Lady Anshara to . . . make arrangements." Horace didn't know what Akeshians did for their funeral rites.

"Mistress Alyra has already taken care of that."

He nodded and started to leave when Harxes stopped him. "Is everything all right, Master?"

He was too tired and sick at heart to discuss it. "Fine. Go to bed, Harxes."

"As you say."

Horace went upstairs to his room, where he stripped off his sweaty robe and kicked off his sandals. He was tempted to call for a cool bath, but he didn't have the patience to wait.

Just as he was about to lie down on the bed, a voice startled him in the dark. "Where did you go?"

Alyra sat in the low-backed chair on the other side of the room.

"Why are you sitting in the dark?" he asked.

"I was waiting for you. Are you all right?"

Horace sat on the end of the bed. "I don't know. I feel bad about Mulcibar."

"That wasn't your fault. I told you before. Lord Mulcibar swam in dangerous waters. He knew the risks and he accepted them as the price of supporting the queen."

He knew that intellectually, but no words could erase the guilt that welled up inside him every time he thought of his old mentor. "It feels like everything is distorted. Like my life has been twisted inside out. What happened? How did it get to this?"

"Nothing here was ever as simple as you wanted to believe, Horace."

That's true. Not even us.

"You brought down the Sun Temple," she continued. "But you couldn't change the reality that this city, and the entire empire, is corrupt right down to its core."

Of course, it always came back to the queen with Alyra. It chafed at him, but he didn't want to fight. Not tonight. "So what can I do to make things right?"

"Maybe you can't."

"So we can't get back to what we had?"

She looked down at the carpet. "I don't know. I care about you, Horace. But to be honest, I'm not sure what I want or where to go from here. We're on different paths."

"Is there someone else? I wouldn't blame you if there was."

"There's . . . is it all right if we don't talk about it tonight?"

So there *was* someone else, and now she was trying to spare his feelings. He had a choice. He could make it tough on her, force her to spell it out. Or . . . "Sure. I went to the Chapter House."

"Horace! Why would you go there?"

"It wasn't the best idea, I know. But I had to strike back at them. The Order killed Mulcibar. I wanted them dead, all of them."

"What did you do?"

He told her about his destruction of the fortress and ended up telling her more than he intended, about how he had admired Mulcibar and how his new duties as First Sword were overwhelming him. He even told her about sending Lord Ubar to deal with the rebels. That last bit seemed to surprise her.

"Did the queen consent to that?"

Horace shrugged and tried to hide a yawn. "Not exactly. But she told me to handle the matter. I took that to mean do whatever was necessary to stop the fighting."

"Horace, Byleth will never make a deal with the rebels. You have to understand that."

"How do you know? Has anyone ever tried? As far as I can see, the empire only has two ways to deal with anything, to kill it or lock it in a collar. I think it's time someone tried a different approach."

Alyra threw her hands in the air. "Don't you think the network would have tried that if it had any chance of succeeding? You have to understand how someone like the queen thinks. She isn't seeking a peaceful resolution. She wants a great victory. No, she *needs* it, because that elevates her in the eyes of the other kings. And she's chosen you to lead this enterprise."

"You think I would go along with such a plan? I shouldn't have to remind you that I actually wore an iron collar, and not one of those pretty golden chokers you got to prance around in while people were dying outside your gilded cage."

Her lips parted, her eyes stabbing at him. "I can't believe you. You, of all people, should understand what I went through all those years. What I suffered for my beliefs. That is, until you came along and ruined everything. Just like you're doing now. You have no idea the trouble you're stirring up."

Horace knew he was being unfair, but he was too angry to take it back. Especially after all the attacks she leveled at him. No one expected him to succeed, but he'd thought Alyra would be on his side. But what if she was right? What if everything he'd been trying to accomplish was impossible? Yet for some reason he couldn't let go of his anger. "And you've been shutting me out ever since that night at the Sun Temple."

"Of course I did! How could I trust you now that you've gotten so close to *her*?"

"Her, huh? Did it ever occur to you that the queen deserves the chance to repair her realm? Or that I could help make that happen?"

"Because you're suddenly so important, right?"

That was it. He could see the truth in her eyes. *I've lost her. Maybe for good this time.*

Harsh words hovered on his tongue, but he swallowed them. They wouldn't do any good. "I'm going to bed."

Her face was ashen as she got up and went to the door. She paused at the threshold. "Horace, I . . ."

She didn't finish her statement, but just walked out and closed the door behind her.

Horace lied on top of his covers and stared up at the ceiling. His heart thumped in his chest like a restless animal. He'd been hoping to reconnect with Alyra, but that had been ruined one step at a time. And now he knew the awful truth, felt it burning deep into his bones no matter how much he wished to deny it.

He had lost her.

Alyra cursed under her breath as the hem of her cloak caught in the closing gate. It refused to come loose when she tugged, forcing her to re-open the iron postern, pull her garment free, and close it again. The resulting clang echoed down the lane behind the manor house, making her grit her teeth in frustration. She took off at a quick walk.

She tried to put Horace out of her mind, but it was impossible. He had hurt her with his words, flung so carelessly as if he couldn't be bothered to understand her position. She had been preparing to leave on an important errand when Horace came home bearing Lord Mulcibar's body. Then when he went out again, she'd waited for him to return despite having someplace else she needed to be, because she'd wanted to make sure he was all right. She'd known he was close to Mulcibar, though she hadn't realized how close until tonight. Although she had never trusted Mulcibar, as she did not trust any Akeshian *zoanii*, she respected their bond. And more than that, Mulcibar's death troubled her. She was accustomed to political murders, but the lord of House Alulu had weathered so many storms, survived so many enemies as the queen's closest advisor, she'd honestly believed he was untouchable. His demise was a sober reminder that no one was entirely safe.

Alyra told herself to focus on tonight's task as she left the Cattle Quarter heading northwest, away from the city center into a series of older neighborhoods. The buildings she passed were more rundown than the newer areas, but the streets were broad with potted trees lining the gutters, and the architecture had a classic style that evoked a feeling of timelessness.

The new safehouse was situated on a smaller lane branching off the main thoroughfare, nestled in the shadow of a five-story tenement. She would've walked right past the innocuous little house if not for Cipher's directions. The entrance was on the side, at the top of a short stoop. She went to the door. It opened with her first knock, swinging inward. No old woman this time. Just a dark hallway beyond.

Enough with the creepy theatrics, Cipher.

She thought the house was empty until she noticed a faint shine of light along the bottom of the door at the end of the hall. Steeling herself, she crept forward. Doorways on either side led to dark rooms.

She got to the end of the hall and pushed the door open. Cipher stood in a large kitchen wearing an apron, humming as he sliced onions on a cutting board. He looked up at her. "Oh, you're early."

"Yes." Alyra let the door swing closed behind her. "I suppose I am. You cook?"

"I'm just making supper. I was hoping to be done before you arrived. Give me a hand, will you?"

He pointed to a second knife and a slab of lamb on the counter. Alyra hesitated. Part of her wanted to turn around and walk out. After the argument with Horace, she wasn't in the mood for games. Yet she needed information that only the network could provide. With a sigh, she picked up the knife and started cutting the meat into cubes without asking how Cipher wanted it done. *Screw you. You'll get what you get.*

"So," he said as he added the onions to a pot simmering over a low fire. "Did your mission go smoothly?"

"Smooth enough. Katara held up her end of the arrangement, though I don't think she's interested in assisting you anymore."

"That's too bad. She's a good asset. But we can work around that. Here, let me have that."

Cipher placed the beef cubes in an iron skillet and began sprinkling them with salt and other spices as they seared.

Alyra took out the letters from Lord-General Qaphanum's house and put them on the counter. "Here's the proof you wanted. At least thirteen houses have pledged their support of a coup in Erugash. Half of them have local ties, so you shouldn't have any trouble applying pressure on whichever side you want."

Cipher picked up the skillet and poured the meat, juices and all, into the simmering pot. "This city is ripe to fall, Alyra. I think you know that. But what would be the repercussions?"

"The nearby cities—Nisus, Chiresh, Hirak—would rush in to claim some share of the spoils."

"Exactly. The same cities that are marching to Erugash at this very moment. At the same time, the Cult of Amur works to undermine the queen from within."

The realization struck her like a hammer to the forehead. "It's all connected. The war, the cult, and rebellion . . ."

Cipher stirred the pot, adding a handful of minced garlic.

"The network did all this?" Alyra asked.

"We had a hand in it, but we've been aided by some unexpected events that turned in our favor. Such as the arrival of your housemate and the curious effect he's had on several key players."

Horace's elevation to the court. The ultimatum leveled on the queen, which led to the fall of the Sun Temple. Holy stars, they've been manipulating everything.

"You're starting a civil war," she said. "It will start here, but other cities will be pulled into the conflict as everyone takes sides. Akeshia will be ripped apart."

"Possibly, although it's difficult to make projections that far into the future. Still, enough turmoil to distract the empire for a generation. That is our mandate, after all."

No, I haven't forgotten. But the cost in human lives will be astronomical. Is this what it takes to save a country?

"And the attack on the Chapter House?"

"Another fortunate accident." He tasted the concoction. "Hmmm. Needs some basil."

"So what comes next? Do you stand back and let the city tear itself apart?"

"Not exactly. There's still one more step before our recipe is complete." He smiled at her. "Forgive the pun."

She didn't want to ask, but the words were pulled from her. "What step?"

"It is time for Queen Byleth to die."

Alyra didn't speak. She didn't move. The words echoed in her mind, but she couldn't quite grasp them. They were too ridiculous, too far beyond reason even for the network. "You can't mean . . ."

"I received the communication this morning. The network believes the time is ripe for the queen to go. Now that Prince Zazil is gone and the Sun Cult banished from Erugash, her absence would plunge this territory into chaos as the *zoanii* houses fight over the spoils. But we need someone willing and able to commit the act. One last mission to preserve our homeland's security for years to come."

Alyra found it difficult to breathe. She had no great love for Byleth, but murder was the furthest thing from her mind. Although she knew the network sometimes authorized assassinations, they were rare. "Even if I thought it was right, you must have someone better suited for the task."

"This is the moment, Alyra. If you wish to rejoin us and share in the downfall of the empire, this is what you must do. As we speak, the queen is planning a major operation. If we're too late, the rebellion might be crushed, and our chance to put our thumb on the scales of history will be lost. Will you do it?"

She tried to answer no, that she couldn't take his offer and never to bother her again, but the words halted on her tongue. The network was right. If the queen died, the city would come apart as all the vying factions fought to take over the throne. If they were left alone, a winner would eventually emerge from among the noble families, but the other cities would never sit back and let that happen. Nisus and Chiresh would both move to take over Erugash, shattering their temporary alliance, and the war would spread from there as every city in Akeshia tried to gain some piece of the cake while preventing their rivals from benefitting. In the past, the priesthoods had been able to keep such internecine wars from getting out of hand, but since the Godswar there was only one cult powerful enough to put a stop to it. And she didn't think they would. *No, the Cult of Amur might even fan the flames, hoping to profit from the devastation. Oh God in Heaven, is this what You want me to do?*

"I'll do it," she said, unable to believe what she was saying.

He nodded without smiling, as if he expected no less.

Alyra held up a finger. "But I want protection."

"We will take care of everything. After the deed, we can get you safely out of the city—"

"Not for me. For Horace. If I do this, the network agrees to protect him."

"Alyra—"

"This isn't up for negotiation," she said. "Once the queen is gone, he'll be targeted by every member of the court. You'll promise me here and now that the network will keep him safe, or you can find another agent."

He stared at her for several seconds, but she didn't flinch. Finally, he nodded. "Agreed. I will do everything in my power to ensure his safety. Once the queen is dead. We will send you the final instructions when everything is in place."

Cipher reached under the counter and retrieved a leather case. "And this is for you. It's everything we have on the Chapter House killings. I caution you not to expect much. We don't know who was behind it. Also in there is the name of a city planner who favors our cause, as you requested."

Alyra tucked it under her cloak. She felt the need to say something, maybe to prove she wasn't just a puppet in their game. That this was her choice. But she was too numb to think of anything satisfying, so she turned and left, stalking down the dark hallway until she got outside.

The cold night played with her hair as she took a deep breath. Why had she agreed? She didn't have Horace's mystical power or Emanon's fanatical zeal. She was just an information gatherer. A spy, not a killer. *What about Rimesh? You killed him. But that was to save Horace's life. I could never . . .*

She felt like she'd fallen into the river and the current was dragging her down, the air dwindling in her lungs. If she did this one thing, would the waters recede to let her go? Or would she die at the bottom?

At least she might be able to save Horace. *If I can only manage to break into the most secure place in the city undetected and kill one of the most powerful sorceresses in history, and then escape in one piece with an entire army on my heels. What's to worry about?*

CHAPTER ELEVEN

Mulcibar's body was wrapped in a white sheet from crown to heels and laid out on a slab of blue granite on the eastern terrace of the Moon Temple. Akeshian tradition usually required four days of mourning before a body was interred, but the unusual circumstances surrounding the death—as well as the unpleasant fact that the body had begun to rot quickly after it was found—had shortened the time to one night and part of the morning.

Standing at the rear of the terrace, Horace shifted his weight and tried his best not to fidget. He was here in his official capacity as First Sword, which meant the full uniform complete with bronze breastplate and sword.

Zoanii and members of the city's higher castes crowded the steps of the temple's ziggurat, while the lessers gathered in the courtyard below. The queen and her retinue stood with Lady Anshara, who wore the traditional white robe of mourning. A young priestess, barely old enough to be called a woman, led the funeral rites. Her voice cut through the morning air like a silver bell, while two acolyte girls in blue-and-white robes paced around the body, sprinkling it with scented oil.

Horace's attention wandered as the prayers went on and on. This reminded him too much of the *Tammuris*. He kept glancing through the crowd for crimson robes. But every few seconds his gaze gravitated toward Alyra, standing with a group of lesser nobles on the lowest tier of the step-pyramid. She was wearing the clothes he'd last seen her in, and he wondered where she had spent the night. He was still angry about their last conversation, especially her insinuations that he was taking the queen's side against the rebels. He didn't need her to remind him what it felt like to be a slave.

She never saw me for who I truly am. I was just a tool, to use and throw away when she was finished. Maybe she had real feelings for me, but how can I be sure? I'm fairly certain she's back to working with her spymasters, even after she admitted they were ready to let me rot in that temple pit because it suited their purposes. I expected more, but I should have known better.

Still, he had to admit he missed her. Worse than that, he didn't know how to mend this separation.

Byleth looked every bit a queen in a floor-length gown of purple silk with gold embroidery. Her double-tiara encrusted with blue sapphires shone like a second sun in the gathering rays of morning. She also looked distracted.

Perhaps, Horace thought, it was how she dealt with grief. She had known Lord Mulcibar all her life. It was natural that she would be stricken by his passing. Horace hadn't been present when news of the body's appearance had reached the queen, but he'd heard rumors that a lot of furniture needed replacing after her reaction. Perhaps that explained why there had been no recrimination from the palace about his destruction of the Chapter House.

There had, however, been a reaction from the citizens of Erugash. Public demonstrations broke out all across the city this morning, larger than ever before. A few reports mentioned new graffiti in the River Quarter depicting him in sexual congress with various animals. Hairy goats seemed to be a main theme.

He glanced at the altar piece. *You were a great man and a true friend. I'm sorry I couldn't prevent what happened to you, but I promise the people responsible will get what they deserve. And I'll do my best to look after the queen, too, because I know you would want that. Although it will make things worse with Alyra and probably get me killed to boot. Farewell, Mulcibar. May you find happiness in whatever paradise you've earned.*

The service ended as the sun was fully above the horizon. One of the attending priestesses set a torch to Mulcibar's body, and it erupted into flames. Horace looked past the pyre at the sun, bathing the rooftops of the city in its radiance. As its beams turned the sky from deepest purple to startling blue, he wiped a tear or two from his stinging eyes. He needed to get control of himself. Only then could he do anything about the Sun Cult. And he would. Beyond his vow to Mulcibar's spirit, he wanted to crush the sect of Amur until there was nothing left.

Horace moved away from the royal entourage looking for Alyra, but he didn't see her. She had disappeared into the crowd descending the temple's sides into the courtyard below and out the gates. He was still looking when a soft touch alighted on his elbow. "I never thought this day would come."

Byleth stood beside him. Her eyes were red, her kohl makeup blurry from hastily wiped tears. Seeing her sorrow, displayed so prominently, struck a solemn chord. It wasn't often anyone would see a queen so genuinely vulnerable. He placed his hand over her fingers and squeezed. "I was thinking the same thing. Mulcibar was so steady. So permanent. I didn't know him very long, but I honestly believed he would always be around."

"We used to jest, my father and I, that Lord Mulcibar would outlive us all. When my father died, I would have been lost if not for him. He became my second father, my protector." She tried to smile. "Now that duty falls to you, I'm afraid."

"I'll do everything I can, Excellence. In fact, I think I'd better get back to the palace. Things have been hectic lately, as I'm sure you know."

She leaned closed. "Put down the rebellion, Horace. The faster, the better. All things will come together in harmony once that threat is ended."

He nodded, and breathed easier when she went back inside the temple with the priestesses.

While the cream of Erugash's society departed, he waited on the terrace, wanting to be alone with his thoughts. The pyre was now mostly burned down to a smoldering pile of bones and charred fabric. Mulcibar was gone, in both body and spirit.

He left after most of the crowd had gone, joining his bodyguards below. They exited onto the main avenue running through the city. At its end was the royal palace, its western face still in shadow. Horace started in that direction until a black carriage pulled by a team of fine horses drew up beside him. He didn't think much of it until the window curtains parted and a voice called out, "Lord Horace. One moment."

Horace started as he saw Lord Astaptah peering out the window. His burnt-copper features were even darker inside the vehicle. The eyes staring out were like pits of amber ice surrounded by deep folds of skin.

"Ah, sure. I suppose . . ."

The carriage door swung open. Gesturing for his guards to remain, Horace stepped inside and sat opposite Lord Astaptah.

The vizier was dressed in his customary black robe, the hood settled around his shoulders. "Pardon me," he said. "I wish only a little of your time."

STORM AND STEEL

Horace sat back and tried to appear at ease, even as his insides were jumping. "Of course. I thought I might see you at the funeral."

That was a lie. Lord Astaptah was notorious for his solitude, rarely appearing at public events.

"I was otherwise engaged." He closed the window curtains and knocked on the roof.

Horace held onto the seat as the carriage started off, rocking back and forth. Since the night Astaptah and Alyra had rescued him from the Sun Temple's abattoir, he'd thought a lot about the reclusive vizier, about why Astaptah had helped him in the first place. Mulcibar had warned him not to trust this man, but no concrete reason had ever been given. For his part, Horace found the vizier to be well mannered and civil, if a little remote. He felt, on account of his rescue, he should at least give the man the benefit of the doubt and judge for himself. "Where, uh, are we going?"

"Not far. Tell me, Lord Horace, how are you finding your new office?"

"Well, to be honest I've been feeling a little overwhelmed."

"That is to be expected. Even for those born to power in this country, the royal courts can be treacherous places."

"Lord Mulcibar said as much before he died."

Lord Astaptah glanced at the window as if he were looking through the dark curtains. "The late lord of House Alulu and I were not great friends, as I'm sure you know. However I respected his temperament."

"He tried to warn me about what I was getting myself into, but it seems no amount of warning could express the sheer madness of it all."

"Madness? No. It can seem chaotic at times, but you must remember there is always a system in play underneath the surface."

"How did you—pardon me, but you're a foreigner to the empire, too. Right? How did you adjust so well to the court?"

"The ways of these Akeshians are not so different from my homeland. I come from a country beyond the sands of Isuran where murder and coercion are tools used by both the high and the low."

"It sounds unpleasant. I'm not surprised you left."

"My leaving was not of my own choosing. I was exiled because I dared to challenge the old ways of my people. I saw a path that would lift us to new heights of knowledge and prosperity. However my message was not well received. My countrymen banished me into the desert with nothing more than the clothes I was wearing and a gourd of water. I was meant to die."

"And you came here?"

"After a long exodus, yes." Lord Astaptah's eyes glowed in the dim cabin. "Byleth took me into her household, and I so came to be in her service."

Although this foreign-born nobleman made him uneasy, Horace thought he might be the only one in this entire city who understood his predicament. "I need your advice and your assistance."

"Ask."

"How can I convince the queen to make concessions to the rebel slaves?"

The vizier leaned back deeper onto the shadows of his seat until his features were all but hidden from sight. "You cannot. The only thing Akeshians respect is strength. Attempting to persuade or barter will only make them more obstinate."

"But I've shown them strength," Horace said. "The personal challenges have stopped coming. So why won't they listen to me?"

"Your experiences prove my point. When you showed your power in the arena, the challenges ceased. When you defeated the priests of Amur, the cult fled the city. You must continue to project strength and authority at all times, in all things. Do not be burdened by feelings of compassion, as they will make you appear weak."

Horace didn't like the advice, but he had to admit it sounded accurate. The men and women of the royal court were an arrogant bunch, constantly seeking to exploit each other for personal gain. If he wanted to impress the queen, perhaps he needed to play by the same rules.

"One more piece of counsel, Lord Horace, if you will allow me to offer it."

"Of course."

"Act swiftly. The city of Nisus, with the backing of the Sun Cult, is sending an army to attack Erugash. It would be regrettable if the priests regained their stranglehold over this city, as I'm sure you're aware."

Horace squeezed the edge of his seat harder. He had enough problems already, and the last thing he needed was for the cult to take back the city. "In that case, I have a confession."

He struggled with opening up about this, but he knew it had to be done. "I've lost control of the *zoana*."

Lord Astaptah leaned forward slightly. "Explain."

So many thoughts tumbled through Horace's head, he didn't know where to start. "Ever since that night at the Sun Temple, the power doesn't seem to obey me. I didn't have the best control before that, either, but at least it came when I called for it. Now it's all over the place. Sometimes it comes, sometimes it doesn't. Or too much comes, and then I end up going too far. I've tried meditating and working with a mentor. Lord Ubar was kind enough to tutor me, and of course, I worked with Lord Mulcibar before his disappearance. But now I feel lost. It's just a . . . a mess."

The vizier rested his chain on his clasped hands. "Is there discomfort when you use the power?"

"Yes. It feels like something is trying to break out of my chest."

"Perhaps I have access to resources that could help your situation. If you are willing to place your trust in me."

"*Ai, ai!* Please. Any help you could give me would be greatly appreciated."

The carriage came to a stop with a slight lurch. "Very well," Lord Astaptah said. "I will send my carriage for you tomorrow at dawn, and we shall begin."

Horace let out a quick sigh. "*Kanadu, Belum*. For everything. I didn't get the chance to thank you properly after the *Tammuris*, but I want you to know I'll never forget what you did for me."

"Perhaps someday I may grant you the chance to repay that debt, First Sword."

"Of course. I look forward to the opportunity."

Stepping out onto the street, Horace was momentarily blinded by the morning light. Blinking away the brightness, he discovered he was back where Astaptah had picked him up. His bodyguards saw him and hurried over. The carriage took off again, its tall wheels rattling across the street.

As he watched it leave, Horace considered the strange conversation in a new light. Lord Astaptah was no fool. Oddly enough, the vizier seemed to understand him better than he imagined was possible, perhaps better than anyone else in Erugash. And that included Alyra, who had returned to her private world of spies and informants without him.

The rising sun cast his shadow far ahead of him as he headed home.

The final images of the scene decayed into sepia emptiness as she withdrew her power. Horace leaving Astaptah's carriage. Standing on the street outside the Moon Temple as the vehicle drove off. Then her First Sword walked away, his head down as if deep in thought.

Byleth released Kelcia's head as the memories evaporated between them. She didn't like seeing her vizier conferencing with her First Sword, especially without her knowledge and consent. Lord Astaptah was difficult to control; she did not want him influencing Horace. Even worse, she didn't want to imagine what kinds of plots the two might hatch together. If there was a more volatile and dangerous pair of men in the empire outside of the Imperial Court, she didn't want to know. Standing up from the chair where she'd been sitting during the mind-scrying, she sent the girl back out into the street to follow Horace. That was as much as she could do at the moment.

Byleth glanced at Lady Anshara, who stood in the doorway of the ante-chamber they had borrowed. "Go home, my dear. Mourn for your uncle."

The woman lifted her chin. "With all respect, Majesty, my place is here. This is where I wish to be, doing my duty. My uncle would expect no less."

"As you wish."

Byleth took a deep breath and walked down the wide corridor bisecting the Moon Temple's second-highest tier. They'd left Xantu and the rest of her bodyguard below in the main chamber out of deference; no males were allowed above the ground floor of the temple. But Lady Anshara was more than enough protection, especially here in the heart of the crown's most ardent supporters. Byleth felt more at ease amid these pale-blue hallways than she often did in her own palace. There was something calming about this place, or perhaps it was the serene looks on the faces of the priestesses here, old and young. She felt like she was among sisters.

The door at the end of the hallway was watched by two ancient priestesses. They sat on stools outside the door, combing flax from large baskets into long strands. Byleth paused for a moment to watch with awe their spindly fingers, working the fibers with amazing dexterity. As they worked, they hummed a tune together. She didn't recognize it as first, but then she realized they were humming a widow's dirge. Frowning, Byleth passed between them.

The high priestess's cell was a plain affair, barely as large as Byleth's bathing chamber. Rough plaster covered the walls and ceiling without decoration save for a coating of light-blue paint, which was chipped and cracked in several places. A narrow cot sat against the far wall, flanked by a chamberpot and a small washstand. In a niche over the bed was a simple idol of Sippa in alabaster. Heat radiated from a small fireplace and two coal-filled braziers.

Three young novices stood around the high priestess, looking as if they were about to cry. They held a sheet of black cloth in front of the bed as Byleth entered. It was an old ceremonial tradition to separate the dying from the living with a symbolic veil of death.

"Leave us," came a wan voice from the bed.

The novices hesitated a moment, until the high priestess waved them away with a frail hand. "Go, my darlings."

The young girls sidled past Byleth and fled into the hallway. The queen closed the door behind them.

"They mean well, the poor children. Help me up."

High Priestess Iltani looked painfully old. The linen undershift hung loose on her bony frame, and the age spots down her cheeks and across the backs of her hands appeared darker in the pale lamplight. Her silver hair tumbled loose about her shoulders. *When did she get so old? She looks like she's about to break apart at any moment.*

Byleth hurried to help her sit up, grabbing a cushion from the foot of the bed and placing it behind the old woman for support. As she did so, she probed the priestess with a trickle of *zoana*. She'd never had much talent for healing. She could do little more than determine whether the old woman's heart was failing, its rhythm fluttering every few beats, causing blood to pool in the large arteries. But the high priestess had already been seen by the best healers in the city. She was simply dying, and nothing could stop that.

The priestess leaned back with a sigh. "Thank you, Your Majesty."

Byleth flicked her fingers. "Please, no titles. Not today."

"As you wish. But if you're going to stay, you'll have to make yourself useful. Fetch me that cup. My throat's as dry as the desert. I can't seem to make enough moisture anymore."

Byleth got the cup and refilled it from a pitcher on the washstand, noticing as she poured that it was wine instead of water. She brought it over with two hands. "I hope this isn't from the goddess's sacred vintage."

Iltani chuckled as she accepted the cup. "That swill? No, this is the good stuff. Lord Mulcibar's steward sent it over yesterday, and I've been sampling it vigorously."

The queen couldn't help but smile at the old woman's words. "I think you're justified."

"Of course I am! I'm dying. Oh, don't bother shaking your head. I know it. I've known for months. I have my good days and bad days, and lately the bad days have been taking over. It's the way of things, that's all."

Byleth sat on the side of the bed and placed her hand on the priestess's arm. The bones felt like kindling under the thin sleeve of the shift. She tried to subdue the feelings bubbling inside her, but they climbed up her throat anyway, putting an annoying quiver in her voice. "You'll be missed, you know? Especially by me. There aren't a lot of people I can talk to."

"Oh, stop feeling sorry for yourself, Byleth. Life is hard, for queens as well as washerwomen and net-haulers. Your father had it harder, let me tell you. He didn't have half your ability with the *zoana*, and he was forever putting out fires inside his own court because of it. He had to forge strong alliances to win the proper respect, and even then most of the nobility were licking their chops to see him fall. No, child. I won't permit any peevishness in here. Lift up your chin! There you go. That's the girl I remember."

Byleth laughed despite the tears spilling down her face. "That's what I mean. No one else tells me the truth. I'm not complaining. I'm just trying to say no one will ever replace you."

"Sadly, that's not true. There will be a new high priestess of this temple soon, and you'd be wise to bind her to you as soon as possible. You're intent on rolling the dice, child. Yes, I can see it in your eyes. You've been planning something, and what happened on the *Tammuris* was only the tip of the spear. I almost feel bad for your enemies. Well, not really. The bastards deserve every bit of what they've got coming."

"Iltani! Cursing in the temple? They'll bury you out behind the refuse pits."

The high priestess took another sip. "It's a distinct possibility. But the goddess is forgiving. She knows we're all flawed vessels."

"This flawed vessel could use some good advice."

"I'm sorry, but that's in short supply these days." The high priestess reached up to pat Byleth's cheek. "Trust in yourself, child. And trust in the gods who created us and breathed the spirit of life into our bodies. These are the secrets of success. Now go. I'm feeling tired."

"Of course. Is there anything you need?"

"No, I'm content. But thank you for coming to see me. It was my last wish, and the Lady made it come true."

Byleth blinked through her tears, nodding as she got up and went to the door. She thought she heard a whisper behind her, the words so soft she couldn't be sure, but they had sounded like a blessing. Or a lullaby.

The queen opened the door. Without looking back, she whispered, "Good-bye."

Horace returned home to find a crowd outside his gates. More than fifty people—men, women, and even a few children—chanted and banged small drums, and a few even danced in feverish circles. Then someone spotted him, and the multitude fell silent as they turned to him.

"Belzama!" a person cried from the crowd.

At once, all heads bowed.

Horace ground his teeth. *What do you want from me? I don't have any answers. I'm not special. I'm not even good. If you only knew the truth. . . .*

But he said nothing. He followed his guards through the crowd, wincing as the gate clanged shut, separating him from the outside.

Once inside the house, he wandered the upper floor of the manor. His brain felt scrambled with all the things rattling around inside it. He was tired but didn't feel like sleeping. He wanted peace and quiet, but he was afraid to be alone.

Alyra's door was closed. He was tempted to see if she was in but pushed the thought away. She wanted her space, and he could respect that. Perhaps if things kept going along this path, he would find her another place to live. A nice apartment in the city, maybe near the royal gardens. Yet the mere thought of her leaving drove a spike through his heart and made everything he was feeling worse.

His meandering took him into the east wing to his solarium. The room was large, but it felt close because of the floor-to-ceiling bookcases built into the side walls. The east wall was dominated by a stained glass window as big as a dinner table. The orange, red, blue, and green slices of glass cast a mosaic of lights across the hardwood floor. The air was warm and smelled of paper.

Most of the books on the shelves had come with the house. They covered a wide range of subjects from farming techniques to astrology. Horace had read a few of them already, using them to bolster his grasp of the Akeshian language.

A long desk of yellow wood sat beneath the stained glass window. It was low to the floor in the Akeshian style, with a padded stool in place of a chair. Since he didn't spend much time in here, preferring to work in his office at the palace, he hadn't taken the time to change the furniture. As he walked over to the desk, he saw the wooden chest he'd brought back from Mulcibar's estate, tucked behind a map stand. Seized by sudden curiosity, and more than a little melancholy since the funeral, Horace pulled the chest over to the desk. He opened the latches and started to lift the lid but paused, remembering the day Mulcibar had educated him on the many devious ways that containers could be trapped with malicious sorcery. He was about to tap into his *zoana* to examine the trunk more closely, but the lethargy that had haunted him since waking up convinced him it would be fine. *I'll take my chances.*

Inside were a variety of items. Two leather-bound books were stacked beneath a bundle of papyrus scrolls. Horace scanned the scrolls as he placed them on the desk. They read like journal entries at first glance, but as he read further Horace got the gist that they were research notes. The topics included religion, astronomy, mathematics, and architectural drafting. He even found a treatise on the construction of a new kind of sailing vessel, larger than anything he'd ever seen. Impressed, he dug back into the trunk.

The books were studies on magical theory, both written by Mulcibar. Horace picked them up eagerly and fanned open the gilded pages. The script was strange—Akeshian but in a style he'd never seen before. There were diagrams as well, showing geometric shapes with lines and labels in the same script. They reminded him a little of engineering plans, but it only took a minute for him to realize these volumes went far beyond his meager understanding of the magical arts. He put them on the desk as well, determined to study them later.

On the bottom were several objects wrapped in oilskin cloth. Horace took them out one at a time. The first was a sailor's sextant in brass, which gave him a chuckle. Was Mulcibar trying to remind him of his seafaring past? Perhaps it was an admonition to never lose your bearings. *Or maybe the old man just liked to collect odd knickknacks.*

The next parcel turned out to be a set of pens in a lacquered box, complete with two inkwells and a pearl-handled sharpening knife. He put that aside also, thinking it would look good in his office at the palace.

When he reached down for the last parcel, a shock ran up his hand. Like a fog scattered before a stiff sea breeze, the lassitude infecting him disappeared as if he had plunged his head into a bucket of cold water. He reached for the cube-shaped package again. It was heavier than he expected. He unwrapped the cloth to find a silver box with four tiny clawed feet. Each of the sides and top were cast with abstract crisscrossing designs that resembled the winding tracks of earthworms crawling through the dirt.

He cleared a space on the desk. Then he tried to tap into the Kishargal dominion to probe the box with thin tendrils of energy. Pain erupted along the backs of his hands and up his arms like steel nails driven into his flesh. With a hiss, he pulled back. His power had left him in a rush, snuffed out like a lamp wick.

Zoahadin.

Why would Mulcibar keep a box made from a metal antithetical to sorcerers? More importantly, what could be inside that needed such protection? He took the knife out of the pen set. Taking a deep breath, he used it to push up on the lid. It refused to budge. Horace pried at it for several seconds until he became exasperated. *To Hell with this. Just take the bull by the horns.*

Dropping the knife, he grabbed the box's lid with both hands and lifted. As if a hidden catch had released, the lid flew open. A small sphere sat inside on a bed of black cloth. Horace leaned forward for a better look. The sphere was completely smooth and translucent. The outer shell was red-gold, but black swirls lurked within its depths. He'd never seen anything like it. Even the material was a mystery to him. Was it glass? Some exotic alloy?

Horace touched the sphere with his forefinger. The surface was slippery and cool to the touch. An engraved silver plate was affixed to the inside of the lid, reading:

> *And thus did Harutuk arm himself with the flame of Endu and go forth to battle the Great Mother of Night.*

Horace looked back in the trunk, but there were no more parcels. Nothing else to explain what this might be. He was stuck in the dark, no closer to knowing why Mulcibar had been murdered than before. Then he remembered the nobleman had visited the royal archives the night he vanished.

Horace plucked the orb out of the box and shoved it into his pocket for later study. He was curious why Mulcibar had bequeathed it to him. Was it another clue about what he'd been studying when he disappeared? *Maybe the archives will have the answer.*

He put the box back in the trunk, repressing a shiver as his skin touched the silvery metal, and closed the lid. He thought about attempting to ward the trunk with some kind of enchantment, but he didn't know the first thing about it. Instead, he shoved the chest out of sight behind the desk.

Leaving the solarium, he closed the door behind him and headed downstairs. Gurita and another guard sat in the atrium playing at sticks, their shields at their feet. They stood up as he came down and followed him out the door.

The royal archives looked different in the daytime. A stolid building as ancient as the city's oldest temples and palaces, it was surrounded by a neighborhood that had moved on with the times, becoming more upscale and lavish even as the archives remained stuck in an older century. The building's flat roof was crowned with a row of statues, limestone icons of mythological beasts and persons, their faces worn away by the passage of time.

Horace walked up the broad stairs and entered the great bronze doors, which stood open during the day. Leaving the heat of the afternoon outside, he looked around the long atrium, trying to decide how to conduct his search. Six wide halls led off the central atrium, each filled with rows of scroll cases and shelves. Scribes, most of them old men, bent over canted desks, scribbling with quill pens. Novices with shaved heads dusted the completed pages with sand before taking them away to be stored.

Horace stopped one of the novices as he hurried past with a sheaf of fresh papyrus sheets. "Pardon me."

The young man blinked at him as if unsure how to react but then bowed from the waist. "*Ai, Belum.*"

In his most formal Akeshian, Horace asked to be announced to the head archivist. The novice bowed again and rushed off. After several minutes, two old men entered the atrium from the south end. Horace recognized one of them from the last time he was here. He raised a hand in greeting. "Good morning, Archivist. Perhaps you remember—"

"The First Sword, Horace Delrosa of Arnos. Can you explain why I was interrupted from a very delicate restoration of a Fourth Dynasty cyclopedia?"

"My apologies, sir. The last time I was here, I was searching for Lord Mulcibar."

The old archivist's head bobbed up and down between his narrow shoulders. "I heard of his death. Very tragic, but I fail to see how this concerns the archives."

"You told me the tomes Lord Mulcibar was studying that night, but I've forgot—"

"The *Gahahag Codex of Theolon Siggaratum*, the Maganu *Book of the Dead* translated by Garoma Parimi, and Ipsu-Amur's *The Ninety-Ninth Day*."

"Ah, yes. Those were the ones. I was hoping I could see—"

The archivist started walking away before he could finish. Horace hesitated for a moment. Then he motioned for his guards to stay behind as he followed the old man.

They passed through a grand hall floored in white marble. Light poured in through rows of square windows high along the walls. Motes of dust danced in the sunlight, but everything was kept remarkably pristine. The archivist shoved open a door at the back of the hall, and Horace followed him into a smaller chamber, dim without any windows. The old man fretted with a lamp on a stand near the door until it sparked to life. "Wait here," he said simply before leaving.

The room had plain walls of cedar wooden paneling, unlike the stone walls he'd seen elsewhere in the archives. Their pleasant, faintly musty scent filled the air. The only furnishings were a low table large enough to seat a dozen people and a single footstool. Not sure what to do, Horace just stood as time passed. After a half a bell or so, the door opened, and three novices entered. Each youth held a large book. They placed them all on the table with special care. Then, after a bow to him, they filed out.

Horace sat down. The first tome to his left was as tall as his arm from wrist to shoulder. Bound in leather so dark it looked almost black, faint characters in gold-leaf read *Nine and Ninety Days*. The other two books were even larger. Their antiquity was evident in the aged pages. Horace began with the first book.

Reading by the single lamp soon made his eyes ache as he leafed through the pages. The book detailed, according to its author, the nearly one hundred days that the gods of the Akeshian pantheon dwelt on earth during the

Annunciation. It was precisely what he expected it to be, a collection of ludicrous myths dressed up as a historical account. What had Mulcibar been looking for in this collection of primitive tales?

He went on to the next tome, the *Gahahag Codex*. The tall leaves of this bronze-bound tome were made from some kind of leather hide, tough yet supple. Because of its age, translating the text was difficult for him, but it seemed to be a testimonial. The author's claims were fantastic—even ludicrous—and Horace found himself skipping passages, though he paused at a section devoted to demonology, which described a host of evil spirits believed to haunt the dark hours of the night. There was even an entry on *idimmu*, the kind of flesh-eating demons that had attacked the palace on a night Horace would rather forget. He was about to move on when he spotted a handwritten notation in the margin of the page, written in Arnossi.

> *We cannot afford to ignore this. The threat is growing.*

Had Mulcibar written that? Beside the notation was a passage about the demons of the underworld. Horace read it quickly.

> *Seven are the lords of Absu, the beings from the Outside who ever desire to enter our world. And their Names are forbidden, for to call upon Them is to invite Death for all mankind. Do not seek to descend the seven Steps down to the Gates of Death. The nether world is formless and contains all the elements of Chaos, unbounded and against which no charm can protect you.*

Below the passage was a disturbing illustration of a huge underground sea. At the bottom of its depths was a serpentine creature—possibly a dragon—that appeared to be asleep. Studying the picture, Horace tried to understand what Mulcibar was trying to tell him. *Damn it, old man. Why couldn't you just tell me like a normal person?*

He read the entire page twice and part of the next section, which talked about how demons had once ruled the world in a time of darkness until they were banished by the new gods of Akeshia to someplace called the "Outside," which was apparently also an ocean deep underground.

He closed the book and pushed it away. The whole matter made him uneasy. He'd never been a believer of supernatural things. Even as a follower of the True Faith, which had its own fair share of spirits, both benign and malicious, he tended to think about such forces in metaphorical terms. However, he'd seen things since coming to this land that had shaken that philosophy. *Hell, I've done* things that would get me exiled from the Church if anyone back in Arnos found out. If not tied to a stake and burned as an agent of darkness. So what am I to make of all this talk of demons and gods? Obviously, the Akeshian people believe these stories, but what's so important about them now in this day and age?

Lord Mulcibar had warned him that he suspected people in the court were working against the queen, although he never offered any names. Was there a connection between the two warnings? It seemed dubious.

Horace held back a yawn as he stretched. He thought about going through the third book, but it looked awfully long, and he was getting tired. He went to the door and found a young novice standing outside. "Pardon. I'm going to need to take these books with me. Can you fetch my guards?"

The novice's eyes almost popped out of his head. Without answering, he ran off. A few minutes later, he returned following the chief archivist, who again was not pleased at being interrupted. When Horace repeated his request, the old librarian had nearly an identical reaction as his young helper. It took some wrangling, but eventually Horace was able to pull rank and get permission to take the books, with the promise that he would be exceedingly careful and not let them out of his sight. Each book was then wrapped in a soft leather sheet and tied up with twine for protection.

By the time he left the archives, the day was mostly gone. Long shadows stretched across the streets as the afternoon waned. He was tempted to go home, but a twinge of guilt convinced him to visit his office.

With his guards, burdened with the bound books, in tow, Horace set off toward the palace.

CHAPTER TWELVE

The sky laughed at him, a low rumble that reverberated down into the ground. Horace dropped his head back to the earth and felt the gritty crunch of the soil beneath him. He was alone on a vast field of dark earth with the gray firmament stretched above him. A zephyr toyed with his hair, but he tried to ignore it as he listened to the sky's murmurings. There was a message in those tumultuous rumblings, he was sure of it. He listened closely until a voice emerged, sometimes as loud as thunder before drifting away to a mere whisper. Yet quiet or loud, the words seared into his brain.

We see you lying in the cold earth, Storm-Lord. Why do you not rise up to meet our call?

Horace heard his voice responding, though it sounded off to his ears. "I can't fly. My wings are gone."

No, you have only forgotten them, as your kind always forgets. In time, you will even forget us, the one who gave you life. We breathed our spirits in you, but you no longer remember.

Horace wanted to reach up, but his arms were stuck to the earth, tied down by a thousand invisible bonds. "Wait! I don't want to go down into the ground!"

It is too late. The darkness comes, and from that we can no longer shelter you. The book of the earth is closing, and a new age dawns.

From somewhere above his head came a deep, angry howl. Horace struggled against the ties that held him, but he couldn't break free. The sky roiled and spat green pillars of light, but the voice was gone. Drifted away on the wind.

The opening of a door woke him. Horace blinked up at the ceiling of his bedchamber. He could still feel his ears straining to hear every note of the thunder in his dream, now fading as he came to full wakefulness.

Dharma entered with a covered tray and placed it across his lap. Under the cover were a small plate of sliced oranges, a brown roll, honey, and a clay cup. Thanking her, he dug in. While he cut open the roll and slathered its hot insides with honey, Dharma opened the curtains. Birds chirped outside his window. The warmth of the sun's rays across his blanket made Horace want to go back to sleep, but the echoes of the dream prickled at the back of his mind.

"What time it is?"

"Just past the first hour, Master," she replied. "A carriage has arrived for you."

Horace suddenly remembered Lord Astaptah's offer to help with his problem. He wolfed down the roll and beer as he got out of bed. He used the water closet and dressed in a simple robe, not sure what would be appropriate attire. He stuffed the orb on the nightstand into his pocket and rushed downstairs.

Gurita waited in the foyer, ready to leave.

"Meet me at the palace," Horace said. "I'll be there in an hour or maybe two."

The guard captain didn't look pleased by the command, but he nodded.

The carriage waiting outside looked the same as the one he'd ridden in with Lord Astaptah the day before. He couldn't be sure if it was the same driver, though. Horace climbed inside and settled back against the firm seat.

The carriage took him on a bumpy ride through the city, east to the Silver Gate leading out of the city. Horace had never been this way. He watched through the window as they passed under the great battlemented gatehouse, through the long stone tunnel, and finally out the other side. The road angled northeast from the gate through sections of empty fields.

He thought about trying to meditate, but the ride was too bouncy, and anyway he wasn't in the mood. His mind was distracted, making him antsy and yet also sapping his energy to do anything. *Maybe it's that bizarre dream. I've been having a lot of them lately. It's probably the stress. I could use some time away from all this responsibility, but this time without anyone trying to kill me.*

Less than a bell later, they turned onto a dirt road. The fields petered out, to be replaced by copses of sturdy cypress trees surrounded by long stretches of open plain. In the distance, high up on a lone hill, Horace saw an old structure consisting of tall pillars with capstones. He thought that might be their destination, until the carriage passed it by. The ride became even more uncomfortable for several minutes as the wheels seemed to find every hole and rut in the road. Then the vehicle jerked to a halt.

Horace let himself out before the driver could climb down from his seat. They had arrived at an outdoor amphitheater. Rows of stone seats were carved into the side of a low hill, encircling one-half of a wide stage. The open end of the theater looked out over a bucolic expanse of meadows and trees. The walls of Erugash gleamed on the horizon.

Two men stood on the stage platform. Horace recognized Lord Astaptah, his black robes an ominous contrast to the gorgeous countryside around them. The vizier stood beside a younger man, possibly thirty years of age or thereabouts, in a gray robe with a leather belt. Horace had never seen him before. The younger man had a solid build and a full head of hair, cut short above his collar.

As Horace walked up to them, Lord Astaptah nodded to the other man. "Lord Horace, this is an associate of mine. You can call him Uriom. I brought him to work with you today."

Horace was a little confused. "I thought you and I would be working together."

"I shall oversee the exercises. Now, step up on the platform, if you will. Opposite your opponent."

Horace wasn't sure he liked the designation "your opponent," but he said nothing. He was trying to be open-minded about this, although he doubted Lord Astaptah or his associate could help much with this particular problem. As he took his place, he noticed several large symbols had been drawn on the stage in red paint. He didn't recognize any of them. They certainly weren't Akeshian characters. "What are these for?"

"Please focus." Lord Astaptah walked off the stage. "I have considered your difficulty. It's my opinion you are unsure of yourself, and thus the power refuses to respond."

Before Horace could respond, the vizier held up a hand, and Uriom attacked. A narrow jet of water shot across the distance between them.

It came so fast Horace almost couldn't react. He grabbed for his *zoana* out of pure instinct and wove it into a crude shield of compacted air. The water struck it with a hissing roar. Horace dug his heels into the stage to keep from being pushed backward by the force.

"Stop!"

STORM AND STEEL

Lord Astaptah's voice cracked over the amphitheater like a whip. Uriom immediately ceased his assault, which left Horace stumbling for a second. He dropped the air shield.

"You must use all the tools at your disposal, Lord Horace."

"I'm not sure what you mean."

"The void! It is your primary weapon and your greatest defense."

"But Lord Mulcibar said that mastery of the Shinar allowed me to use all of the dominions."

"Exactly, but the true strength of the Shinar comes from incorporating it into every other element. Only by blending them together will you achieve this so-called mastery."

Horace remembered the flow of void energy that had merged with his sorcery to bring down the Chapter House and how effective it had been. And also how frightening. He didn't relish feeling that loss of control again, not to mention the intense pain that ate at him every time he tried to use the power. He took a deep breath and let it out slowly. *Breathe. Mulcibar always said to focus on your breathing. You can do this.*

Lord Astaptah gestured again, and Uriom resumed his attack. This time, he hurled two jets of focused water across the stage. Horace focused on his flows. He drew out the Imuvar, as before, and this time pulled a thread of Shinar along with it. Knitting them together into a new shield of air and void, he was surprised by how easily the power came to him. He became so enraptured by the simple joy of using the magic that he almost jumped when Lord Astaptah shouted again.

"Stop!"

The water vanished. Horace allowed his shield to linger for a moment before dropping it so he could appreciate the fineness of the weave. He was rather proud of himself, though a dull ache throbbed behind his breastbone. "What now?"

Lord Astaptah smacked his palm with a closed fist. "You must turn back the attack. Defending merely encourages your opponent to continue his attack. After all, what price does he pay?"

Uriom stood still as blood dripped from a long cut on his left hand. Horace watched it splash on the platform, drop by drop. He swallowed. "All right."

"Again!" Lord Astaptah called out.

They ran the exercise over and over. Each time Horace met the attack and turned it aside, and each time Lord Astaptah exhorted him to press harder, to strike back faster, to go for the kill. With every bout, the pain in his chest grew. After an hour, he could hardly stand upright. Uriom was only in slightly better shape. Though the *zoanii* had managed to evade all of Horace's counterattacks, his gray robe was soaked in his own blood. It poured from his face, chest, and both arms. A strange sort of pride filled Horace. Yes, he was suffering, but he had pushed past the pain again and again, proving that it was not his master.

He also noticed the odd sensation he'd felt at the Chapter House. The feeling of being watched, only it was stronger now. It almost felt like a presence was lurking inside his mind, listening to his thoughts. He'd tried to shove it out, but it was like pushing wet sand. It just oozed around his mental grasp. The symbols on the stage seemed to shimmer for a moment.

"Enough."

Horace drew in a ragged breath and winced as the pain in his chest burned. *Is it really supposed to hurt like this?*

Lord Astaptah approached the stage. "That pain is the cost of power."

A little unnerved that the vizier could read him so easily, Horace replied, "It didn't feel like this before."

As he stepped up in the stage, Lord Astaptah indicated Uriom, who was wrapping his hands and forearms in thick bandages. "Most *zoanii* suffer the immaculata. Practitioners of the Shinar, however, pay a different price. An internal price."

"Why?"

"That is the way it is. The sooner you accept that, and *embrace* it, the sooner you will find the control you seek. Until then, you will be a danger to those around you."

Horace didn't need to be warned about that. "Lately, whenever I use the power, I get this weird feeling. It's hard to describe, but it's like I'm being watched." He touched the back of his head. "But from *inside* my mind. Does that make any sense?"

"That is you, watching yourself. It is called the inner eye. Do not fear this presence. Instead, like the pain, you must draw it closer and make it one with you. I suspect this is what happened on the night of the *Tammuris*, though you did not realize it at the time. Now you feel the power more keenly."

They started walking back to the carriage. Horace was exhausted and glad to be done. Lord Astaptah walked with his hands folded behind his back and his head bowed. "This is a difficult period of transition, Horace. But you will do better if you refrain from fighting it."

"That's not easy. The pain becomes so intense—"

"Focus on that pain. Breathe it into your body and merge it with your essence. The more you resist, the harder your path will be."

They came to the carriage, and the driver opened the door.

"*Kanadu, Belum*," Horace said. "This has given me a lot to think about."

"We will try again tomorrow."

Tomorrow? God in Heaven, I don't think I can go through this again. Yet he replied, "You honor me with your attention."

The vizier bowed his head. "The honor is mine, First Sword."

Horace climbed into the car and sagged gratefully into the seat. He hurt all over, but the pain in his chest was slowly fading, leaving behind an ache that seemed to punch straight through to his spine. He considered going home for a nap or a soak in the tub but called up for the driver to take him to the palace instead.

As the carriage rattled over the bumpy dirt road, Horace closed his eyes. He thought back over the training, reliving it in his memory. Some of the things Lord Astaptah said conflicted with Mulcibar's teachings, but he couldn't argue with the results. He'd exhibited more control and confidence with the power today than he had since . . . *since the battle against Rimesh and his priests. Why does that moment haunt me so? There was no other way to stop them.*

Sometimes he thought life was just one huge challenge against the universe. If that was so, he was going to win.

Shifting onto his side, he felt a bulge in his robe pocket and pulled out the orb from Mulcibar's trunk. The slick coolness of its surface was soothing. He'd forgotten he'd picked it up on his way out the door.

Crimson light swirled with the black inside the small sphere, like an early morning sky over the ocean as night's cloak slips behind the horizon. He gazed into its depths as he considered what to do about his troublesome powers.

The sun beat down, flogging everything that walked or crawled across the earth's surface. It wasn't even midmorning yet, and already the temperature was insufferable. The river looked inviting, green and cool, but danger lurked in the hidden currents beneath its rushing surface, currents that could grab hold of a man or even a full-grown ox and drag it down to a watery end. Abdiel wiped his forehead with a damp cloth. All of nature, he observed, was a killer of one kind or another.

He stood behind his master on the high promontory, gazing down as the combined army of the three kings crossed the Typhon. He had heard his master speaking with the military commanders of the army. This was only the first crossing they would need to make. A second crossing across the northern branch of the river would happen later, once they were closer to their target.

Lord Pumash had remained behind in Nisus to see to his business concerns. However, true to his word, the noble merchant had coaxed the rulers of three cities to finally begin their march toward Erugash. Progress was slow, but that was to be expected with a force of nearly fifteen thousand soldiers, not including the train of attendants and camp followers that accompanied the army. He himself had been born in an army camp. His childhood had been one long struggle to find enough to eat, of wearing rags his mother had sewn herself from whatever scraps could be found. He'd not worn his first pair of sandals until he was ten years of age, and those had been taken from a dead man's feet.

As small skiffs ferried units across the turbulent waters, Mebishnu raised a hand to shade his eyes. Abdiel squinted against the sun's glare. His eyes were not as good as they once had been, but he spied something happening on the northern shore. Parties of scouts had been sent ahead to secure the far side, but the initial reports said that all was clear. Now at least one of those parties was standing on the other shore, waving to gain the attention of the skiffs.

Time seemed to crawl as the boats made their way across the river and unloaded their human cargo. Once the scouts had boarded, the vessels started back on their return trip. Mebishnu started down the rocky path to the river embankment. Abdiel followed after him.

The river was so swollen that the desert ran right up to its silty shores. As they approached the bank, a group of officers spotted his master's arrival and turned to bow. Lord-General Xalthus, commander of King Moloch's army, gestured toward the river. "We're waiting to hear the latest report from the far shore, Your Eminence."

Mebishnu waited silently, and Abdiel began wishing for some shade. He was tempted to ask his master if he wanted something to drink, but he did not want to embarrass him in front of the officers, all of whom sweated as they stood together, watching the boats.

Once the skiffs finally made shore again, the scouts poured out. They were a motley lot, looking as rundown and filthy as a pack of dogs, but it was what they brought with them that had everyone's attention. Three men tightly bound and gagged. Two had the look of soldiers themselves, though they wore no colors over their travel-worn leathers. Empty sheaths and scabbards hung from their belts. The third man cowered in his bonds, his fine silken clothes torn and ruined by the sweat leaking out of him. His hair was shaved to mid-scalp and the rest pulled back in a tail that mimicked a warrior's queue, but this man was clearly no fighter. He looked soft despite his sun-bronzed skin.

"We were hunkered down beside a road on the far shore when this caravan came rolling along," one of the scouts said. He was a grizzled man with thick black stubble covering his chin and long hair that hung down in greasy locks. "Three wagons pulled by oxen. We sprung an ambush, and these are the ones that survived."

Mebishnu inspected the captives. "What were the wagons carrying?"

The lead scout had the good sense to duck his head in a sketchy bow. "Food, mostly, Your Lordship. Fish packed in salt. Barley. Beer."

"No arms? No siege equipment?"

"Just food. This one," he poked the soft-looking man in the back, "says he's a trader from Sekhatun."

The man in the spoiled silk outfit nodded emphatically as he tried to speak behind his gag.

"Lord-General," Mebishnu said. "Bring these men to my ship. I will interrogate them personally."

Xalthus appeared uneasy at that command, but he bowed nonetheless. "Yes, Your Eminence. Right away."

Soldiers from the legions took control of the captives as the scouts left, talking about finding something to eat and a cool patch of shade where to take a nap.

The master's cabin on the ship was too small for a proper interrogation, so Mebishnu had the captives taken down into the hold. After sending the crewmen out with orders to make sure he wasn't disturbed, Mebishnu directed the soldiers. The prisoners were bound to the posts that held up the deck above, and then he sent the soldiers away, too.

Abdiel expected to be ordered out as well, but his master said nothing. He just stood in the center of the room and studied the captives. All three were trying to speak now. Even though he couldn't hear their words, Abdiel knew they must be proclaiming their innocence. He waited with patience, and his patience was rewarded.

Ribbons of smoke rose from the leather vests worn by the two guards. Both men struggled against the ropes holding them, and their movements became more frantic as the smell of burning filled the air until they were thrashing and writhing. Their outer armor turned black, yet never burst into flames, such was his master's control. An incision opened across Mebishnu's face from right cheekbone nearly down to his chin. Blood welled from the open immaculata. Abdiel hurried to offer a clean cloth, which his master pressed to his face as he continued his work. Abdiel chanted under his breath. *Blessed is the holy offering, shed that we may suffer the Sun Lord's grace.*

The guard's clothing had begun to flake away, revealing singed flesh underneath. The men screamed into their gags. The soft one was not being affected, but tears ran down his plump cheeks as he glanced back and forth at his companions.

The torment seemed to last for hours until Abdiel started to develop aches in his old knees. However, he endured in silence.

Finally, the guards stopped struggling and hung limp. Abdiel couldn't tell if they were dead or merely unconscious, though he could not imagine anyone surviving such torment. All the flesh of their bodies below the neck was charred black. Mebishnu had left their faces intact though. *So they could continue to scream to the end.*

The soft one was drenched in sweat, so wet his clothes hung from him in sodden folds. He moaned behind his gag, shaking his head. Abdiel almost felt a touch of compassion, but this had to be done. They were on a holy mission. There could be no chance of failure, no precaution left untaken.

Still not having said a word, Mebishnu stepped forward and ripped off the last captive's gag.

"My lord! My lord!" the man spoke in a rush. "Thank you, my lord! I am only a humble merchant. I know nothing of arms or armies! Please believe me!"

"I do," Mebishnu said. "I believe you are telling me the truth. And as long as the truth comes from your mouth, you will not have to feel the pain your comrades suffered. Do I make myself clear?"

The man's head bobbed up and down. "Yes, yes, yes! Anything! Anything at all! Please, just don't hurt me!"

"Your name."

"Melip, my lord. I live in—"

The man yelped as Mebishnu removed the cloth to reveal the long gash down his cheek, seeping blood. "Answer only what I want to know, Melip of Erugash. Yes, I know you're one of hers."

The merchant opened his mouth as if to protest, but said nothing.

Good. You have broken this dog already. Now extract what you need, just as I taught you as a child. You must be cruel to serve a god. Feel nothing and ensure your place among the stars in the next life.

"Now," Mebishnu said, "tell me why you were racing so swiftly out of Erugash. Do you carry a message?"

The merchant shook his head. "No, my lord! Rumors say that the town of Sekhatun has been under attack by the rebellious slaves and may soon close its gates until the matter is settled. I hoped to make one last delivery before that happens. The prices, you see, are astronom—"

"Do not lie to me!"

The merchant shrieked in a high voice like a woman, though Abdiel couldn't see what pained him.

Mebishnu stepped forward to lean close to the merchant's face. "Tell me why you were going to this town."

"I swear it, lord! Please make it stop! I swear, I swear! I was only trying to make the sale. Please!"

Abdiel frowned as Mebishnu turned away from the man, who was most likely lying. *Do not falter now, my master.*

His master surprised him by opening a new line of questioning. "What is the queen doing to stop the insurrectionists at Sekhatun? We know that the bulk of her legions remain at Omikur. So what is her plan?"

"I don't know! I'm only a simple trader, lord. No, wait! I heard something. A rumor! The queen is sending the First Sword to Sekhatun to handle the uprising. The rebels are monsters, lord! Beheading people, killing peasants, stealing everything in sight. Please, I meant no harm!"

Mebishnu lifted a finger, and the merchant's babbling ceased at once. Abdiel heard a faint pop, and then the merchant sagged against his bonds, his neck bent sharply to the side.

Abdiel watched his master for signs of what he was thinking, but his face was a mask, occluding everything that was happening within. *I taught him well. Perhaps too well.*

Though it galled him to ask, Abdiel cleared his throat. "Master?"

Mebishnu dropped the bloody cloth and started toward the door. "Have these bodies disposed of, Abdiel. I'll be meditating in my cabin. Make sure I am not disturbed."

With a bow, Abdiel replied, "Of course, Master."

STORM AND STEEL

Horace sat back in his chair and ran his fingers through his hair, feeling the urge to tear out his follicles by the handful. The desk before him was covered in field reports from all across the province, all of them complaining with some variation of the same theme: the slave uprising. For the past four hours he'd been trying to wade through them, but his mind kept returning to this morning's training.

The pride he'd felt earlier had been eclipsed by feelings of abject failure. Just as when he'd trained with Mulcibar or Ubar, his reactions were too slow, his control too tenuous. He had faced down chaos storms—something no other living *zoanii* could claim—and yet he struggled with the basics. Everyone said it took years to master the art, but he didn't have that kind of time.

With a sigh, he put down the report he'd been trying to get through for the last half an hour and turned around to the long table behind his desk. He'd had the three tomes from the archives brought here so he could study them. *And since I'm not getting anywhere with those reports, I might as well dig in.*

He still didn't have any idea how these books tied together, but they kept nagging at him, whispering of veiled secrets held within their pages, secrets that would reveal the answers to the problems facing him. *I doubt they have anything to say about suppressing a rebellion without killing anyone, or convincing a queen to be reasonable.*

He opened the *Book of the Dead*. He didn't know much about the country of Maganu except that it was on the southern continent. Sailors often talked about it with an air of mystery, where the women were as beautiful as they were untouchable and death was the preferred penalty for any offense.

The book's pages were a darker form of papyrus than the Akeshians used, and the ink was as black and crisp as if it had just been written, even though he could tell by the cover that this tome had to be decades, if not centuries, old. The translator had included the original text; the Maganu used pictures in their writing instead of letters. While he read, Horace took the orb from his pocket and rolled it around in his hand.

After a little while, he closed the book and slumped back in his chair. It was page after page of prayers to deities he had never heard of and instructions for preparing corpses for burial. Just more ancient myths and death cults and fantastical journeys to the afterworld.

Horace was about to reach for the *Codex* when the outer door of his office slammed open. Mezim's voice rose for a moment as heavy footsteps trod across the floor and then fell quiet. Horace jumped up. He didn't get halfway to the door before it flew open to crack against the wall. A huge soldier, tulwar in hand, stood in the doorway. Startled, Horace began to reach for his *zoana* until he saw the royal livery of the Queen's Guard on the soldier's chest. As he let go of the power, the soldier moved aside as the queen strode past into the office.

Horace bowed, lowering his face to cover his shock at her dramatic entrance. "Good evening, Excellence."

"Have you seen the report, First Sword?"

Her voice was angry, almost raw, which added to his surprise. Although he'd heard her use that tone before, it had never been leveled at him before. "I received a lot of reports today, Excellence? Which one are you—?"

Her attack was so swift he didn't even have time to react. One moment he was talking, and the next he was thrown up against the wall behind his desk. A stiff wind scattered his papers across the room. Horace almost reached for his power, just to pry himself free, until he saw Lord Xantu and Lady Anshara enter the room behind the queen. He hung in the grasp of the invisible air fist holding him upright without struggling.

"The report," Byleth said, "from the governor of Sekhatun. The one detailing the *six* separate attacks in that region in the last two moons. Forty-seven of my soldiers have been killed and more than a hundred injured. Ambushed by rebel slaves, First Sword. The same slaves you are supposed to be bringing to heel. Instead, they are running wild across my lands. Even worse, they are setting slaves free wherever they strike. Do you understand how that makes me look?"

The fist of air tightened around his chest. Horace gritted his teeth against the pain. "I'm doing every—thing—I can."

"My nobles are anxious, First Sword. They want to see retribution for their loss of property. They want blood."

STORM AND STEEL

The pressure across his chest increased. Horace started to push the queen's power away, but then he noticed the presence in the back of his mind again, watching this incident unfold. He got the strange feeling it was . . . amused.

Byleth's delicate brows came together in a frown, faint lines creasing her forehead. She waved her hand, and the force holding Horace against the wall vanished. "No more excuses!"

Horace landed on his feet. His knees shook as he took a moment to catch his breath. "Yes, Excellence."

She beckoned over her shoulder with a finger. "By the way, this came for you today with the afternoon reports. I thought I would deliver it in person."

Lord Xantu carried in a wooden box. The queen crossed her arms over her chest as it was placed on his desk. "It's a gift," she said. "From the rebels."

The box was square, about a foot wide on each side, and made from some light wood like cedar or pine. Xantu flipped open a latch at the top, and one side of the box fell open. Horace scrambled back as the contents stared back at him. He turned aside and vomited into the corner, unable to get the sight of Ubar's severed head from his mind. Especially the eyes. Shiny like glass, they stabbed at him.

When he stopped heaving, Horace sat on the floor with his head in his hands. He couldn't bring himself to look at the box. "What happened?"

"Apparently Lord Ubar went to meet with the rebel leadership on a mission of peace. I don't know who gave him the idea such a mission was sanctioned by myself. In any case, they killed him and sent this back. What do you think that means, First Sword?"

Horace couldn't answer. He didn't want to believe Jirom would do such a thing. Ubar had been young and bright, the perfect emissary to carry his message. There must have been some miscommunication. The only other alternative was that he had made a grave mistake trying to reach an accord with the rebels.

"Pack your belongings, First Sword," Byleth said as she turned to the door. "My sources inform me that the rebels will strike for Sekhatun itself next. Tomorrow you leave to take care of this matter once and for all."

Lady Anshara gave Horace a curious look, as if she were trying to empathize with him but found the chasm between them too great to cross, before she followed the queen out of his office. The rest of the royal entourage filtered behind. Lord Xantu was the last to leave. He glanced at the box and said, "He deserved better than this."

Watching them go, Horace could only agree. *Yes, he did. He deserved the chance to grow up and experience life, perhaps have a family. Now all that is gone, eradicated with the stroke of a sword. And for what? It accomplished nothing. His death was meaningless.*

The box flew off his desk and shattered against the wall. The contents smashed into a pulpy red mass. Horace clamped down on the *zoana* burning through his veins, afraid he might truly lose control. Sharp pain seared through his skull.

Mezim poked his head in the door and then darted out again without a word.

Horace picked himself up. His head was pounding as if tiny hammers were working the inside of his temples. He spared a glance at the mess he'd made, at the red trails running down the wall, and left. Mezim stood by his desk in the outer room, his face pale.

"Go home," Horace said.

"Pardon, but I will stay. I have much work to complete before—"

"It can wait. We have a trip to prepare for."

"I overheard. I will make the necessary arrangements. May I ask, what should be done with Lord Ubar's remains?"

"I've made a mess of that, too. Have it cleaned up and burn whatever is left. Send a letter to his family. No, wait. I'll write it myself. You can send it by courier tomorrow before we leave."

"As you wish. I shall see you tomorrow at first light."

Horace left the office, with his guards trailing behind. Lost in his own thoughts, he kept his head down as he walked out of the palace. Though he didn't meet anyone's gaze as he left, he imagined he could feel their eyes upon him, weighing him down like chains. Or another collar.

CHAPTER THIRTEEN

The brown liquor swirled like river mud around the bottom of his glass. Horace sat alone with his thoughts in the parlor. A fish-shaped bronze lamp on the table illuminated the empty room, but there was nothing worth seeing. Faded carpets, furniture that had belonged to the manor's previous owner, dark niches in the walls—the remnants of another person's life left behind to molder in the dark.

Dharma entered the parlor on soft footsteps with another amphora and set it on the table. Horace finished his glass as she broke the seal on the jar. She made to pour, but he shook his head and told her to go back to bed. He fixed himself another glass, splashing a little of the plum brandy on the floor as he settled back in the chair.

After returning from the palace, he had ensconced himself here and started drinking to relieve the crushing pressure that hung over his head. He was certain he was finished at the royal court, having failed the queen, his only ally. And tomorrow he was being sent west to deal with a problem that had no solution. *That's not true, old boy! There is a solution! Blood, and lots of it. Rivers of blood spilt from rebel veins. Enough to wash the entire city clean of its sins and buy a queen enough time to launch her bid for the empire's highest prize.*

He wished he'd taken the queen's offer to go home months ago. *Maybe it's not too late? No, she's in no mood to do me any favors now.*

A roll of papyrus sat on the table between the lamp and the brandy jar. He wanted to write the letter to Ubar's family himself, rather than delegate it to a scribe. He owed them that much, at least. But how did you tell someone that their loved one, a young man barely old enough to be out on his own, was dead? And not just dead but murdered, all because he had been sent into a situation without understanding the danger. Should he write that he understood how they must feel? How could he? And yet, he did on some level. Perhaps even worse. He had lost a son, right before his eyes.

Jirom, I thought I knew you better than that. I believed we could work together to solve this problem. But now my hands are tied. I either try my best to stop you, or I lose everything.

He took another gulp from his glass, no longer tasting the brandy, only craving the oblivion it promised. He knew he would pay for it in the morning, but he'd gladly embrace the pain tomorrow if he could just escape the emptiness lurking in his heart for tonight.

The front door opened, and the guard stationed in the atrium murmured something. Horace slouched back in his chair, fighting against his first impulse, which was to rise and greet her.

She stood in the parlor doorway, facing him in the shadows. He imagined her features, drawn tight in condemnation. *She'll stand there a moment longer, and then she'll go upstairs to enclose herself in her room until the early hours of the morning. When I awake, she'll be gone again, just like a ghost floating in and out of my life.*

Alyra started to move, and he braced himself to be alone again, but then she was crossing the room. He swallowed the last splash in his glass as she stopped in front of him. Her hair was slightly tangled as if she'd been caught in a fierce wind. Her clothing was plain and simple with muted colors, unlike the bright, airy things she liked to wear during the daylight hours. Despite having just drunk himself into a mild stupor, his mouth was dry.

"I heard about Ubar."

Her voice broke through the haze hanging around his brain, threatening to shatter him into a thousand pieces, but he held it together. "I . . . I'm supposed to write his family, but I don't have the damnedest idea what to say."

"You should go to bed. You'll feel better in the morning."

He let out a long sigh. "I wish I could, but I keep thinking about the last time I saw him. He was giving me advice about the queen and other things. He was always helping me, Alyra. You know? And he never asked for anything."

"Sounds a lot like Lord Mulcibar."

Yes, Ubar had taken Mulcibar's place in his life, as both a teacher and a confidant. Even though he was younger, he had been so mature for his age, and so understanding. Now he was dead, just like the old man. *And I'm responsible for both their deaths. Maybe I didn't send Mulcibar to his doom, but his helping me surely played a part in his murder. Is this all I have to look forward to? Everyone that I care about dying?*

Looking up at Alyra, so beautiful in the lamplight, he wondered if she would be next. By the tightening around her eyes, he could tell she was hurting. He wanted to put his arms around her, but they remained by his sides as if tied down. Despite seeing her pain, echoing his own, Horace couldn't help himself from asking, "Where have you been?"

He tried to soften the question with "I've been worried," but he saw right away it didn't help.

"You look like a ghost, Horace. You need to take better care of yourself. All this stress isn't good for you."

"Now you care?"

"I'm tired. I'm going upstairs."

He jumped to his feet, swaying as a rush of blood flooded his brain. "No! I need to talk to you now. Tomorrow I'll be gone. . . ."

He clamped his mouth shut. He hadn't meant to reveal his special mission right away, hoping to work things out with her before he drove that wagon home. He kept talking to explain. "The queen is sending me to Sekhatun in the morning. I don't know when I'll be back."

Her eyebrows inched closer together as she regarded him. "I know."

He didn't know why that should surprise him. She always seemed to know more about the happenings at court than he did. "So were you going to just let me leave without saying anything?"

"I hadn't decided yet."

"Well, that's what you're best at, isn't it? Not deciding anything."

"If you're talking about us—"

"Of course I'm talking about us! What else is there to discuss? You've got one foot in the door here with me and the other planted in your precious network. It's obvious you can't or won't make a decision about where your priorities lie. What do your spymasters think about that?"

Alyra's eyes turned cold. One of her hands came up to rest on her hip. "Do you really want to know? Because up until now you've been happy to play house with me while blissfully ignoring what's going on around you. I told you that you were playing with fire, but you didn't want to listen."

"How can you stand there and say that? I've done nothing except shovel shit since the day I got here. For you, for the queen, for the court, for the rebels."

"That's the problem, Horace. You don't have the courage to choose a side. You want so badly to please everyone that you end up blundering into one catastrophe after another. *That's* why I wasn't sure if I wanted to talk to you, because I knew this would happen. You've been blaming yourself for the things you did right and rejoicing in the things you did wrong."

He threw his hands into the air, almost losing hold of his empty glass in the process. "What the blistering fuck is that supposed to mean?"

"What happened to Ubar was horrible, but you did the right thing by trying to negotiate with the slaves."

The pain in his chest went from hot and raw to icy cold. "How can you say that? I sent him to his death, all because I trusted a mob of murderous traitors more than the people who have helped me and given me a place in this city."

Alyra didn't move, but she seemed to be watching him from a greater distance, as if a gaping chasm had opened between them. "That's not you talking, Horace. That's her."

"Who? The queen? She's angry at me and she has every right to be. I should have listened to her and dealt with the rebels the right way from the beginning."

"How is that? With whips and wooden stakes? Is that the answer you've been seeking? Or is that what she wants? Think about it, Horace. You've been a slave. You should understand what the rebellion wants and why they won't quit until they get it."

"I thought I understood, until they sent me Ubar's head in a box."

Alyra fell silent, her face flushed, eyes dropping away. "I don't know why that happened, but you have to trust me—"

"No, I don't. I can't be sure who you're really trying help. Me, the slaves, or the people who sent you here to spy. But it's clear you don't care about what I'm trying to accomplish here."

She murmured something, too low for him to hear.

"You're so secretive," he continued. "I can't even talk to you anymore."

She lifted her eyes, which were moist with pent-up tears. "I can't talk to you either, because I don't know you anymore. You've changed."

"You've changed, too. We used to——"

Alyra left before he could finish his statement, marching out with swift strides back to the atrium and up the stairs.

Horace sighed, wishing she'd just avoided him from the start. He felt worse than before, even emptier inside, like a vast hole had opened inside him. He poured himself another brandy, not caring that some of it spilled over the rim of the glass and drenched the table. As he drank deep, he watched the liquor soak into the papyrus roll like a tide of brown blood.

Alyra got to the top of the stairs before her legs gave out, dropping her to her knees on the cold marble landing. Her sobs came in big, ragged gasps. She'd held on as long as she could in the parlor, but now her emotions crashed down beyond her control, dragging her down into a pit of misery. She hated the things she'd said to Horace but couldn't stop herself. She knew she was losing him to the queen, day by day. And now he was leaving Erugash to strike against the very people he'd once professed to want to help. It was the worst kind of betrayal.

Yet she couldn't deny her feelings. As much as she hated what he was doing, she still loved him. *Night was right all along. He knew Horace would be the end of my usefulness to the cause. Now, after all I've done, I have nothing left. I'm alone.*

With several shuddering breaths, she forced herself to her feet. She wiped her face as she hurried to her room. She couldn't stay here any longer. Every time she saw Horace it was like reopening a wound.

She went through her wardrobe, picking out the things she had to take with her. So many of the beautiful clothes she'd been given would have to stay. It was difficult to pack without knowing where she was going, so she took her sturdiest everyday clothes and sandals. Then she realized she had nothing to put them in, and the tears threatened to start falling again. A soft knock came from the door before Dharma entered with an unhappy expression. "Pardon, my lady. But we heard the master's voice, and . . . are you all right?"

Alyra nodded, and the young servant girl rushed into her arms. They hugged until their sobs settled, and then Alyra told the girl her problem. Dharma left and returned a few minutes later with a canvas bag. "Cook uses this when she goes to market. I cleaned it, but it still smells a little of barley."

"It's fine." Alyra took the bag and started filling it with her possessions. "I'm sorry I have to leave like this, but . . . well, I just can't stay."

"I understand, my lady. We all do. We know it's been difficult for you and the master. We'd hoped you two might hop a broom together, but Cook says sometimes these things just don't work out."

Alyra nodded, not really wanting to talk about it. "Please take care of yourself and . . . him."

"I will, my lady."

"Alyra. Please, call me Alyra."

"Yes, ma'am. You take care, too. And don't fret about the master. We'll keep him safe."

Alyra smiled through her heartache. "I know you will." She went to her vanity and took the things she needed—a comb, two brushes, a hand mirror, and a pouch of hair ties. She picked up the carving of a sea turtle Horace had given her. Then she put it back down and took up her bag. After another hug, she sent Dharma away.

Alone once more, Alyra set the bag on the floor and reached under her bed. She pulled out the leather satchel that held the tools of her trade. She also felt something else and pulled out a small teakwood box she didn't recognize. Goosebumps rose up and down her arms as she placed the box on her bed, knowing what this had to be. She opened it with baited breath, hoping she was wrong, and exhaled with a noisy sigh when she was not.

A dagger rested on a bed of purple silk. The weapon was gorgeous, the lamplight shimmering along its silver blade. The handle was white ivory carved to resemble a prowling jungle cat. A small scroll bound in red ribbon sat beside the dagger. Her instructions, no doubt, for a mission she didn't want to take. *But this is my last chance to do right by the network and possibly alter the fate of the empire.*

She closed the box and put it inside her bag along with her tools, feeling the added burden as she slung it over her shoulder. After one last look around the room, she left.

The household staff waited at the bottom of the stairs. Alyra bit her bottom lip to keep it from trembling as they quietly spoke their farewells. She silently cursed Dharma's loose tongue even as she melted into one embrace after another. Even Harxes gave her a hearty squeeze as he pressed a small leather purse into her hand. Feeling the coins inside, she tried to give it back. "No, I couldn't. I'm fine, really."

"Shhhh," he shushed her. "Take it, my lady."

She kept her gaze focused straight ahead as she passed the parlor entrance. She thought she heard something from within. Perhaps a glass setting down on a table. Then she was at the front door. Gurita opened it for her. Head down, she left the manor.

Horace reached for the amphora as he heard the front door close. Alyra was gone, possibly for good. He could have tried to stop her. There were a thousand things he might have said to change her mind. Yet he'd chosen to sit in his chair and finish his brandy instead. *She made her choice. I never should have believed she could love me. We were too different, and both of us too damned stubborn to change. Why should I choose between her and Byleth? I never asked her to choose. No, she runs off whenever she wants to pursue her mission, but I'm stuck here, cleaning up the mess.*

He tipped the jar and frowned when only a trickle rolled out into his glass. He sighed, not wanting this drunk to leave him, especially now. In fact, he might just stay here all night and keep at it. What was the point in sobering up? He knew what awaited him when the mystical spell of the liquor left him. A world of pain, a life without love or friendship. He pictured the rest of his days as one long parade of disappointments and failures until, at last, he succumbed to one of his many enemies. There would be no one to remember him fondly, no loving family to visit his grave.

He was considering a call to Harxes for another jar when a light itch nagged at the back of his head. He tried to brush it away, but the feeling only intensified. *It's just the brandy. It'll go away.*

Frowning at the traitorous tumbler, he set it down on top of an unlit candle beside the door and went out into the atrium. There was no one there except Gurita standing watch. Horace saluted him with a pleasant chuckle and looked around, wondering why he'd come out here. Then the tickle returned at the nape of his neck. It seemed to want something, and that something was above him. *Perhaps the Prophet is calling me home. Wouldn't that serve Alyra right? Me up and dying on the night she leaves me. Oh, to see her face when she finds out. She'd know right away what a mistake she made. Or maybe not. The woman is as stubborn as a . . . as a . . .*

He stumbled up the stairs, following the lure of the itch that refused to leave him alone. The steps were trickier to navigate than he remembered, but holding tight to the bannister he eventually reached the top. He heard someone moving around downstairs. *Probably Cook up late. Or Harxes in the larder doing a midnight tally of the house stores. He's a good man. Better than I deserve, like Mezim. Where would I be without them? I should pay them more. Yes! Starting tomorrow they both get double wages! Not just them. All my servants! Because they're more than just servants. They are my family, the only family I've got.*

He pushed open the door to the roof. Like many of the homes in Erugash, his had a flat top. The stars wheeled overhead, brighter than he could remember seeing in a long time. Not since he was a boy and his father had taken him boating out on the bay. That night the stars had seemed like magical companions. Their reflections in the inky water had made it seem like they were sailing across the sky even as the familiar constellations floated overhead. The itch pulled his gaze directly to the queen's palace, rising like a blade of a golden dagger from the city's heart.

Horace noticed, distantly, his heart was beating faster. A film had formed over his eyes, blurring the starlight into a vast pale haze. A cool feeling enveloped his right hand. He looked down to see he was holding the orb.

It glowed, filling the rooftop with a deep red-gold brilliance. The swirling patterns he'd seen before were more evident now beneath its surface. Horace leaned closer to watch the play of light and shadow inside the sphere. The itch on his neck vanished, and so too did the headache that had been plaguing him all night. He blinked, realizing he was stone-sober all of a sudden, and a cold tingle ran down his spine. *What in the names of the saints is happening to me?*

The manor shuddered, and the orb nearly fell out of his grasp. Horace clutched it to his chest with one hand while fighting to maintain his balance. Then he felt the swell of power, like a chaos storm had erupted right above him. His teeth rattled as the shaking settled. Horace went to the southern edge of the roof and looked down into the courtyard, half-expecting to see a cadre of robed sorcerers outside his door. There was nothing to see except swaying tree branches, dappled with moonlight. Yet in his head he imagined a vast cyclone of lights swirling above the city.

No, not above the city, he realized. It came from underneath, deep down in the ground. He suddenly felt sick to his stomach.

Only stumbling a little, he went back inside to find a drink.

"This reminds me of that time we got conned into protecting that shithole on the border of Haran." Three Moons swatted at an insect buzzing around his head. "What was it called? Poleez or something like that. You remember we were stuck inside those walls with that urban militia. We hated each other's guts something fierce. Then most of our crew came down with a flux, just shitting and puking their guts out for days. And that's when the raiders decided to hit the town, of course. Had us surrounded for two whole days. We nearly ended up with our heads on sticks before we broke out of there."

Jirom ducked under a low branch, heavy with moss, and stepped over a pool of murky water. They marched at the tail of the rebel column through the marsh. They had almost arrived back at the main camp. The hills towered before them, giant masses huddled against the night sky. Moonlight cast moving shadows through the trees.

"It was three days, not two," he said. "And I remember you were so drunk when the final attack came that you almost couldn't tell us from the enemy."

"Maybe. Who can say? In any case, this situation is just like that."

"You're drunk again?"

"Sadly, no. I ran out of my homebrew two days ago, and none of these louts will share. But stop changing the subject. This situation—us and these escaped slaves—it's just the same. We're stuck with allies we can't trust and surrounded by an enemy thirsty for blood. Whatever way we turn, it's gonna get messy."

Jirom didn't disagree with the assessment. His thoughts had been clouded with visions of Lord Ubar's murder, of the knowledge that he and Emanon were still outsiders. When he saw Neskarig get up from his blankets and hurry off into the trees alone, he had been compelled to follow. And what he'd discovered had shaken his faith. The admiration he'd felt for the rebel leadership was gone, replaced by a cold fury. Emanon had been right.

The captains spoke little on the return journey to the gathering. The General kept a close watch over him and Emanon. Jirom got the impression Neskarig had argued for their executions, along with Lord Ubar's, and it was possibly due to Ramagesh's voice that they were still alive.

They arrived at the northern ridge of the hidden basin just before nightfall. Passing through the picket of sentries on the short climb, Jirom and Three Moons reached the summit. If anything, it looked like more campfires burned below than when they had left. Several bonfires dotted the vast bowl, each surrounded by a crowd of people. The sounds of drums and singing spilled out into the night.

As they entered the camp, Ramagesh told several fighters to seek out the other captains. "We are meeting." He looked back at Emanon and Jirom. "Now. We have much to discuss."

Emanon sighed under his breath. "Sounds like it's going to be a long night."

"Watch your back," Jirom told him.

"You're not going?"

Jirom watched Ramagesh stalk away. "Better if I don't. I'll get the band ready to travel while you're gone. Best if we leave before daybreak."

"Aye. Round up our boys. I want them sober and ready to march."

They parted ways, with Emanon heading toward the council area and Jirom going south along the eastern ridge. He'd wanted to say something to Emanon before they split up but hadn't been sure how to put it into words. Now the moment had passed.

Striding under the drooping branches of the mangrove trees with Three Moons, Jirom watched the throngs of reveling former slaves and wondered if Emanon and he were going to last. It wasn't easy finding a man he could trust with his feelings, someone he could love and respect in a world that seemed to value neither. He cared for Emanon, deeply, but the past few days had made him question how much of that love was returned.

He tried to put Emanon out of his mind as they approached their band's camp. The flames of a feeble fire cast a ruddy glow over the faces of seven men sitting around the hearth.

"Anyone got anything to drink?" Three Moons asked.

The men stood up as they arrived, and a few more faces peeked out of the lean-tos. Longar tossed a bulging skin to Three Moons.

"Where is everyone?" Jirom asked. He only counted two dozen heads in all.

"Mahir and Jerkul took out a few to hunt," a burly Nemedian slave replied. They called him Red Ox. There was another heavyset northern rebel called Black Ox in their band, but Jirom didn't see him. "And a couple are out at the latrines."

"The rest left," Longar said.

"Left? For where?"

"They went off to join some of the larger bands." Longar pointed his thumb to the west, toward the council area. "Mostly the newer recruits, from what I could tell."

Jirom scanned the faces around him. They were mainly fighters who had been with Emanon since the army camp or longer. Even counting the hunting party, they had lost at least a score of fighters.

"That's not the worst of it," Partha said. He looked awful, as if he hadn't slept in days. "A group of Ramagesh's men came by and tried to take the treasure boxes."

Jirom felt his jaws clench into hard knots.

"Weren't nothing we could do 'bout it," Partha said. "Until the sellswords came over to back us up. Then the bravos slunk away with their tails tucked."

Captain Ovar shrugged as he came over. "We weren't about to let someone make off with our pay chest, so we put on a little show of force."

Jirom nodded, but the news added to the fury building inside him, feeding on his frustrations like they were dry kindling.

"Ah, shit," Three Moons muttered, lowering the skin's nozzle from his mouth. "I know that look."

Jirom glanced at Longar. "How long ago did Jerkul's hunting party leave?"

"Before midday. We were expecting them back soon."

"It can't be helped."

"What can't?" Partha asked, looking around.

"Everybody get your best killing weapon," Jirom said. "Red Ox, you stay with Partha to guard the money boxes. If anyone tries to come for them, split their skull open. Everyone else with me."

"Mind if we tag along?" Captain Ovar asked.

"No, but I'm doing the talking." When Ovar nodded in response, Jirom looked to Longar. "Make us a path to the council fire. Oh, and Three Moons . . ."

The sorcerer sighed as if he knew what was coming. "Aye?"

"Brew up something nasty."

Jirom started walking. No, he was *marching* like he was going off to war. Longar moved people out of the way, heading straight toward the large bonfire raging against the foot of the central hill. Jirom didn't bother checking behind to see how many of the rebels were following.

People noticed them pushing through the crowd. By the time they strode up to the row of totems, the council's guardians were waiting. The fighters stood in a row behind the carved fetish-woven poles with their spears held out. Longar glanced back when he arrived at the barrier, and Jirom gave a firm nod. A cry went up as Longar shoved a spear aside and jammed the heel of his palm into the soldier's face, shattering his nose in a crunching spatter of blood. Another spearman tried to swing his weapon at the scout's back, but Jirom caught the weapon with one hand and flattened its wielder with a clout to the forehead with his bare fist.

Before the rest of the sentries could react, Three Moons stepped forward and growled at them. A stream of fluttering black shapes poured from the warlock's open mouth, flapping leathery wings. Bats. Hundreds of them, screeching as they swarmed over the sentries. Slapping at the flying creatures, the council guardians were overrun by Jirom's band of fighters. Jirom didn't pause to watch, but marched toward the bonfire.

The captains were all standing as he advanced. Emanon frowned in clear confusion, but Jirom could tell by his stance—his knees bent slightly with one foot a bit farther back than the other, like a cat ready to pounce—that his captain was ready to react if necessary.

Neskarig glared from his position at Ramagesh's right side. "You break the peace of this gathering, Red-Blade! Before the eyes of the gods and m—"

"Shut up," Jirom growled. "I know you're in league with the queen of Erugash."

Questions broke out among some of the captains, but others remained silent, and Jirom marked them in his mind. They were Ramagesh's chief supporters, which didn't surprise him. This entire assembly had been devised to channel power into the hands of these individuals.

Ramagesh raised a hand, and the talking quieted. "I do not know what you think you heard, but now is not the time. We're finalizing our plans to attack Sekha—"

Jirom cut him off. "To the lowest hell with your plans. We're going to settle this now."

He told them all how he had stalked after Neskarig the night of Ubar's murder, how he had seen the General meet with two agents of the queen. The memory still burned bright in his mind, every word seared into his consciousness.

"Her Majesty sends her appreciation," the first agent had said in fine

Akeshian, "for your excellent work. The death of Lord Ubar serves our purpose. And now you have your cohorts precisely where we want them, eh?"

"And we shall have what was promised," the General had replied. "Do not try to play us for fools."

"Of course." The second agent had been a woman. Her voice was even more cultured than her partner's, as smooth as eastern silk. "You and Captain Ramagesh shall have fine estates in the countryside, with slaves and bodyguards—"

"And horses, you said." Jirom looked over at the General, who stood in Ramagesh's shadow. "You demanded a stable of horses. All in exchange for killing the rebellion."

Ramagesh smiled, though the expression didn't extend to his eyes, which were focused with hard intensity. "Where is your proof? Do you expect this council to simply accept your lies?"

Jirom drew his sword. "This is my proof. I challenge your right to rule."

Shouts called out from beyond the totems where a crowd had gathered to watch. Captain Ovar's mercs spread out in front of the mob, making sure that no one interfered. Emanon stood apart from the rest of the rebel captains, his hands by his sides.

Neskarig came up beside Ramagesh. "Just order our fighters to kill them all and be done with it."

Jirom adjusted his grip on the *assurana*'s hilt. His heart beat hard and steady, the blood thrumming in his ears. "Take the coward's path if you want. Let every man and woman see the fear in your heart."

Ramagesh's face hardened into a scowl. He reached behind him, and Smerdis hurried forward to put the war-mace in his hand.

"Think!" Neskarig hissed at him. "Order an attack and wipe them out!"

Ramagesh shoved the General away and raised his weapon over his head. The knobbed iron ball at the end of the thick handle gleamed black in the firelight. "Red-Blade, I will give you one last chance to—"

"Save your breath," Jirom said. The din of the people crowded around the council area was rising higher like the rumble of an earthquake. "You don't have many left."

With a glower, Ramagesh advanced on heavy footsteps. Jirom didn't move. He didn't raise his sword or strike a martial stance. He simply stood there as the rebel leader came toward him. Ramagesh's steps quickened as he approached, swinging his war-mace. At the apex of his downward strike, Jirom burst into action. He slid to his left, out of the path of the falling weapon. At the same time, he brought up his sword in an upward diagonal slash. He expected to feel the bite of steel into leather and flesh, but Ramagesh rotated away at the last instant, following the momentum of his swing. Jirom took his sword in both hands, preparing to make a horizontal cut into Ramagesh's back, but the rebel leader completed his turn out of range. The war-mace swung again, this time coming at a flatter angle. Jirom stepped back to avoid it, gauging his opponent with every move. With a hefty weapon like a two-handed mace, he expected Ramagesh to need significant time to recover after each swing, but the rebel leader wielded the massive weapon as if it were no heavier than a cane. Ramagesh reversed his weapon's course and brought the broad head around again. Jirom, caught in mid-step, couldn't duck away in time, so he shifted the *assurana* sword into the mace's path.

A jarring clang resounded as the two weapons collided. Sharp vibrations shot up Jirom's hands, numbing both wrists. He half-expected his sword to be bent by the powerful blow, but the blade retained its crescent shape. Ramagesh's brows rose as he staggered back. His breath coming in deep grasps, he lifted the war-mace into a guard position. Jirom forced himself to smile, an old trick from the arena. When your opponent holds back, mock him into making a mistake.

"Kill him!"

Jirom didn't know who the encouraging shout came from and tried to block out the noise. *This is no different than the arena. Just imagine that Thraxes is watching in the stands, waiting for you to win him a fat purse. Damn, I wished I'd killed that son of a whore when I had the chance!*

He deflected another swing of the mace, but this one came low and without much force behind it. Ramagesh was tiring. *Or he wants me to think he's tired. Let's find out.*

Jirom brought his sword up and around in a circular cut. Although the technique was a bit of flourish, it was easy to defend against. Ramagesh backed away a couple steps and kept his mace held before him. Jirom advanced with a high-to-low cut, which also fell short as Ramagesh continued to retreat. Some of the calls from the crowd were turning into jeers. Jirom raised his sword overhead for another downward swing but froze as Ramagesh charged forward, jabbing his war-mace ahead of him like a battering ram. The iron ball caught Jirom squarely in the chest, driving the air from his lungs and shoving him back several steps. Loose earth flew as he tried to maintain his balance, but Ramagesh didn't allow him time to set his feet. The rebel leader followed up with a powerful haymaker. Jirom fought to draw in a breath as the heavy iron ball sailed toward his head. He felt sluggish, his legs too heavy to evade the blow, his arms too slow to block it. Swaying back, he felt the wind of the mace's passage, just inches from ripping off his face.

Now Ramagesh was the one smiling as he brought his weapon up and over for the final attack. Jirom's heart hammered against the inside of his rib cage. He saw death approaching as Ramagesh prepared to bring down his war-mace. He hesitated a moment, just a bare instant, as Jirom smiled and then winked. Replying with a scowl, Ramagesh stepped forward to lend his body's weight to the attack. Jirom leaned forward, and his smiled widened as the point of his sword slipped into Ramagesh's knee joint, slicing through the tendons below the kneecap. He twisted the blade sideways and ripped it out, cutting through the outer side of the joint. The blade emerged, followed by a string of mangled sinews dripping blood.

Ramagesh's scream was a garbled roar as he collapsed, his right leg folding uselessly beneath him. The war-mace thunked on the ground beside him. Jirom placed the tip of his *assurana* to his opponent's throat. "You fought well. Now you will die well."

Struggling to contain his agony, Ramagesh lifted his chin. The crowd was silent. Jirom didn't draw it out. He raised his sword and brought it down sharply, and Ramagesh's head joined his mace on the ground.

The gathered captains stood silent. A few shared meaningful looks, but none spoke up. *Dogs, every one of them. What will they do now that their pack leader is slain?*

"No!" Neskarig took a step toward Ramagesh's corpse. "Do you know what you've done? You've damned us all!" He turned to face the captains. "Why are you all just standing there? Ramagesh was our best hope to defeat the Akeshians. Now he's dead because of this foreign barbarian!"

Smerdis nodded to Rurtimo Lom and the couple other captains that Jirom had marked as Ramagesh's chief lieutenants. They fingered their weapons as if gathering their courage. Jirom held his sword by his side. His blood coursed hot and wild through his veins. Some part of him wanted to kill them all. But he held back, not wanting the bloodlust to take control. *Let them make the first move.*

Neskarig shouted at the captains, "Kill him! We'll strike him down togeth—!"

The General gasped, unable to finish his words as he twisted around. The shaft of a spear protruded from between his shoulders.

"That's enough of that," Emanon said as he lowered his throwing arm.

Jirom put on his fiercest glare. "I name Emanon the new leader of this council. Anyone care to challenge that?"

None of the assembled captains said anything, which Jirom chose to take as compliance. Emanon looked at him for several seconds, his face unreadable. Then he faced the rest of the council. "Anyone who wants to leave can go. But if you're still here at sunrise tomorrow, that means you and your men are with us. We'll meet tomorrow to discuss . . . the future. Until then, get out of my sight."

The captains scattered into the crowd. Men came to take away the bodies of Ramagesh and Neskarig as the onlookers dispersed back to their campfires. Jirom saw a renewed respect in some of their eyes as they turned away, but he also heard comments of discontent. He estimated they would lose three-fourths of the fighters come the dawn. Maybe more.

Emanon sat down by the abandoned bonfire. He looked like Jirom felt—exhausted, frustrated, and unsure what to do next. Jirom cleaned his sword and put it away as he went over to sit beside his captain.

"You didn't have to do that. Name me the leader. You could have kept that for yourself. Gods know, these men would rather follow you than me."

"That's not true," Jirom said. "I think most would of them would prefer we were both dead."

Emanon grinned the wolfish smile that Jirom loved, halfway between a snarl and a laugh. "You're probably right. So what do we do now?"

"That's what I was going to ask you, O Great Leader."

Emanon's gaze wandered over to the bloodstained ground where Ramagesh had died. "He's wasn't all wrong, you know."

"You defending him now? Sooner or later, he would have had you killed."

"I'm not defending his methods, but he had a sharp mind for strategy. We still have the intelligence on Sekhatun, and the other captains have already agreed to the attack."

"The queen has laid a trap for us there."

"Aye, but a trap is only a trap if the prey doesn't suspect it. And we do. Moreover, with Erugash focused on Omikur and the army from Nisus, this could be our best chance to strike a real blow."

Jirom looked down at his hands, sticky with blood. "Those that decide to stay, which won't be many. Once they leave, we'll be lucky to field two hundred men. Not enough to assault a town that size, even if they didn't know we were coming."

"You let me worry about that, all right?"

"Sure, Em. Whatever you want."

"What's that mean?"

Jirom wiped his fingers on the ground. "It feels like we're drifting apart, and all this trouble with the other bands hasn't helped. I don't know what to do about it."

Emanon reached over to squeeze his forearm. "You need me to say it? I need you. More than ever. You're my rock. When things are insane all around me, you're the only one I can count on."

Jirom looked into his eyes. "So I'm a rock, huh?"

"Hey, I didn't mean it to sound like—"

Jirom smiled and winked. "I know what you meant."

Emanon laughed as he leaned over to offer his lips. Jirom hesitated a moment. He looked around the encampment. A dozen of his fighters crouched under the totems, keeping watch alongside Captain Ovar's mercs, but no one seemed to be watching them. *To hells with it. I love him, and anyone who can't deal with that can go burn.*

Jirom went in for a kiss and lost himself in the tenderness that Emanon usually only displayed when they were alone. When he leaned back, they both took deep breaths.

"So what do you think?" the new rebel leader asked.

"I think we should find an empty tent and try that kiss again."

Emanon shoved him playfully. "I mean about the attack. Your approval will go far with the others."

"I don't know about that, but I'm with you. Good or bad, I'm not leaving your side."

Emanon stood up and offered his hand. "Then let's go find that tent and lose some of these clothes."

"I thought you were tired."

Emanon arched one eyebrow. His lupine grin was back. "Suddenly, not so much."

CHAPTER FOURTEEN

The desert was a vast sea of gold and brown. Long ago this land might have been thriving grassland or even a great forest before the sands had come to cover everything. Occasional dust devils spun across the dunes like elemental children at play. Squinting down at the barren landscape sailing past far below, Horace wondered what dead civilizations lay beneath its bleached sands. *And someday the Akeshian Empire might be one of them, destined to be forgotten by the annals of distant history.*

The Typhon River was a fat brown serpent along the southern horizon, glinting in the morning light. Its banks overflowed on both sides to cover hundreds of square miles of farmland. Come spring the waters would recede, and workers would rush to plant the next season's crops in the newly silted fields, and the cycle would begin again.

They'd left Erugash with the rising sun onboard one of the queen's flying vessels. When he first stepped onto the ship, he'd felt a pang of anxiety as memories of the crash gripped him, but he'd managed to put them aside. Once they set off, the exhilaration of flight had washed his concerns away. They headed northwest, straight as an eagle's flight, over fields and scrubland and long stretches of open desert.

He couldn't help comparing this trip to his excursion to Omikur. Every time he turned around, he expected to see Byleth or Lord Mulcibar standing behind him. But the only people accompanying him were soldiers. A full company of the queen's finest. And he was expected to use them to enforce Her Excellence's wishes, no matter how he felt about it. *You took the post. Now you have to perform the duty. Or take the other route.*

He placed a hand on the hilt of the sword at his side. His sword now, though it still felt alien to him, like wearing another man's shoes. He imagined what its oiled blade would feel like sliding into his stomach, ripping him open as a sacrifice to erase his obligation.

He shook his head to clear it. His skull felt three sizes too big today.

Thankfully, his servants had prepared everything for him, with Mezim meeting him at the palace with the day's reports. Standing at the bow of the flying ship, his secretary appeared to have recovered from Horace's outburst the day before. *He's probably having the time of his life. I should apologize for my behavior. Maybe when I feel a little better.*

It didn't improve his mood that he was still haunted by his fight with Alyra. Recent events had him all mixed up inside. The recovery of Mulcibar's corpse. His new duties as First Sword. Ubar's death. Alyra's mysterious absences. He could see it clearly now, but he didn't know what he could've done to create a different outcome. He couldn't seem to please anyone. *Or protect them either.*

A shout from the bow made him look over. Fingers pointed ahead to a brown smudge on the horizon. Sekhatun. From all the reports of rebel attacks, he almost expected to find it under siege, but there were no outward signs of trouble. In fact, it appeared much the same as the last time he'd seen it, arriving at the tail end of a slave coffle.

The sight of the town's walls filled him with both relief that the journey was nearly over and regret. He had brought the letter to Lord Ubar's family with him. He didn't know whether he could summon the courage to deliver it in person or have Mezim handle it. He imagined what they might say to him, and how he'd respond, but there were no words to soothe such a hurt.

He tugged on the sleeves of his tunic, dark purple to match his skirt. He'd chosen to wear the queen's colors today, hoping it would send the right message to the town, that perhaps they might see the First Sword of Erugash instead of an anxious, pale-skinned foreign devil. He wasn't holding out much hope.

Mezim came back with his leather valise. "Master, do you wish to see the dispatches before we land?"

"No. Later."

The secretary gave a short bow and started to leave, but Horace halted him. "Wait. I'm sorry about yesterday. I didn't mean to frighten you."

"There is no need to apologize. You were understandably vexed by the unfortunate demise of Lord Ubar. I myself felt tremendous sorrow."

Mezim bowed again and backed away as the ship's captain approached with heavy strides. A former legionnaire, Captain Muranu had retired from service with a rank of regiment commander and parlayed his status into a captaincy in the queen's air service. They'd spoken only briefly during the journey, but by his stern gaze and obvious love of sailing, Horace guessed the captain would have made a fine naval commander if not for his self-professed terror of the open sea. Considering the great fall beneath them, Horace thought the man must be insane.

Captain Muranu held out a white tube capped with silver at both ends. "For you, your lordship. My instructions were to hand it over as we arrived."

As the captain excused himself to prepare the ship for landing, Horace examined the tube. The silver caps were sealed in red wax and stamped with the royal sigil. Inside was a letter written in the queen's own hand. He read through it quickly, his blood cooling with each line until he got to the bottom where she had signed it simply, "Your Queen."

When Horace finished reading, he handed it over to his secretary.

"Her Majesty sounds . . . ah, concerned, Master."

Horace grunted. Concerned wasn't the word for it. Byleth was angry, bordering on irate. He could almost feel her wrath coming through the document. It said, in so many words, that she was unhappy with his performance as her First Sword, and that he'd better make up for it now. The threat was implied, thankfully. The letter went on to reassert that Sekhatun was a place she had to hold or else lose the entire western half of her realm. As such, he was commanded to defend it to his last breath, and so on. In essence, he had to succeed or die. Her final line had been the most confusing. After the lengthy harangue, she ended it by saying she had faith in him in this, "her time of direst need."

The pressure is getting to her, the same as me. I guess we're in this together, though that doesn't make me feel any better. I don't know if I can do this. I didn't like the way she said it, but Alyra was right. I understand what these slaves are fighting for. If I can't find a solution everyone can live with, then what?

The ship touched down beside the roof of the central palace. It was odd returning as an official emissary. He felt almost like a deceiver masquerading as a nobleman.

STORM AND STEEL

The gangplank was extended between the vessel and rooftop, where stood a party of men. The wind whipped their long robes, all except for man standing in the forefront who wore a military uniform with numerous gold hashes on his shoulder.

Horace was the first to disembark along with the officers of his detachment. The welcoming party came forward to greet him.

"This is a great honor, First Sword," said the man in the uniform. "I am Governor Arakhu il'Huwanu."

The governor's shaved head gleamed with a light sheen of oil. His eyebrows were thick and dark, almost touching over his protruding nose. He made a short bow that the others in the party emulated.

Horace bowed back to them. "I am honored by your greeting."

Governor Arakhu introduced the rest of his group, who turned out to be the town's council of elders. Horace repeated how pleased he was to be there several times, even though he didn't exactly feel it, until the governor invited him to accompany them inside for a reception in his honor.

Horace instructed Mezim to assemble their luggage and selected four of the Queen's Guard to stay with him as his personal guard, sending the rest to the local militia barracks. Then Horace followed after the welcoming party. He spared only a single glance back at the ship before he descended a flight of stairs into the interior of the building. Captain Muranu stood at the middeck, watching him go. *He's probably wondering how long before I make a mess of everything.*

Nodding to the ship's captain, Horace went down the stairs.

They arrived at the large, magically cooled room on the top floor where he had first met Lord Isiratu. Even as he was greeted by more old men in robes, Horace couldn't help from looking to the center of the floor where he had grappled with Ubar's father. It seemed like a lifetime ago.

The governor escorted him around the reception, introducing each person by name. Their remarks were brief and polite, even deferential, but they weren't quite welcoming, as if there were an unseen barrier that they dared not cross. All except for Arakhu, who appeared genuinely glad to have him there.

The last in the greeting line was a man a few years younger than Horace.

Stocky for a youth, though not very tall, he wore his hair slicked back into a queue, and his clothing was of the highest quality. Governor Arakhu bowed to the young man and received a nod in response. "May I present Master Naram of House Nipthuras."

Horace had heard that family name before. Then he remembered with a chill. It was Isiratu's clan. *But Ubar was his only legal son. So this must be his . . . nephew?*

"Ah," he fumbled for the correct greeting. "It is my honor to make your acquaintance."

He almost added "your lordship" at the end of his greeting but then recalled the Nipthuras clan had been stripped of its nobility because of Isiratu's action.

The younger man bent from the waist in a miniscule bow. "I greet you, First Sword of Erugash."

Horace hadn't spent enough time among Akeshians to read the intricacies of their facial expressions, so he couldn't tell what lay behind the man's neutral features, but he imagined it must be pure hatred. It made for an awkward meeting. Fortunately, the governor steered him away after another bow to Naram, and Horace tried to put it out of his mind. Mezim brought him a cup of wine, which he sipped to wet his tongue.

"I've been wondering," Horace said, "why the queen didn't select a member of Lord Isiratu's family to take over his position."

"Who can guess the mind of a goddess such Her Highness, the Great Queen of Erugash, may she reign forever? No, simple folk such as we—pardon me, I do not include you—can only hear and obey. I am honored by Her Highness's trust and wish that her holy ancestors continue to shine their light on our good country forever."

"Uh, yes." Horace followed the governor past another group of old men, all of whom bowed and smiled as if meeting him were the best thing to ever happen to them.

They certainly weren't so friendly a few months ago. I doubt they even realize I'm the same crazy slave who attacked their former lord and almost got himself executed.

"So," Horace continued, "you're aware of my mission here?"

STORM AND STEEL

"Of course! You have been sent to deliver us from the odious threat of this uprising. Our people are very concerned. No one is safe outside the town walls. And . . ." He lowered his voice to a conspiratorial whisper. "I've even heard there are rebellious elements inside the town as well, hiding among us. Do you see my dilemma? How can we defend against what cannot be seen? But now you are here to deliver us to safety!"

As if on cue, the assembly clapped vigorously at these words. Horace wanted to find a hole in the floor and crawl inside, though he smiled as if he were enjoying the attention.

"Forgive me," Governor Arakhu said. "I have several duties to attend. Might I suggest that your lordship take my quarters for himself? They are most comfortable."

"No, I couldn't do that."

They walked together, out of the large chamber and down a wide hallway decorated with thousands of tiny colorful tiles.

"Please, I insist. You will tell Her Highness, may her beauty bless us for ten thousand generations, that we are completely loyal, lending you every assistance, yes?"

Horace found himself agreeing. "Of course. You've been . . . very helpful."

The governor smiled, showing his bright, even teeth. "Your lordship is too kind. Please take your ease and rest after your long journey."

"Actually, if you don't mind, I would rather meet with your militia commander about the town's defense."

"Of course. Perhaps after supper? You will dine with me, naturally. I am most eager to hear of your plan to protect our town from these rapacious rebels."

"All right." Horace winced as he found himself agreeing. "That would be fine, I suppose."

"Very good. My servants will come for you when all is ready."

They stopped at a red door trimmed in brass accents, which a servant opened with a bowed head. Inside was sumptuous chamber with pale hardwood flooring, silken wall hangings, and a bed large enough to fit a family of six. The governor bowed and left.

After telling Mezim and his guards to remain outside, Horace approached the massive bed but didn't sit down. It felt odd to stay in his host's room, with all his personal effects still here. Horace went over to sit in a chair beside a tall window. Although he hadn't done much except stand all day, he was tired. The now-familiar ache had returned behind his eyes, stretching from temple to temple.

He closed his eyes and enjoyed the cool breeze blowing in from the window. *I'll just rest for a couple minutes.*

Horace sat up with a start as a heavy hand knocked at his door. He had the vague sense they had been knocking for several seconds before he heard it. "Yes! One moment, please."

His mouth was dry, as if he'd been sleeping with it open. His sword was digging into his side. Wiping his lips with the back of a hand to make sure there was no drool, he answered the door.

Mezim stood outside with the bodyguards. And not just the four men Horace had selected for his escort. The corridor outside his door was filled with at least thirty men-at-arms, all standing at strict attention.

Mezim peeked inside the room as if expecting to see someone else. "It is time for your dinner engagement. May I enter?"

Horace nodded, and his secretary swept inside, closing the door behind him. "Why are there so many soldiers out there?" Horace asked.

"Governor Arakhu assigned them to your personal detail, Master. Judging by his behavior, I would guess the governor is extremely concerned for your well-being."

Horace didn't like the way that sounded, but he supposed he couldn't insult his host by refusing the extra protection. Mezim got to work. In seconds, he had Horace's luggage open and selected a fresh tunic of green silk.

"Who are we going to see again?" Horace asked. His mind was still a little fuzzy. He couldn't believe he'd fallen asleep.

"The governor and several members of the town council." Mezim made several swipes at Horace's hair with a comb before giving up. "They await you downstairs."

"Fine, fine."

STORM AND STEEL

Horace followed Mezim out into the corridor, the guardsmen falling in behind them. The tromp of their nailed boots reverberated off the walls.

"I have the latest figures and analysis of the town, Master," Mezim said as they turned a corner.

"Can you boil it down to the basics?"

Mezim paged through a sheaf of papers from his valise. "In short, Sekhatun is not adequately prepared for a protracted siege. The walls encircle the entire town, but they are old and not in the best repair. There are numerous places where an enemy with the right equipment—catapults and the like—could make a breach with relative ease."

"How did you discover that?"

"I spoke with an engineer with the royal garrison, Master."

"All right. How does the garrison look?"

"Not good, I'm afraid. There aren't enough soldiers to man the entire length of the walls. Even if citizens are conscripted, the armories don't have enough weapons or armor to equip them."

Horace didn't like the news, but he supposed it could be worse. "Is that all?"

"Not quite, Master. Although the region is bountiful, not enough stores have been put aside. My estimate of the current supply is that the town could feed itself for one week. Possibly two if stringent methods are applied, although that brings the added risk of poor nutrition, which would likely breed illness among the population. Which would—"

Horace put up a hand to stop him. "I understand. Is there any good news?"

Mezim shuffled a bit more. "Well, there haven't been any reports of brigandage on the river, so we still have a reliable route of resupply and, if necessary, escape."

Escape. Why bother? If I fail here, Byleth will have my head. Unless I could grab a boat headed west to the coast. No, I'd never make it. The queen would catch me in that flying ship, as sure as the sun rises tomorrow.

As much as he wanted to deny it, Alyra's words had pricked his conscience. He could not order the slaughter of the slaves. However, the queen's life balanced on the edge of a precipice, and she could be deposed if the rebellion continued much longer. *Why am I stuck in the middle of this mess? I hate politics and I've no training in warfare. Yet here I am, in charge of the defense of an entire town. And if I fail, it's more than just my head. A lot of people are going to die.*

"And there is this, Master."

Mezim showed him a notation on an inventory of the town's resources.

"All right," Horace said. "I want you to gather the officers from the garrison and the local militia, and our men as well. We're going to have a meeting tonight. We'll draw up a plan and put it into action."

"I think I know just the place. Do you require my attendance for dinner?"

"No. Go take care of that. Oh, and send a message to the river master, or whatever they call the person in charge of the docks. I want all incoming and outgoing vessels searched, starting now."

The secretary hurried away, and Horace continued on his way to dinner. He wasn't looking forward to this meal. There was too much going on in his head for him to focus while being entertained by strangers. He wished he could think of a way to bow out, but then he was ushered into a huge dining chamber.

Twenty-foot-high pillars supported a vast domed ceiling, its smooth underside painted sky-blue with a golden sun at the center. The chamber's enormity was underscored by the small, almost intimate, table set up in the middle of the floor. Three men stood beside the table with drinks in their hands. One was Governor Arakhu, who turned with a broad smile as Horace entered. "Ah, our honored guest has arrived! *Dam parasut, Belum.*"

Horace returned the greeting with all the cordiality he could muster, and the governor in turn introduced the others to him. "First Sword, I present to you Elder Damuggah, one of Sekhatun's most celebrated and beloved leaders, and a family friend."

The elder was a tiny man. At least sixty years old, he had a hunched frame and walked with a polished cane. His skin was like aged parchment, wrinkled and sagging. He smiled as he bowed his head, revealing rows of brown teeth.

The governor gestured to the other man, who was quite a bit younger, probably in his late thirties. He stood a couple inches taller than Horace, with the rugged build of a professional soldier. His head was shaved bald except for a single lock of hair plaited at the nape of his neck. "And this is *Kapikul* Shu Tural, the commander of the royal garrison."

STORM AND STEEL

The commander bowed with one hand over his chest. "*Sobhe'etu, Belum.*"

Horace nodded to both men as they were seated at the table. Slaves entered the chamber with carafes of wine and platters of olives, dates, and sliced goat cheese. Seated at the governor's right hand, Horace was given the full treatment of an honored guest. Arakhu served him first, pouring the wine with his own hands, and the slaves started each course with him.

"I have heard," Elder Damuggah said as he lifted his wine glass, "that you are from the city of Avice, First Sword."

Horace wiped his mouth with a silk napkin as he nodded. "*Ai*, Elder. Although I'm originally from Tines, which is a smaller port."

"Ah, and how do you find Erugash, compared to these great cities of the west?"

"In truth, sir, I think Erugash is a magnificent city. Antiquity oozes from its bricks and stones, staggering my imagination with all the great artisans and scholars who have dwelt inside its walls over the centuries. We certainly don't have that intimacy with living history in Arnos."

The elder chuckled, sounding like an owl hooting, as he tapped the table with two fingers. "'Intimacy with living history.' How well-spoken! I did not know the First Sword was a poet as well as a mighty warrior."

"Well, I wouldn't say I am much of either. I spent most of my life building and maintaining ships. Working with my hands and whatnot. But I've had very good teachers since Her Excellence took me under her wing."

Governor Arakhu smiled. "I understand the First Sword has his own . . . unique . . . manner of addressing Her Majesty the queen, may she grace us with her heavenly light for a hundred thousand years."

The elder's eyebrows rose. Just a fraction of an inch, but Horace caught it. *He thinks I'm sleeping with the queen. And he's probably not alone.*

Trying to ignore the insinuation, Horace changed the subject. "I've been sent to protect Sekhatun, which may soon be the target of a rebel attack. I'm glad the *kapikul* is here, because I have a few ideas about how we can shore up the defenses."

Governor Arakhu said, "We would all be interested in learning your plans."

"First off, the walls need to be repaired. From what I understand, there are some weak points."

Elder Damuggah shook his head. "They are in a poor state, but we don't have the stone to repair them properly. And even if we did, the masons' guild refuses to negotiate an equitable price."

Governor Arakhu nodded. "This is true. There are no local quarries worth mentioning. I have sent many requests to Erugash, but there has been no reply."

"Are you saying someone in the royal court has been obstructing your requests?" Horace asked.

"Of course not, *Belum*." Governor Arakhu shook his head with emphasis. "We would never disparage Her Majesty's trusted advisers in such a base way."

"Never," Elder Damuggah chimed in. "But perhaps the governor's messages have not reached the proper eyes yet?"

"Well, what about using sorcery to rebuild the walls? A few *zoanii* working in shifts could do much."

"Unfortunately, Sekhatun suffers a dearth of *zoanii* with the power necessary for such feats," the governor said. His expression of regret was so sublime that Horace felt the urge to pat him on the back.

"All right. But the walls are only part of the problem. *Kapikul*, how many soldiers do you have?"

"Fifty-four. Including the officer staff."

"And how many in the militia?"

"About sixty. Though they are of a decidedly lesser quality than the garrison troops. More suited to policing the streets than defending the walls."

The servers returned with roasted duck on a bed of mushrooms. Horace leaned back as they loaded his plate. "Governor, we'll need to recruit more men. Five hundred, at least."

"Five hundred!" Elder Damuggah shook his head. "Pardon me, but we cannot afford to feed and train that many soldiers. Not to mention the terrible burden a conscription of that size would place on our markets."

"The markets?" Horace asked.

"*Ai, Belum.* Sekhatun is, above all, a center for trade. We produce goods in ceramic, bronze, and tin, and trade them across the empire. And to foreign interests, too. If you take all our young men, who will continue our trades?"

"Not to mention the planting season will soon be upon us," Governor Arakhu said. "If we don't start on time, we'll lose the entire harvest. Surely the queen does not wish to disrupt the flow of goods and services that Sekhatun provides."

"What the queen wants," Horace said, trying not to growl, "is for Sekhatun to survive. Trade will resume when the danger has passed."

Elder Damuggah exchanged significant glances with the governor. The *kapikul* focused on the duck, chewing slowly.

Horace felt his jaws tighten as he ground his teeth. "Gentlemen, let me be perfectly clear. The threat of the rebellion is real. They do not care about your trade or your quarries. They want to bleed the empire any way they can. You need to prepare for battle before it arrives."

Elder Damuggah nodded several times. "Of course, of course. But there must be a way to make preparations that do not disrupt the town so onerously, eh?"

All three men looked at Horace as if they were being perfectly reasonable. And perhaps they were, from their perspective. The threat of war must seem a distant prospect to those who had enjoyed peace and prosperity for so long. Yet he was here to stop an attack, not to make friends. "Sirs, tomorrow at dawn you will send forth these instructions, to be obeyed to the letter on pain of imprisonment. First, all able-bodied males will submit themselves to *Kapikul* Shu Tural to reinforce the garrison. Weapons and armor will be issued to them from the town armory."

Horace endured their stares, which had turned cold as he spoke. "In addition, all goods and materials inside the town are hereby confiscated by the order of the queen."

Elder Damuggah's eyes nearly popped of his withered skull at that, and the governor's mouth gaped open. Horace didn't give them a chance to object. "Those materials will be used by the town's craftsmen, all of whom are ordered to fashion shields, weapons, helmets, and whatever else the defense requires. Shu Tural, see my man after you finish dining. We're holding a meeting tonight with all the military officers, and I want you to be present."

"As you command."

Horace stood up, and the others did as well, each of them bowing to him in turn. He returned their obeisance with a firm nod before he left the chamber. His guards took up position behind him as he walked through the corridors, not really sure where he wanted to go.

He found Mezim in a wide hallway lined with marble pillars and beckoned him to follow. "Let's go for a walk."

After a couple wrong turns, they found the ground-floor exit to the palace. Sentries thumped the butts of their pikes on the stone floor of the foyer as he departed, out into the grand square.

"Where do you wish to go, Master?"

Horace paused to take a look around. The plaza was mostly empty, with just a few trading booths still open. Pedestrians strolled amid the buyers and sellers. In the center of the square, a huge statue was half-finished. The artisans had completed the lower portion of a wide body, supported by four powerful legs like tree trunks, but he still had no idea what it was supposed to be. *Probably some demon or god from their myths.*

"Let's just walk about," he replied. "I want to get a better view of the town's layout."

Without a clear destination in mind, Horace set off across the plaza heading west, and his retinue followed on his heels.

Everything looked different than before. The buildings were taller and more impressive than he remembered, with little flourishes in the architecture he hadn't noticed the last time he was here. Sekhatun was obviously a wealthy town. New construction mingled with the old in a pleasing manner that suggested growth and prosperity. The atmosphere was vibrant, with people in bright clothing greeting each other on the street and often stopping to banter. They seemed so friendly that Horace actually got a little homesick, wishing he knew some of these citizens so he could join their conversations, no doubt discussing family and friendships, the joys of life.

After half a bell, they came to the edge of town. The walls rose amid the blocky rooftops. The gatehouse dominated the view, flanked by square towers on either side. Though not as huge as the gates of Erugash, they looked plenty strong to Horace. On a whim, he headed toward one of the towers. He couldn't locate the entrance at first, so he stopped a passing guardsman and asked for directions. The soldiers looked him up and down, his gaze settling on the sword at Horace's side, and then pointed out a doorway inside the gate-house. Horace had to get past a guard post to get inside the massive fortified structure and a watch-sergeant to enter the tower, but finally he climbed the flights of interior steps to the crest of the tower.

He exited onto a narrow parapet connecting to the wall's segmented allure. A sentry turned his way, gave a nod, and returned to his vigil.

The view of the town was amazing. From up here he could appreciate the precision of Sekhatun's architects. The town was a perfect square. The streets ran at right angles to the walls, creating a crosshatch of arteries. At its heart was also a square delineating the town center, dominated by the palaces and government buildings. And temples. The largest was the temple to Kishar, the Earth Mother and protector of women. Yet the largest crowd filled the courtyard of a smaller temple, crowding around the rust-red ziggurat at the epicenter. The temple of Hinurat, its iron gate thrown wide open. Smoke rose from the flat crest of the temple where hecatombs of oxen were being offered to appease the war god. If this were Arnos, the church bells would be ringing as the clergy led services to pray for the Prophet's blessing on the armies. Another example of how they were not so different.

On the other side of the wall, fields stretched along the banks of the river, peppered with farmhouses and storage hives. People traveled on the road. Some walked, but many drove two-wheeled carts. They might be farmers heading back home after a day at market. Horace reminded himself that the gate sentries would need to be more attentive in the coming days in case the rebels tried to infiltrate the town, though he didn't know how he could stop them. After all, they'd been able to enter Erugash and make their attacks without being caught, and that was done under the nose of the last First Sword. *Who paid for his mistakes with his life.*

He could also see how sparsely manned were the walls. Along the western ramparts, he counted only a dozen sentries. He saw, too, several places where the walls were in poor repair, with crumbling allures and missing battle-ments. One of the watchtowers south of his position sagged as if it were about to topple over at any moment.

Horace tried to imagine how an attacker would view the town's defenses. The leaning tower and vacant merlons were a dead giveaway, but he thought many of these weaknesses could be disguised in a short amount of time. If he could present a more intimidating posture, perhaps the enemy would seek another target. That didn't necessarily solve the queen's problem, but it might get him off the hook. Best of all, it would mean he didn't actually have to kill anyone.

The biggest problem with trying to formulate a defense plan was that he had no idea how many fighters the rebels could field. The reports he received varied wildly, with some commanders claiming numbers that had to be inflated to disguise their own inability to stop the slaves. At least, Horace hoped so. He put his hand in the pocket of his tunic, feeling the cool smoothness of the orb. He rolled it around with his fingers. *I can do this. I'll stop the attack, whenever it comes. And maybe afterward I can convince the queen to show some leniency. Yes, she'll have to listen to me after I deliver such a victory.*

"All right," he said. "We're done here."

As they left the gatehouse and headed back to the palace, his uncertainty returned. The town walls, which had been a source of comfort just minutes ago, now felt confining.

A soldier in a militia uniform hailed them on the main street leading back to the palace. He bowed and held out a scroll with both hands. "Lord Horace," he said, his face still pointed toward the ground. "I was bid to deliver this to you."

Mezim took the scroll and broke the wax seal. Unrolling it, he read quickly. His features were grave as he presented it to Horace.

Horace read it for himself and felt a growl lurking in the back of his throat. The message was a challenge to duel, sent by Naram et'Nipthuras. He crumpled it into a ball and tossed it back to the militia trooper. "I don't have time for this. Tell him to stay away from me."

The soldier bowed again, even lower, as Horace stalked past him. He was thirsty. He hoped the governor's wine cellar was well stocked.

STORM AND STEEL

Byleth strode through the palace corridors, her anger nearly overwhelming her composure with every clack of her heels against the marble flagstones. She was being tested, challenged from every direction, mostly by foes she could not see or touch. It was maddening. She already regretted unleashing her wrath on Horace in her letter.

Well, not entirely. He did shoulder much of the blame for Lord Ubar's death, but she should have seen it coming. Her First Sword was no hothead like her brother Zazil. Horace had a brain. And a heart, too. *I'll deal with him tomorrow. Right now, focus on the more important target.*

Lord Astaptah had been avoiding her since their last conversation. The Nisusi coalition forces were advancing, and she needed them dealt with. Now, not later. She wasn't going to accept any excuses this time. Astaptah would fulfill his obligation to her or . . .

Or what? I'll cast him back into the desert like a deformed infant? By the gods above, I would if I could, but I still need him. His machine is the only thing between Erugash and a complete collapse.

She had just left a meeting with her other advisers. Demonstrations were appearing all over her city, and there were also reports that some of the militia had lain down their weapons to join the protests. She'd ordered the executions of the protest ringleaders and any soldiers who participated, and then thrown her council out of the throne room. Things were getting out of control, and she needed some good news. A victory to put her back on the path to glory.

They came to the black iron door to the catacombs. Byleth reached out with her *zoana* and pulled. Hard. The portal resisted for a moment, as if sensing her ire, but then gave way with a raspy screech. She beckoned for her entire complement, a dozen of her finest guards plus Xantu and Anshara, to follow as she entered. She intended to make a statement her vizier could not misunderstand today.

Plunging into the hot, dark tunnels beyond the doorway, she surrounded herself in a cocoon of *zoana*. The winds caused by her power rolled out ahead of her and returned laden with the stenches of brimstone and ash. She charged into the central cavern that housed the storm engine, ready to unleash her anger, and halted on the top catwalk. The chamber was empty except for the device, which was covered under a black canvas sheet. By its look, the place could have been deserted.

"Come," she said as she descended the metal ramps to the ground floor.

Wrapped in her power, she hardly felt the intense heat of the magma at her feet. A couple of her soldiers gasped until *zoana* flickered from Xantu, and they quieted. She walked onward, trusting them to follow.

Her first thought was to check the cells where Astaptah kept his captives. She was heading toward that tunnel off the main cavern when she caught a trace of power coming from another direction. It had a strange texture that made her stop in mid-stride. Something flitted in the shadows, too quick to be seen. *What has Astaptah been doing down here? The air is charged with a different energy.*

"Do you feel that?" Byleth asked her *zoanii*.

Lady Anshara shook her head, her face solemn. "No, Your Majesty. I feel nothing . . . except the stink of this place makes my skin crawl. I fear I'll need a bath to get it off."

Xantu looked ahead down the tunnel from which the sensation seemed to emanate. "A trickle of *zoana*, but it feels . . . odd. Like biting into a rotten fruit."

Byleth headed toward the mysterious tunnel. It dipped down slightly, almost causing her to stumble in the gloom as the luminance of the central chamber receded. Byleth formed a small globe of white light and sent it floating ahead. The tunnel extended farther than she first imagined, dipping a second time before sweeping to the right in a long curve. As she traversed the arc, the sound of a voice came from ahead.

The tunnel opened into a cave. It was mammoth, extending at least a hundred yards to the other side and more than half that distance across. The walls were roughhewn but somewhat smooth with striations of brown and red and gold running through the gray basalt. Their surface reflected the light from dozens of black candles set around the chamber.

Lord Astaptah stood in the center. Before him knelt a young man in a simple gray robe, head bowed as the vizier chanted above him in an alien tongue. Byleth looked to the ceiling, and her insides turned to ice as she spied the seven statues of black stone lurking above. They were huge, like giants watching over the chamber. Astaptah had constructed a new shrine to his dark gods. *Holy Lady, how did he manage it? Right here beneath my feet. What else is he hiding down here?*

Byleth wanted to barge in, but she waited at the entrance of this subterranean temple and watched. Six of Astaptah's odd servants stood in a ring around the kneeling man. They swayed back and forth, the hoods of their shroud-like robes pulled down over their faces. There was *zoana* present in the chamber. She couldn't see its flow, which was strange in and of itself, but she felt its passage.

Lord Astaptah ceased his droning chant, and the young man rose to his feet, almost stumbling before he caught himself. A short exchange passed between them, and then the youth left by a passageway on the other side of the chamber, his head down in genuflection with both hands clasped before him. The unseen thread of *zoana* vanished.

As if that were a signal, Byleth crossed the threshold. Lord Astaptah looked over as she approached, dismissing his gray-mantled servants with a few words. The whispering irritated her further. "Lord Astaptah!"

He bowed smoothly. Byleth decided to show her displeasure the same way she had displayed it to Horace. Some men, it seemed, only responded to one tactic. She drew deep on her *zoana* and channeled it into a massive vise of solid air. She tried to remain impassive as she closed it around the vizier, although she had to admit to herself that it was a pleasure to exert her powers. So much of being a queen was about remaining in control. It felt thrilling to unleash herself.

The thrill dissolved as the power failed to contact Lord Astaptah. Something interfered, like an unseen bulwark. Her first guess would have been a shielding of Imuvar, but she saw nothing with her eyes, nor her Sight either. It threw her off-kilter for a moment. She felt Xantu and Anshara fill with power behind her. Though part of her wished to test Astaptah's defenses, she threw out both arms toward her bodyguards, stopping them before they moved to protect her. Something flared in Astaptah's eyes. A look of readiness, just for a brief moment but so supremely confident it convinced her to stay her hand. As quick as it came, the look left his gaze, and he bowed again, this time a little lower. "Majesty," he intoned. "I welcome you to my new sanctuary."

Byleth glanced at the tall black statues around them. Yes, that was the secret behind his newfound power. This place was sanctified in some way that protected him. She rebuked herself in silence. Astaptah was resourceful in the extreme. She should have known better than to confront him here in the seat of his power. Forcing her herself to appear calm, she walked around him in a slow circle. "It is quite impressive, my lord. I wasn't aware you were making alterations to these old catacombs."

She stopped on the other side of him, glancing toward the narrow passage his charges had used to leave. "Was that the son of Lord Arkhandun?"

"Yes. He is now committed to our cause. To your continued rule, that is."

Why do I doubt you recruited young Uriom for my benefit, Lord Astaptah?

"A new sanctuary. New followers. What else have you been doing down here? Specifically, what have you been doing to carry out my commands? I hope you haven't forgotten the *army* on its way here to slaughter us all! Why is the storm engine covered up?"

Astaptah turned to remain facing her. His overall appearance had reverted to nonchalance, with his hands pulled up inside his long sleeves. "I did not wish the heir of House Arkhandun to see it and begin asking the wrong questions. Not until he is fully indoctrinated. As for the larger problem, I have been studying it."

"Studying?" She bit her tongue to keep her voice from rising into a shout. "I did not ask you to study it, Astaptah. I gave you a direct command to destroy the army before it reaches our gates. Yet you have not done so. What is the delay?"

"I cannot risk using the engine for such a task without a suitable source of energy, Majesty."

"I told you I would see to getting you more subjects, but I cannot conjure them out of the air. You will strike now using what resources you have at hand."

"That could prove unwise—"

"At once!" She allowed the *zoana* to fill her once again, imparting its power to her voice.

STORM AND STEEL

Lord Astaptah stared at her for several heartbeats. He didn't blink once, his amber-gold eyes unwavering as if he were trying to penetrate her will. Just as she prepared herself to take the clash of wills to the next level, he nodded. "As you command. Will you stay to witness it?"

The question surprised her. "Yes. I would like to see—" She almost said "you" but switched in mid-speech to, "your invention in action."

With Astaptah's floating onyx light leading the way, they left the sanctuary and headed back to the central cavern. The heat returned as they entered, washing over Byleth like the breath of the furnace. Several of the vizier's minions appeared and crossed the narrow bridge to the island at the center of the magma pool.

At Lord Astaptah's direction, his men took down the cloth covering the storm engine. As the inverted pyramid of silver and black struts emerged from under the cover, Byleth went over the bridge as well, waving her bodyguards to stay back.

"What has gotten into you?" she hissed at Astaptah on the other side, low enough that no one else could hear. "You know our plans hang in the balance. If the Nisusi reach the city . . ."

He bent over a metal box of lights and switches, adjusting some of them. "I understand my responsibilities in our relationship. Yet I am beginning to wonder if you understand yours."

Stunned by his words, it took her a moment to recover. "What are you talking about? I've given you everything you have. Even this—" She waved her hand at the machine. "—this monstrosity was created with funds and materials supplied by me. Don't dare to speak to me of responsibilities. You have no idea the pressures I face, while you tinker down here in the dark."

"Of course. I apologize."

Astaptah pulled a lever on the side of the metal box, and a deep vibration traveled through the rock island. Byleth felt it in her chest, too. Above them, the engine began to hum with an occasional crackle. Tiny sparkles appeared in the heart of the metal lattice, like strands of diamonds hung in midair. A swirling purple haze formed around the sparkles, muting their brilliance. Then an arc of green electricity ran through the miniature cloud with a sharp sound like a cracking whip.

Her heart beat faster as the little storm brewed inside the machine. It was stimulating, knowing that this incredible power was at her disposal. *I will destroy the Nisusi and their allies in one stroke, and then every city will fear me. I will drive the Sun fanatics—*

A loud pop erupted from the metal control box, followed by a stream of black smoke rising from its rear.

Astaptah jumped to the panel and started flipping switches, his hands flying across the board. Inside the silver lattice, the purple cloud pulsated. Tiny green bolts of lightning flickered within so fast Byleth could barely follow their movements. "What's happening?"

Astaptah went around to the back of the box. Wrapping the cuffs of his sleeves around his hands, he reached down. More smoke and the acrid stench of burning skin poured from the engine as he tugged. The crackles and pops grew louder. Byleth took a step back. Just as she was about to repeat her question, something exploded within the lattice.

A long branch of silver metal flew past her head. Heavy droplets of magma splashed into the air as it plunged into the molten pool.

Xantu was suddenly at her side.

Byleth watched the interplay of electricity within the machine. Showers of orange and yellow sparks rained down from the ends of the broken strut near the top of the engine. Lord Astaptah was almost completely occluded by the cloud of smoke issuing from the controls. Byleth considered helping him, but self-preservation overrode her sense of altruism, and she allowed Xantu to pull her away, back over the stone bridge where her soldiers were already rushing up the ramp to the catwalks above.

The pyrotechnics continued as she was hustled up and around the chamber. She paused for a moment at the tunnel mouth leading back to the surface. The bottom half of the chamber was shrouded in smoke. Then movement on the catwalk caught her eye. A tall figure in black stumbled up the ramp.

Lord Astaptah caught up to them as they climbed the long tunnel to the outer door. A burning haze followed them, making every breath more difficult than the last. Finally, they reached the black door, and Astaptah shoved it open with a strike from his palm. Half-carried out by Xantu and Anshara,

Byleth gulped the fresh air of the corridor beyond. Once everyone was out, Astaptah started to close the door.

"What . . . ?" Byleth asked between coughing. "What about . . . your people?"

Lord Astaptah shook his head as he pushed the door shut with his shoulder. He didn't cough, but his face was slightly green. His eyes were sunken even deeper into their sockets. The ends of his sleeves were blackened and burnt. She couldn't see his hands, which he kept pulled up inside the garment, but she suspected they must be badly burned as well.

Once Byleth had recovered enough to stand on her own, she asked, "What happened down there?"

"The engine was pushed past its capacity," Astaptah answered. He had drawn himself up to his full height, the color returning to his features.

"How long before it will be fixed?"

"I do not know."

Gritting her teeth, Byleth sent her guards down the corridor. Then she turned back to her vizier. "By every god and spirit, Astaptah, I swear if you—"

"The storm engine is destroyed."

"Destroyed? You mean it's broken, but you can repair it. Correct?"

He sighed. It was the first disappointing sound she'd ever heard from his lips. "I will need to begin again. New materials . . . new conductors . . . new every-thing. It will take a significant amount of time. Several months, at the least."

Byleth sagged against the cool stone wall of the corridor. Of all the things he could have said, that was the one she'd been the least prepared to hear. All of her plans . . . ruined. Gone up in smoke before her very eyes.

She hit the wall with her fist. "No! I don't accept that. You *will* repair it. Use whatever you need, on my orders. Commandeer any person and anything you need, but fix it. The army could be at our doorstep within days. Without that machine, we're finished. Both of us."

He did not answer, his back to the door, eyes downcast toward the floor.

CHAPTER FIFTEEN

A cool breeze wafted down the street, scattering stray leaves and blowing someone's old straw hat into the gutter. A squad of soldiers marched in formation, spears on their shoulders, down the avenue and around the corner at the end of the block. Alyra held still in the shadow between two vacant fruit stalls until she could no longer hear the stomp of their boots. Then, after a quick glance around, she stole across the street and pressed herself against the base of the high wall. She willed her heart to quiet its incessant thumping. This was just another mission. *Keep telling yourself that.*

With another look in both directions and a scan of the buildings across the way, she turned and climbed. The outer face of the wall was brick. Her fingers and toes found purchase in the mortar joints, and within twenty rapid heartbeats she reached the top. The crown of the wall was canted outward and capped with barbed spikes. Alyra grasped two of those spikes and, springing from her heels, bounded over the barrier. She folded her legs as she landed on the other side and rolled to a halt flat on the ground. The grass of the courtyard's broad sward tickled her ears as she held her breath, listening for signs she had been detected. All was silent. *All right. That was the easy part. Get up before someone spots you.*

Operating by faint starlight, Alyra approached the royal palace from the south. She'd spent all day going over the instructions left for her by the network, trying to find the flaws in their plan, but had finally been forced to admit it was solid. She would enter through the servants' wing where, at this time of night, there should be little traffic. Assets inside would ensure she didn't meet anyone on her ascent to the royal apartment. The queen's last official duty had been evening vespers, meaning she would likely be in her residence when Alyra arrived.

The weight of the new dagger on her belt reminded her of what was to come. She had dealt with soldiers and miscreants, people with more than a little blood on their hands, but this time she would be the one dealing the killing blow. *Don't think about that. Just focus on what's in front of you. One step at a time.*

She stayed low as she ran. These inner grounds were patrolled by soldiers, but none were in sight. She got to the door set in a deep alcove in the palace's bottom tier. Sheeted in dark iron, it was an imposing barrier. She held her breath as she pushed on the cool surface. The door swung inward on silent hinges. Alyra ducked inside.

She entered a small antechamber where deliveries of food and sundries were received. Stealing across the tiled floor, Alyra peered through the doorway on the other side, into an empty hallway. The kitchens were off to her right, but they would be empty until the morning bakers arrived a couple hours before dawn. Alyra bypassed the first set of stairs she encountered, which led up to the various reception rooms and dining halls on the second floor. Instead she headed for the private stairs at the inner edge of the servants' wing, the stairs reserved for the royal handmaidens. A brief fit of anxiety fluttered in her stomach. There was always a member of the Queen's Guard stationed here, day and night. Yet the corridor was empty. Things were going according to plan. And that made her even more nervous.

As she started up the steps, she strained to hear any sound coming from above. The stairs were narrow with no place to hide should someone come upon her suddenly. Her hand kept straying to the dagger under her cloak as if it were a talisman. *I'm going to do this. And then I'll get Horace out of the region, far from the tentacles of the Sun Cult. But what would he say if he knew I was doing this? Would he hate me?*

Apprehension clamped around her throat as she reached the top tier of the palace. The stairs stopped at the handmaidens' quarters, in the common room they shared when not attending the queen. Alyra eased the door open, wincing as it squeaked faintly. However the space beyond was empty. Starlight through the lone window provided just enough light for her to navigate past the plush floor pillows and a twenty-squares board, its round tokens scattered on the thick carpet. Four other doors exited the common room. Two led to sleeping chambers for the handmaidens, one to a pantry and wine room, and the last to the queen's quarters. Alyra was halfway across when the wine room door opened. Her dagger was out in an instant. She lowered it as Sefkahet appeared, a candle in her hand.

Alyra returned the dagger to its sheath, not liking the way it fit so well in her hand. "You scared me," she mouthed with a soft whisper.

"The other girls are already gone. I'm the last one here, and I'll be going once the deed is done."

Good thinking. Whether I succeed or fail, there will be interrogations after tonight. "No, leave as soon as I go inside."

"If something goes wrong—"

There was something in Sefkahet's eyes, a bitter anguish that reached out and squeezed Alyra's heart. She did her best to shunt it aside. "You won't be able to help me. Is the queen abed?"

"In a manner of speaking. She is joined by the new captain of her guard. With luck, they will finish soon. Don't worry. She never lets them stay the night."

"How many guards?"

"Six in the hallway. Alyra, I'm sorry this deed was given to you. I tried to tell them I was in a better position to—"

"Don't be silly. It's my honor to serve the cause. After tonight, everything will be different."

Sefkahet nodded, though she didn't look happy about it. "You'll have to leave Erugash, won't you?"

"I suppose so. What will you do?"

"Cipher hasn't told us what's next."

Alyra put a hand on the woman's arm, feeling the softness and warmth. Many nights she had lain in those arms back when she was a handmaiden, taking what little comfort she could in a place where life was often cruel. "Be safe, Sef. Whatever happens . . . I'll always care for you."

Sefkahet smiled, her eyes suddenly wet in the candlelight. They embraced. Alyra tried to be comforting, but she was so tense she could only manage a halfhearted squeeze before she pulled away. "All right. I'm ready."

Sefkahet went to the door to the queen's chambers. "May the gods smile on you."

Then she blew out the candle.

As the door opened, Alyra started forward. Her legs were heavy, as if she were walking through mud. She paused beside Sefkahet. "Lock it behind me. And don't open it again no matter what you hear. If I fail . . ."

Sefkahet touched her gently on the cheek. "You won't."

With a nod, Alyra entered the dark suite. Her shoulders tensed as the latch clicked behind her. There was no turning back now. Faint light from the floor-to-ceiling windows allowed her to make out the furniture arranged around the room. A light breeze rustled the gauzy drapes.

The bedroom door on the opposite wall was open. Sounds issued forth, a combination of moans and sighs that Alyra remembered all too well from the times the queen had made her be present during her lovemaking bouts. Thankfully, Her Majesty hadn't requested spectators this night.

After a quick glance at the windows and the balcony beyond, Alyra inched up to the doorway. Candles flickered on the long vanity that extended the entire length of the left-hand wall, their flames reflected in the many mirrors to light the room in a hazy glow. The bed curtains were tied back, giving Alyra a clear view of the queen straddling her lover, rising and falling in a frantic rhythm as her moans grew louder. For a moment Alyra felt a twitch of irritation. She knew about Byleth's incessant attempts to lure Horace into her bed, and for a moment she imagined him under the queen before she shoved the image to the back of her mind. As Sefkahet said, there was no one else in the suite. Alyra slipped the dagger out of its sheath.

This was it. The moment of truth. Her heart beat strong and steady. All fear had left her. Now there was just one final act to propel her into a new future. One death in service to the world. Could she do this?

As she slipped into the bedroom, her eyes focused on the queen's naked back, the heaviness she'd felt earlier returned. Lifting the dagger took all of her strength. Her feet halted halfway across the room, rooting her in place. *Is this some enchantment? Does she know I'm here?*

The queen continued to writhe atop the guard captain, both of them completely oblivious to Alyra's presence. This was her own body betraying her. The sounds on the bed changed tenor, and Alyra stumbled back, reaching the cover of the doorway just an instant before the queen rolled off the bed. The soldier got up, too. He was quite tall and good-looking despite his shaved head, but the queen dismissed him without a good-bye kiss. He gathered his uniform, boots, and sword belt from the floor before he left. Alyra pressed herself against the wall as he strode past. When the outer door opened and closed again, she released the breath she hadn't realized she was holding. The worrisome tightness had returned around her neck, now extending down into her chest like iron bands around her lungs. Glass clinked in the queen's bedroom. Alyra peered inside.

Byleth stood at the bar with her back to the doorway. Shadows played across her coppery skin like the caresses of a spectral lover. The queen set down the crystal glass and tilted her head to the side as if listening to something far away. Alyra stood completely still.

The queen went back over to the bed. She wiped between her legs with the coverlet and dropped it to the floor before crawling onto the mattress. A minute later, her head was on the mass of pillows, and the low drone of her breathing filled the room.

Alyra considered her approach. *Just go in and do it. Now while she's drowsing. A quick stab in the chest. That's all it will take.*

Yet, as she tried to convince her feet to carry her inside, Alyra felt the doubt rising up again. This didn't feel right. She'd done a lot for the network over the years, endured things she never thought she'd have to experience, much of it at the hands of this woman. But murder didn't seem justified. *If the network wants to get around Byleth, there are better solutions than this. And if they don't like that, they're welcome to do it themselves.*

The pressure around her chest eased as she retreated from the doorway. She started to turn away until she saw something move out of the corner of her eye. A shadow detached itself from the room's darkness and glided toward the bed. Candlelight flashed off a short blade in its hand. Alyra froze, unsure what to do. Was this another assassin? Who sent him? *Did the network set up a contingency in case I failed?*

While Alyra debated what to do, the shadow slid up beside the queen. The blade rose and fell with startling swiftness. The queen stiffened, her eyes opening in pain, and then a scream erupted from her throat. The shadow flew backward as if swatted by a gigantic hand, the blade falling from its grasp. It was a dagger, exactly like the one she carried.

Alyra ran toward the windows. On her way out, she reached inside the satchel under her cloak and dropped a bundle of papers on the floor. Then she dashed onto the balcony, unwinding the rope bound around her waist. She tied one end to the railing of the stone bannister and tossed the rest over the side. The silken line hissed as it played out down the side of the palace.

Her hands shook as she grasped the line. She swung a leg over the bannister. When she got to the bottom, she would—

The front door of the suite cracked open with a terrific crash, its panels sheathed in frost. Lady Anshara strode through with a squad of guardsmen at her heels. As the sorceress hurried to the bedchamber, something detonated inside with a massive thump. Alyra took that as her cue and jumped.

Her feet touched down on the palace's sloped wall four spans beneath the balcony. The rope played out between her fingers, not too fast or she would lose control, but always with haste in mind. She needed to get to the ground before she was seen. She was going over her plan to get out of the city when a sudden gust swirled around her. She almost lost her grip on the rope as she rolled across the face of the palace wall. Holding on tight, she waited for the wind to die down, but it remained, making the line quiver. Her fingers cramped around the rope.

She started to look down, trying to gauge the risk of rappelling down in this wind, when an invisible force grabbed her around the middle. Its fierce hug squeezed the air from her lungs. With clenched teeth, she let go of the rope with one hand and tried to draw the dagger sheathed at her waist, but the unseen power held the handle tight against her body. As her fingers cried out in pain and her shoulder started to ache, she tugged at the bottom of the sheath. Inch by inch, she worked it free. The wind's pitch rose to a keening screech, and then the power let her go.

The sudden release almost made her fall. Shoving the dagger back into its sheath, she grabbed onto the line with both hands. She shimmied down as quickly as she could manage.

She couldn't help from letting go of a long sigh as she touched down on the roof of the next tier. Feeling the stone under her feet was almost enough to make her cry with relief, but she wasn't done yet. She went to the edge of the tier and looked over the side. Taking another deep breath, she stepped off.

By the time she finally touched down on solid earth, the palace grounds were filled with soldiers. Torches raced around in the night. Alyra let go of the rope and ran across the courtyard to the nearest section of wall. She didn't even pause to look around before she jumped up, her tired legs protesting, and hoisted herself to the top.

Her drop to the other side wasn't as graceful as her entrance had been, but she landed on the street without breaking any bones. She just wanted to close her eyes for a minute. *Get moving! You can sleep when you're dead.*

Ignoring the aches in her arms and legs, she took off. Across the street and down a gap between an upscale brothel and a counting house. She had entered the palace from the south, but she left heading north and slightly east, moving parallel to the Great Canal. She paused at the far side of the alley, peering out into the dark streets of Erugash. The sounds of activity had fallen behind her.

She had a safe place to spend the night, the home of a friend she'd made outside the normal network channels. Come morning, she intended to find a way to get to Horace. With the queen dead, he just lost his most powerful protection against the political factions. The Sun Cult would come for him. She intended to convince him to leave Akeshia. *I only hope he doesn't get the notion of avenging Byleth into his head.*

"Where are my physicians?!"

"Be still, my queen. I have sent for them."

Gods blind them, they'd better hurry.

Byleth hissed as pain ripped through her. She almost clutched her *zoana* and swatted Lady Anshara, who held the bed sheet to her bleeding shoulder, but the woman was only trying to help. Instead, she focused on the face of the dead slave lying on her bedroom floor. She didn't recognize him, but there were scores of slaves in the palace she didn't know.

Then there was the matter of his accomplice. She'd sensed someone else in her bedchamber during the attack, but they had fled. After killing the first assassin, she'd sent her power questing for the second and found someone descending the outside of the palace. Her guards found the rope tied to the balcony. Quite daring. Yet her magic had failed to capture the culprit, for some reason she hadn't understood at first. Not until she saw the shiny dagger on the floor beside her would-be killer. *Zoahadin.*

The other assassin must have been armed with the same magic-defeating metal. She didn't know why the second killer hadn't stayed to finish the job, but their incompetence probably saved her life.

"All right." She pushed Anshara away. "All right! Go lead the search. I want that second assassin found before daybreak."

Lady Anshara left at a quick jog, almost bowling over the captain of her guard. Orthen bowed to the lady's back as she departed, then bowed to Byleth. His full lips were pulled down in a frown as he addressed her, making him look like a melancholy fish. "Majesty, I've put a double guard around your suite. Every other available man is searching the palace and surrounding neighborhood. Also, your handmaidens' apartment is empty. I found the door locked."

"Of course. The killers did not wish to be disturbed."

"It was locked from the inside, Majesty."

Oh, you naughty girls. Plotting against your queen, are you? Not of all you, certainly. But I'll find out which of you helped these men.

"Close the gates and docks, Captain! I want them found!"

"Yes, Majesty!" Captain Orthen saluted and raced out.

Byleth pounded the carpet with her fist. She doubted locking down the city would help. The conspirators were probably gone already, back to their masters. She suspected King Moloch was behind this attack, though the *zoahadin* blade was a new tactic. Few *zoanii* would deal in such methods. Even poison was more honorable.

"Wine!" she yelled.

As a low-ranking guard fumbled to fill a goblet, Lady Anshara returned. Byleth was about to lash out at her for returning empty-handed when the lady held up a handful of papers. "What is that?"

"These were found on the floor of the sitting parlor, Your Majesty. It is possible one of the assassins dropped them."

Dropped them or left them on purpose.

"Give them here."

After a brief inspection to make sure the pages held no latent enchantment or poison dusting, Byleth took them from the lady's hand. They were letters between Lord Qaphanum et'Porranu and several nobles, some living here in Erugash and others from around the empire. She read with growing dread the details of their conspiracy against her. An awful taste spread from the back of her throat as her stomach threatened to revolt. She dropped the letters on the floor, unable to believe what she had read. She had known Lord Qaphanum since she was a child.

"Gather them up," she said. "Arrest everyone mentioned in these papers and bring them to the palace."

Lady Anshara bowed and left once again. Byleth called for a scribe as she leaned back against the foot of her bed. A cold wind laced with the scent of rain blew in through the bedroom window. She breathed it in.

Now she had names. Now she had something substantial to grapple with instead of gossip and knives in the dark.

Lightning flashed outside the window, followed by the sharp crack of thunder.

Cambys, Kasha, and Yadz were standing behind Corporal Idris as Ismail entered the alley.

"I'm back."

"About time," Cambys said with a lopsided grin. His blind, white eye was an uncomfortable sight. "We were about to leave, with or without you."

STORM AND STEEL

Ismail wiped his face with his sleeve. Despite the chill of night, he was covered in sweat under the heavy wool robe he wore. Beyond the alleyway, the towers and rooftops of Sekhatun crowded the skyline.

"Did you get a look inside the militia hall?" the corporal asked.

"Ah, yeah. For a couple seconds. I counted fifty bunks, but about half of them were bare. I think maybe there's another guard house somewhere we don't know about."

"No one asked you to think." Idris turned his head, and Ismail looked away from the nasty yellow bruise covering the side of the corporal's face. Ever since the fracas with Ramagesh's men where he took a nosedive into the sod, the corporal had been even more of a hardass than before, and no one thought that was possible.

"What took you so long?" Kasha asked in a whisper.

"I was waiting for Seng," Ismail said. "He just disappeared on me at the guard hall."

It was after curfew. By standing order of the governor, anyone caught out of doors after sunset was placed under immediate arrest.

"I heard one of the scouts saying they had a different mission than us. Sergeant Mahir is probably taking them to spy on the palace or something."

"We're moving out," Corporal Idris announced, and he started down the alley in the direction of the River Gate where a skiff was waiting for them.

"What about the captain?" Ismail asked.

Emanon had led them into town disguised as peasant fishermen with a haul of river trout to sell. Once inside, they spread out to check on the town's defenses. Sergeant Jerkul's squad went to investigate the walls. Ismail's squad was responsible for counting the militia. Another squad was checking the food stores. Yet Captain Emanon had gone off on his own.

Corporal Idris shouldered past him. "We got our orders, trooper. Get moving."

Ismail looked to the others, but they were quick to follow the corporal, filing down the alley in their threadbare disguises. Ismail tagged along at the end, grumbling to himself. His superiors led and he followed. It was the story of his life since he'd been a child, and he didn't know how to break the chain.

Idris stopped at the other end of the alley and looked out. Then, with a quick motion of his hand, he waved everyone along. Ismail paused when he got to the alley mouth, wanting to say something but without a clue what it might be. *To hell with you! Stop treating us like children. We're supposed to be soldiers, not slaves.*

They all sounded good in his head, but they crowded on the back of his tongue, unable to come out. "Your turn," Idris said. "Walk slow but don't stop. I'll be right behind you."

Nodding in spite of his resentment, Ismail started out. They were crossing a long plaza that led back to the southern half of the town. Remnants of the market—loose garbage, a pile of broken lumber, an abandoned cart wheel—were scattered around the open space. Faint smells lingered in the air, of cooking meat and animal pens.

Kasha walked twenty paces ahead of him, and Cambys another thirty paces in front of him, both of them hugging the side of the plaza. Ismail tried to remain quiet the way Seng moved. He was getting a little better at it. He reminded himself with every step not to appear conspicuous. *Just keep looking ahead and walk naturally. You're just a fisherman on his way home.*

Kasha and Cambys had reached the far side of the plaza, and Ismail was almost there when shouts echoed behind them. Remembering the corporal's instructions, he kept moving but couldn't help himself from glancing back over his shoulder. Several men in militia uniforms were converging on someone. Ismail ignored Idris's gestures to keep moving and stopped for a better look.

The man fleeing from the soldiers wore a long brown robe with the hood pulled up over his head. *We should help him. Maybe he's a slave trying to escape or a—*

Ismail almost swallowed his tongue when a militiaman caught up to the runner and snatched the hood off his head. It was the captain.

Emanon reacted with a punch that knocked the soldier to the ground with a smashed nose. Next he deftly spun out of the path of a spear butt swung at his head and kicked his second attacker in the stomach, following up with a knee to the chin that sent the militiaman reeling.

STORM AND STEEL

Ismail thrust his hand under his robe to grab his dagger as he stepped toward the fight, and collided with Corporal Idris, who stopped him dead in his tracks. "Keep moving, trooper!" the corporal snarled in his ear.

"But the captain needs our help!"

Corporal Idris shoved him. "You have your orders. Follow them or I'll put you down where you stand."

Ismail staggered back a step. In a hot flash of emotion, he considered drawing his blade, but the corporal slapped an open palm over his knife hand, trapping the weapon in its sheath, and pulled him into a close embrace. "This is part of the plan," Idris mouthed. "Just keep moving."

Amid the growing circle of onlookers, Emanon was struck across the back of his shoulders by a baton. A second blow knocked him to his knees.

His heart hammering against his breastbone, Ismail allowed Idris to steer him out of the plaza. The sounds of fighting stung his ears, but he fought the temptation to look back.

Once they were in the next street, the rest of the squad huddled around. "What should we do?" Yadz asked, his face pale and dripping sweat.

"We get out of here," Corporal Idris said. "And fast."

Ismail wiped his forehead with his free arm—his right hand still gripped tightly to his knife handle—as he followed them down the street.

CHAPTER SIXTEEN

"*U*nderstand that the Gates of the Stars must be entered in their proper order and at their proper times. And that the spirits of the Outside require a sacrifice of fresh-spilt blood. If they be denied this gift, they shall take it from the summoner, for so it is writ in the ancient pact that our forefathers forged with the celestial Spheres.

"Understand that the Fallen ever seek to return, and if that should happen an age of eternal Night will come to the world. The Dragon shall return with fire. The seas will boil with Her infernal wrath, and the skies will be made as dark as sackcloth. Be ever vigilant, for this is the goal of every acolyte of the Dark Ones.

"Remember your amulets and sigils, lest you be the victim of evil sorcery. Remember to honor the Sun and the Moon and all the heavenly bodies, for they were placed in the sky to guide us. Remember the waters of the rivers and seas, for they once gave us life, and so shall all life someday return to their womb.

"Remember . . ."

Horace sat back in his chair and rubbed his eyes. The air in the governor's reading room was deathly still and smelled of roses. The administrator of Sekhatun had a penchant for the flowers; every room in the palace had a vase of fresh-cut roses, and the reading room had *two*. Horace was beginning to abhor the scent.

He sat at the governor's rosewood desk, reading from the borrowed tomes he'd brought from Erugash. He still had the feeling they held an important clue about what happened to Lord Mulcibar.

He'd started this morning with *The Ninety-Ninth Day*, but after an hour without seeing anything that pertained, he switched to the *Codex*. Horace paged through it, pausing now and again to make out a passage, but it was more of the same. He was about to move on to the third book when he came across a drawing he'd seen just a few minutes ago. He flipped open *The Ninety-Ninth Day* until he found its match, and he put the books side by side. Two pictures of a sleeping serpent at the bottom of a subterranean sea, nearly identical.

The written passage above the drawing in the *Codex* spoke of a time before the world was made, how Erimu—the "chaos mother" if he was translating correctly—gave birth to the gods, who in turn created the world of men. The gods repaid their mother by placing her in an enchanted slumber and chained her to the bottom of a vast ocean in the underworld.

He shoved the tomes away. It was all nonsense, and he was a fool for thinking some old books were going to tell him why Mulcibar had been killed. He suspected he knew the reason anyway. The nobleman had been investigating the demon attack on the palace. Whoever conjured those things must have discovered this and put an end to his snooping. *And here I am following in his footsteps, reopening this old wound. But I can't just let it go. Whoever sent the creatures had been trying to kill me. And the attacks haven't stopped with Mulcibar's death. If anything, I fear more for my life now than ever before.*

He was closing both books when a small mark in the *Codex* caught his eye. He almost took it for an ink smear until he realized it was two very small characters written close together. The characters for the sounds *hur* and *ris*. Those characters meant nothing when put together as far as he knew, but say them aloud and they made . . .

Horace.

Beneath the characters was a notation written in a hand Horace recognized. Another message from Mulcibar from beyond the grave. It simply said "dead book," and a number. One hundred twenty-four.

Horace dragged over the *Book of the Dead* and turned to page one twenty-four. Most of the page was filled with cabalistic diagrams, circles and lines and squiggles that made no sense to him. At the bottom were a few lines of text.

> *Seven are the Lords of the Abyss,*
> *Seven the evil fiends who tear at the souls of men.*
> *Seven are the steps on the ladder down to the underworld,*
> *Seven the watchers at the Gates of Death.*

Horace sat back in his chair. What was Mulcibar trying to tell him? *He knew he was being targeted, and he counted on me to track down these clues. All right. So what are they supposed to mean?*

He was poring over all three librams again, looking for more notes, when Mezim entered. Horace looked up. "Do you have those new reports?"

Much to his surprise, the town council had actually begun the work he'd ordered last night. He'd asked Mezim to keep an eye on the wall repairs and the recruitment drives specifically, because he considered them the most vital aspects of their defense. The rebels usually attacked with small bands—no more than fifty or sixty fighters. They'd have a difficult time assaulting a town this large with sturdy ramparts manned with a couple thousand soldiers.

"Nothing to report just yet, Master," Mezim said. "But the militia officers are confident they will sign up three hundred able-bodied men before day's end. Barracking and outfitting them will likely be the biggest problems."

Horace nodded as he returned to his study. "I trust you to make the necessary arrangements. Just tell everyone you speak with my voice."

"Ahem. As you wish. Two messages arrived for this morning." He held out one scroll. The royal seal was stamped across a blob of purple wax. "This came by flying ship. Captain Muranu will wait to carry back your response."

The queen is running that man ragged. It must be important.

Horace took the message and started to peel it open. "You said two?"

The queen's letter was brief. She was beset on all sides by enemies. She wanted him to finish in Sekhatun and get back to Erugash as soon as possible. Her final line tugged at him.

You are the only one I can trust, Horace. Return to me before I falter.

Mezim cleared his throat. "The other was from Master Naram of House—"

"Just burn that one. Maybe he'll leave me alone."

"It's interesting you say that, Master. The message wasn't another challenge. Master Naram has invited you to witness his death."

"What?" Horace stood up. "What's that supposed to mean?"

"The heir of House Nipthuras intends to immolate himself this evening. At sunset."

"Is this because I won't fight him?"

"I believe so. The act is meant to shame you."

Horace sat back down, shaking his head. *I'll never understand these people. No matter how hard I try, I can't fathom their fascination with dying.*

"Fine," Horace said. "Send his family a note with my condolences."

"That will be viewed as a grave insult—"

"I don't care. Do it. And get those progress reports for me."

Mezim bowed and left, closing the door behind him. Horace let out a deep breath as he tried to get back to his reading, but the mood was gone. He needed to get some fresh air. He went through the bedchamber to put on sandals before heading out.

The soldiers in the corridor came to attention as he stepped out the doorway. Horace nodded to Captain Gurita, glad to see a familiar face among the now fifty-strong escort Governor Arakhu kept adding to his retinue.

They went down to the ground floor. Functionaries stopped and bowed as Horace passed, but he didn't know any of their names. As he went out the front entrance—with ten more soldiers holding open the doors and saluting— Horace wished he'd thought to ask Mezim where the wall repairs were being done so he could supervise the work. *I'll just poke around.*

The sky was somewhat overcast with banks of low, gray clouds covering large swathes of the firmament. The sunlight was dampened as if it couldn't be bothered to show up today.

Horace strode through the great plaza fronting the palace, noting that it was emptier than it had been the day before. A few clusters of people stood together, but otherwise the square was vacant. Even the labor crew working on the statue was absent.

The sense of emptiness persisted as he led his horde of guards west down the street. It occurred to him that it might be a holy day—the empire had dozens of them—and the people might be at worship.

When they reached the western gatehouse, Horace asked for the officer in command, and a lieutenant of the militia was brought before him. The man bowed several times. "How may I serve, First Sword?"

"I've come to see what progress you've made in the fortifications."

"Very good, Great Lord. Please, come with me."

The large gates were opened. Horace and his guards followed the lieutenant outside and south along the wall. Up close, Horace could see the many pits and cracks. Though the wall appeared sturdy enough to repel common bandits, he worried how they might hold up if the rebels got hold of some siege weapons. He suspected the ancient brick would crumble under a concerted attack.

As they passed the base of a square tower, Horace spotted a chain gang up ahead. Twenty men shackled together at the ankle, most of them also wearing iron collars. They were hauling large bricks from a pile over to the wall where a crew of masons worked at creating a new layer to the existing bulwark.

The crew stopped working and climbed down to bow as Horace approached. The handful of guards watching the slaves forced their charges to kneel in the dirt, heads down. Horace used both hands to gesture for everyone to get up. After a moment's confusion, the guards dragged the captives to their feet.

"Who's in charge of this work?" Horace asked.

One of the workers stepped forward. He was one of the few not wearing a collar. "I'm the foreman, your lordship."

Horace looked along the wall, which followed the lay of the plain as it sloped down to the river. He counted four more crews working down the line, laying fresh brick. Gangs of slaves carried pots of mud from the river to a site where it was mixed with crushed gypsum and sand. The resulting mortar was then hauled to the crews at the wall. "How long will it take you to finish?"

"Fourteen days for the walls, your lordship. And another eight days for the tower facings. After that, we've been ordered to begin reconstruction on the main gatehouses."

Twenty-two days. I don't think we have that long.

He considered using his power to augment the repairs. He might be able to use the Kishargal dominion to strengthen the brickwork, or Mordab to dry the mortar faster. But considering his recent problems with the *zoana* . . . *I'd probably do more harm than good and set the schedule back even farther.*

"Foreman," Horace said. "Tell your superiors I'm authorizing you to recruit every craftsman in the town to assist your effort. I want these walls finished in six days. Is that understood?"

The foreman bowed. "I will tell the guildsmen right away."

As the crew returned to work, Horace continued to look around. He felt bad for them, especially the slaves, but he couldn't afford to be merciful right now. They needed this wall fixed right away. *After I figure out how to defend this town, I'll do something about the slaves.*

He had no idea what that "something" might be, but he was serious about tackling the problem. If he was given a town like Sekhatun to rule as he saw fit, he could free the slaves and show Byleth how much better things could be.

He was dreaming of this plan when he noticed one of the workers walking past him carrying a stack of bricks. The man didn't look like the others in the chain gang. For one thing, he wasn't undernourished. He had the tall, lean body of a warrior. Horace also noticed the man didn't wear a collar, although he had scars around his neck suggesting he may have once been a slave. Thinking of Mezim, who had bought his freedom and risen high to a post in the royal palace, Horace addressed the man. "You, worker."

The man stopped and turned with a hard look in his eyes.

"What's your name?" Horace asked.

When the man didn't respond, the nearest guard struck him across the back with a baton. "Answer his lordship!"

"Goram," the man muttered. His voice was deep and surly.

The squad leader of the guards hurried over. "My apologies, Great Lord! This one has been nothing but trouble. I shall have him executed at once."

Horace held out a hand to forestall the man. "No. That's not necessary. Why is he a prisoner?"

"I believe he was out past the curfew, Great Lord. He might have avoided a labor sentence, but he fought against the men who arrested him and hurt one of them very badly."

It was a shame to have man like this in chains, fixing the walls when he should be manning them. Horace stepped closer and looked him in the eyes. "If I freed you, would you fight for this town?"

The man smiled. It wasn't a kindly grin. It was the sneer of a wolf right before it lunges for your throat. "I wouldn't fight for you if my life depended on it."

The guard lifted his baton for another strike, but Horace shook his head. "All right. I respect that. But when a thousand blood-hungry rebels come over these walls, you might regret not facing them with a spear in your hands instead of those bricks."

As he motioned for the guards to get the workers moving, Horace saw something change in the man's gaze. Just a subtle shift, but he wanted to believe it was a measure of admiration, however small and begrudged.

He wished he had more time to complete these defensive measures, and then he wished they weren't necessary in the first place. Leading his entourage back inside the town, he thought back to that day in his office when the queen had shown him Ubar's head. He still couldn't believe Jirom was responsible for such a thing. *Perhaps he wasn't. After all, I'm part of the queen's inner council, but I can't be blamed for every decision Byleth makes.*

Praying there was more to this entire affair than he could see, Horace headed back to the mountain of work waiting for him.

Alyra studied the house from the shadow of an abandoned glassblower's shop.

The moon was a pale sliver above the crooked street, here in the west end of the Bronze Quarter. *It's an odd place for a safehouse.*

The Bronze Quarter was home to many of the city's artisans and businesses. Its streets were patrolled day and night by militiamen, and laws broken here often incurred a harsher penalty than anywhere else in the city except the royal palace. *So why would the network risk discovery?*

She'd spent the day trying to sleep, but her mind kept racing, going over the events of the night before again and again until she started to think she might be losing her sanity. As soon as the sun went down, she came to track down Cipher. She needed to know what happened. More importantly, she needed him to know that she didn't appreciate being treated like a toy. If the network sent the second assassin, then either they didn't trust her or they didn't have faith in her abilities. She was certain about one thing: she was glad she'd held onto some of Lord Qaphanum's letters. It had been just a hunch, but leaving them in the queen's suite might lend Horace some cover. In spite of everything, she'd decided to trust him, come what may.

Moving cautiously through the city, she'd gone first to the house where she was given the mission, only to find the place empty. She'd even broken inside to make sure. The place was a dead end with no furniture, no clothes, no pots in the kitchen, nothing. Just a decoy. Cursing herself for not being more scrutinizing, Alyra had hurried to the Dredge to the old safehouse. She arrived just as Cipher, in a long skirt and cloak, was leaving the house through the side door and heading down the alley. Her first thought had been to accost him right then and there, but by the time she reached the alley she'd decided to follow him.

So she shadowed him through the River Quarter and into the Bronze, and finally to this street. He'd gone right inside without knocking or giving any special signal that she could see from her vantage at the end of the block. Welcoming light poured out of the doorway as he entered and promptly vanished as he closed the door behind him, returning the street to its moonlit gloom.

Alyra leaned against the wall of the glassblower's home. She still wanted answers, but she wasn't keen on breaking into an unknown location. The place looked innocuous on the exterior—just a two-story townhouse with yellow shutters and a flat roof—but there was no telling who or what was inside.

Taking a deep breath to calm her jumping nerves, Alyra eased out of the shadows. She went around to the side of the house and peeked in a first-floor window. What she saw cooled the ire running though her veins.

Cipher stood in a parlor room, embracing a woman a few years older than Alyra. Two small children, a boy and a girl, climbed on them. *Holy Father, this is his home!*

Alyra watched as the family moved to another room where a meal was set up. They sat down to eat, the children talking while their mother filled the bowls and cups, and Cipher smiling as he broke a bread roll and gave half to his daughter. Alyra found it all so surreal. Her idea of bursting into the house, waving her knife, died a quick death.

She went around to the back of the house where a small plot of grass was enclosed inside a low brick wall. Children's playthings were scattered about the yard—wooden soldiers, a ball of stitched hide, a doll with a missing eye. There was also a rear door. Alyra sidled up onto the short wooden porch and tried the latch. It opened smoothly without a sound. She slipped inside.

She moved through a small, cozy kitchen that smelled of olives and fresh herbs, into a hallway leading toward the front of the house. An archway on the right opened into the dining room. She went to the archway and paused, hand on her knife, considering her options. *Damn me, I don't want to scare the children.*

Steeling herself, she leaned her head into the doorway. Cipher sat with his back to her. "Eat your cabbage, Dir," he said to his son.

"I don't like it!"

Alyra was about to reach out and tap Cipher's shoulder when his wife looked over. The woman almost jumped, her mouth falling open. Alyra placed a finger on her lips. Then she pointed at Cipher and gestured for him to come out. The woman didn't move for a moment.

"Kissare?" Cipher said. "What's wrong?"

"Go to the kitchen, husband," the woman said. "I left some figs on the cutting table."

"Of course."

Alyra darted back to the kitchen and waited. When Cipher entered, she pulled back her hood, and he halted in his tracks. "Alyra, how did you—?"

Alyra half-drew her knife from its sheath. "Keep your voice down. We wouldn't want to alarm your family."

She felt guilty threatening his loved ones, until she heard shuffling feet and the closing of the front door. They had escaped, probably figuring her for a burglar or worse. *Damn me!*

"Are you all right? What are you doing here?" he asked.

"You sound surprised to see me again. Was that not a part of your plan?"

"I've spent every minute since last night trying to locate you. What happened?"

"That's what I'm here to find out. I have questions, and you'd better have the right answers."

"All I know is what Sefkahet told me when she reported in. She let you into the royal apartment and locked the door behind you. Evidently, she waited for a few minutes—against her orders, by the way—until she heard a commotion. A scream, followed by some kind of struggle. When you didn't return to the door, she assumed you had succeeded and were on your way out. I didn't find out until hours later that the queen survived. At that point, I started searching."

"Why did you send a second assassin? Not sure I could handle the job?"

He frowned, his eyebrows forming a solid line above his eyes. "I know nothing about a second assassin."

"Don't lie to me, Cipher. I'm not in the mood."

"I'm telling you the truth. We don't have anyone else we could trust with that mission. No one with such an intimate knowledge of the palace and the queen's habits and—to be perfectly honest—with the personal fortitude to carry it out. That's why we came to you."

But I didn't have the fortitude, did I? Does he know that, too? That I faltered at the final step, unable to strike when I had the chance.

"There was someone else there to kill the queen, too, Cipher." She lifted the dagger. "And he had one of these."

"Alyra, please believe me. We didn't send anyone else but you. Whoever was there, we didn't send them."

"So who did?"

"I don't know, but I'll find out. You have my word on that."

She didn't want to believe him, but she did. She'd known him for years, and she didn't want to believe he could fool her so completely. "All right. You already know the mission was a failure. Byleth is alive and well, and no doubt she's going to comb the entire city for us. Well, for me."

"We'll get you out, just like I promised."

"And what about Horace?"

"The First Sword is in Sekhatun. I can try to get a message to him, but we don't have a strong presence in that town. What else can I do to help you?"

"Find me a way out of Erugash. Not the normal gates. Something secret and safe."

A flicker of a smile tugged at the corners of his mouth. "So that's why you wanted the city planner."

"Yes. But I can't very well go strolling into a public forum now, so you'll have to do the legwork yourself. Whatever you find, keep it to yourself."

"You're going to evacuate the First Sword when he returns."

"I'm going to try."

"Alyra, I don't think you'll be able to get near him. If your suspicions are correct and he is in danger with the queen, there will be too many eyes on his every move."

She lifted the latch on the back door. "Let me worry about that."

Cipher leaned against the kitchen wall, an expression of pure exhaustion settled across his face. "I'm sorry about all this. When Night sent the offer, I had serious doubts, but I swallowed them like a good soldier. Now everything's gone to hell."

"Yes, it has. But now you get the chance to make it right."

She went out the door, hopped down from the porch, and hurried off into the night.

CHAPTER SEVENTEEN

"Y ou sure about this?"

Hunkered down behind a low stone wall in a field of black soil, Jirom winked at Three Moons. "Not at all, but it's a good day to die. Right?"

The comment belied the anxiety stirring in his gut. He gazed around at the squads of rebel fighters hiding among the folds and ridges of the vast farmland west of Sekhatun. Every squad had a lantern, kept shuttered so as to not give away their position, but they provided enough light for the fighters to assemble in the darkness. By the lay of the stars, it was almost midnight.

Roughly a mile away, Sekhatun loomed in the darkness. The town's ramparts were studded with square towers every hundred paces. It was only a single wall, which was difficult to defend from a concerted attack. More modern cities employed double or even triple walls, with an added fortress inside to serve as a final holdout against attackers. Sekhatun had no donjon, only spacious palaces that would be impossible to protect once the rebels got inside. The scouts had returned from the town with news of an important personage guesting at the governor's palace, but they couldn't get close enough to determine the identity of this grandee. News of additional security made Jirom nervous, but not as much as Emanon's idea to get himself captured, which was the most moronic tactic Jirom could imagine. But it was done, and now he had to follow through with the rest of the plan.

Jirom swallowed the uneasy feeling that he'd done this before. Many times, in fact. Looking back over the course of his life, most of its biggest moments were found in times like this, the quiet prelude before a fight. *This is what I know. I guess fighting is my purpose in life, no matter how much I wish I could leave it behind. Maybe settle down somewhere with Emanon on a nice little farm.*

He snorted as he tried to picture Emanon tending a flock of goats.

"You're a twisted man." Three Moons opened the sack slung from his shoulder and began rooting around inside. "I've heard of laughing in the face of death, but I've never actually seen it done."

"I was just . . . never mind."

The sorcerer pulled out a flat box and put it down gently on the top of the field wall. Very gently.

Jirom kept his distance. "What's inside?"

"My guardian demon. Very big and very hungry."

A young rebel named Garga kneeling on the other side of the sorcerer scooted away from the tiny container. Three Moons chuckled as he took out a slim wand and set it on top of the box. "Gets them every time."

Jirom shook his head. The morning after he slew Ramagesh, he had been shocked to discover that more than half the rebels in camp had stayed. Emanon called a council meeting and asked the remaining captains to renew their support for an attack on the Akeshian town. Every man had pledged his fighters to the endeavor. The next couple days had gone by in a blur as they prepared. Most of the camp followers—wives, children, tinkers, whores, and so forth—had been commanded to stay behind, but that still left almost a thousand warriors to move. Emanon sent them north to the river in small groups with strict orders to stay out of sight. Crossing the Typhon's northern arm hadn't been an easy task, either, but they'd managed without losing a single fighter to the sometimes-treacherous currents.

Based on the intelligence gleaned from the scouts, Jirom had decided the main thrust of their attack should come from the west, where the town's walls were taller but in worse repair.

Checking the positioning of the men under his command, he felt his anxiety starting to return. Seven hundred fighters. Almost two full cohorts. He'd never commanded this many men before. The responsibility was crushing. He tried to distract himself by bothering Three Moons.

"You know when to start, right?"

The sorcerer looked sideways at him, a stoppered glass bottle in his hand filled with what looked like blood. "You want to hold my cock while I piss, too? Go find someone else to torment."

Smiling to himself, Jirom took a lantern and crawled up the line. The plan was simple. While his force attacked from the west, Jerkul and the other three centuries of their fighters were stationed on the riverbank to the south.

Jirom had wanted to keep a company or two back as an auxiliary, but they didn't have enough troops for that. He was betting all their resources on a single toss of the bones.

Jirom suspected the odds of success were slim. For one thing, Lord Ubar's murder had squandered away the element of surprise. The town's sentries would be on high alert. Also, the rebels didn't have any experience assaulting a town of this size, and they didn't have any siege weapons, either, which would have made things easier. *Everything adds up to a defeat. The only question is how bad will it be?*

He kept his expression neutral as he walked, speaking a few words to each squad along the way. He'd been trying to learn their names, but there wasn't enough time. In any case, forming personal relationships wasn't his forte. Emanon's words from the previous night, as they ate a cold supper and discussed the last details of the plan, still lingered with him. *Just lead them, Jirom, and they'll follow. The men respect you, maybe more than you realize. Just do what you do best.*

Jirom got to the end of the line where the Bronze Blades were positioned. Emanon had suggested putting them front and center to absorb the brunt of the initial assault, but Jirom had seen that strategy fail as often as not because any soldier, mercenary or otherwise, who was treated like fodder would turn worthless as soon as the fighting began. So he'd placed them on the left wing in the hopes that their experience and superior armor would anchor the assault. Plus, any counterattack from the town would likely come from the north, so the mercenaries would protect his flank.

He spotted Longar lounging at the rear of the unit and went over. "You're not out snooping around?"

Longar looked up from something in his hand. It was a twisted piece of wood and twine. "Nah, they don't need me to tell them this is going to be one hell of a buggering. I hope your rebel slaves brought plenty of grease."

Jirom sat on the embankment beside him. "This reminds me of Haran."

"The siege of Amab-Hecth?" Longar let out a short whistle. "That was a hairy affair. I remember we lost most of our sappers when the eastern barbican collapsed before they finished the tunnels."

"Aye. We lost a lot of brothers there. And at Bylos, too. Seems like we've left pieces of ourselves across most of the world, doesn't it?"

"That's what soldiering is, Jirom. Bleeding for other people. That was always your problem, you know? You wanted to get something more from it, but there ain't nothing else."

Jirom wanted to ask why Longar kept at this life if it was so futile, but he already knew the answer. *Because fighting and killing are the only things we do right. And a man needs a vocation, a body of work to give his life meaning.*

They exchanged a long look that said it all.

Then Longar returned to his palm-gazing, and Jirom stood up. It was time.

He made his way back to the center of the formation. Snagging Three Moons' attention, he nodded. The sorcerer waved back and got to work with the strange implements he had dragged out of his wizard-bag. Next Jirom drew his sword and signaled his squad leaders.

The assembled fighters hopped over the wall and began a slow jog toward the town, the tips of their spears and pieces of armor glinting in the starlight. As he ran beside them, the blade of his *assurana* sword blazed like a living flame in his hand.

The moist soil crumbled underfoot as they advanced toward the town. Jirom listened for the bells or horns that would tell him they'd been spotted, but they crossed the invisible halfway point and still there was nothing. The walls rose higher with each step, their details becoming sharper. From a hundred yards away, Jirom could make out the dark arrow loops in the towers and the stylized designs along the battlements. Then a sound interrupted the stillness, the keening cry of a lone horn. Someone had finally noticed them.

Jirom shouted, and the entire line of rebels accelerated into a full-on charge. Torches appeared atop the wall. From somewhere inside the town, a gong rang out in a fierce rhythm. Memories of Omikur flashed through his thoughts as he sprinted the last fifty paces. The incandescent burst of lightning. The stench of ozone mingled with burning flesh. The roar of thunder overhead. He saw Czachur's body lying on the sandy ground again, with his eyes boiled away and flesh peeling in black strips. Swallowing his bile, Jirom turned his head back to the field they had just crossed. *Come on, you old warlock. They're going to cut us down any second now.*

Something struck the ground at Jirom's feet—probably an arrow—digging a divot into the earth. Another flew over his head. Archers took aim from atop the wall. He and Emanon had chosen a spot midway between the main gate and the northernmost tower. According to the report, it was supposed to be the weakest spot on the western wall. Jirom prayed the information was right. *Or else this is going to get ugly.*

He was fifty yards from the base of the wall when he looked back again. He was trying to mentally project a sense of urgency to his company sorcerer when a dull thump vibrated through the ground under his feet. He barely had time to shut his eyes before the explosion occurred.

Shards of bricks and clay flew past him as a forty-foot section of the wall collapsed in a cloud of dust. Steadying himself, Jirom plunged into the breach. Coughing and squinting against the particles swirling in the air, he climbed the low hillock formed by the fallen material.

The harsh breathing of the men behind him was a welcome sound. For a moment, he'd had the terrible fear he was assaulting the town alone. He peeked over his shoulder to see several squads fast on his heels, with the others crowding behind, some with bows taking shots at the guards on the walls.

Jirom kept his head low as he reached the top of the rubble mound. A multi-floor building must have abutted the inside the wall, but Three Moons' sorcery had demolished it as well, spilling bricks and broken timbers into the town's baked-mud streets.

Jirom turned and waved his sword at the men climbing behind him. "Up, you curs! Up for freedom! Up for blood!"

"You sure about this?"

Ismail grunted to Yadz as he looked over the low ridge. He wasn't sure about anything, but he kept that to himself.

STORM AND STEEL

The town looked huge this close up, masked in the darkness except for pools of light where torches flickered atop its stone walls and lofty watchtowers. Lined up by squads behind the low field wall, the rebels waited for the signal. The call that would send them charging into the maw of death, hoping to somehow come out victorious before it snapped shut on them. The wind was picking up, piercing his clothing and making him shiver. The stars were muted overhead. *Aye, this is madness. We don't have near enough men to pull this off. And if we fail, it might be the end of the rebellion.*

He looked to the indistinct silhouette of the lieutenant, sticking out like a hunk of granite against the night sky. He hoped the higher-ups knew what they were doing. He thought back to how the lieutenant had picked a fight with Ramagesh, the thrill of watching Jirom cut the rebel leader down like so much cordwood, as if Jirom had been fighting for them all. But somewhere between then and now the old doubts had resurfaced. Why were they doing this? What difference would it make? They couldn't defeat an entire empire.

"At least this ain't as bad as Omikur," Yadz said. "With the lightning and the thunder raining down like all the gods were shitting on us at once. I tell you, Ish, that—"

Before he could tell Yadz to shut up about Omikur and thunderstorms, a long blade waved back and forth from the lieutenant's position, glimmering in the darkness like a red-hot brand. That was the signal.

"Let's go!" Sergeant Partha bellowed, louder than Ismail had ever heard him shout before. It shocked him for a moment, but then he was on his feet and jogging alongside the rest of the unit.

The sergeant fell behind after a few hobbling steps, his leg betraying him. But Corporal Idris ran with the squad, urging them on with colorful comments such as "Move that fat ass, Katha, before I skewer it from behind!" and "Run, Cambys, you blind goat-fucking son of a whore!"

Ismail focused on not tripping as they crossed the unplowed fields. More than one rebel stepped into a hole and took a tumble.

As they neared the town, a gong began ringing from within. Its deep tones were like the drums of the underworld, calling out for them. Ismail clutched his spear tighter, and, for the first time in a several years, he found the words to pray. *Father Endu, protect me this night. And if I should die before the morning comes, guide my soul to its eternal rest in your home.*

Arrows fell from the ramparts, and screams cut through the air. Ismail's throat dried up as Theom fell face-first on the ground beside him, with an arrow through his neck. The big man didn't even twitch but lay perfectly still in the soil as if he were taking a nap.

"What are we going to do?" Yadz yelled. "Climb it with our bare hands?"

The wall grew closer with every stride, filling their vision. Their squad leaders hadn't told them how they were going to get on the other side, only to have faith. But having faith was near impossible when they had no siege equipment, not even ropes or ladders. As more arrows flew past him, an awful dread settled in Ismail's stomach.

He was about to ask the corporal what they were going to do when the earth jumped up under his feet. He flew a couple feet into the air, the sick feeling in his stomach turning over and upside down. Then he landed hard on both feet. Stinging vibrations ran up through his ankles, and with them came a deep rumble, so powerful it made his teeth chatter.

A long bowshot away, the torchlights atop the town walls quivered like they were trying to fly away. Then they fell, swiftly, straight down. A harsh wind filled with grit blew out from the wall's crumbling foundations. Ismail stumbled to a halt, covering his mouth. A mammoth hole had been punched through the town's ramparts. Then an unmistakable voice pierced the cacophony.

"Up, you curs! Up for freedom! Up for blood!"

A chorus of cheers rose above the tumult as the rebels charged toward the newly formed breach. Ismail found himself caught up like a leaf in a raging river, jostled about and carried along at dizzying speed. The mound of rumble where the wall had stood was not as high as he imagined, though all the broken bricks and jagged edges made for treacherous climbing. He breathed in a mouthful of dust right as he reached the summit and spent a few seconds hacking it back up. When he could breathe again, he slid down the other side.

They were inside. Lights from windows and tower tops flickered before him. It seemed like a miracle, and for a moment he wondered if he was dreaming it. Then Corporal Idris was there, shouting orders.

STORM AND STEEL

Ismail's squad formed up in the shadow of a three-story building that looked to be some kind of city office. Besides the corporal and sergeant, there was himself, Yadz, and Cambys. He started to ask where the others were when Idris barked at him to shut up.

Suddenly the lieutenant was among them. The sergeants clustered around him like kittens surrounding their mother. They talked for less than ten seconds before they split up. Calls to "form up!" rang up and down the street.

Sergeant Partha returned to the squad. "We're heading to the center of town. Our goal is to seize the palace and hold it. Corporal, lead us out."

Lieutenant Jirom had already started down the street. It was a wide avenue with deep gutters along both sides. Ismail's squad joined the column following the lieutenant, which included the entire company of mercenaries. Captain Ovar led his men from the point of a diamond formation, pikemen on the outside and crossbowmen in the center.

They traveled two blocks without spotting a single citizen or foe until they came to an open square, much like the plaza where Emanon had been arrested. The merchant stalls were empty, the windows facing them shuttered tight. He had begun to wonder when they were going to find some resistance when a flight of javelins flew overhead. Ismail ducked as a wall of Akeshian soldiers erupted from a side street and carved into the rebel flank.

Men died in a heartbeat as spears and swords flashed. The scant light of a few lanterns was barely enough to make out friend from foe. Corporal Idris was shouting orders, but Ismail's legs had locked in place. Unable to move, he could only watch as his comrades fought and died before his eyes.

Then the lieutenant was there, in the thick of the fray. His crimson-bladed sword rose and fell like a reaper's scythe, cutting a clear space around him. Ismail couldn't believe the fury with which Jirom fought. It was primal, verging on animalistic. Inspired, he took a step after the lieutenant, and found his paralysis was lifted. Raising his spear, he ran after his squad.

Corporal Idris and Yadz were trading blows with a pair of beefy Akeshians. Ismail dipped between his squad mates with a stabbing lunge. The point of his spear struck Yadz's foe in the midsection. He leaned into his lunge as he'd been taught, and the spear tip slid through the layered armor. A slippery sensation crawled inside Ismail's stomach at the sight of his weapon splitting through leather and skin, with the blood spurting out around the wound.

The soldier bent over as if he were bowing to them and made a gasping groan before collapsing on the street. Ismail stared down at the body of the first man he'd ever killed. Numbness had entered his brain, making his thoughts slow and clumsy. Who was this man? What was his name? Did he have a family somewhere, here in town perhaps, waiting for his safe return?

Warm blood pelted Ismail's face, shocking him out of his morbid reverie, as Corporal Idris chopped down his opponent. "Stand and hold!" the corporal yelled at them.

Ismail settled his spear in a defensive pose. Yadz bent over, hands on his knees, breathing hard, and Cambys grinned like a fool on the other side of him. Focused on the task at hand once more, Ismail could see that the militiamen, after the surprise of their initial attack wore off, were poorly trained. What's more, their armor was thin, their shields only oxhide stretched over wooden frames. As the Akeshians fell back, he wondered why he'd been told to stand in place. With a concerted push, they could whip these foes. Then men strode up behind him on either side. Mercenaries, with their crossbows held ready. At Captain Ovar's command they aimed and shot. Dozens of Akeshians fell where they stood, their armor no protection at all against the powerful quarrels. A militia officer slid off his sleek roan mare with three bolts in the chest and another through the side of his helmet.

Lieutenant Jirom charged in behind the crossbow barrage, brandishing his bloody sword. With a lusty yell, Ismail ran after him, straight at the enemy. He thrust and slashed with his spear at every militia face he saw. His shoulders grew tired, and yet he pressed forward, following the lieutenant's example until finally there were no more foes to fight. The last of the Akeshians had fled, some of them throwing down their shields and weapons as they ran.

Leaning on his spear, Ismail took several deep breaths, though it didn't help much. The air in the side street had turned hot and putrid with the stench of death. His front was covered in blood, but somehow he had emerged from the battle without suffering a scratch. His pulse thumped in his ears, filling him with a heady vitality. Now that he had tasted victory, he wanted more.

STORM AND STEEL

A few paces from him, the lieutenant stood alone. He, too, was drenched in gore. Blood streamed from the lowered point of his sword into a puddle on the street. His eyes were downcast as if he were lost in thought, but to Ismail he looked like a hero out of the old legends.

Among the milling rebels, the sergeants were taking over, getting everyone back into formation. As men returned to their units, the dead and wounded were left behind with a handful of field barbers and leeches.

Ismail spotted Cambys first, looking as old as a grandfather but still smiling despite a long cut across his lined forehead. A little lower and it would have blinded his good eye. Yadz was with him, pale-faced and atypically quiet but otherwise none the worse for wear. He tried to find Corporal Idris but didn't see him until he glanced back at the wounded. The corporal was being dragged by two troopers. A trail of blood followed him. Ismail gestured, and his squad gathered around their superior.

When he got out of the gutter, Corporal Idris shook off his bearers and propped himself against the side of a building with a harsh grunt. Sweat ran down his face in heavy drips. There was something odd in the way he moved, and then Ismail realized the corporal's legs were just dragging as if they'd fallen asleep.

"You all go on," Idris said. "Get back in formation."

"Not without you, Corporal," Yadz said with a grin. "No one kicks our asses like you do."

"Ismail." Idris coughed and winced. A trickle of blood ran out from under his back. "He'll take you shit stains the rest of the way."

Ismail didn't believe his ears. Yadz evidently had a problem with it, too. "Where's the sergeant?"

Corporal Idris shook his head as he lowered himself to a reclining position, every movement evoking a grimace of pain. "He took an arrow to his good knee. He's out of the fight. Funny, huh? Some people got so much fucking luck it's spilling out their ears."

He rested his head on the street and closed his eyes.

Ismail's insides churned as he stood over the corporal. All of a sudden, his legs felt too weak to support him.

Yadz was looking around as the main force prepared to march off. "We could just stay here," he said. "With Idris and the sergeant gone, who's going to notice?"

"No." Ismail surprised himself with the forcefulness in his voice. "We're going on with the others."

"But Ish—"

"Form up, Yadz." He hefted his spear. "Before I skewer you between the ass cheeks."

Cambys grinned as they hurried to find their place in the rebel formation. Ismail grimaced as the sick feeling resurfaced in his stomach.

Jirom studied the sky as rebel fighters surged through the gap in the wall. Banks of black clouds had appeared out of nowhere to cover more than half the sky. A cold wind blew down from the north.

Captain Ovar strode over with a pair of his platoon leaders. Jirom pointed down the street toward the center of the town. "You're with me. We're heading straight for the heart."

"Understood."

Jirom waved forward three centuries of rebel fighters and led them behind the mercenaries. The rest of the rebels would thrust north and south into the town, but those assaults were mainly for distraction. The palace of the local governor was the plum that would, hopefully, deliver the town to them. He had no idea what they would do if they succeeded. The rebellion had been hatched in the hidden shadows of the empire's underbelly, but now they were out in the open. Did any of these former slaves know how to administer a town this size? The situation reminded him of a fable his father had told him as a child, about a greedy hyena that had brought down an elephant without a clue how to eat it. *Worry about that later. Concentrate on your duty.*

Rain began to fall as they passed through a section of the town that appeared to be an extended bazaar. There were no people about, and most of the buildings on either side looked abandoned.

STORM AND STEEL

Jirom was thinking of Emanon, hoping he was all right, when a column of Akeshian soldiers emerged from a side street. Shouts rang out as the enemy plowed into the rebel formation. Calling for the mercenaries in the vanguard to hold position, Jirom plunged through the milling chaos toward the threat. He arrived as an older rebel named Qan took a spear through his ribs. Jirom leapt over the body, swinging his *assurana* in a horizontal arc. He struck Qan's killer on the temple, knocking off his iron helm and sending him reeling backward.

Spears stabbed out at him, but his sudden charge cowed the Akeshians long enough for his fighters to engage. Jirom traded blows with a husky, black-eyed corporal for a dozen heartbeats before they were separated by the press of bodies.

The rebels slowly pushed the enemy back down the street until at last the town militia broke off in full retreat. By that time, the rain was coming down in sheets.

Jirom turned to see the mercenaries were likewise engaged with a foe at the front of the column. A runner found him with a report from Captain Ovar. A single company of defenders had obstructed the street, but the captain was confident they would clear the roadblock in short order.

Those words proved to be prophetic as the mercenaries rolled over the militia with barely a pause in their stride. Within a few minutes, the rebels were stepping over scores of dead Akeshians as they resumed their march. Crossbow quarrels jutted from the corpses.

He sent a squad ahead to scout the street, with orders to fall back at the first sign of trouble. He could feel time rushing by like the drip of sand in an hourglass, urging him to move faster. They had an opportunity here, but they couldn't give the Akeshians time to regroup. This entire plan hinged on a series of swift strikes. He wished he knew the progress of the other groups, Jerkul's in particular. *And where the hell is Emanon?*

After they pushed past the deserted bazaar, the street widened before them into a broad thoroughfare. Jirom recalled something similar on his last visit to Sekhatun. The buildings here were built with a finer brand of architecture, and many of the windows on the lower levels were protected with iron bars. Jirom caught glimpses of faces in some of those windows, and a few signs of hurried flight—dropped baskets spilling foodstuffs on the ground, an abandoned cart with a broken wheel, open jars of paint and a brush left beside a half-limned wall.

Suspecting an ambush, Jirom ordered his units to spread out as they marched down the quiet avenue. He was watching the rooftops when Red Ox ran back to him. The Nemedian's left eye was bruised and swollen shut. "Lieutenant, the point squad has found something."

"More militia?"

"Not sure, sir. You should come take a look."

Jirom called over one of his sergeants, a lean ex-gardener from Nisus. "Pulla, you're in charge until I get back. Keep them moving."

Satisfied that the rebels would survive a few minutes without him, Jirom followed Red Ox through the ranks of mercenaries.

They found the advance squad crouched at the edge of an intersection. An obelisk carved with hieroglyphs commemorating a long-dead general's victories stood in the center of the crossing. Jirom knelt beside his men. "What have you found?"

Mahir pointed down the opposite boulevard. "Just as we arrived, I saw movement in that direction."

"This would be a good place for a trap," Captain Ovar said.

Jirom hadn't noticed the mercenary commander standing there. The man was good at staying out of sight.

Jirom peered around the corner. The street was clear as far as he could see. The sound of a door opening caught his attention. He whipped his head around when a small group of people emerged from a doorway to his left. He started to order defensive positions until he got a better looked at them—a man and a woman with three small children. With startled glances at the rebels, the family scurried into a nearby alley and disappeared. Jirom sighed as the sudden tension drained from his body.

Seng appeared out of nowhere to squat beside Jirom. The slender easterner's face and clothes were coated in wet mud that had an unpleasant odor. "Lieutenant," he said in his soft voice.

"Ugh!" Red Ox whispered. "You stink like a stable!"

"Very close," Seng said with a mocking smile. "I found a sewage channel that crosses this street one block to the south. I was able to get across without being seen and search ahead. There is a plaza at the end of the next block. The palace is two blocks farther down."

"Did you see any resistance?" Jirom asked.

"No, sir." Seng tilted his head slightly. "Though there was a sense of . . . observance . . . when I scouted past the plaza."

Mahir shifted his bulk. "What the fuck does that mean?"

"We're being watched." Jirom didn't see anything threatening across the intersection, but an entire legion could be hiding in the town's maze of alleyways and dead ends. "But we don't have time to be cautious. Mahir, take your men across the way and search for threats, but keep your heads down. If there's an ambush coming, we want to spring it on our terms."

"Understood."

While the scouts raced across the street, Jirom waited with Red Ox until the rest of the column caught up.

"So you think we're going to survive this, sir?" Red Ox asked.

"No one lives forever. If this is your day to die, then do your best to make it worthwhile."

Red Ox chuckled. Jirom turned as the first units of rebel fighters appeared behind them. He waved to Pulla, who nodded and brought the men forward. As he took back his command, Jirom ordered the fighters into a tight wedge with the mercs up front and archers in the back.

They crossed the intersection. Jirom held his breath as they entered the street on the other side, waiting for an attack that never materialized. They reached the end of the block to find the plaza Seng had reported. The street's mud pavement gave way to fire-hardened bricks in a long rectangle, about eighty paces wide and almost twice that distance lengthwise. The space was empty save for several large puddles and a water well near the center.

The buildings facing the square were all temples to the Akeshian pantheon. Jirom wasn't an expert on the gods of this country, but he recognized the prominent sunburst design inscribed above the bronze doors of the largest temple on the plaza, the fane of Amur the Sun Lord.

As he surveyed the area, he discovered the sense of observation Seng had mentioned. The feeling of being watched was intense, as if a hundred pairs of eyes were focused on him. He looked to the many windows surrounding the open space and into the mouths of tributary streets, but saw nothing suspicious.

Growling under his breath, he sent the scouts ahead with a squad of spearmen to secure the far end of the plaza. Then he gathered his sergeants together.

"This is the final leg of the assault," he told them. "Stay tight together, but don't bunch up. If there's an attack, keep control of your men. We'll be fine as long as we stick together."

With that Jirom stepped out into the plaza. The squads fell in behind him. The feeling of being watched intensified, until he could have sworn someone was standing behind him, peering over his shoulder. It made the hairs at the nape of his neck stand up. Judging by the mutterings behind him, he wasn't the only one experiencing it.

What if it was sorcery? Jirom almost tripped as that thought crossed his mind. What if this battle was going to be Omikur all over again?

Just as he was about to order his men to step up their pace, a shout echoed across the plaza. Up ahead, the scouts had reached the entrance of the opposite street. He saw Mahir look back, his mouth wide as he yelled something, but Jirom couldn't make it out. He held up a fist for the column to halt.

Shock ran through him as Mahir fell to the pavement. Jirom started to run, forgetting for a moment the men following him. His scouts were falling back behind a shield line formed by the heavy squad he'd sent with them, and that decision appeared to be the only reason any of them survived as flights of arrows showered over them. One by one, he watched as the mercenary infan-trymen fell under the onslaught.

Jirom sprinted into the melee, finding an opening in the shield line and plunging into the gap. Two Akeshian soldiers with war-axes were squeezing through at the same time. Jirom lowered his shoulder and slammed into the soldier to his left, and followed up with an overhand chop at the other. His sword deflected off a round iron shield, but his shoulder-slam caused the other Akeshian to stumble backward, buying Jirom a moment's respite.

STORM AND STEEL

The soldier on his right came at him with a low chop. Jirom parried and drew the *assurana* sword up along the Akeshian's midsection, starting at the pelvis and ripping the blade upward across the ribs. Iron scales and the leather backing underneath parted beneath the sharp edge as it sliced a long furrow through skin and muscle. The soldier spun around as he fell back, his torso split wide open.

Jirom had just enough time to lift his weapon before the other soldier charged back into the fray. He braced himself, but one of the mercenaries beside him caught the axe on his shield and turned it aside. Jirom nodded his thanks. The Akeshian was carried away by the flow of battle as more soldiers tried to fill the gap.

Jirom parried a khopesh sword that swooped toward his head and riposted with a slash that cut through his attacker's cheek-guard to shatter the bone underneath, spattering the soldier and those around him in blood and splinters of broken teeth.

Then the rest of Jirom's unit joined the fight. The reinforcements shored up the holes in their line and allowed the rebels to hold their ground, but Jirom could see they were stalled. He didn't have enough fighters to break through the Akeshian formation, and there was no room to maneuver in the street. It was only a matter of time before enough reinforcements arrived to finish them.

As if answering his fears, shouts echoed from the rear. He turned to see enemy units entering the plaza behind them. A company of Akeshian spearmen. *They've got us boxed in tight. All they need are sharpshooters on the roofs to make this a perfect killing box.*

Fortunately, he didn't see any archers, but that was a small comfort. Jirom called for the rearguard to engage the new arrivals and looked for an escape route. If he couldn't get his men out of this trap, the battle was over. Then a commotion broke out among the echelons of approaching spearmen. It was difficult to hear over the clash of fighting, but Jirom thought he heard cries and gnashing steel. The Akeshian formation scattered, the soldiers dropping their weapons and shields as they frantically tried to strip off their armor. *What in the name of the seven hells . . . ?*

Then Jirom saw the insects. Massive hornets as long as a man's thumb hovering around the soldiers. They attacked every piece of exposed skin and got inside their gear. The Akeshians stripped off their armor and rolled around on the wet bricks in their attempts to dislodge the vicious creatures. Jirom spotted Three Moons in the shadow of a building on the north side of the plaza, doubled over with laughter while he swung some small object around in circles over his head. Jirom thought it was a mercy when his fighters put the writhing Akeshians out of their misery.

With the threat from the rear neutralized, he wheeled around to deal with the roadblock ahead. His blood coursed like liquid fire in his veins as he pressed forward, striking at any enemy he could reach. Silfar's squad pressed in around him. He saw the strain on the faces of the rebels as they tried to regain their earlier momentum. But they couldn't make much headway as the mercenaries ahead of them got bogged down.

Jirom was about to call for Three Moons to conjure up some new sorcery when a file of fresh fighters rushed out of an alley behind the Akeshians holding the street. Jirom spotted Emanon at the head of the screaming warriors as they crashed into the enemy from behind.

"Forward!" Jirom shouted.

Crevices split the Akeshian formation from the pressure at both ends. Jirom bashed a swordsman in the nose with the pommel of his sword and pushed forward, only to find himself alone on the other side of the line. His hands and wrists were numb from the frantic combat. He gulped for fresh air while he scanned the street for more threats. The way before him was clear.

A minute later, Emanon came over to him with a smile on his lips. He was drenched from head to toe in rain and blood. "I was hoping we'd find you at the palace already, accepting the governor's surrender."

"We ran into some trouble. I see you got out of prison all right. And brought some friends along, eh?"

"It was a bit tougher than I expected," Emanon admitted. "They kept us chained up at night, but I managed to get hold of a key. After we overwhelmed the guards, most of the work crews decided to join the cause. Still, I don't know if we would've pushed through them in time if your pet wizard hadn't shown up with some of his magic tricks. He's handy to have around."

"Aye, as long as he's sober."

"You ready for the last push to victory?"

"We're ready as soon as we mop up this engagement."

"All right. Let's get to work."

Emanon left, shouting orders for their combined force to finish off the last Akeshians. Many of the surviving enemies had thrown down their weapons to surrender. Jirom faced away as the rebels and mercenaries dispatched them without quarter.

He was studying the palace, only a couple blocks away now, when he spotted another enemy unit approaching from that direction. It was a much smaller contingent. Perhaps fifty soldiers at most. Then he noticed the man at the head of the formation. He wore a long purple robe and leather boots. His complexion was pale for an Akeshian, his brown hair hanging in damp locks about his shoulders.

Jirom started forward, thinking this might be a town official or minor noble worth taking prisoner. He hadn't taken two steps before the street quaked beneath his feet. Then—impossibly—the mud pavement rose up before him, creating a wall twice the height of a man across the entire street. Jirom heard other rumblings to the north and south, and guessed that similar walls were rising in those directions.

Emanon shouted something, but it was lost in a boom of thunder. Jirom clenched both hands around the hilt of his sword. "Over it!" he shouted, waving his men forward. "Up and over!"

Jirom started toward the wall, but before he could reach it another boom of thunder burst above their heads. A shock of electricity tore down his back, followed by a flare of intense heat. Rebels and mercenaries were knocked to the ground.

Jirom blinked against the white spots swirling in front of his eyes. A prayer rose to his lips as he saw the jagged hole that had been blasted through the newly erected wall. It was wide enough to drive a wagon through. Jirom didn't know what god or goddess was looking out for them, but he wasn't about to waste this opportunity.

"Forward!" he shouted, his blood boiling with the need to finish this battle.

He was the first one through the smoking breach. On the other side, he saw the enemy only a bowshot away. The temperature suddenly dropped as the wind became so fierce he had to lean into it. Each step became harder to take against the mounting gusts. Then his sword's handle became warmer in his grip, and the winds died down. Jirom almost tripped as the resistance vanished before him. Rain hissed as it fell on the blade of the *assurana* sword, which glowed cherry-red in the gloom.

Then the robed man stepped forward, and Jirom's momentum faltered. It could only be one person.

CHAPTER EIGHTEEN

Horace shot up straight in the chair as the crackle of thunder echoed outside. He looked around, not sure where he was at first. Then he remembered. The governor's chambers in Sekhatun.

City plans and troop displacements were scattered across the desk where he'd fallen asleep. Right before retiring, he had used his authority to declare martial law over the town. He ordered the search of all persons entering or leaving, no matter their station. Suspicious persons were to be detained for questioning, which he would undertake himself. He didn't want the troops to be overzealous, but they couldn't afford any mistakes.

He'd had a strong drink before retiring. One drink quickly became two, and after that he lost count as he pored over the paperwork. Now a pounding headache had set up residence behind his eyes. Every flicker of lightning made him want to bury his head. He was about to do just that when an explosion detonated outside. Orange light shone through the window as the pane rattled.

Horace bolted out of the chair. A moment later, the chamber door flew open and Mezim rushed in. "We're under attack!"

Horace found his sandals and slipped them on. "Get a message to the *kapikul*. I want to know how many are attacking and where."

Mezim started to leave when Horace stopped him. "Wait! Find the governor, too. Have him join me on the roof."

"The roof, Master?"

"Yes! Now run!"

Horace's guards were waiting for him at the door. "Which way to the roof?"

The officer in charge, a young *hazari* with a shaved head, saluted. "This way, *Belzama*!"

Horace followed the officer down the corridor. They had just reached the stairs when a messenger for the town militia ran up, holding a slip of papyrus. "First Sword! I've been sent by Governor Arakhu!"

STORM AND STEEL

Horace took the note. It was a brief invitation to join the governor and his council of elders in the grand hall. He slipped it into his pocket beside the orb, which pulsed coolly against his fingers. "I've already sent instructions for the governor to attend me on the roof of this damned building. Go tell him. Quick!"

The messenger ran off, and Horace started up the stairs with his guards in tow, only realizing halfway up that he hadn't thought to bring a rain cloak. He reached the door to the roof and shoved it open.

Thunder boomed as flashes of white lightning forked above the town. The stars were now hidden behind a blanket of clouds.

He went to the roof's edge and peered over the side, west toward the explosion he had seen from his bedroom. Havoc echoed below him. Civilians were out on the streets, running in every direction. Something huge burned at the edge of town. It took him a moment to realize it was the western wall. He didn't know that stone and brick *could* burn, but the flames roaring into the sky attested that it was indeed possible. He couldn't see the source of the fire from here. What should he do? If this was the rebel attack, he needed to be there. *To do what? Fight them? I can't do that. Those people, whatever their crimes, are only fighting for their freedom, the same as I was. They need my help.*

His headache returned like a spike pushing through the center of his skull as he tried to figure out a way to both satisfy the queen and aid the slaves. *I can solve this. Just think!*

A tingle ran down the back of his neck. Horace opened the gateway of his *qa* and reached out with his inner senses to try to find the source. Yet what came back to him was only a feeling, like an elusive flicker of warmth. It was only there for an instant, then it vanished.

One of Sekhatun's biggest weaknesses was its lack of *zoanii*. Shu Tural told him in confidence that Isiratu had systematically driven them away during his reign, possibly to negate any challenges against his authority. Most of the *zoanii* with holdings in Sekhatun lived in Erugash, and some in Nisus. In any case, when it came to magical protectors, the town was in short supply. He was on his own.

Horace turned to his guards. "Go find a militia commander and tell them to send soldiers to reinforce the west gate right away!"

The *hazari* frowned. "*Belum*, we're instructed to stay with you at all—"

"Forget that. Pass along my command or be prepared to tell the queen why you disobeyed her First Sword."

The officer saluted and dispatched a runner. As Horace turned back to the chaos below, the elusive flicker of *zoana* out in the city returned, like the momentary spark of a firefly. Even as he reached out again to identify the source, another explosion erupted from south of his position, ruining his concentration. Fiery orange light illuminated the dock quarter of the town. The River Gate was now burning, too.

Horace stared at the new inferno for a dozen heartbeats before he noticed Mezim standing beside him. The secretary was soaked and appeared short of breath as if he'd been running for his life. "Mezim. Good. Listen, we need everyone we can find working on putting out those fires."

"Master, the governor has ordered the militia to surround and protect the palace."

"What? No, no! We need those men at the gates. That Prophet-damned fool and his shortsighted pack of idiot elders!" Horace glanced at the guards, but none of them so much as batted an eye at his disparaging remarks. "All right. We can still salvage this mess. I need you to find *Kapikul*—"

The roof trembled as a loud roar echoed through the town. Horace looked west, not believing what he saw. An entire section of the western wall was collapsing, spilling into the adjoining streets in an avalanche of flaming stone. He couldn't move, too stunned to speak or even utter a curse. He thought of all the soldiers who had been standing on those ramparts, now buried under tons of debris. All dead. Just like Ubar. Just like Mulcibar. His anger, which had been banked like a hearth of cold embers in his chest, sprang to life anew.

"Find Shu Tural," he said. "And tell him to concentrate his men around the breach."

Mezim ran to obey, and Horace left the rooftop behind him. He couldn't do anything from up here. He needed to be down where the fighting was happening. He and his guards hustled down the stairs to the clatter of armor. He passed through the main hall, which was filled with slaves and servants running errands. He didn't see any military uniforms among them. He considered for a moment going to see the governor and taking the man to task, but there wasn't time.

The grand doors of the building's entrance were closed tight and guarded by a platoon of soldiers. Horace waved at them as he approached. "Move out of the way!"

The soldiers didn't move. At least, not fast enough for him. Horace summoned his *zoana*. He meant to push them aside with a gentle gust of air, but the soldiers flew apart as if they'd been caught in a typhoon. Horace bit his tongue but only offered a mumbled "I'm sorry" as he strode past them. He shoved with the power, and the doors swung open to reveal a scene of pandemonium.

Beyond a double cordon of militia troopers, townspeople flooded the plaza. Families, many with small children, fought through the press to some perceived place of safety, although Horace had had no idea where they thought that might be. The sight hurled his mind back to the day he, Sari, and Josef had fled the plague in Tines. The same shouts filling the air, the same tableau of terror as people were confronted with the specter of death.

"You!" Horace shouted to be heard above the pouring rain. He pointed to the sentry with the most rank hashes on his shoulder plate.

The officer took one look at Horace, and then saluted.

"Get your men out into the streets to protect those people! Try to move them east, away from the fires."

As the troopers broke formation to rush out among the people, for a few heartbeats their presence only amplified the anarchy, but slowly they started moving people in the right direction.

Once the crowd in the plaza thinned, Horace plunged out into the rainstorm, heading for the western wall. One of his guards threw a cloak around his shoulders, but he was already drenched. He wasn't entirely sure what he was going to do yet, but he knew he needed to be in place if fighting broke out. As he walked at a swift clip, he felt something ahead. Still far away, but it made the back of his neck tingle.

He slowed his pace and concentrated. It was back, the same elusive sensation in the distance. It flickered ruby-red in his mind's eye. Then he noticed a second one, identical to the first, moving up from the south. And another to the northwest, which had to be inside the town walls. They moved fast, making it difficult to pinpoint them. Every few seconds one would vanish, only to reappear somewhere else. *How are they doing that?*

He counted six of them now. None felt extraordinarily powerful, but the number alone was making him nervous.

Water rushed around his ankles as he resumed his march. His guards came up to surround him on all sides, and for once he was grateful for their presence. They passed the temple of Kishar where a crowd of people were massed around the stone ziggurat, praying and kneeling in the mud. A handful of young priests in soaked robes stood atop the edifice, their arms raised to the stormy heavens. Horace ground his teeth at the sight. He understood that people wanted security, but they wouldn't get it in a temple. If the town fell, no place would be safe.

Flickering light appeared at the end of the street. Horace squinted to see what was happening. A swarm of shapes with slivers of metal in their hands advanced in his direction. *Heading for the governor's palace.*

His guards formed a cordon in front of him as he slowed down. He could see that the town's militia couldn't contain this threat. It was only a matter of minutes, perhaps, before the defenses crumbled. He knew he should intervene. Yet he was afraid. Afraid that his powers would surge beyond his control. Afraid to fight these men and women who only wanted their freedom. Could he be that monstrous? *I can try to stop them without hurting anyone.*

Lord Astaptah's teachings nagged at the back of his mind, urging him to unleash his full potential. *No, not here. Not now.*

He opened his *qa*, but only just a fraction of its capacity. The *zoana* surged behind the gateway, pushing to flood him with its energy. The strange presence reappeared in the back of his mind, as if it, too, wanted to experience the power. Horace reached through to the Kishargal dominion and directed it downward into the street. Suddenly he felt the weight of the buildings on either side, felt the solid bedrock far below. The first idea that came to mind was a new wall, cutting off the rebels from the town's citizens. He pulled at the mud and stone with his *zoana*. A titanic crack resounded, battling with the din of the storm, as a sheet of limestone thrust up from the ground two blocks in front of him, cutting off his view of the invading forces.

Horace's hands shook from the effort. The power flowed through him, similar to what he'd experienced working with Lord Astaptah. Without a second thought, he reached out to adjoining streets and erected fresh bulwarks there as well, forming a line of defenses between the rebels and the rest of Sekhatun.

It was exhilarating. Each conjuration sapped his strength for a few heartbeats, but then the energy returned even stronger. He felt invincible, like he had been born to do this. Even the strange presence hovering at the back of his mind didn't bother him much anymore.

He was admiring his handiwork when lightning struck, so close the emerald-green flash seared through his eyelids. Roaring thunder drowned out his shout as the ground bucked beneath him and dropped him hard on his ass. Water ran around him like the tide. When he could see clearly again, he was confronted with a sight that infected him with a sense of dread. The stone wall he had just created was shattered, a gigantic hole punched through its center. Trails of smoked issued from its blackened edges.

Horace tried to stand up, but his sense of balance was off. He got to his knees before the sudden vertigo forced him to pause. His guards recovered slowly as well, some of them holding their heads. Shouts rang out down the street. Horace groaned as he tried again to stand. His legs were shaky, but he managed to get up by leaning on a guardsman. A big man passed through the hole in the stone wall. The large sword in his hands glowed bright like a bar of steel pulled right from the forge. Horace reached down to help another soldier to his feet. "We have to retreat."

"Go, *Belum*," one bodyguard said. "We'll hold them here."

More men were clambering through the broken wall. Arrows hissed through the air, though he couldn't see them in the dark, nor tell which side was firing at whom.

Horace looked to the east. The street behind them was clear, no sign of soldiers or citizens. "Get back!" he shouted. "Behind me!"

Trusting the guards to follow his command, Horace called upon the

Imuvar dominion. It rushed into him, swift and cold like the breath of an Arnossi winter. He gathered it around him in a miniature cyclone. Puffs of wind swirled about him, tugging at his clothes, growing from a breeze to a strong gust as he exerted himself. His headache returned as he worked, but it wasn't bad enough to distract him. He sent the wind down the street, channeling it into a continual flow of air.

All of a sudden, a ripple coursed through his *zoana*. The winds faltered like an old man gasping for breath. Horace focused harder. His *qa* was open, his connection to the Imuvar unchanged, but the magic wasn't behaving, as if something was blocking it from taking the proper shape.

Horace delved deep to find every last shred of *zoana* inside him. The pain in his head increased. The big man was striding closer, followed by a pack of armed fighters. Horace knew his guards couldn't hope to stand against that mob. The presence urged him to call upon his power, but the stone wall hadn't kept the rebels out, and his winds were faltering. He doubted if a shield of *zoana* could withstand whatever trick the enemy was employing.

Horace wracked his brain for a solution that didn't involve mass slaughter. Then a lightning flash from above illuminated the street in ghoulish light, and Horace froze. The big man stopped, only a stone's throw away, and their gazes met.

It was Jirom.

Jirom lowered his sword. One of the rebels, a brawny man with short black hair and a stubbly beard, came up to stand beside him. A shock ran through Horace as he realized he'd seen the man before. Today, in fact. He'd been part of the crew working on the wall outside of town. *Is that the mysterious rebel agitator Emanon? And we had him in chains just hours ago.*

Numbness climbed Horace's legs as he started to realize how little he understood what was happening here. Then the lightning faded, plunging the street once more in gloom.

He wondered what would happen now. He hadn't seen Jirom in months. What if the man had changed? What if he had forgotten their brief friendship? Horace took a chance.

"Jirom!"

STORM AND STEEL

Lightning flashed above the town, highlighting the townhouses and shops along the street in stark relief. Jirom studied this man he had once called a friend. He was surprised by how much Horace had changed over the last few months. The fine clothes. Soldiers at his command. The confidence in his steady gaze. *He's not a slave anymore. He's the First Sword of Erugash, right hand to a queen.*

The two of them stood there, just staring at each other.

Emanon came up beside him. "You all right, Jirom? You look like you're seeing your own . . ." He peered down the street. ". . . death. Take a rest. I've got this."

Jirom put out an arm to halt his paramour. "No. That's Horace."

"I know. I saw him when I working on the wall. How in the six raging cocks of Enkath did he get into Sekhatun without us finding out?"

"Stay here."

"Where the hell do you think you're going?"

"I need to talk to him."

Emanon grumbled under his breath but didn't try to stop him. Jirom studied the man he had once called a friend as he thought back to that hellish march through the desert and all that they'd shared.

Tightening his grip on his sword, he called back.

Finally, after several long seconds, a familiar voice shouted back. "Horace! That you?"

Horace allowed himself a moment to smile. "It's me. I'm coming out to talk. All right?"

"All right. Just you and me."

Horace turned to his guards "Stay here. No one do anything stupid, like launch an attack while I'm over there. Understand?"

Heads nodded, rain pinging off their helmets. Horace walked out beyond the formation alone. Drenched to the bone and feeling terribly exposed. If this was a trick to kill or capture him, it would probably work, especially if the magic-dampening effect remained to thwart his powers. Without them, he was just an ordinary man.

One of the rebels had a shuttered lantern that shone a small circle of light on the front ranks of the mob. There were more of them than he realized. He stopped suddenly, halfway between the opposing frontlines.

Jirom came out to meet him. He was covered in blood and stank like a butcher's stall. The long, red sword in his hand made Horace nervous. "I've been trying to find you. The trail went cold after Omikur."

Jirom nodded, his mouth a grim line. The rain mingled with blood on his face. "There's been rumors you're working for the queen of Erugash. That you're part of her inner circle."

"She's the one who sent me."

"Are you her executioner now, Horace? You come to kill us? Put us back in chains?"

"No. I'm here to forge a peace. We don't want any more violence. There has to be a peaceful way to end this."

"What if peace isn't possible? We won't go back to bondage again. Not ever. We'll die before that. Is your queen willing to accept that?"

"I don't know. But I'm here to offer you and your men a chance to live. You don't have to die in vain."

"It's not in vain. Freedom is worth fighting for."

"Is it worth killing for? Is that why you murdered Lord Ubar? He was a friend of mine. He trusted me, and I trusted you enough to make that peace offer."

"That was not my doing."

Despite the hardness in Jirom's eyes, Horace wanted to believe him.

"He was killed by traitors in our midst to make it look as if—"

Jirom looked up, his eyes narrowing. Then he shouted over his shoulder. "Ambush! Take cover!"

A heartbeat later, a hail of arrows scoured the street. Horace glanced skyward and saw rows of figures with bows in their hands on the rooftops on both sides of the street. Tortured screams cried out as rebels fell, their blood pouring into the rainwaters that sluiced between their feet.

Horace looked back to Jirom with panic. "I didn't do this!"

But Jirom was already sprinting back to the rebel lines. Horace was tempted to go after him, but strong hands gripped him by the shoulders as his bodyguards surrounded him.

"This is a death-trap!" one of his guards shouted over the clamor. "We have to get out of here!"

Horace allowed himself to be pulled back. Down the street, Jirom and the bearded man directed their men to get out of the street. They battered down doors, only to find Akeshian soldiers waiting inside the homes. The fighting grew savage. Horace had retreated to the end of the block when a tingle ran down his spine. He felt the buildup of energy a split second before fire exploded in the street. Men howled as they were burned alive.

Horace traced the trail of *zoana* up to the roof on his left and saw a tall figure standing there, his robes beating in the stormy winds.

Lord Xantu.

This was a critical moment. Did he go to Jirom's aid, possibly even attack Xantu to help the rebels escape? If he did, he'd be branded a turncoat forever-more. Yet, if he did nothing, the rebels and Jirom were going to die.

Above the town, the sky was awash in roiling thunderheads. The spitting lightning was almost continuous, striking near and far. Its staccato repetitions bolstered his resolve. *To Hell with it. I'm not going to watch them be massacred. If Byleth doesn't like it, then she can have my head.*

The rain on his face gave him an idea. Xantu was attuned to the Girru dominion. Fire magic. Horace took a deep breath and reached down to his *qa*. He summoned as much power as he could handle, feeling it course and sear through him as he worked it to his will. Both Mulcibar and Ubar had warned him that playing with the weather was a dangerous and unpredictable thing. *Well, it's the best answer I can come up with. So here it goes.*

He threw the conjuration into the sky as high as his mind could project. He felt it soar straight up like a bird through the ethereal tether still connected to him. When he judged it was high enough, he sent a jolt of *zoana* up that line, praying it would do what he intended.

The sky opened with a crackling roar. Gale-force winds blew down on the town. Roof tiles and loose shutters tore free of their moorings. And then the rain came. Not just a downpour but a deluge. Water fell from the dark heavens with the fury of a hurricane. The street vanished under the tide of water, washing away the blood and bodies of the fallen combatants.

Up on the rooftop, Lord Xantu bent under the power of the storm with one arm thrown over his head. Horace felt the sorcerer's gaze directed down at him, but he stood tall. *Yes, I did this. Now, if you want to strike at someone, I'm right here.*

Part of him wanted Xantu to attack, craved something that resembled a fair fight in all this mess. Yet the queen's bodyguard turned and disappeared out of sight.

Horace glanced down the street. Jirom and his crew were putting up a fight, but they were still being pushed back step by step. His gambit had worked to some extent. At least the rebels had a chance now.

He eased the flow of energy into the sky. The storm, however, continued to hurl rain and lightning. Then a shiver ran through him from crown to heels. A billowing of green radiance was growing inside the clouds like a gangrenous tumor.

Oh, Lord. Oh, no.

"Back! Get back! Stick tight, damn you!"

Jirom shouted over the roar of the storm. An old battle hymn thrummed in his head, rising to the quickening beat of his pulse. The grip of the *assurana* sword coaxed him to unleash his anger on the armored masses of his enemies. Arrows continued to sting his men. The ambush had been executed with precision. He should have seen it coming, but he never would have guessed that Horace would be a party to such a ruse.

STORM AND STEEL

Maybe he wasn't. He looked as surprised as anyone when the archers appeared. But then fire rained down on us and I know I saw something in his eyes. He knew it was coming, or he suspected, which is just the same. Now we're good and fucked.

Jirom stooped down to rip a rectangular shield from the arm of a fallen Akeshian. Holding it over his head, he looked for Emanon. The rebels, caught out of formation, scrambled around as the flights of arrows showered them. Screams ripped the air, adding to the confusion. The mercenaries held together with minimal losses and returned fire in orderly volleys.

Columns of uniformed soldiers emerged from several side streets into the avenue. Jirom could tell at a glance that they were better armed and armored than mere militia. They marched in tight formation behind a shield wall, long spears jutting before them. Akeshian legionnaires. The cream of Her Majesty's army. *Blistering fuck! Where did they come from?*

Ramagesh's intelligence report hadn't mentioned anything about reinforcements in Sekhatun. If anything, they had focused on the sorry state of the local militia forces. *Killing that envoy was a big mistake.*

Anger burned in Jirom's stomach, but Ramagesh was already dead and there wasn't time for casting blame. He called for his heavy infantry to advance and was relieved when two half-strength squads complied. An arrow struck his raised shield as he shouted commands to the infantry sergeants to plug the street against the Akeshian advance.

A bang of thunder was the only notice he received before the clouds burst overhead. Rain fell like an entire sea had opened in the sky. Stumbling in the violent swash, Jirom ushered his fighters in the most organized retreat they could manage, but it was a losing battle. The enemy had the weight of numbers, not to speak of their sorcerous advantage. With his rearguard in place, Jirom turned to Emanon for an answer. His captain was ordering a faster retreat, sending scouts ahead to find safe way out. *I doubt there is one, Em. They caught us. Now they're going to grind us into meal.*

Suddenly, Emanon sprinted toward him with his sword upraised. Jirom tensed at the intense look on his lover's face. Jirom started to turn around just as a noise rushed up behind him, a hissing roar like the gathering of a massive wave on the verge of crashing.

An inferno exploded in the rebel formation. Smoke filled the street as men flew in all directions. From out of a cloud of smoke emerged a long burning arm, and then another. It took Jirom a moment to realize they were serpents. Huge pythons of fire. He didn't even have time to curse before they lunged at Emanon, closing their burning mouths around his arm and shoulder. Jirom leapt to protect his man from the foul things, but a third flaming serpent emerged to strike at him. Jirom swung the *assurana*, and the fire-snake reared back as if it had hit a stone wall. He took a step, intending to press his attack and save Emanon, but something clubbed him from behind.

He staggered to one knee. Fighting through the pain, he tried to stand up. The fiery serpent lunged, its jaws opened wide. Jirom surged upward to meet it with a two-handed slash. Intense heat flowed through the hilt into his hands as he split the creature in two. With a soft hiss, it dissipated in a puff of acrid steam.

He started to run to Emanon, but the unseen attacker struck from behind again. This time his vision blacked out, replaced by a panorama of swirling lights. A rock landed on the street beside him with a splash. Not a stone, but a brick. Bits of broken mortar stuck to its edges as if someone had torn it out of a building and hurled it at him.

Jirom looked over his shoulder and up. Another robed man stood on a nearby building. The man gestured, and an oblong object flew off the roof. Jirom raised his shield just in time to meet the flying masonry. The impact sent a shiver up his arm as the shield's wooden facing split. *Damn all wizards to hell!*

Jirom lifted his sword, but a sharp pain ran through his wrist. Stony shrapnel stung the side of his face as he dropped his sword. The shield buckled as pieces of stone and brick poured down, tearing into his shoulders and back. He tried to crawl to Emanon, but the fire-snakes lashed out with vicious snaps. His lover hung in their embrace, his eyes closed. The rebels tried to form a barricade, but they were getting slaughtered under the spears and arrows of the Akeshian legionnaires.

Jirom started to yell for them to scatter, to get out any way they could, but something struck his lower back before he could get it out. It hit right in the spot where he'd taken a spear, so many years ago he couldn't remember where it had happened anymore. His entire lower body went numb from the shock. He fell forward on his chest, arms splayed out before him.

Tongues of bright flame filled his vision as searing pain dragged him down into a bottomless abyss.

Horace stood atop a mound of rubble, barely able to hold himself upright. His head and chest were killing him, the aches penetrating into his core.

Akeshian soldiers scoured the streets, pulling the dead and wounded from the piles of bodies. Captives were disarmed, cobbled together, and led off under guard. The rebels were bedraggled and soaking wet, most of them bearing at least one bleeding wound, but they weren't beaten. They walked with their heads up, a challenge written in their eyes. *You may have won*, those hard gazes said, *but you'll never beat us.*

He understood. It wasn't so long ago that he had trod in a similar line, battered and bruised but refusing to let his captors defeat him. It tore at his heart to see the former slaves in bondage once again. But this time, he knew, none of them would be given the choice of serving the empire again. The queen had been true to her word, even if she hadn't been completely honest with him.

Jirom had already been carried away, either unconscious or dead. Horace hadn't been able to tell which, and he grieved for his friend. This had been a cruel blow.

Gravel crunched underfoot as a tall man in sodden robes came to stand with him.

"First Sword. I have sent out skirmishing parties to track down the remaining rebels beyond the walls."

Horace kept his fists clenched tight by his sides. "Lord Xantu. I didn't expect any . . . assistance with this matter."

"Her Majesty thought you could use the reinforcement."

Is that it? Or did she suspect I wouldn't be able to complete the mission?

He waited for Xantu to comment on his actions during the battle, especially the cloudburst, but the sorcerer merely stood quietly. Rain plopped in the puddles and rivulets that filled the street. After a minute, Horace couldn't stand the silence. "So what happens now?"

The *zoanii* raised his glance to the governor's palace. A flying ship hovered next to the roof. "We are ordered to return to Erugash."

"And the prisoners?"

"The survivors will accompany us."

And be executed as an example, no doubt. Damn you, Byleth. Why couldn't you trust me to handle this my way?

Lord Xantu led the way. After a couple seconds, Horace followed him through the ruined street. As he stepped over a wide gash filled with muddy water, Horace felt a faint itch down the back of his neck. In his mind's eye he saw a flicker of red. That mysterious aura again, farther off than before.

Ismail squatted behind a section of broken wall as mayhem raged around him. Cambys was dead, lying not five paces from him, with a dent in his forehead deep enough to fit a man's fist. His good eye had rolled back up in his head, but the bastard was still grinning.

Arrows flew down from the rooftops, invisible in the darkness. Just sticking his head out was enough to draw a withering hail. Worse things rumbled in the night. Things that shook the ground and flooded the streets. Things that weren't natural. That meant sorcery, but he didn't want to think about it. He had enough problems already.

He'd seen the captain and lieutenant taken. Seen the fire-snakes and the green smoke, things he never thought he'd see in his lifetime. Now he didn't know if anything would ever be the same.

Someone ran up. Ismail turned, his spear set to receive a charge, and almost impaled Yadz through the gut. The rebel trooper dove to the ground beside him. "It's crazy out there! I can't tell who is who except for those fuckers on the roofs. You think they'll run out of arrows anytime soon?"

Probably not before they've killed all of us.

"Did you find the other units?"

Yadz gestured down the street. "I think I saw one. Silfar's squad, maybe. But they ain't looking too good either. Only got a couple warm bodies left."

Ismail squinted in the dark, trying to determine whether a shadow on the street ahead was an enemy crawling toward them or just his imagination. "That's better than nothing."

Yadz held up a crossbow, glistening wet. "And look what I found!"

Ismail leaned his face away from the head of the quarrel loaded in the weapon. "You know how to use it?"

"It looks pretty simple. Just point and shoot, right?"

If anyone would understand simple, it's you. "Fine. Just don't point it in my direction. Like I was saying—"

Ismail flinched as the crossbow's string catapulted forward, shooting the quarrel high into the air. Yadz smiled like a six-year-old with his first honey stick. "Yowee! Did you see that?"

"Do you have any more ammunition for it?"

Yadz's smile faded. "Uh, I guess not."

Ismail shook his head and kept scanning the street for foes. He still couldn't believe that Lieutenant Jirom had stopped in the middle of the battle to parley with that *zoanii*. Even more unbelievable was the rumor that the pale-skinned man was the foreign wizard they'd all heard about, the one who served in Queen Byleth's court. But before anyone had a chance to stop and think about what was happening, more Akeshians showed up. These new ones wore the royal colors and were a heck of a lot better armed than the town militia. The mercenaries had gotten to work, setting up a sturdy defense in the intersection to four streets. When they started pushing into the buildings underneath the roof archers, Ismail had gathered his squad to join them. They had almost gotten to the street-level doorway when a terrifying *crackle* erupted from above. Seconds later, the building came tumbling down in a rush of bricks and mortar dust, throwing him and his mates into the street. That's where Cambys had died with a brick through his forehead.

After that, they'd been lost on their own, pinned down and surrounded by enemies. Yadz had run off, against his orders, to "find help." Ismail gave the man credit for guts, if not much smarts. "All right. We're going to make a break for it. We'll join up with Silfar's squad and get out of here."

Yadz gave him a lazy salute. "After you, Corporal."

"You might want to find a weapon."

"Oh, yeah." Yadz crawled over to Cambys and pulled a shortsword out from under the body. "Sorry, old boy. Since you can't pay me that money you owe, I'll just take this in trade."

Ismail suppressed the urge to leave Yadz behind. "You ready yet?"

"Yep."

They set off down the street. With every step Ismail got a better view of the carnage. Bodies lay all around, their blood mixing with the rainwater. Arrows occasionally flew in their direction. They crawled over a mound of debris from another semi-collapsed building at the end of the block.

Silfar's crew was coming out of a ruined eatery, all four of them. Their sergeant led the way; broken arrow points jutted from his shield. Corporal Uchan took up the rear.

Sergeant Silfar called out to them, his shield held ready. "What unit?"

"Partha's squad," Ismail answered back in a loud whisper.

The two squads met in the lee of a municipal building with a marble overhang supported by a row of pillars. "You two the only ones left?" the sergeant asked. His face betrayed a flicker of despair.

"Yessir. I hope you guys are heading out of here."

"Sure. We've already overstayed our welcome. You two take rearguard and stay on us like—"

"Like flies on shit?" Yadz asked.

For a second Ismail thought the sergeant was going to punch Yadz square in the nose, but he merely nodded and turned away.

They made their way through the wreckage, swathed in darkness. Every so often someone would trip over something, usually a dead body, or brush against a wall, and the resulting noise made Ismail duck his head as he imagined hidden marksmen drawing a bead on them. *Where are all the people of the town? Did they evacuate, or are they hiding all around us? Watching and waiting for us to die.*

Just then, doors opened on either side of the street, filled with dark shadows. "Watch—!"

Akeshian soldiers poured out of the buildings before Ismail could finish his warning. Corporal Uchan dropped immediately with a javelin through his side. Another of the troopers in Silfar's squad took a spear through the thigh and fell on his ass, screaming as blood spurted from the wound.

Ismail blocked a war-axe aimed at his head and pushed hard. The soldier stumbled back a step, and Yadz darted in to stab him under his armpit. Yadz flashed a tight smile and almost got his head caved in by a soldier swinging a two-handed maul. Ismail extended his spear in a lunge, hoping to catch the blow in time. But the soldier fell back, a thick quarrel punched through his chest.

The mercenaries arrived like steel-clad ghosts, rushing in to engage the Akeshians. Ismail stuck close to Yadz as the furious melee unfolded, pitting them against one visored face after another. He was stabbed twice and took a mace to his left shoulder, hard enough that he saw stars and thought the socket was ruined for a few seconds before feeling returned.

There was no place to retreat or advance with the mercs surging behind them and the enemy in front; they were stuck like two refugees on an island while the battle raged around them. An Akeshian came at him with a pair of long knives, sawing at the air like a deranged man. Ismail didn't think. He just bent his knees and leaned forward, letting the point of his spear lodge in the soldier's abdomen beneath the breastbone. The spear shaft flexed for a moment as the soldier came to an arrested halt, then the knife-wielder sagged and slid off to the bloody street.

As the flow of soldiers trickled to a halt, the mercs pushed inside the doorways with murder in their eyes. Ismail leaned against the side of the building. His nerves were shot. He just wanted to give up and let someone else deal with the situation. Yadz leaned beside him, smiling and gulping down fresh air. Then the rebel straightened up. "Oh no."

Ismail looked and almost swallowed his tongue as he spotted the old mercenary warlock. What was his name? Two Stars? The elderly merc stood in the street, humming something as he waved his hands back and forth. His gaze was focused on the building behind them.

"Ishy," Yadz said.

"Move!"

They both ran. Ismail got six steps away before a violent wind swept in behind them, lifting them up and shoving them forward. He landed on his side and rolled over several times until he crashed against a tenement building across the street. His ears rang like he'd been rabbit-punched repeatedly. Across the street, the building's upper floors were engulfed in flame. Pieces of wall fell to the ground in smoldering piles. Groans echoed from every quarter.

The old warlock slumped, and Ismail sincerely hoped he was out of magic power or whatever wizards used to fuel their enchantments. He started to get up until he saw Yadz lying on his stomach a couple feet away. Ismail crawled over to jostle him but stopped as his hand hovered above the motionless figure. Yadz's entire face had been ripped away. Mangled shreds of muscle and bone stared back at him, the eyeballs melted away.

Ismail sat back. He'd lost his spear, but he didn't care. He was the last of his squad. Perhaps the last rebel left alive. It was over.

"Come on, soldier," a grim voice spoke beside him.

Ismail looked up to see Captain Ovar standing over him. The mercenary captain had lost his helmet. His uniform was stained with blood and what looked like soot, or maybe it was dark mud. Fresh gore stained the hilt of his sword and its scabbard. Any other time, Ismail would have hurried to obey, but at this particular moment he didn't care. Other mercs moved around the rubble-covered street, dispatching the wounded enemy.

Suddenly, Ovar grabbed his arm and heaved him to his feet. Ismail didn't have the energy to resist, so he stood on numb legs. "I don't understand," he said. "Some of your men were inside. He killed them, too."

Captain Ovar held him steady. "They knew going in, son. Someone had to hold off the enemy while Three Moons worked his mojo."

How is that possible? What kind of men are these mercenaries?

"Where is your commanding officer?" Ovar asked.

"My sergeant and corporal are dead. The bosses got taken."

He left it at that. No use in trying to describe things he couldn't explain. Captain Ovar nodded as if that was enough. "Fine. You'll come with us then."

The captain stripped a demilance and a dented round shield from the corpse of a young soldier and shoved them into his hands. "Here. Strap up and get moving, son. We're not out of this yet."

Ovar shoved him toward the group of mercs assembling at the far intersection. A hulking brute of a man at least a foot taller than Ismail spotted him and called out. "Fall in! Second rank!"

After some jostling, Ismail found himself hustled into a square formation. The pikemen on the outside lifted their great shields and they began marching, back through the street the way they had come.

Ismail spared a glance over his shoulder, but there was nothing to see in the gloom as the smoke and darkness of night swept in behind them.

They knew going in. Gods damn us, didn't we all?

The first traces of dawn shimmered across the sky as the rebels scrambled over the dark fields, dragging their wounded with them. Stepping over a low wall that divided the fallow plots, Ismail set down his weapons and sat on the stone hedge. Exhaustion pulled at every muscle in his body, begging him to lie down and close his eyes.

The rest of the rebels kept moving. There were precious few of them left alive, hardly enough to fill out a platoon. The mercenaries had fared a little better. On the final push out of Sekhatun, another wave of Akeshian legionnaires struck them from the rear. Captain Ovar had sent half of his remaining force to hold them off while the rebels escaped. *What a disaster. Most of us dead. Our leaders captured. This is it, the death of the rebellion. There's no way we can come back from this.*

Captain Ovar came over to stand beside him. Ismail craned his neck to look up. The mercenary captain wore a strange expression, appearing both relieved and disheartened. Ismail tried to think of something to say, some way to boil what they had just experienced down into a pithy sentiment, but his mind was a blank.

As the survivors shuffled past them, Captain Ovar pulled off his bloody gauntlets and tucked them in his war-belt. "Don't give in to it, son."

"To what?"

"After a bad defeat, there's a tendency to wallow in the despair. To see it as an omen that things are going to only get worse. You have to fight that. If you stay in this game long enough, you're going to lose every once in a while. Sometimes a lot. But my outfit's fought back before and we'll do it again."

Ismail lifted his head in a nod, but the gesture didn't extend to his heart. The dark feelings remained, weighing him down. "What do we do now?"

"Well, I figure they're going to take your captain to Erugash. I know a few people, so we'll see what we can piece together."

Erugash? That's insane. Just walk right into the lioness's den.

After a few seconds, Ismail took up his weapons and rejoined the silent procession filing away from the town.

CHAPTER NINETEEN

His eyes strained as he reread the passage for the fourth time. Then, with a sigh, Horace gave up and closed the *Codex*. Bright light poured in the window of his solarium. His tunic was undone to allow some air to get to his sweaty chest. *What is she waiting for?*

It had been three days since he returned to Erugash, only to find the city awash in a heat wave. Hot, sultry air lingered on the streets, hardly moving at all. Lord Xantu had invited him, quite firmly, to return to his home. "Until Her Majesty has need of you," were the *zoanii*'s exact words.

And so he did, returning to his manor, where he discovered more piles of offerings and gifts outside his front gate. This time, though, there were no petitioners, for which he had been eminently grateful. He didn't know if he could deal with them right now. His world was crumbling apart. The rebellion had been crushed, ruthlessly, and Jirom was again in chains, awaiting what Horace feared would be a ghastly death.

Left alone with his worries, Horace went over his argument again and again, why he had attempted to parley with the rebel slaves, how mercy and understanding would soothe the country's wounds. But he was barred from seeing the queen. He'd found out about the assassination attempt on her life from his chambermaid.

He wished he had someone to talk to, but all his friends were gone. Mulcibar. Ubar. Even Alyra, although in her case he was somewhat glad she wasn't here. Anyone close to him was at risk.

And now he awaited a summons from the palace, where he would learn his fate. Lord Xantu, no doubt, was informing the queen of everything that had happened at Sekhatun. *If he convinces Byleth I'm a traitor, I may be sharing Jirom's sentence.*

I can't sit around any longer. I need to talk to Jirom.

He took down the sword of his office from the wall and went to his room. When he was dressed in his finest robes and properly coiffed, with the sword hanging from his hip, he went downstairs. Captain Gurita, sitting by the front door, got to his feet. "Going out, sir?"

"Please call for a litter."

Horace paced back and forth through the foyer while he waited. He didn't have much of a plan. He thought about sending a message to Mezim, but there wasn't time. If he waited too long, he'd lose his nerve.

When Gurita returned, Horace followed him outside. A litter car waited in the courtyard with four stout bearers. Fighting his distaste for such vehicles, Horace climbed inside. "Stay put, Gurita. I won't need you today."

Harxes rushed out of the house, his long robe dragging on the pavestones. "Master, shall I summon the rest of your bodyguard?"

"No, Harxes. Please make sure the three books in my study are returned to the archives if anything should happen."

His steward frowned but then bowed. "As you say."

Horace rapped on the roof of the litter. "To the royal palace."

The bearers picked him up and got underway. The heat was unbearable. Horace opened the curtains for some air, but it hardly helped. The ride reminded him of his first time in Erugash. Only a few months ago, but it felt like years. In that short time the city had somehow become as much a home to him as Avice had ever been. Gazing upon the tall tiers of buildings with their balcony gardens and painted domes, he felt a sense of pride. He wanted to believe he had done some good while he was here. He smiled at the people he passed on the avenue, nodding to the tradesmen and the laborers, the acolytes and students, the sailors and devas, as if they were old friends. *Yes, I'm one of you now. And I will meet my fate with the proper dignity.*

A row of heads on spikes greeted him at the outer gate of the palace. Most of the flesh had been picked from the skulls, making it impossible for him to identify anyone, but he didn't think any of them were Jirom.

Horace put on a stern face as a gate warden came over. "First Sword," the officer said. "We weren't expecting you today."

This was exactly what he had feared might happen. If there was an order to keep him out of the palace . . .

However, before he could form a reply, the sentry barked for the gate to be opened and waved the litter onward. "Have a good day, *Belzama*."

"Uh, and you as well," Horace mumbled.

Thank you, Lord. Or Lady Sippa. At this point, I'll take all the help I can get.

Only once he was inside did Horace notice the lack of protestors around the palace. Suddenly, the row of heads made more sense.

Horace got out of the litter. As he climbed the steps to the main entrance, he glanced up at the summit of the pyramid and was almost blinded by the sunlight reflecting off the great golden dome. The sentries at the inner gate stood aside as he approached.

Once inside the Grand Atrium, Horace let out a little sigh of relief and set off to find Jirom. He went to the north wing, to an access hall with a sturdy door at the far end that led to the dungeon level. Two soldiers of the Queen's Guard flanked the door. Their gazes focused on him.

Clearing his throat, Horace marched over to the door. "I'm here to see a prisoner."

The guard on the left said, "No one is allowed entrance without a writ from the queen."

"I am the First Sword. I have the authority—"

"Sorry, your lordship," the guard on the right said. "But this order comes directly from Her Majesty. No admittance under any circumstances. Please leave this chamber."

Horace stared at the men, but they did not waver. Finally, with one hand on the pommel of his sword, he stalked out. For half a moment he had considered forcing his way through but then thought the better of it.

Horace was exiting the hall when he saw Lord Xantu approaching at the head of a dozen guards.

"First Sword," Xantu said. "You are to come with me by the order of—"

"The queen," Horace finished for him. "*Ai*, I had the feeling you might say that."

He followed them through the Grand Atrium, up several flights of stone steps. At first, he thought they were taking him to the queen's rooms or perhaps one of the upper council chambers, but Lord Xantu led him to a small room on the second-highest tier, a room devoid of furniture or decoration. Just plain white plaster walls and a stone floor. A single, narrow window pierced the wall two arms' lengths above his head.

"You are to remain here," Xantu said. There was no emotion in his voice, no inflection at all. Then he closed the door and left Horace alone.

Horace heard the clank of metal as the guards took positions outside the door. He was tempted to try to the latch to see if it was locked or enspelled, but he didn't want to know. As long as he wasn't certain otherwise, he could pretend he was a guest instead of a prisoner.

So he stood in the center of the room, perfectly still, for as long as he could stand it, which was about half a bell. Then, propelled by his nerves, he began pacing. He walked back and forth across the room, examining his situation from every angle.

If the queen wanted him detained, or even dead, there wasn't much he could do to prevent it. He had no powerful allies to protect him. Even his *zoana* was refusing to cooperate. He was entirely in Byleth's power. But then again she knew that, and he still lived, which meant she wanted him alive. He stopped pacing. *Or she needs me. But why? She can handle the rebellion without me. Lord Xantu proved that at Sekhatun. That was a test—which I failed—but nothing more. No, she needs me for something else. Something more important.*

He tried to wrap his mind around her possible motivations. He discarded love right away. Byleth was no naive debutante. She played at seduction the way a cat toys with mice. Another bell passed by, and still he had no idea what the queen wanted from him. However he did come to one realization. *If she needs me badly enough, maybe I can use that to help Jirom.*

He wished he knew where Alyra was this very moment. He felt lost without her. Even fighting with her was better than being alone. *Maybe that's a side of love I've never known before. Maybe it doesn't always need to be peaceful. Did she leave because I didn't fight hard enough to keep her?*

He jumped when the door opened but then breathed a sigh of relief as Mezim walked in. He hadn't seen his secretary in person since they returned to the city. "What's going on?"

Mezim bowed from the waist. "I have been sent to fetch you."

All the warmth left Horace's body. Trying to mask his apprehension, he started toward the door. However, Mezim held out his hands. "My apologies, but I am ordered to take the weapon."

Horace looked down at the sword at his side. *So they don't expect me to take my own life. Is that because no one believes I possess the honor necessary to carry it out? Maybe they're right.*

He took off the weapon with care and handed it over. Mezim accepted it with another bow. Horace opened his mouth, thinking to give some last command as First Sword, some way he could make things better. But nothing came to mind. "Mezim, I think you'd better go home."

"I will accompany you—"

"Not this time. I'll handle this. Whatever happens, you're not to involve yourself. Understood?"

The secretary nodded, his face impassive. Horace patted him on the shoulder before he strode out the door, into the hall where Lord Xantu and Lady Anshara awaited. The lady made a nod in his direction. Xantu simply indicated for Horace to come along. He did, walking between the two body-guards. An entire platoon of the Queen's Guard closed in behind them.

His escort took him down the central stairs to the main audience chamber. The huge golden doors were open when they arrived. The coolness of the audience hall wafted over Horace as he entered. Members of the upper castes stood along both sides of the hall, leaving a broad aisle clear to the dais where the queen already waited.

Horace tried to gauge the mood of the assembly as he approached the throne, but the faces turned to him were impassive. That was something about the Akeshian culture he hadn't been able to breech, their ability to convey entire conversations just through gestures and expressions, or hide their thoughts so completely when they wanted. Byleth was no different. Wearing a long white gown that left her arms bare, her hair piled up in a tower bedecked with golden chains and jewels, she looked every bit a queen. She sat, hands resting on the arms of her throne, eyes focused on him.

Horace stopped a few paces from the bottom step of the dais and made a formal bow. He was considering whether he should go down on one knee or make some other obeisance when the queen addressed him. "Lord Horace, take your place with us."

He glanced up in surprise and saw a slight upturn of the queen's lips as she indicated a spot to her left. Horace climbed the marble steps, careful not trip, and turned to stand beside the queen. *Maybe she's not angry with me. Maybe I can escape this with my hide intact—*

His composure threatened to buckle as a square of soldiers marched into the audience chamber. The stomp of forty nailed boots sent loud echoes throughout the hall, amid the chorus of jingling mail and the rhythmic stamp of their spear butts on the floor. In their midst were two prisoners. Horace swallowed against the painful knot that had formed in his throat.

Jirom and the rebel leader, Emanon, stood in the center of the formation. Iron collars around their necks were joined to wrist manacles by lengths of heavy chain. Likewise their feet were shackled together. Both men sported numerous bruises, Jirom also having terrible burn marks across his head. Emanon's wounds seemed more concentrated on his body, and he walked with a shambling limp. Yet, despite their injuries, both men stood tall as if this were a parade in their honor. Jirom's eyes locked on Horace, and he swallowed again.

The platoon leader held out a long, curved sword in a beautiful scabbard adorned with gold filigree. Lord Xantu took the weapon and presented it to the queen. "Queen Byleth, I present the leaders of the slaves who so heinously rebelled against your divine rule. And also this *assurana* blade, which was found with these men. It belonged to *Kapikul* Hazael of House Tanunak, who was slain at the Battle of Omikur."

"Kill them, my queen!"

The shout rang out through the hall, and other voices rose to match it, raking the captives with vicious threats. Jirom stood quietly, still staring at Horace. The other man laughed out loud and was clubbed in the face by a soldier. Spitting blood, he wobbled for a moment but remained on his feet. Horace tore his eyes away from the prisoners to watch Byleth. She sat calmly, saying nothing for a few heartbeats. Then she lifted a hand, and the crowd fell silent.

"We thank you, Lord Xantu, for these prizes. By the efforts of our most trusted servants . . ." Byleth turned her head slightly in Horace's direction. ". . . the rebellion has been crushed. For their actions, the captives will be put to death."

Appreciative noises rose from the crowd. Horace could imagine what cruel tortures they were devising in their heads for these men who had dared to fight against the natural order. It made him burn with anger, which combined with the frustration in his stomach to make an unsettling brew. He could feel Jirom's gaze upon him, as if willing him to do something. Horace couldn't take it. "Excellence, may I speak?"

Byleth gestured to him. "Very well."

Horace struggled to find the words. "Your Excellence, I was not born in this country. I do not understand all of your customs, nor am I an expert in your laws. However, it would seem to me that executing these men would not serve Your Excellency's best interests."

Angry voices called out from the assemblage, but the queen quieted them with a look. "Continue."

"I was myself a slave, as I'm sure you recall. I remember the hopelessness and degradation that haunted my steps during those days. Yet there are people in your city who have spent years in bondage. Even their entire lives. Is it any wonder some of them chose to take up arms and fight to be free?" He looked out over the crowd, at the sea of seething faces. "Wouldn't any of us do the same if we were the ones in chains? If we saw our families bought and sold like property? Is there a single person here who wouldn't kill, or even die, to stop that from happening?"

"He's a traitor!" a man shouted from the back.

"Let him share their fate!" a woman called out.

The shouting began anew, so loud Horace couldn't make himself heard again. He searched for someone—anyone—who might join him in protesting this judgment. Yet he only saw condemnation. "Excellence, please," he said. "They have fought for their freedom. At least allow them the chance to fight for their lives."

The queen stared at him for several seconds. Then she stood up. A hush fell over the crowd. "These men," she said, "are sentenced to the Grand Arena, where they will fight to the death for our amusement. Take them from our sight!"

Cheers resounded from the nobles as the captives were dragged away. Jirom held his ground for a moment as two guardsmen pulled on his arms. Then he spat on the floor and let them haul him out.

"Put us against some of your pretty soldiers, Majesty!" Emanon shouted as he was wrestled toward the door. "We'll send them back in bloody pieces!"

Horace's legs shook so he could hardly stand. This was his fault. He'd had a chance to help Jirom and the slaves at Sekhatun. He could have defied the queen's command. Yet he'd stood by and allowed this to happen. Jirom's blood was on his hands. His stomach clenched, threatening to bring up his breakfast. He clutched the back of the throne for support, not caring about propriety. Fortunately, the queen didn't seem to notice as she walked out the hall, with Lord Xantu following in tow.

Horace took deep breaths to try to calm his stomach. His head ached again, bad enough he wanted to lie down. He didn't notice Lady Anshara standing behind him until she called to him. "Her Majesty would like a word in private."

I'll bet she does. Going to dress me down behind closed doors. Maybe I'll be back in chains before the day is through. Not that I deserve any better. I let Jirom and the slaves down, so now I should join them.

As the audience chamber emptied, Horace followed the lady out the back. The queen and Lord Xantu waited in the corridor. Royal guards flanked them. Horace kept a tight rein on his uneasy stomach as he bowed. "Your Excellence."

"I have decided to remove you from the office of First Sword, Lord Horace. Tomorrow at daybreak you will leave the city."

Again?

"The army of our enemies has crossed the Typhon River," she continued. "You will stop them by any means within your power. This is your final chance to convince us that you remain our loyal servant."

Horace didn't have the will to argue. It wouldn't do him any good, in any case. He'd once believed his elevation to the *zoanii* caste was an accolade, a reward for his services. Now he realized it was a leash. An invisible collar. He might have a nice home and fine clothes, servants, and all the rest, but he was still a slave.

"But tonight," Byleth said, "you will escort us to the Grand Arena where we shall watch the end of the rebellion together."

Horace bowed again. "As you wish, Excellence."

She stepped closer. "I think I like this side of you better. Perhaps when you return from your mission, we shall find more . . . pleasant . . . ways for you to serve us."

He said nothing as she walked away, surrounded by her guards. He waited until they disappeared up a flight of stairs, then left in the opposite direction. He needed to talk to someone, and only one name came to mind.

He didn't exactly know where to find Lord Astaptah, but he'd heard plenty of rumors about the vizier's personal chambers under the palace's foundation. Many of those rumors also speculated about the nefarious things Lord Astaptah did in those subterranean chambers, but Horace had no reason to believe them. The man had saved his life at great personal risk, and he knew the royal court like few others.

He went deeper into the palace. Once past the outer ring of halls, the natural light dwindled, and the corridors were illuminated by torches in iron cressets.

As Horace turned down a corridor he hoped would take him to the central section, a pair of young slaves stopped and bowed low.

"Pardon me," he said. "Can you tell me how to get to Lord Astaptah's quarters?"

The slaves exchanged a glance, and then both shook their heads. "*Neh, Belum*," they said in unison.

"I think," one said, with obvious hesitation, "there is a door." He pointed the way from which they had come. "Straight until this hallway ends. And then take two right turns. But the way is unlit."

"*Kanadu*." Horace nodded to them and proceeded on his way.

The corridor went on a good deal longer than he expected before ending in a junction. He turned right and stepped into a dark hallway. As the slave had said, there were no torches on the walls here, nor any brackets to hold them. Those who came this way were expected to bring their own illumination. He concentrated to channel trickles of Imuvar and Girru, and a ball of blue light appeared above him. It hovered over his shoulder as he continued on his search.

This hallway was shorter, running only about twenty paces before it arrived at an intersection. He started turning to his right when a looming figure emerged from the darkness ahead. Horace recoiled, both hands coming up before he recognized the other. "Lord Astaptah! I was just on my way to see you."

The vizier stopped and peered at him from down his long nose. "Lord Horace. This meeting is propitious, for I was coming to call upon you as well."

"Oh? What did you need with me?"

They walked back in the direction Horace had just come. The vizier had a long stride, forcing Horace to take quicker steps.

"I have just been informed of your return to the city," Lord Astaptah said. "And the events in Sekhatun. I was coming to inquire about your health. I heard there was a battle."

"That's what I was coming to see you about." Horace told Astaptah about his role in the fighting and how he tried to parlay with the rebels. He left out that he knew Jirom from before, not sure how the vizier would look upon a ranking member of the queen's court having such a tie to the slaves. "And now the leaders of the rebellion are sentenced to die, and I feel like it's my fault. The queen should—"

"Be wary, Lord Horace. It is not wise to presume to judge the actions of Her Majesty. Especially here at the seat of her power."

"I'm sorry, but these men don't deserve death. They were only fighting for the right to be free, the same as any—"

"If that is how you feel," Lord Astaptah interrupted him again, "then you must do your utmost to stop these executions."

Horace almost tripped. He had been prepared for anything. A rebuke to mind his betters. Or a lecture about the duty of the people to obey their ruler. Anything except agreement. "I'm pleased to hear you say that. So . . . how do I go about that? Without insulting the queen and losing my head, that is."

"With extraordinary care. Her Majesty is beset by many enemies. If you oppose her directly, she will strike you down as surely as the night falls. When I was a student, my *hasseba*—my teacher—set a task for me. Every morning I had to catch a toad from the river and throttle it with my bare hands, and then bring the dead creature to my teacher as proof of the deed."

Horace tried to get the image of Lord Astaptah wringing a toad's neck out of his mind. "Uh, I'm not sure what you're getting at. Are you saying I should let Jir—the rebel leaders die?"

"I did not finish my tale. On the third morning, I brought no toad, and my teacher beat me quite viciously. The next morning before dawn, I went to his house and killed him in his sleep."

A chill ran up Horace's spine. He didn't know how to respond to that.

They had reached the corridor junction. Horace stepped into the torch-light, but Lord Astaptah stopped at the edge of the darkened passage. "Every so often, Horace, we come to a moment when the decisions we make will impact the rest of our lives. When such a time comes, the most important thing is to be true to yourself. Or else you will be lost forever."

Horace nodded and started to reply, but Lord Astaptah's footsteps retreated into the darkness, leaving him alone once again.

"I'll keep that in mind," Horace whispered under his breath.

With hurried steps he made his way back to the sunlit portion of the palace.

CHAPTER TWENTY

The roar of the crowd brought back memories, none of them good. The Grand Arena. Its vast oval pit covered in sand, soaked with the blood of countless men, women, and children. The torches along the top of the stadium with their crimson tongues waving in the cool evening breezes. Even the stars high above. They all conspired to remind him of that night not so long ago when he had stood in the pit below and fought for his life.

"Horace."

He turned as Byleth entered the wooden box. She wore a floor-length *kalasiris* gown in dark green that, despite covering everything except her head and arms, showed off every curve. A fan-shaped neckpiece of gold plates complemented her other jewelry, the rings and earrings and bangles. Horace made a bow as she slinked into the throne at the front of the box. At her nod, he sat in the chair to her right. Lord Xantu and Lady Anshara stood behind them. It was to be an intimate affair, by royal standards.

Sitting beside the queen, he wore a neutral expression like a mask. It was the only defense he had against the conflict brewing inside him. He knew what was expected of him tonight, to sit at Byleth's side while his friend died. He told himself there was nothing he could do, with the queen and her bodyguards and all the *zoanii* in the other elevated boxes around the arena, any of them ready to burn him to ashes if he so much as raised a finger in Jirom's defense. *But he wouldn't hesitate for a moment if it were you, and you know it.*

That knowledge pained him most of all. It shattered every excuse he tried to use to convince himself that the situation wasn't hopeless.

A line of drums below the royal box rumbled to life, filling the stadium with a thunderous roll. One of the pit gates opened, and a procession entered the fighting area. They were priests and priestesses of Tammuz, wearing their white death garb, complete with dark iron masks. The people in the stands took to their feet and touched their foreheads. Even the queen. Horace stood out of respect but kept his hands by his side.

STORM AND STEEL

"I want you to know, Lord Horace," Byleth said as she sat back down. "Your loyalty means a great deal to me. There are not many I can fully trust. I hope I can count on you."

"You can, Excellence. But if you expect me to fall on my sword, I can tell you right now—"

"Perish the thought! I removed you as First Sword because the role never suited you. After you deal with the Nisusi, you'll return to Erugash as my High Vizier."

"I'm not sure I'm the man for the job." He paused before adding. "With all due respect, Your Excellence."

She gazed around the arena, seeming to take delight in the crowd of people preparing to witness their blood sport. "And why is that?"

"I'm not sure we share the same vision for the future."

Her laughter grated on his raw nerves. "Oh, Horace. Why do you persist in believing there is justice in the world? Honor, duty, justice. These are merely words we who rule devised in order to enslave our inferiors in webs of conflicting desires. Even the gods cannot be bothered to punish the wicked or reward the righteous. The rebellion is over, and balance is restored to the realm."

Horace struggled to form a reply that wouldn't get him executed, but he was spared by a sudden roar from the stands. A party of gladiators had emerged onto the sand. The pit fighters were outfitted in a variety of armors and helms to resemble different cultures. There was even a "western soldier" in mail with a shortsword and round shield. They lifted their weapons to the multitude while they paraded around.

Horace considered a silent prayer. *God or Gods. Whoever is watching this. Jirom is a good man. Please find some way to spare his life.*

After a moment's hesitation, he added one more thing. *And if you wouldn't mind, I could use a little help keeping my own head attached to my body.*

The second gate opened, and several men stumbled out. Horace looked closely, but he didn't recognize any of their faces. Jirom certainly wasn't among them. The new arrivals looked disheveled and malnourished. Several sported half-healed wounds and dark bruises. Each man carried a round shield the size of a dinner plate and a shortsword; none had any armor. *This isn't going to take long.*

The gladiators, whom Horace took for professionals, had arrayed themselves in a semicircle surrounding the rebels. They played to the crowd, banging their weapons together, waving the men to come forward. The rebels stayed together in a tight cluster, their eyes darting back and forth. Horace squeezed his hands tight together. *Come on! Spread out a little!*

He gritted his teeth as a gladiator darted forward and thrust his spear through a rebel's thigh. The victim collapsed, screaming as he clutched his injured leg. A second spear jab took him through the throat.

"Well done!" Byleth called out. She leaned toward him. "I know you tried to make an accord with these men."

Ice slid through Horace's veins. He tore his gaze away from the fight. "Excellence, I never intended to disobey your—"

"You aren't the first man to try to find his own solutions, Horace. You should have seen the calamities my brother would get himself into, always trying to maneuver himself to greater heights. But remember this. You aren't a prince of the blood. You're not even Akeshian. There is only so much I am willing to forgive. Oh!"

Down below, three of the rebels were lying in the sand now, unmoving. The rest were trying to fight back, but they were outmatched by the professionals. Another rebel fell, holding onto the stump of his left wrist. His vanquisher lifted his weapon to the stands. Live or die? Their calls were riddled with derision. The gladiator put his sword cleanly through the downed rebel's chest.

"Mercy?" Horace winced at the plaintive tone in his voice, but he pressed forward anyway. "To honor their bravery, Your Excellence."

Byleth's smile widened as another rebel was killed, kicking his legs as he bled out from his stomach. "My darling, why would I want to honor such a pitiful thing?"

Horace seethed as another scream echoed from the pit and the crowd roared with delight.

Byleth observed him as she beckoned to Lady Anshara. "Wine, Horace?"

He shook his head. He was leaning over the railing, staring down at the combat as if wishing he could be down there, too. He was thinner than he had been, almost as scrawny as when she first met him, fresh out of the collar.

"There was another assassination attempt while you were gone." She tried to sound as if she were discussing something entirely mundane. "They actually got into my bedchamber, which you've never seen."

Horace nodded but said nothing. She saw a brief flash of emotion cross his face, but she couldn't tell if it was concern or simple annoyance.

She took a sip of wine. "I often feel my death approaching. Moreso these past couple months. I know a queen should not fear anything. Yet I cannot help myself. I don't believe there is anything waiting for me after this life. What do you think about that?"

Horace frowned as he glanced over at her. "Do you taunt me, Excellence?"

"Of course not, Horace. I want your honest opinion."

"Men are dying before our eyes. By your order. Pardon me if I'm not sympathetic to your newfound fears of mortality."

"And if I agreed to spare their lives?"

"Will you?"

She shook her head and smiled. "No."

His gaze returned to the pit below. His knuckles were bone-white as they gripped the railing.

It was just like old times. The roar of the crowd. The smells of blood and sweat and fear mingled with leather and old sawdust dredging up primal urges inside him, diminishing all of life down to one elemental equation. To kill or be killed.

Back where I started.

Jirom clenched and unclenched his hands as the gate opened and two slaves dragged Jerkul's body inside. The sand-caked corpse had been hacked until its arms were barely attached to the shoulders. A ghastly wound sliced across the lower belly, spilling out brown entrails. Sadly for Jerkul, it had not been a quick death.

"Fucking hell," Emanon said, standing beside him. "How can you be so calm?"

They were chained to the tunnel wall, awaiting their turn with the rest of the rebels who had been captured at Sekhatun. Jirom watched as Lappu was unchained by a pair of guards. He struggled with his captors, which was admirable, but after several blows to the back and shoulders with their truncheons the guards hauled him up the ramp. The gate opened again, filling the tunnel with light and fresh cheers from the spectators, and then slammed shut again, plunging the rest of the rebels back into darkness. It was a cycle he remembered well, like the chime of prayer bells marking the hours of the day.

"You cannot deny the fear," Jirom said. "You must use it."

Emanon swore. "That doesn't make an ounce of sense. And I'm not afraid. I'm pissed off and ready to tear someone's heart out."

Jirom looked to the closed gate. At least he had some small hope that Three Moons and Longar may have escaped, as they weren't among the prisoners. Thinking about them made the feelings in his chest stir. "Then you'll soon get your wish."

"And you can forget about your friend, the First Sword, coming to save us. I saw his face. He belongs to the queen now, heart and soul."

Jirom didn't respond to that. There was nothing to say. He still trusted Horace, however it appeared. He knew what he'd seen in the man's eyes.

"Jirom, look at me."

He didn't want to. He was angry, too, but nothing could overcome the feeling he was to blame for this. He had agreed to the assault on Sekhatun. He had led them into the jaws of the trap, and then failed to get his fighters out. Now he was forced to watch as they were butchered one by one for the sport of the crowd.

"Dammit, Jirom! Look at me!"

With difficulty, he turned his head.

Emanon's deep-green eyes stared at him. "Jirom, I want you to know that no matter what happens, I've never loved anyone as much as I love you. I never thought it was possible. You opened my heart, and I'm forever grateful."

Forever isn't going to last much longer, my sweet man.

Jirom opened his mouth to say he felt the same way when the gate opened with a rumbling shudder. Lappu's remains were dragged inside. Terrible wounds covered the body, parallel tracks that looked like they'd been inflicted by large claws. Most of the face had been chewed off. Jirom swallowed a curse. Lappu was the last of the crew who'd been with them at Omikur. Now it was just him and Emanon.

The cheers of the crowd rolled above the tunnel. As the guards came for them, Jirom spied a slim figure lurking at the bottom of the ramp. The person wore a long cloak with the hood drawn up. Staying to the shadows that obscured the bottom of the tunnel, the figure moved its hood far enough to show her face. He caught the gesture she made.

"What the fuck are you smiling at?" Emanon asked.

Jirom nodded to the figure before she disappeared. "Things just got more interesting. Tell me more about how much you love me."

The guards grabbed them by the arms and hustled them up the ramp. Emanon snarled at them and wrenched himself loose. "We can walk, you goat-lovers."

Jirom didn't bother struggling. His mind and body were focused on the fight to come.

Torchlight washed over them as the gate opened, and the screams of a thousand Akeshians greeted their arrival. Jirom's heart beat faster. Weapons and bucklers were dropped at their feet. He hefted them. Cheap iron and wood.

"Shall we give them a show?" Emanon asked.

Jirom showed his lover a grim smile. "Aye. A show they won't forget."

The gate slammed shut behind them.

They strode out into the arena like conquering heroes, crossing sands drenched in the blood of their comrades without flinching. Two men against six armed and armored killers. Jirom looked fearsome, despite wearing only a tattered tunic and skirt. Emanon was no less intimidating, the broad stripes of burn marks across his arms and body making him look like some exotic beast. Each of them saluted with his sword, not toward the royal box, but to the men aligned against them. Horace held his breath at the sight.

"Ah," Byleth said, sitting back in her throne as she swirled a cup of wine. "Now come the leaders of the insurrection. I wonder if they'll die as well as their henchmen."

Horace clutched the stone railing at the front of the box. He wanted to jump over the bar and race down to join Jirom. He imagined the gasps of shock that would spring from such a bold gesture. He also imagined the queen unleashing hell on earth. With a deep breath, he sat back and tried to appear calm.

In the pit, the gladiators had moved to surround the two men. Jirom and Emanon stood back-to-back with readied weapons. Horace prepared himself for the violence, yet he was shocked by the speed with which it arrived. Jirom went from standing completely still—his legs bent, small shield raised to chest level—to rushing forward in a flash of steel. One gladiator fell in the opening blows, his lower jaw nearly sliced clean off in a fountain of bright blood. A gladiator lunged with a spear, aiming for Jirom's legs, but the weapon was caught by a deft dip of a wooden buckler. As its wielder pulled to free it, Jirom followed up with a swift thrust that took the spearman through the stomach. The gladiator fell and curled up in a bloody ball.

Jirom's partner moved just as quickly, putting three gladiators on the defensive with a series of attacks. The hollow ring of iron on bronze rang throughout the stadium. Second by second, the crowd began to show its approval. Murmurs of excitement grew to loud cheers with every blow struck.

The western-style gladiator collapsed from a blow to the temple that dented his helmet. A heartbeat later, Emanon sliced off several fingers on a swordsman's hand and kicked him in the face when the fighter doubled over in pain. Jirom and Emanon stood together and waited. Each bore a couple scratches, but no serious wounds. *That's it. Finish the last two and it's over.*

STORM AND STEEL

Yet the two remaining gladiators appeared to want nothing to do with the rebels. They had backed up almost to the gate by which they had entered. Jirom and Emanon didn't chase after them, which Horace thought was wise. They controlled the battlefield. *Maybe the queen will grant them amnesty after seeing this. Not even her own killers want to face them.*

His heart beat faster as Byleth stood up. The drums below began to pound to a quick beat. He waited for her to say something, but the queen merely gestured to across the arena. He thought she was just playing to the crowd, but then a third gate opened. His heart stopped as a massive shape scuttled out. He couldn't believe his eyes. A similar reaction rippled through the crowd as cheers turned to shouts of horror. *It's not possible. It can't be.*

The creature emerged slowly onto the sands. First a pair of pinchers, unbelievably huge, followed by a wedge-shaped body supported by six segmented legs. Over its back poised a hooked tail with a dangling stinger the size of a sickle blade. Torchlight gleamed from its black carapace. A thicket of long spears appeared behind the gargantuan scorpion, prodding it ahead. They pulled back quickly as the gate closed.

One of the gladiators tried to chop through his gate. The portal shook under the frantic blows, chips of wood flying, but it held fast. The other gladiator ran to the wall directly beneath the royal box, opposite from the monster. The sudden movement must have triggered some primal instinct, for the scorpion darted forward, kicking up a cloud of sand. Jirom and Emanon held their ground, shields raised, and the monster passed them by. The running gladiator, who wielded a long-handled axe, saw what was coming and sprinted faster around the pit's curved edge. He almost made it halfway around when the scorpion reached him.

A pincher lashed out and gouged a divot in the brick retaining wall. The axe-fighter jumped out of the path of the second pincher, which barely missed taking off his head with a quick snap. Then the stinger shot forward, so fast Horace almost didn't see it move. Once. Twice. Then the gladiator fell writhing on the sand with two deep punctures through his chest.

Horace didn't believe his eyes. The creature moved so fast and with such power, it was like watching an avalanche of death. He glanced sideways at the queen. A cruel smile played on her blood-red lips. He'd been a fool to think Jirom would receive any mercy from her. This was exactly what she wanted, a gruesome death, the tale of which would spread through the empire.

The scorpion turned around with more grace than seemed natural for a creature so large. The last gladiator knelt beside the closed gate, his head pressed to the wood as if trying to push himself through the boards. Jirom and Emanon hadn't moved, standing side by side with their swords held by their sides. They took deep breaths as if bracing themselves.

The next attack came in a furious rush. The scorpion came at the rebel leaders, its pinchers extended before it. Jirom shouted something—Horace couldn't hear it over the tremulous rumbles of the crowd—and the two men split apart. Jirom ran left and his partner went right. The huge arachnid turned to chase Emanon. A burst of relief filled Horace until he saw Jirom stop and run after the beast. *No! Don't follow it, you idiot!*

"Did you say something, Horace?"

He shook his head without taking his eyes off the fight. "No, Excellence. Not a word."

But he was having trouble containing the frustration building inside him. He was furious with the queen and angry at himself, but a part of him was also irate at Jirom, for joining up with this rebellion and putting him in such a bind where he was caught between loyalties. The compounded feelings ate at him, making him want to lash out.

Emanon got to the wall. He jumped aside as both pinchers reached for him. The stinger leapt forward, quicker than an arrow's flight, and hit the man's buckler with a heavy thunk. The stinger retracted for a second thrust, but it jerked to a halt as Jirom leapt onto the monster's tail. With one arm wrapped around the massive limb, he wrenched it backward, and Horace couldn't stop himself from smiling. Then the pinchers snapped again, and this time one of them clipped Emanon, catching him by the hip for a moment before the man smacked the huge claw away with his sword. The other pincher closed on his shield and crushed it with a fierce snap. Emanon let go of the buckler and struck a blow to its armored head between the two arching feelers, but a sideways swipe from the scorpion knocked him off his feet.

STORM AND STEEL

Horace jumped to his feet.

"Lord Horace?"

Down on the sands, Jirom tried to haul the scorpion away from his partner by brute force, but the creature was just too big. Its next attempt to grab Emanon missed by mere inches. Horace's heart thumped hard as he grasped the railing so hard his finger joints started to ache.

"Lord Horace!"

The steel in the queen's voice pulled him away from the spectacle. She was staring at him. He almost reached for his *zoana* but stopped himself before his *qa* opened. He felt the power pulsing behind the mystic gateway and turned away from it.

A groan from the stands made him turn back. Emanon was down, unmoving on the sands, with a nasty puncture in his chest. The monstrous scorpion turned in circles, reaching for Jirom with its pinchers as it simultaneously tried to shake him off. Jirom had already ditched his buckler, possibly to get a better grip on the beast's tail, but he still had his sword. He dug the point into the scorpion's hide, but the thing was too well armored. Then the scorpion jerked its tail forward, and Jirom flipped up and over onto its broad back.

Horace almost bit his tongue as Jirom kept rolling, barely avoiding a quick jab from the stinger as he tumbled over the scorpion's head and fell right in front of it. Before the monster could grab him, Jirom scrambled between its pinchers and got underneath the body. He thrust up at the armored underbelly, but again his weapon could not penetrate.

"At least you could have given them proper weapons," Horace muttered.

"I'm sure I heard you say something this time," Byleth said.

He nodded without turning his head. "I was just remarking on the merits of this demonstration. What a fitting testament to the crown of Erugash, to allow these prisoners to display more courage and integrity than those who hold them captive."

"You forget yourself!"

Horace felt Xantu and Anshara step closer to him, and he smiled without humor. He wanted an outlet for his rage. He craved it. *Give me a good reason to stop playing nice.*

The scorpion skittered around in circles as it attempted to get at Jirom, but the big man was too quick. Then Jirom did something that caused Horace to almost swallow his tongue. He threw away his sword. It struck the nearby retaining wall with a metallic clatter. As the scorpion spun toward the sound, Jirom darted away, out from under the creature and across the sands. *What are you doing? There's no place to go. No place you can—*

Horace pounded the railing as Jirom picked up the axe from the body of a fallen gladiator. It was a fearsome weapon, two-handed with a double-edged blade.

At the same time, the giant arachnid discovered its prey had escaped and charged straight at him. Horace expected Jirom to evade it with some intricate combat maneuver, but he just stood there, axe held across his body as the scorpion reached out with both claws. An instant before those fearsome pinchers snapped, Jirom brought the axe down in an overhand chop. He hit the joint holding the right pincher, and the gigantic appendage drooped. A second chop to the same spot severed the pincher completely. The crowd roared with approval.

The scorpion's remaining pincher, however, snatched Jirom around the waist. It lifted him close, and a thousand voices filled the stadium with their horror. Jirom wasn't struggling. *No, no! You can't die this way. Not now!*

The axe came up again in an arc of bright steel and crashed down on the monster's head. Pieces of chitin flew as the blade bit deep. The scorpion trembled from antennae to tail. Horace lifted his fist, ready to proclaim victory. Then the monster bucked like an unbroken stallion, and the stinger jabbed out. Horace's cry was lost in the clamor.

Jirom stood rigid in the scorpion's grasp. Then he flopped to the floor of the pit. He thrashed for a few seconds before he lay still.

Horace stared down in disbelief. Jirom lay dead in the sand as a dozen wranglers armed with ropes and polearms herded the limping scorpion back toward the gate. Second by second, his disbelief turned to anger, and the anger burned white-hot. Torches flickered as the wind picked up.

For some reason, Lord Astaptah's last words to him came rushing through his brain.

STORM AND STEEL

Every so often, Horace, we come to a moment when the decisions we make will impact the rest of our lives. When such a time comes, the most important thing is to be true to yourself. Or else you will be lost forever.

The stone railing twisted in his grip like wet clay. With a start, Horace realized he was filled with *zoana*. It seethed inside him, formless and wild. Thunder boomed overhead, a long slow rumble that grew louder by the second, building until it shook the stadium. The dark presence appeared, so close it felt like it was looking out through his eyes. He didn't care. The power felt different. More personal. He could feel it flowing through his body with new clarity, as if his anger was a focusing lens. His head swam with euphoria, and yet he remained perfectly clear.

He turned around to see Byleth staring at him. Lord Xantu stood at the queen's right hand, Lady Anshara on her left. Both bodyguards watched him. He thought about admonishing the queen but kept his mouth closed. There was nothing to say.

Pins and needles raced down the back of Horace's neck as a shimmering globe of solid air formed around the throne. At the same instant, an ice-cold knot formed around his throat, choking off his breath. He felt the thread of power leading back not to the queen, as he'd expected, but Lady Anshara. The icy noose around his neck tightened, restraining him in place. He pushed back against it, but she was too strong to be dismissed, her *zoana* shining around her like a brilliant white cloak. Hoarfrost spread across the floor, ceiling, and bannister of the royal box.

Lord Xantu lifted a hand toward Horace as if to touch his face. Flames moved along the lord's fingers, hopping from one digit to the next.

With a grunt, Horace struck back. Just as Lord Astaptah had taught him, he drew more power through his *qa* directly from the Shinar dominion in its raw state and sent it at Xantu. The eruption was like a release. The bodyguard doubled over as if he'd been shot in the chest with a crossbow bolt. Then he dropped to his knees.

Horace formed the Shinar into a sword and sliced through the thread connecting him to Lady Anshara. The knot cutting off his breath evaporated. A kernel of pain blossomed in his chest as he sucked down a gulp of fresh air.

Shaking it off, Horace called upon the Girru dominion to surround himself in a wreath of fire. He split the flow of *zoana* to create a large bubble of solid air around the entire box so no one else could interfere. Then he split it again and made that strand as thin and sharp as a stiletto's blade. He put the tip of that invisible blade against the shield protecting the queen and pushed.

You dare to toy with people's lives as if they existed solely for your amusement. I'm going to show you what that feels like, Your Excellency.

Byleth stood up, a sharp frown creasing her features. "That's enough, Horace. Release your connection to the *zoana* or I shall be forced to—"

He shoved harder, and the shield burst in an explosion of twisting winds that battered everyone inside the box. Before Horace could take advantage, Lady Anshara stepped between them with both hands extended. Knife-like fans of ice flew at Horace, one after another. He batted the first few aside with puffs of hardened wind, but the icy blades spun faster and faster. A couple slipped past his guard to encounter the fiery nimbus he had formed around himself. They melted on contact, but with each touch he felt his defenses weaken. The pain was growing inside him like acid eating through his innards.

Thunder reverberated throughout the arena. The stands were emptying as the crowd fled. The wind howled and brought down a deluge of rain that sluiced between the rows of seats and spattered against the shield he had erected.

The dark presence in his head stirred a heartbeat before invisible bands clamped around his wrists and ankles. Byleth gestured, and the bindings yanked Horace's arms and legs in four directions. At the same time, Lady Anshara had stopped her ice knives attack to gather a ball of spinning white frost between her hands. She breathed into the sphere, and with every breath it grew in size. Horace started to reach out with his *zoana* to sever the bonds holding him when the sphere shot from the lady's hands. A wintry gust blasted his face, shredding his aura of heat and numbing him from head to waist.

Horace strained against the pain to free himself, but the *zoana* was bundled inside him, refusing to obey. The presence thrashed with frustration inside his head.

A streak of green lightning blinded him as a crash like shattering stone rocked the royal box.

STORM AND STEEL

Consciousness flickered. He felt himself fall, the bindings suddenly gone from his arms and legs, but he couldn't control his limbs. The sour reek of blood and burning flesh clogged the air.

After a few seconds, feeling returned to his body. Horace lifted his head. The royal box looked like a typhoon had passed through it. The roof was ripped away. Rain drenched the scorched carpet. The queen's throne was destroyed, charred to burnt sticks and ashes.

Byleth lay beside the wreckage, her gown torn and water-stained, her beautiful coiffure unraveling. Lady Anshara sprawled beside the queen. Horace thought the women might still be alive, but Lord Xantu was clearly dead. Most of the skin on his left side had peeled away in blackened strips, exposing layers of seared muscle and tissue. His face was melted like candle wax around two bloody holes where his eyes had ruptured.

Horace pushed himself upright. His legs were shaky, but the *zoana* still coursed inside him. The presence nestled close, opening all his senses. He could feel the storm overhead and the winds as they cut through the city. Through all of it ran a common thread of unpredictability, of lovely chaos. The entire universe rotated on a wobbling axis, spinning through the limitless darkness of the void.

He looked down at Byleth. Her chest rose and fell in a jagged rhythm. He had only to reach out with his power and end the threat she represented forever. *Strike. Strike her down. Do it now. You will never be free as long as she lives. You know this is true.*

Was it the truth? The queen was powerful and sometimes difficult. She had sought to use him, even seduce him, but she had never compelled him against his will. Until Sekhatun. His anger returned in force. She had forced him to choose between his loyalty and his conscience, and people had died because of it. Now he could add Jirom's name to the list of friends who had been lost. Their blood stained his soul. The *zoana* grew inside him, seeking a target. He focused on the queen, defenseless at his feet.

With a sigh, he let go of the power, forcing it back through his *qa* into the great beyond from whence it came. At once, the rage drained out of him and took the dark presence with it. A tidal wave of pain rushed in to fill the void of their leaving, tearing through his chest and dropping him back to his knees. A horrible stench like dead things moldering in the dark filled his head and made him want to retch.

He reached out his hand but stumbled sideways as a massive surge of wind collided with him. His shielding collapsed as thunder crashed again, directly above him. The power closed around his chest and squeezed, forcing the air from his lungs. With a rasping wheeze, he fell senseless to the floor.

The tunnel stretched out before her, a long passage of darkness with no end. A red glow wavered on the ceiling, its malevolent face watching as she floated beneath it. She had the sense of being carried—feeling the hands under her legs, hips, and shoulders as distant things, devoid of warmth or tenderness. Tall shapes hovered over her, their outlines amorphous in the darkness. There was something familiar about her whereabouts, but her thoughts were slow to form.

She was alive. Somehow. She recalled a battle. Horace's face, distorted with a rage like she had never seen before. Had he truly tried to kill her? She couldn't believe it. Of all her court, he was the one she'd least suspected of betrayal. *I pushed him too far.*

She was drained and battered. It was no exaggeration to say she'd never experienced such a defeat before. Even during the most vigorous periods of her early training, when her instructors pushed her the hardest, she'd never been the victim of violence, physical or otherwise. All her life she'd been assured of her own potency. Had it all been a convenient lie, meant to pacify her? Or was Horace truly that strong? It was a question for another day. Right now she was going to return to the palace and gather her court. Before daybreak, she intended to have him in chains. And this time she would never be so foolish as to let him out of her grasp. *Perhaps it would be better if he didn't survive capture. The lords of the stars know I felt something for him, but he's too dangerous to let live.*

A faint moan came from beside her. With great effort Byleth managed to turn her head. Through the spaces between her bearers she saw Lady Anshara, likewise being carried. The lady's eyes were closed, and her face was marred by purple bruising.

STORM AND STEEL

As her vision sharpened, Byleth saw the rough walls of the tunnel, the piercing red runes spaced along the ceiling. The catacombs under the palace. A sigh escaped her lips. She was almost home. She looked around for Lord Xantu, thinking he must be the one who had saved her, but the robed figures carrying her wore cowls over their heads, so long she wondered how they could see where they were going. She was about to command them to stop and put her down when a sepulchral voice reached from the darkness.

"Good evening, Majesty."

A chill ran down Byleth's spine as Lord Astaptah appeared, impossibly tall in the ambient light. "Astaptah," she said. "You saved me?"

The vizier stepped closer. His robes swished softly across the stone floor. "I suppose that is the case, although not by intention. I assumed you would be dead when I sent my underlings to collect you and the lady."

"Collect us?" Byleth tried to sit up, but she didn't have the strength. Gasping, she collapsed back into the grasp of her gray-shrouded bearers. "Take us up to the palace at once. The First . . . Horace must be apprehended."

Her vision began to spin. She could barely make out Lord Astaptah as he reached down and placed his hand over her face. Harsh words filled the tunnel, piercing her skull like red-hot irons. Byleth thrashed, her stomach arching toward the ceiling until she thought her spine would snap. She tried to fight back, but the *zoana* remained out of reach.

"This gives me no pleasure," Lord Astaptah said close to her ear. Softly, almost like a lover's whisper. "Yet it was always inevitable. A pity I cannot add you to my test subjects. However you are more valuable to me as a martyr."

Byleth shivered within the cocoon of agony encasing her as something sliced through her bowels, up through her stomach, burrowing toward her heart. "But the machine is . . . destroyed! I saw it . . ."

"I must apologize for that deception, Byleth. The storm engine remains functional, as I shall soon prove. Farewell."

Lord Astaptah turned to leave, and Byleth struggled to call after him. A curse formed on her lips, but only a strangled groan emerged, rising into a scream. She feared it would never end, even as the veil of darkness fell over her.

CHAPTER TWENTY-ONE

*V*oices *drifted down from the black sky, calling to him in deafening rumbles. Ancient beings born in the hearts of stars and flung across the endless gulfs of space and void. Destroyers of a thousand worlds, cast down eons ago by their upstart children. But the forces that had bound them for eons were eroding, and now their baleful eyes were turned once more to this realm.*

The old gods were returning. . . .

Horace's eyes shot open. He lay in darkness, a darkness so quiet he thought he had awoken inside a tomb. His tomb, for he had died. Hadn't he?

But this place was stifling hot. He was lying on a hard surface, probably a stone floor. His shoulder ached like a spike had been driven through the joint. He tried to sit up and was stopped by bindings. They were unyielding, holding down his ankles, wrists, waist, and around his neck. He swallowed against the metal pressed there.

Fighting to keep calm, he focused for a moment to create a light. The *zoana* slipped through his mental grasp. He tried again, this time concentrating harder. He felt the power coursing beyond the gateway of his *qa*, but it refused to come at his command. Then an awful suspicion twisted inside his mind like a rusty blade. The bindings might be made of *zoahadin*. If that was the case, then he was well and truly fucked.

A door opened beyond his feet, and light poured in. Fierce and ruddy, carrying with it a gust of hot air. The walls and ceiling of a small stone room surrounded him. He appeared to be on a table, not the floor. Some kind of metallic apparatus with handles and silver hoses dangled above his head.

Horace tensed as a familiar figure entered the room. "What am I doing here?"

Lord Astaptah walked to the head of the table. "Forgive me not being present when you awoke. Other matters were pressing. This . . ." He gestured around the cell. "Is the first part of my grand design. You're here because the queen is dead. The people of Erugash mourn her passing. Were you to walk onto the streets above, you would find the air filled with their lamentations. Byleth the Blessed, struck down by the foreign devil she had protected."

Horace couldn't believe it. "I didn't . . . the lightning, the storm . . . I didn't do it. I mean, I was just trying to make her understand. I didn't mean to hurt anyone."

"I know, Horace. That was my doing."

The hairs on the back of his neck stood up. At first he thought it was just a mirage, but as his vision cleared he saw it, a field of energy surrounding the vizier. The power radiated from him in crackling, black waves. Horace tried to swallow, but his mouth had gone dry. "You're a sorcerer."

"Of course. We share a connection, you and I. Akeshia hasn't known a master of the void dominion in centuries. Now there are two. Quite the coincidence, no? Unfortunately, that is one too many."

A sinking feeling filled Horace's chest, as if all his internal organs were collapsing in dismay. Of course Astaptah had blamed him for the queen's death. A thousand witnesses had seen him battling her at the stadium. "So now you kill me and get rid of the last obstacle, you fucking bastard."

"There is no need for such vulgarity, Horace. After all, we've become quite close of late, haven't we? Yes, I believe I've come to know you as well as you know yourself."

Lord Astaptah reached up to the apparatus on the ceiling and pulled a handle downward. One of the silver hoses was attached to the top, but on the bottom end—the end coming much closer to Horace's face than he was comfortable—jutted three sharp prongs like tiny claws. The round end of the handle was serrated. The vizier leaned over him and peered into each eye. "Perhaps better."

"You don't know me at all, and you sure as Hell aren't the man I thought you were. Mulcibar was right about you."

"*Ai*, it's unfortunate that he warned you. It forced me to move sooner than I intended."

"You . . . you killed him." Horace looked at the handle swinging over his forehead and knew why it had looked so familiar. He'd seen the wounds on Mulcibar's body and didn't want the thing anywhere near him. "You killed him here with this contraption."

Lord Astaptah held the handle with both hands. "In this very cell. This device drains the subject of the vital essence that feeds our bodies, our brains, and especially our power. It is, in essence, a pump. Your energy will fuel my ascension. I wish I had time to show you the engine. I think you, above all others, might appreciate its elegance."

"Then you don't know me at all! I'm nothing like you. I don't care about—"

"Power? Don't be foolish. Of course you do. Ever since you had your first taste of the *zoana* in the desert, you've craved more of it. Power is freedom, and everything must submit to its inexorable tides. Pain is the key. I tried to teach you that, but you stubbornly refused to learn the lesson." He leaned down closer and placed a hand on Horace's head. "Pain is what sustains us and drives us to excel. You must embrace it or perish."

Astaptah pulled the metal handle lower.

Horace turned his face as far away as possible as the pronged end descended toward him. "The other kings will never let you keep the throne! You're just as much an outsider as I am!"

"Perhaps. However, I told you these Akeshians revere only one thing. Strength. And with my device operating at peak capacity—thanks to your contribution—I now control the strongest power in the empire."

Astaptah grabbed his chin and held him tight. The sharp claws bit into his forehead. Horace fought against his bindings, even knowing it was futile. The ache in his shoulder redoubled, but he continued to struggle. The handle had latched on tight.

The vizier reached out to the wall. "I wish events could have been different, Horace."

He flipped a switch, and a high-pitched whine started within the handle. Horace braced himself, but nothing could have prepared him for the bolt of electric agony that shot through his body. It centered around the spot where the device was attached to his brow, waves of pain like he'd never known washing over him in a river of torment that wiped his brain free of all other concerns. He could feel the warmth of his body being pulled out, and with it his life, like grains of sand falling through an hourglass. He gritted his teeth, fervently intending not to give his torturer the satisfaction, but his resolve vanished in a matter of heartbeats, and a ragged, guttural shout was ripped from his throat.

The vizier started to leave. Horace wanted to beg him to turn off the device, though he knew it would be in vain. Yet he couldn't form the words. His teeth rattled with the violence of the pain surging through him.

Astaptah paused at the door. He looked back, his face expressionless. "Prince Zazil held out for three days before he succumbed to the engine's hunger. Lord Mulcibar lasted four. I have high hopes you will prove more durable than either of them. Good-bye, First Sword."

He closed the door behind him, leaving Horace alone in the dark with his pain.

Jirom awoke on a bed. A real bed with a mattress. Too soft to be straw, it had to be stuffed with feathers. The coverlet underneath him was cool linen. A pillow cradled his head. He tried to sit up, and a sharp pain pierced his forehead.

Three Moons leaned over him. "Easy there, Sarge. Take it slow."

Jirom grimaced as he touched his head, which ached like it had been cracked open with a sledge. "Did I get demoted again?"

The sorcerer shrugged. "Sorry. Old habits die hard. And, to be honest, I never really saw you as officer material."

"You and me both, brother."

A familiar voice chuckled on the other side of the bed. Emanon placed a hand on his shoulder. "Well, you did lead our army into the mother of all ambushes, get us both captured and sent to the Grand Arena where we had to fight to our deaths."

Jirom mustered the strength to smile. He was in a fairly large room, better appointed than anything he'd seen in years. The walls were painted burnt ocher with a border of red scrollwork along the top. "True. How are we not dead?"

Emanon nodded to Three Moons with a wolfish grin. "Your friend here is full of surprises."

"You're not telling me anything I don't already know. How did you escape capture at Sekhatun?"

Three Moons winked. "A little sleight of hand in the midst of the confusion. The Akeshians were so busy rounding up you hard-chargers they didn't have time to worry about us cockroaches."

"That'll teach me to lead from the front. So where's Longar?"

The sorcerer's mouth twitched as if an invisible line were tugging on his lower lip. "He didn't make it. You know Longar, always trying to be the hero. He insisted on covering our retreat, but he got caught up in the fracas. It was a good death."

In his mind, Jirom saw the faces of all the men who had died at his side, adding Longar to the list. *A good death. Is there such a thing?*

Alyra came over from a doorway on the far side of the room. She was carrying a bag, which clinked as she set it down beside the bed. "How is he?"

"I'm f—" Jirom started to answer.

"He took a lot more venom than I originally thought," Three Moons interrupted. "So it took two treatments to bring him around. Sorry, old friend, but your head is probably going to hurt for a while."

Jirom looked to Alyra. "I saw you in the tunnel under the arena."

"I was able to cash in a few favors," she replied. "The Nemedian network got you and Emanon and the rest of your surviving fighters out of the pits. We brought you to a safehouse in the city."

Jirom tried to sit up again and was rewarded with a new slice of agony shooting down from his right temple. He clamped his jaws shut and spoke through gritted teeth. "You managed to just spirit us away without anyone noticing? That must've been some trick."

"Everyone was distracted by the big mojo flying around," Three Moons muttered.

"Big mojo?" Jirom asked. "What's that supposed to mean?"

Alyra and Emanon exchanged glances, and then she said, "After you fell, Horace attacked the queen."

"He did what?" Fierce throbbing erupted over Jirom's temple, but he ignored it.

"The queen was killed," Emanon said, sounding as if he was irritated he hadn't gotten the pleasuring of doing the deed himself.

"It's all my fault," Alyra said. "Three nights ago I was sent to kill the queen while she slept. But I couldn't do it. If I had, your men would be alive today and Horace would be free."

Jirom shook his head. "Don't blame yourself. Killing in battle is one thing, but a knife in the dark is no way to fight."

Emanon raised an eyebrow in disbelief, but Jirom ignored him. "What happened to Horace?"

"He was captured by Lord Astaptah." Alyra's mouth tightened into a frown. "After the queen's demise, Astaptah took control of the court. I would have thought some of the other *zoanii* might challenge his right to rule; however, it seems he has cowed them all."

"Where did he take Horace?" Jirom asked.

"By every fucking god and demon in this festering land!" Emanon winced as he put a hand to his forehead. "Jirom, I know you're concerned about this friend, but haven't you been listening? The queen is dead. The city's hierarchy is in disarray. This is the chance we've been waiting for. We can finally deal a decisive blow."

Jirom was about to launch into a tirade about how Emanon had been promising him the chance to rescue Horace for months now and never once tried to make it happen, but Alyra spoke before he could get it out. "I'm not sure about that, Emanon," she said. "We can't afford to underestimate Lord Astaptah. He obviously bided his time for this opportunity. If the *zoanii* get behind him—"

"But we don't know if they're supporting him," Emanon argued. "They may be waiting to see how this new regime shakes out before they pick a side."

"Even if the major houses are waiting in the background, he still commands the palace and the ruling apparatus—"

"Which is why we must strike now, before he consolidates his power—"

"Quiet!" Jirom yelled.

Alyra and Emanon, both red-faced, shut up. Jirom took a deep breath and let it out in a loud sigh. "Listen, both of you. If Horace is alive, we need to get him out. Emanon, I know you don't think he's worth the risk, but you're wrong. This is the right move. Alyra, he's right about the timing."

Emanon snorted. "So I'm right *and* wrong?"

Jirom held up a hand to silence him. "The timing may be right, but we're suffering from a serious lack of manpower."

"I've got some good news on that front," Alyra said. "Your hired swords arrived last night after what must have been one hellish forced march, and they brought along the rebels who survived Sekhatun. The network is smuggling them into the city at this moment."

"How many?"

"Twenty-four mercenaries and twice that many rebels."

Jirom let out another sigh. Less than a hundred fighters. Not enough to stage a decent assault on a place as fortified and well guarded as the royal palace. "What other assets can we count on? What about your friends?"

"The Nemedians will provide what information they can," Alyra replied. "But I don't think they'll involve themselves in actual fighting." Emanon started to growl at that, but she overrode him. "They are taking a longer view of the situation. Erugash is only one city of the empire."

"But if one city falls," Emanon said, "the others will weaken."

She gave him a wry look. "Try convincing *them* of that. King Moloch's army is only hours away. Once they arrive, Erugash will be under siege."

"That's going to make things difficult," Emanon muttered.

Three Moons chuckled. "I always knew you were the brains of this outfit."

"I have a way to get us all out of the city," Alyra said. "But I won't go without Horace."

Jirom tried to come up with a strategy that would get them inside with minimal conflict. Stealth would be the key. "We need a plan."

"It better be a damned *good* plan," Three Moons muttered.

"Agreed," Jirom said.

Emanon and Alyra exchanged glances. "Actually . . . ," Emanon said.

"We have an idea," Alyra finished for him. She picked up the bag from the floor and dumped its contents on the bed.

STORM AND STEEL

An avalanche of metal fell over his legs. Jirom picked one up and turned it around in his hands. *"This* is your big idea?"

Emanon planted a kiss on his forehead. "Don't say I never bought you jewelry, darling."

While Emanon took Three Moons out of the room to find "something decent to drink," Jirom stared down at the pile of iron collars in his lap.

The walls of Erugash rose higher than he had remembered. Her lofty battlements bristled with powerful engines—scorpions, catapults, and mangonels. Yet the most lethal weapons could not be readily seen from this distance, the *zoanii* amid the ranks of soldiers manning those walls. The sorceries on both sides, more than any other factor, would decide this battle.

Abdiel eyed the rows of purple-black clouds gathered against the northern horizon. *Or perhaps not. Of all the days for a storm to strike, why do the gods choose today? Must they see him suffer more?*

He looked to his master, Mebishnu, standing tall at the front of the flying ship, resplendent in a long robe of blood-red silk, with his hands clasped behind his back like one of the great men of the past. *Yes, after this day my master will take his place among those fabled names. Praise Amur!*

Mebishnu had been different these last few days. More withdrawn and introspective. At first, Abdiel had attributed this to the responsibility of his new command. Leading thousands of soldiers, not to mention three independent-minded kings, was no easy task. However, the more time went on, the more Abdiel suspected that something else was at work. His master had hardly slept since the first river crossing, and his appetite had dwindled to almost nothing, as if he were now subsisting on air and sunlight. *It all started after those interrogations. But there was nothing unusual about them, nothing out of the ordinary.*

Abdiel considered for a moment as another piece of the puzzle slid into place. *No, it wasn't until after he emerged from his meditation, after the interroga-*

tions. He was clearly troubled when he went into his cabin. But when he came out, he was changed. More determined.

Abdiel put the matter out of his mind. Whatever decisions his master had come to while cloistered in that cabin, everything came down to today.

They floated half a league west of the great city. The flying ships of the three kings were strung out to the north like mountains of gold and silver. Colored flags waved on the decks of each ship, passing messages back and forth and down to the ground where the army had assembled, awaiting the final order. Abdiel's heart beat faster in anticipation.

Finally, Mebishnu turned his head and nodded to an officer standing nearby. The officer nodded to the signal leader, and a moment later the ship's massive fanlike flags extended. Far below, a clamor of rustling armor and weapons arose as the army began to march toward the walls.

The Erugashi had not challenged their approach to the city, which the generals agreed was a grave error. They expected skirmishing parties harrying them along the way, dampening their morale with every foot of ground they covered. Or so the generals said. Mebishnu remained silent during these discussions, giving no opinion either way. *He sees farther than they do. Something in the air tells him this will be no ordinary battle.*

Abdiel glanced again to the north where the storm clouds were rolling closer. Then the eleven Brothers of the Order came up on deck, their red robes billowing in the breeze, and took their places beside Mebishnu. Abdiel smiled with pride.

Down below, massive spears and tumbled stones rained down from the walls in a hail that intensified as the combined legions of the three kings advanced. The armies sloughed through the devastating attack until they got close enough where their archers could return fire.

Abdiel appreciated that he was witnessing an extraordinary event. For all their bickering and squabbling, seldom did the city-states of Akeshia engage in full-out war with each other. The last had been shortly after the Godswar when this same city, Erugash, had attempted its ill-fated march to hegemony, only to be fiercely defeated by her sisters. A defeat that had cowed any similar ambitions along the same lines.

STORM AND STEEL

Explosions detonated along the front ranks. Steel and flesh flew through the air, away from the smoking patches where soldiers had once stood. The city's *zoanii* were finally getting involved. He saw them, men and women in fine raiment scattered along the wall. Abdiel waited for Mebishnu and the Order to react, but they merely stood by and watched the battle unfold. *Saving their strength, no doubt.*

A disturbance ran through the army below as a massive construction was trundled forward from the rear. This contraption, which was basically a huge log on wheels, rolled with increasing swiftness through the ranks on a direct path toward the city's western gatehouse. Abdiel's first reaction was disdain. How could the generals think such a crude battering ram would make a dent in the city's heavily reinforced gates? Evidently, the city's defenders didn't think much of the approaching attack either, as they made no special effort to stop it. When the rolling log neared the gates, arrow fire from the battlements picked off the men pushing the vehicle one by one. Yet, by the time the last pusher fell, the log had enough momentum to carry it the last few yards to the gates. Abdiel strained his ears, expecting a faint thud as the ram made contact.

Instead, a massive fireball erupted with a thunderous roar. The sound of shattering wood and tearing bronze rocked the flying ship. When the black smoke cleared, one of the titanic gate doors hung loose on melted hinges. The opposite door remained more or less intact, but a breach had been made.

The army surged forward with a loud cry while the conflagration engulfing the sagging gate continued to burn. Mebishnu spoke to his adjutant, and the message was relayed by flag. The ships of the three kings began to sail forward. *Now comes the second attack, descending like a hammer blow from the gods.*

He felt the deck shift as the ship moved forward at a sedate pace. The Order brothers raised their hands as if they were praising the Sun Lord. Perhaps they were. Abdiel imagined the fervent prayers whispered silently in their minds. Oh, to be a part of that brotherhood! The rapture of their sacred bond brought tears to his eyes.

When they lowered their hands, a torrent of combined elements burst from their fingertips. Abdiel made out streams of fire and water, the rippled gusts of wind and tumbling blocks of stone. The power swept across the gatehouse battlements. Soldiers were thrown off the wall, burning, frozen, crushed, and battered. Here and there, an enemy *zoanii* resisted the sorcerous scourge, and a battle began between the brothers and those magicians. Multichromatic waves passed back and forth, ripping through the mist-shrouded air. One by one the enemy was defeated, picked off and crushed.

Through it all, Mebishnu remained still. Unmoving except for his eyes.

Down on the ground, the army's advance bogged down as it met resistance at the gate. Defenders blocked the breach, but how long could they hold?

Abdiel looked back to the north and was startled to see the thunderheads had extended across the plains. Faint rumbles echoed from their depths amid a flicker of lights. *How long can we hold out against that creeping chaos?*

A ripple of lights flashed from the city walls followed by a string of sharp blasts. Tiny black packages were falling from the kings' ships, which now floated above the battlements. Everywhere a package touched, it exploded with a violent orange burst. Flames spread across the top of the city walls as soldiers were incinerated where they stood. Siege engines went up in columns of oily smoke.

Abdiel leaned forward over the railing for a better view. The initial attack of the firebombs was a resounding success, but the fires soon dwindled and went out on their own. And more defenders flooded the battlements to replace the losses. Queen Byleth's defenses were surprisingly effective.

"She cannot hold out forever," he said.

He hadn't meant the words to be overheard, but Mebishnu turned his head. As always, no emotion showed on his face. They could have been watching a theatrical performance in Thumon Park. "Byleth is dead."

Dead? What joyous news! It's a miracle sent by Father Amur.

"What we face now," Mebishnu said, "is the product of another mind. Perhaps not as keen as the late queen's in a purely strategic sense." He turned back to the battle below. "But certainly one more willing to sacrifice its resources. It's an interesting challenge."

Abdiel watched with growing apprehension as the defenders fought back. The army had so far failed to get past the gate. It withered under the incessant storm of defensive fire. Abdiel did not mourn for the fallen soldiers, who would be remembered with glory for their small part in this clash.

A powerful gust of wind rocked the ship. Abdiel clutched the railing with one hand and caught his cloak's flaps with the other. Shouts called out across the deck as the pilots attempted to adjust for the sudden squall. Two Order brothers lost their footing and fell overboard, and Abdiel squeezed his eyes shut.

As the ship slowly returned to level, Abdiel risked a glance up, and his heart nearly gave out. The storm had moved over the city. Crackling groans like the war cries of ancient titans echoed from within its ink-black depths. He jumped when the first bolt of lightning flared from the roiling masses. It struck King Ramsu's vessel near the rear. The afterimage seared his retinas a fraction of a second before the resulting thunder slammed his eardrums.

Ramsu's ship listed onto its side, flames exploding from between the seams of its hull. With a groaning shudder, the grand barge careened into a section of the wall and exploded in an eruption of fire and shattering stone.

Abdiel looked to his master and wondered what he was waiting for. *You know what you must do. My master. My son. Don't let this moment slip from your fingers. You may have come from humble birth, but you can still emerge as the brightest sky the empire has ever seen. Take that wonderful gift your poor departed mother and I gave you, and grasp your destiny with both hands!*

"Forward!" Mebishnu shouted above the roaring winds. "All speed!"

Abdiel laughed, filled with elation as the ship surged ahead. This was the moment, the decisive cusp. His son, his master could still win the day. The first cool drops of rain were a balm on his soul.

CHAPTER TWENTY-TWO

The agony was never-ending. Raw sensation scraped along Horace's nerves, spreading fire across every part of his body. It went deeper than his flesh, tearing into his organs and muscles, deep into the marrow of his bones, a fire that burned away all other thoughts.

The constant whine from the device caused a torment all its own. The stone table beneath him was like a slab of ice. Yet, despite the cold, he was drenched in sweat. His joints were swollen knots of anguish, crying out with every jerk and quiver. He could feel his *qa* pulsating as the power was drawn from it, through him and into the machine. Instead of the ecstasy he normally associated with the *zoana*, this was a violation of the deepest kind.

At the same time, something grew in the midst of his torment. Like a shadow lengthening as the sun goes down. The dark presence. As agony rippled and twisted inside him, it coalesced behind his eyes. He tried to shove it away, but it would not budge. He sensed it was . . . amused . . . by his efforts.

The pain.

Astaptah had told him to embrace it. He almost laughed through the growls wrenched from his throat. Embrace it? The agony was excruciating, and there was nothing he could do but struggle. It was driving him out of his mind. Blood filled his mouth as he ground his teeth back and forth, serrating the sides of his tongue.

All the while, the dark presence burrowed deeper. It was a second torment, just as incessant and horrifying as the machine sucking out his power. He writhed back and forth, pulling at the bonds holding him in place. Images flashed through his mind, of Sari and Josef, of Jirom and Alyra, of Ubar's severed head staring at him. Everywhere he looked it was death and pain. They were his inheritance, and part of him was glad he no longer had a child so he couldn't pass these dread gifts on to another generation. *No, let this die with me!*

For he was going to die. He had no illusions otherwise. Astaptah had won. Byleth was gone, the rebellion was crushed, and the vizier had this monstrous machine that could control the chaos storms. But what did he want? Even in the midst of his agony, Horace puzzled over that question. What did Astaptah want? To rule? That seemed too petty. Too far beneath him. The man was megalomaniacal. He was aiming higher.

Pain is the key.

Horace focused on his *qa*. In his mind's eye, it appeared as a glowing golden portal. The glow was muted now, the aperture covered by a murky gray screen. He pushed on it, but the screen was unyielding. He might as well have been trying to dig through a sheet of solid iron with his bare hands. He kept working at it nonetheless. He divided his mind into two parts. While the one part suffered and thrashed, the other remained focused on the task. The knowledge that he was dying, bit by bit, honed his concentration to a razor's sharpness.

In the Akeshian treatises about magic there were descriptions of the effects on *zoahadin*, how it separated the sorcerer from the source of power. Horace hadn't paid much attention to those passages, and now he wished he had. It seemed there must be a way to defeat it. He tested every spot of the gray curtain again and again. He pushed and tugged at it, he tried to slip past its edges. Each time it defied him. It was flawless in its simplicity. Then he felt something. A tiny imperfection in the screen like a pinhole, but so small he wouldn't have ever noticed it if he hadn't been so completely focused. If his life hadn't hung in the balance.

He pushed against the flaw with his mind. Not with blunt force as if to smash it down, but with sharp, precise hits like he was chipping away at a stone wall. As the machine buzzed and dug into his flesh, he worked at the task. Every instinct pressed him to push harder. Doubts whispered in the back of his head.

Your life is running out with every beat of your heart.

Too slow! We must hurry!

What if Lord Astaptah returns before you've gotten through?

Hurry, you fool!

Horace refused to give in. The pinhole was widening. Slowly, so very slowly, but it was widening. After a time—a few minutes? an hour? he couldn't tell—the pinhole had grown enough for him to get a firm hold on it with his mental touch. Reaching through, he grasped the edges and pulled. The flaw gave way all of a sudden, and his *qa* yawned open.

Horace basked in the heat of the power rushing into him. With the power came more pain as the *zoana* put everything into sharper clarity, and with the pain returned his anger, burning so hot he thought it would consume him. And he didn't care if it did.

He released it all with a shout that tore at the raw tissues of his throat. The room shuddered, and the slab underneath him became searing hot. Fiery pain exploded in his head and also at his neck, wrists, ankles, and across his stomach. The pronged handle bore harder into his forehead. Horace yanked at his bindings and cried out as they burst open.

Rolling off the table, he landed hard on the stone floor. The metal handle dangling from the ceiling glowed cherry-red. Glowing streams of melted *zoahadin* ran down the sides of the slab. Globules of molten metal clung to his skin. He hissed as he rubbed them off his wrists and stomach. With every welt that rose from his seared flesh, his rage grew.

Horace swayed for a moment as he got to his feet, holding onto the edge of the table for balance. The glow of the superheated metal was fading, or perhaps it was his vision. He didn't feel well. Emptiness welled in the pit of his stomach, a pit too deep for even the power surging inside him to fill. The dark presence slithered down his spine, an icy touch under his hot flesh. It spread out through his nerves down his arms and legs, penetrating through his bones. Everywhere it touched, the pain exploded, rising to new heights. Yet this time he didn't fight it. He embraced the bitter torment like a brother. He was one with the void.

He flexed his *zoana*, and the door flew off its hinges. He had no idea where he was going, but he had to keep moving. He paused in the doorway. An incredible buildup of power called to him from above this chamber. Faint vibrations ran through the stone walls and floor. Strange sounds croaked in his mind. Then the sound of footsteps jarred him out of his fugue.

The presence stirred inside him, and a radiant globe appeared above his head.

STORM AND STEEL

Did I do that?

The orb's white light threw shadows down the roughhewn tunnel outside the door. Dark shapes approached from his left. Three of them, their gray robes rippling as they ran with an odd, shambling gait. Hooked knives jutted from their gnarled fists.

Horace's hand lifted of its own accord, and three fiery lariats shot down the tunnel to seize the robed assailants and pull them to the floor. The men made no sound as they writhed, smoke rising from their charred flesh. Not a single gasp or groan. Horace, goaded by the presence, reached into the stone and sent it protruding upward. A dozen rock spikes shot up from the floor, spearing his attackers neatly. Their movements ceased.

More figures in long robes came at him from the other direction. He burned them with fire and throttled them with vises of solid wind, riddled their bodies with barrages of speeding rocks and sent javelins of ice through their skulls. When he was done, the tunnel was littered with their corpses. All done without a hue or cry from a single mouth. Not even his own. What did that mean?

A deep roar echoed down the passageway, followed by a blast of crimson light. Horace closed his eyes as the power washed over him. It only lasted a few seconds, but he luxuriated in the unrestrained freedom of the *zoana*. Then it faded, returning the passage once more to gloomy darkness.

Horace shivered as the dark presence directed him past the sprawled bodies.

Emerald lightning slashed the sky, illuminating the black thunderheads in sharp relief. Each levin bolt was accompanied by a discordant crash that echoed through the heavens and shook the timbers of the barge. Less than twenty yards beneath the ship's keel, they passed over the city battlements. Arrows and other missiles struck the bottom of the hull, rattling like hail against the enchanted hardwood.

Clutching fast to the railing, Abdiel was battered by the winds and rain, yet he grinned hard into the face of the storm. The western gatehouse was destroyed, parts of its structure on fire as the army of the three kings pushed inside. Shouts and screams rose from the ground where the fighting was the thickest.

The great pyramid of the queen's palace sat in the center of the city, a slate-gray mountain rising up through the fog. Such a pity Byleth was no longer alive to witness this moment. Instead, her lackeys would pay the price for her disastrous reign. Especially the outlander sorcerer. Mebishnu would cleanse the entire city with fire and steel. Nothing else would do except to burn the rotten tree down to its roots so it could be rebuilt into a shining example of peace and piety. *Thank you, Lord of Light, for blessing me to see this day.*

Another bolt of lightning struck near the ship, making him flinch. He glanced back in their wake. King Sumuel's ship was limping away, south and west, away from the battle with smoke trailing from its decks. *Coward! You flee at the moment of our triumph!*

For Abdiel could see how this would end. His master had taken a huge gamble, but that was the way of a true leader. Big risks garnered vast rewards. If they captured the palace, resistance among the city's defenders would disintegrate. The battle would turn in their favor, and with it would come peace. An abiding peace in the shelter of his son's—his *master's*—hands.

The ship rocked sideways as something struck the underside. Abdiel peered over the side, but he couldn't make out anything through the smoke and mist covering the city. Mebishnu never even glanced down, his attention fully focused on their destination. *Yes, I must have faith in you. I must trust in your—*

The flying ship bucked like a cat dropped into scalding water. One moment they had been sailing through the sky, the next a wave of light—there was no other way to describe it—washed over the airborne vessel, blinding Abdiel as it passed over him. The deck leapt under his feet at the same time as a sonic boom exploded around him. Then the ship was failing, sinking like a lead weight. Red robes fluttered like moth wings as more of the Order brothers slid off the deck.

Abdiel wrapped both arms around the railing. Through half-closed eyes he saw his master stagger against the golden bowsprit. Mebishnu swayed for a moment, his hands grasping for the spar, and then he went over the side.

"No!" Abdiel screamed into the storm.

He let go of the railing and tried to run to the front, but his sandals slipped on the slick boards, and he rolled across the deck. His back slammed against the forward railing. Gasping and coughing, he tried to squirm to his feet, but there was no purchase.

The ship lurched again, tilting even farther forward. Abdiel looked down. At first there was only the mist. Then a slanted rooftop appeared, rushing toward him at a fantastic speed. He remained conscious until the very moment the ship crashed to the earth.

Rain filled the gutters of Erugash, making the streets treacherous. Thunder crackled overhead. A flicker of lightning illuminated a dog in an alley standing over a mangled cat. Blood and bits of torn flesh flecked its black muzzle.

Jirom tried to put the image out of his head as he marched down the boulevard of lesser gods. The pole of the palanquin dug into his shoulder with every stride. He and Emanon and two rebels carried the chair with Alyra inside. Another dozen fighters from their strike force followed behind, carrying furniture and other household goods they had liberated from the safehouse, all in a performance they hoped looked like a wealthy noblewoman fleeing with her possessions.

Captain Ovar's mercenaries, or what remained of them, had gotten inside the city last night. After hours of planning and debating, this was the best scheme they could come up with on such short notice. Emanon had called it the "walk right up and ring the bell" plan. The rest of the rebels and mercenaries had left before dawn, under cover of darkness, to stake out the objective.

So far they had passed by two companies of Akeshian troops tromping through the rain in the opposite direction—*toward* the fighting at the western gates—without being stopped. He took that as a good sign, but all it would take was one overly suspicious soldier to ruin everything.

Wiping the water running down his face, Jirom resisted the urge to tug at the collar pressing around his neck. He had sworn never to wear one again, to die before he submitted, and although it was only for show the collar chafed his spirit. *You agreed to this. It's the only way to get close to Horace.*

The royal palace dominated the city skyline. From Alyra's instructions, he knew that the temple district would be followed by the government ward. The queen's palace was fronted by a large brick plaza decorated with stone monuments. Emanon had suggested they use a series of secondary attacks to distract the Akeshians, but it turned out they didn't need to create their distractions once the enemy army showed up outside the city. From the safehouse they'd witnessed units of city militia and Queen's Guard soldiers hurrying to reinforce the walls. Fate, for once, had worked in their favor.

A sharp crack of thunder split the sky. Two knocks rapped from inside the palanquin, signaling a change of direction. Jirom steered the chair to the right, down a narrower street. This was the part of the plan he wasn't sure about, mainly because it required putting his trust, and his life, completely in Alyra's hands. They'd known from the start there was no way they could assault the gates of the palace directly. They didn't have the manpower or resources. Three Moons, who lagged at the rear of the procession carrying a jewelry box, couldn't hope to match the court's cadre of sorcerers. Yet Alyra had found an answer.

They followed the street for two blocks before another knock drew them to a halt. They had stopped beside what looked like an abandoned business. Broad stone steps climbed to a tall bronze door that might have been impressive if not for the patina of verdigris that covered its face. Its large windows had been shuttered tight, and the shutters boarded over, except for a window on the left side of the upper facade where one shutter hung by a single hinge. Over the entryway was a stone carving done in bas-relief, depicting a woman reclining on her side.

They set the car down on the street, and Jirom went over to help Alyra. She laid a hand on his forearm as she stepped out of the palanquin. She looked beautiful in a sheer dress of white silk that showed off her legs. Jirom was admiring her when Emanon came up and planted a stiff elbow in his ribs.

STORM AND STEEL

"Put your tongue back in your mouth, lover," the rebel leader whispered.

Jirom grunted and rubbed his side. "I never took you for the jealous type."

"Now you know."

Jirom went up to the door. He tugged the handle, but it didn't budge. He could tell just by touching the corroded surface that it was strong enough to withstand anything short of a battering ram, but Alyra had told him a secret way to open it. Running his fingers along the bricks along the left side of the jamb, he found a small hole at waist height. He stuck a finger inside and felt something give. The door swung open several inches. He pulled it ajar and peered inside to see a dark hallway on the other side.

"Hurry, hurry," Alyra whispered as she came up behind him. She had a gray cloak wrapped around her shoulders and a knife on her belt.

Jirom went inside. Emanon and Alyra waited in the entryway as the rest of rebels entered. Scores of weapons were unpacked from the palanquin and furniture—axes, swords, maces, and a bundle of spears. Jirom picked up a long axe from the pile. He missed his *assurana* sword, but he felt better with a weapon in his hands. *Now if I can just get this damned collar off.*

Three Moons wiped the sweat from his forehead as he sat on the box he'd been hauling. He looked old. Too old to be following younger men on foolhardy missions. Jirom remembered Longar and felt bad. He'd seen too many friends die over the years. It would nice to think some of them would live to a ripe old age. *But that's not the life we signed up for, is it?*

Outside on the street, Captain Ovar's mercs had emerged from the nearby alleys. Jirom started to call for them when Emanon stopped him. "We're not going."

Jirom frowned at his lover. "What do you mean, we're not going? That's the plan. We get Horace out and then we escape the city."

"We talked it over," Alyra said.

Jirom looked from her to Emanon. "Who talked about what? And where was I during all this talking?"

Emanon laid a hand on his arm. "Jirom, this is for the best. While you and Alyra go after your friend, the boys and I will keep the royals busy."

Jirom dropped his voice. "I thought we agreed no more changing plans. I need you with us."

"No, you need stealth." Emanon jerked a thumb over his shoulder toward the doorway. "And you know what's happening out there. That's *our* war. We need to make sure it ends the right way."

Jirom started to snap an angry reply but stopped himself. He knew Emanon well enough to realize when he couldn't be budged. "Fine, you stubborn bastard. Have it your way."

He held his lover's gaze and tried to think of something to say that would convey everything he was feeling, all the love inside him combined with the painful fear of losing it, but it was impossible to put into words.

Emanon grinned at him in the way that set Jirom's heart to thumping. "Tonight we eat and drink in hell, brother."

"Take care of our boys. And if you must die . . ."

"Then I'll take a bunch of the fuckers with me," Emanon finished. "Go on now. Fetch your friend. He'd better be worth all this trouble."

Jirom nodded. *I hope so, too.*

He stood at the doorway as Emanon left. The rebels picked up the litter car and carried it down the street. Jirom wanted to run after them. He turned from the doorway feeling that the better part of him had just left and was not sure how to handle that. *Seventy men against an army? I love him, but my man is a reckless fool. If I ever see him again, I'm going to knock out all his teeth.*

Three Moons stood up with a sigh. "Well, we might as well get this over with."

"Follow me," Alyra said.

She led them down the hallway. They passed several doorways leading into rooms of varying size. Some had furniture—a loveseat, low chairs, a table on its side—but all looked as if they hadn't been used in years. A layer of dust covered the floors, though Jirom detected faint footprints on the hallway floor running ahead of them. He thought to ask Alyra about them but held his tongue. He was willing to let her keep her secrets as long as she held up her end of this mission, and so far he couldn't complain.

"What was this place?" he asked.

"A temple brothel," Alyra replied over her shoulder. "The priestesses were moved when the new temple of Ishara was built ten years ago."

She stopped at a dusty kitchen in the rear of the first floor and opened a tall cabinet that might have been a pantry. Empty shelves filled the upper half of the space, but Alyra knelt down and touched something on the floor. A cubby door popped open at the back of the pantry. Waving them forward, she crawled inside.

Jirom got down on his knees and peered into the darkness behind the small door. A faint odor issued from inside. It was dry with a metallic taint, like the air inside a smith's forge. He followed behind Alyra, moving on his hands and knees into a square tunnel about a yard across. Three Moons grumbled at the indignity of crawling like a dog, though Jirom didn't see the point in complaining. He and the sorcerer had done more demeaning things back in their mercenary days. "It's not as bad as that battle in the midden fields outside Gallean, eh?"

"Ugh!" Three Moons said. "Don't remind me. I had to burn a perfectly good pair of boots after that debacle."

Jirom focused on staying with Alyra, but he couldn't see anything after a few feet. The head of his axe clanked on the floor with every step. Without any light, he couldn't tell how far the tunnel extended, and only by occasionally touching Alyra's feet by accident could he be sure she was ahead of him. Then the smooth wood of the floor gave way to rough stone under his palms and knees, and, if he wasn't mistaken, the tunnel took a slight downward slant.

A touch on his shoulder made him stop.

"You can stand up now," Alyra said. Her voice was hushed.

With exaggerated slowness, Jirom got his feet under him. He reached out to find the tunnel had widened as well. The floor had a definite tilt here, making him feel like he was going to tumble forward in the dark. There was a rustling of cloth, and then a light appeared.

Alyra held a glowing rod above her head. Its yellow light illuminated a rough tunnel that ran straight ahead of them at a gentle slope.

"I would kill," Three Moons said as he climbed out of the cramped cubby-tunnel, "for a strong drink. Or even a smoke of *kafir* grass."

"Keep your head on straight," Jirom grumbled, a little harsher than he intended, but he didn't bother to soften the words.

They got underway again down the gentle slope. The tunnel had rounded sides, making Jirom feel like they were marching into the gullet of some massive beast. The hot, bitter air scoured his throat with every breath. After about fifty or sixty feet, he noticed another light ahead, a faint ruddy glimmer. He also noticed the tunnel was getting warmer. He thought it might be just the exertion until he reached out to touch the wall and jerked his hand back before his fingers got singed. The rock felt like it had been baking under the desert sun all day. He anticipated more complaints from Three Moons, but the sorcerer kept quiet. Alyra also said nothing. In fact, she had increased her pace, still holding the shining rod before her like a mystic guide into the depths.

They came upon the red light, which turned out to be a large mark—like a character of a language Jirom had never seen before—etched into the ceiling above their heads. Alyra passed under it without looking up. Jirom would have followed her example except he heard Three Moons mutter behind him. He turned back. "What?"

Three Moons stood under the glowing mark and stared at it. His lips moved as if he were having a whispered conversation with the thing.

"What is it?" Jirom repeated.

"Bad mojo, Sergeant. Very bad. I don't think we should be down here."

No shit, my friend. But it's too late to turn back now. Or is it?

"Are you two coming?" Alyra asked from farther down the tunnel.

"Aye," Jirom said, mostly to himself. "Come on, old man. We need you to keep the spirits of this place from devouring our souls."

He'd meant it as a joke, but just then a tremendous crash echoed from down the tunnel. Jirom froze, envisioning the entire palace complex collapsing on top of them.

Three Moons jumped as if a horsefly had bit him someplace tender and hurried ahead down the passage. Jirom followed as they caught up to Alyra. A few paces ahead of where she'd paused, the tunnel curved to the right and took a steeper downward slant. There was more light coming from around the bend, but it was more yellow-orange than red. For the first time, Jirom noticed that Alyra's face was pinched, her mouth scrunched up, eyes crinkled. "You all right?" he asked.

"Fine. Just keep up."

"Understood. Let's go."

They walked around the bend and entered a long section of tunnel running thirty or so paces that ended at a cave mouth. The yellow light poured out of this maw, along with waves of heat that made Jirom break out in a sweat. The entire tunnel shimmered like the inside of an oven.

Alyra's pace slowed just when Jirom wanted her to speed up. He almost told her to get moving before they fried like eggs on a griddle, but he bit his tongue. This was her area of expertise. He followed close on her heels.

Jirom thought Alyra was going to lead them into the yawning cave, but she turned to a door set in the left-hand wall. The door had an iron facing, but it opened when she lifted the latch. Jirom followed her inside. "How much farther?" he asked.

"Just ahead. This tunnel leads up to the palace."

She said something else, too, under her breath. He bent closer to hear better when a loud noise echoed the passageway, and they all froze. Jirom lifted his axe. The noise had sounded like a scream. Perhaps more than one. Whatever it was, he wasn't in a hurry to meet the person or beast that had made it.

Alyra didn't say anything when Jirom moved ahead of her. Three Moons came up beside him. The old warlock was drenched in sweat, but his expression was intense. "Be careful, Sarge. There's some big—"

A roar like a hurricane filled the tunnel. Jirom looked back, but there was nowhere to go, so he shoved Three Moons behind him and braced himself. A powerful wind rolled over them, searing hot and stinking of ozone. Alyra called out, but he couldn't risk turning around without losing his balance, so he stayed in place, hoping his presence would block the brunt of the gale.

After several long seconds the wind died down, but the sense of dread remained in Jirom's gut. Three Moons was pressed against the tunnel wall, his withered face as white as snow. Alyra knelt on the floor but appeared unhurt.

Jirom started down the tunnel. He was tired of playing it safe. He was ready to face this threat head-on.

The passageway bent to the right. Jirom stalked the last few steps on the balls of his feet, his entire body tensed to react at the first sign of danger. He peered around the bend. Two men stood in the tunnel beyond. The nearest one wore a ragged gray robe. He was bent over as if suffering from some ailment, with both hands reached out before him, his fingers curled into talons. The other man was half in shadow farther down the tunnel. He held out one hand, and a barrage of tiny green balls shot from his open palm. They struck the gray-shrouded figure in quick succession, each one erupting in a fierce explosion. The man in gray fell to the floor, smoke rising from his garments.

Sensing an opportunity, Jirom charged the sorcerer still standing. With each stride, he prepared himself to be incinerated alive or killed in some other gruesome, unnatural fashion. The shadow-swathed sorcerer pointed at him, and Jirom was struck in the chest by an invisible force. It felt like a sledge had slammed in his breastbone. The air rushed from his lungs as he catapulted backward, his back scraping across the rough stone as he landed. He started to get back up when Three Moons was suddenly beside him. The hedge-wizard was chanting in some guttural language as he wove his fingers in arcane configurations. Small shapes sprouting black wings darted from Three Moons' clothing. Crows. Scores of them. They flew at the enemy sorcerer in a stream, their sharp beaks glistening black in the tunnel's ruddy light. The sorcerer waved his hand, almost dismissively, and the flock of birds veered to collide with the wall. Painful squawks and clouds of feathers filled the air.

Three Moons reached into his satchel, but before he could launch another attack, the enemy gestured, twisting his hand in a circle. Three Moons was picked up and flung against the wall. Jirom gritted his teeth as his friend slumped to the floor.

Growling through his teeth, Jirom rushed at the sorcerer. Anger churned inside him, erasing all semblances of fear. He focused on his enemy's head, still half-hidden, and envisioned chopping it from his shoulders. Then the sorcerer stepped forward, and the light fell upon his face. Jirom slowed to a halt with his axe raised and gazed upon the last face he'd thought to see.

Horace looked right through him with no recognition in his expression. A nasty circular incision marred his forehead, with trails of dried blood running down to outline his eyes. His clothing was worn and bloodstained.

Before Jirom could react, Horace flicked his fingers, and a swarm of rock shards rose from the floor and shot toward him. Jirom flung an arm over his face as he spun away. The stone slivers tore into his back and side. *How can I fight the man I came to rescue? But if I don't, he might kill us all.*

A large rock ripped free from the wall and struck him in the shoulder, knocking the axe out of Jirom's hands and sending him to the floor for the second time in a dozen heartbeats. The tunnel shook as more stones flew above his head. He covered his head with one arm as he reached for his fallen weapon with the other.

His fingers had just found the handle when Alyra's voice rang out down the tunnel.

Horace stared at the ghastly figure shambling toward him. It looked like Jirom, but he knew it couldn't *be* him. Jirom was dead. Somehow this hellish place had conjured up a demon wearing his friend's face to torment him. He called upon his power, driven by the dark presence inside his mind, and prepared to incinerate this warped doppelganger.

"Horace!"

A familiar voice sliced through the fog of pain and confusion filling his head. The presence retreated as clarity returned.

He stood in a winding tunnel. Alyra stood before him. She was trembling, and in an instant he realized she was shaking with fear. Fear of him. Two men lay on the floor behind her. One was an old man in a shabby robe with blood running from a gash on his scalp. The other was Jirom, holding an axe.

"How—?" Horace started to ask.

Alyra ran into his arms, and he staggered, almost falling over as his legs threatened to buckle. He was exhausted and covered in cold sweat despite the stifling warmth of the tunnel. He couldn't remember how he'd gotten here. The last thing he remembered was the arena and watching Jirom battle the huge scorpion. He opened his mouth to ask what had happened, and then it all came rushing back. The cell, the stone slab, Astaptah's diabolical machine. And the pain. Memories of the torment haunted him. He could still feel it drilling into his bones. But the presence was gone. He took a deep breath and clung to Alyra like a drowning man to a lifeline.

Behind her, Jirom went over to check on the old man. Horace cringed, guessing he was responsible for the damage. "I'm sorry. I didn't mean to . . . Alyra, I didn't realize. . . ."

She shushed him and held him tighter. "It's all right. We're here now."

When she leaned back, he didn't want to let her go. "Oh, Horace. You're a mess."

His clothing was ripped and burnt. He remembered an explosion—it seemed like it had happened years ago, in another lifetime—but nothing after that.

Alyra touched his forehead. "This wound looks exactly like—"

"Yes. Like Mulcibar. Lord Astaptah tried to kill me with the same machine."

"The machine. You saw it?"

"No, just something that attached to it . . . somehow. I don't know. My brain feels like its cut up into pieces. How did you get down here? And who's the old guy? And we skipped the part where you tell me how Jirom's alive."

Jirom helped the old man to his feet, and together they came over. "How do you feel?" Alyra asked.

The man rubbed his head. Blood matted his short, bristly hair, but it didn't look too serious. "Like I got sat on by a hippopotamus. Remind me to never volunteer for a mission again. Ever. But you two look happy, so it must have been worth it."

"Horace," Alyra said. "This is Three Moons."

"He's an old friend," Jirom added with a shrug.

Three Moons squinted at Horace. "This is the one you said stopped a chaos storm all by himself? I can believe it. We've gone up against a couple heavy-weight spell-slingers back in our day, even some imperial-trained wizards once, but I've never been trampled like that before. I felt like a guppy caught in the jaws of a river shark."

Horace tried to listen, but he kept staring at Jirom, still not sure he could trust his eyes. "You were dead. I saw you die."

Jirom looked to Alyra. "It's her fault. I thought I was headed to the underworld, too. Then she and this old coot conspired to bring me back. I've got to say it's good to see you again, brother."

Jirom reached out, and Horace grasped his hand. Just like that, it was as if they'd never been parted. "What happened to you down here?"

Alyra answered for him, "He was brought down here by the queen's vizier, Lord Astaptah. He's extremely dangerous."

"Astaptah killed the queen," Horace said. "I think he's still down here somewhere."

Alyra nodded. "When he told the court you were responsible, most of the larger houses lined up behind him. They elevated him to Lord Regent for the time being. And with that machine under his control, no one will be able to stop him."

Jirom exchanged a glance with Three Moons. "We'd heard the queen might be using the storms as a weapon. We just weren't sure it was possible."

"It is. The queen had her reasons, but now it appears that Astaptah was just lying in wait until he could get rid of her."

Three Moons snorted. "Had her reasons? Damn, son, that madwoman was aiming to kill a lot of people in her quest for power."

"You didn't know her," Horace said. "You didn't know what she was up against. Trust me; she had cause to be afraid."

The old man started to reply, but Alyra held up a hand. "Now isn't the time. We need to get out of here."

Horace shook his head. "Leave? To hell with that. I'm going to find that bastard and end this, right now."

"You can barely stand without falling over."

"Better listen to her, son," Three Moons said. "You might be the biggest hammer in the workshop, but that don't count for squat if you can't hit the nail."

"I'm not sure what that means," Jirom said. "But I agree with Alyra. I need to get back to my men. There's a battle being fought in the streets. What's the fastest way out of this maze?"

"The quickest exit is up to the palace," Alyra answered.

Horace took her hand. "We *need* to destroy Astaptah's machine before it causes any more devastation."

Three Moons spat on the floor as he looked between the three of them. "Well, it looks like we need to decide what's more important. And fast, I suggest."

Jirom let out a deep breath. "No, we can't choose one over the other. The rebels need Three Moons and me, but the machine has to be stopped as well. We have to split up."

"Split up?" Alyra repeated, her voice rising. "Are you mad? We just found each other."

Horace had to agree. "He's right. I'll deal with the contraption while the rest of you—"

"No! You're not doing it alone. I know what you're thinking. That you have to make this sacrifice, but you don't. We can do it together."

Jirom nodded. "Right. You said you had a way out of the city."

"It's at an old race track in the Garden Quarter," she said. "There are tunnels underneath, one of which is supposed to lead under the city walls."

"Supposed to?" Three Moons asked.

Jirom clapped the old man on the shoulder. "We'll find it."

Horace's throat tightened as he looked at Jirom. Would they ever see each other again? He reached out his hand. Jirom looked at it for a moment, and then pulled Horace into a tight embrace. "Take care of her," Jirom whispered in his ear.

"You go find Emanon," Horace replied. "And we'll meet you on the other side."

Jirom winked before he headed back down the passageway with the old warlock at his side.

Alyra put an arm around Horace's middle. "Let's go. If we're going to try this, we need to hurry."

Horace held her close as they descended deeper into the catacombs.

CHAPTER TWENTY-THREE

"**P**ikes set! Here they come again!"

Ismail gripped the strap of his borrowed shield tighter and hefted his lance into position alongside the battle line of mercenaries. Weapons flashed in the dying sunlight as they readied for another attack, shields locked into a wall of steel. Rain sluiced across their ranks, rattling against armor and forming wide puddles underfoot. Ismail stood still as the crossbowman standing behind him took aim over his shoulder.

Two hundred paces away on the far side of Slaver Square, the Akeshians were forming in front of the marble-faced buildings that housed the head-quarters of the city's top slaving companies. This group of guards, hirelings, and laborers weren't particularly well armed or armored, but their numbers were growing by the minute. And they looked angry. *For damned good reason, I suppose. We've been killing their bosses and freeing all their property.*

Ismail tried not to think about the image of an Akeshian slave-merchant, his bald pate drooling with sweat as a score of newly freed slaves dragged him out of his litter and stomped him to death in the street.

Captain Ovar strode down the line, eyeing the enemy. "Stand fast and don't give these city rats a fucking inch! Funuk, where's your helmet? Well, find one!"

When he got to Ismail, the captain paused. "Your boys doing all right, son?"

Ismail touched the bloodied head of his lance to his helmet in a salute as he glanced at the eleven rebels under his command. "Yes, sir. We'll hold."

"I never doubted it, son. Carry on."

Ismail blinked a trickle of rainwater from his right eye. *Where in the Seven Hells is Captain Emanon?*

After breaking open a mess of slave pens, their leader had split off from the main group with just a few fighters. His last instructions had been to stay with the mercenaries and hold the square. So far they had beat back two attacks, but as the afternoon waned, he began to wonder how long they could keep going. Not to mention the rumors about the army attacking the city from the outside.

The assembled Akeshians were forming into ragged lines. Ismail tried counting them but stopped at a hundred. More than two-to-one odds in the enemy's favor. A group of men observed from atop the marble buildings. They didn't appear to be worried. *Gods, if even one of them is* zoanii, *this battle is already over.*

He had the sudden desire to eat a fine meal. A big slab of beef perhaps. No, his mother's chicken kebobs with peppers and baby onions from her tiny garden. He could taste them on his tongue.

The attack came without any fanfare. The armed ruffians simply started running across the square's worn flagstones in a great, heaving mass. Ismail bent his knees and lowered the point of his lance another couple of inches. He spared a look down the line to make sure his men were doing the same. They looked nervous, but just the ordinary nervousness that he was learning everyone felt before a fight. The sudden need to piss was annoying, but he focused on the approaching fighters in front of him. He picked his first target and shifted half a step to his left. They were seconds away from first contact when a blast of thunder shook the square.

Ismail squeezed his eyes shut as lightning flashed overhead. He opened them as soon as he could, thinking the enemy would already be upon him, but the Akeshian charge had dribbled to a halt, more or less, the men blinking their eyes and looking to the boiling sky.

"Fire!" Captain Ovar's voice bellowed above the tumult.

The crossbow resting on his shoulder bucked, and a dozen soldiers fell to the opening barrage. "Forward!" the captain commanded.

Ismail surged ahead, thrusting his weapon before him. The man he had chosen to target was half turned around in the milling confusion that was the Akeshian force. Ismail experienced a moment of hesitation at striking a distracted opponent, but he swallowed that feeling as the two forces closed. He missed on the first thrust as his target stumbled backward, but his second attack took the Akeshian in the hollow of his throat. There was very little blood as the lance head pulled out and the man collapsed. Squinting against the driving rain, Ismail found his next target.

The Akeshians recovered quickly. Within a few heartbeats they were raging again. A stone club struck the helm of the mercenary on Ismail's left with a reverberating clang. He tried to stab the club-wielder, but he was too close to get his lance's point around, so he swung the shaft sideways instead. He struck the man hard in the shoulder, but the Akeshian spun and returned with an overhand swing.

The club fragmented on the top edge of his shield. Shards of stone bit into his face as he drew back his arm. Blood dribbling in his eyes, he thrust hard. His hand holding the lance slipped as the tip made contact. Still, the point bit, and he leaned into it, fighting for a better grip. The Akeshian screamed, but Ismail couldn't tell if it was from pain or fury. Then the man was gone, swallowed up in the ebb of battle. Another foe appeared with a hooked sword that almost took off his head before he ducked behind his shield. The impact produced a heavy thud that jolted his arm. Ismail's legs and shoulders were tiring, making every movement more sluggish and painful. He plied his lance as best he could in the wild fray but could hardly tell if he was hitting anything.

Then, all of a sudden, the wave of Akeshians receded like the tide going out. Ismail lifted his gaze to see that a new influx of fighters from the north side of the square had drawn the Akeshians' attention. He breathed easier when he spied Captain Emanon leading the wedge of new warriors. A couple rebels stood at the captain's shoulders, but the rest of the combatants behind them looked like newly freed slaves in their iron collars. Many were half-naked as they attacked with sticks and knives and, in some cases, their bare hands. Regardless of their garb, they fought with unrestrained fury.

Ismail glanced back at his squad. "Form up on me! Shields high!"

Trusting them to guard his back, he plunged back into the melee. Weapons and rocks rebounded from his shield, rattling his arm and shoulder until they were numb. His lance dipped out again and again. Once, the head fouled in the straps of a guard's breastplate, but the squad moved up to protect him as he freed his weapon. Then they went back to work.

After a long slog of sweat and blood, they joined up with Captain Emanon near the center of the square. Ismail expected to see concern and fatigue in the slaves' faces, but they kept fighting as if possessed by devils, chasing down fleeing thugs and hacking them apart. The captain grinned like a demented god through a mask of gore and grime. Blood encrusted his left ear, but otherwise he appeared hale.

"Which direction, sir?" Ismail asked.

Emanon shook his head. "What?"

"Which way are we retreating?"

Their plan had been to free as many slaves as possible and smuggle them out of the city. The captain supposedly knew a secret way to get them all outside the walls, although Ismail didn't see how that would be possible with Erugash being under attack. Still, he was eager to be on his way.

"We're not retreating, Sergeant."

Ismail swallowed hard as Captain Emanon turned to the east, gazing in the direction of the slaver syndicate headquarters. *Oh, shit on a stick.*

"Sir, you don't mean . . ."

"Indeed I do. See to your men."

Ismail turned to regroup with his squad when he noticed a circle of mercenaries standing around a man on the ground. He pushed through until he saw who it was, and his chest grew tight. Captain Ovar's head was propped up on a fallen shield. His sword lay by his side. The head of a spear jutted from his side, the shaft broken away. Broken chain links surrounded the wound, from which poured a steady flow of blood.

"Chirurgeon!" Ismail shouted as he knelt beside the mercenary captain.

Pressing his hands around the injury, he called out again. Hands rested on his shoulders, gently pulling him away.

"He's done for," a stocky merc said with a heavy voice. "Ain't nothing to be done."

Ismail shook his head, his vision suddenly blurred. Then Captain Ovar reached out. The pain was obvious on his face, though he made no sound. He just smiled as he patted Ismail's forearm twice. Then he closed his eyes and took his final breath.

Lieutenant Paranas, the mercenaries' second-in-command—now their commander—shouted for everyone to fall into formation.

Standing over Ovar's body, Ismail felt time melt away, along with the sounds of the battle. He tried to think of a prayer to say, but all he could remember was an old charm his mother had taught him when he was frightened of the dark. *Farewell to the light. Come, Spirits of the Stars, and protect us from the hallows of the Night.*

With a bitter taste in his mouth, he lifted his lance in a final salute. Then he went to find his squad. As Captain Ovar would say, they weren't out of this yet.

Veins of white and gold riddled the tunnel walls like the trails of drunken earthworms, reminding him that they were traveling far beneath the earth's surface. Every time his mind started imagining the tremendous weight hanging over their heads—not just the earth and stone of the ground, but the huge mass of the palace, too—Horace snapped his attention back to the task at hand. The prospect of finding and destroying Lord Astaptah's mystical creation was daunting enough to take his mind off anything else. Except the woman leading him.

Alyra stalked ahead with his ball of magical light following over her shoulder. This was the second time she'd risked her life to save him. *After the way I talked to her, she had every reason to abandon me. God, what have I done to deserve her? Nothing.*

For some reason, realizing his own shortcomings made him feel more secure with her. If she could accept him for what he was, wasn't that enough?

"I want to say I'm sorry."

She kept walking with long, purposeful strides.

"Alyra! Alyra, I said I—"

"Shhh!" She held out a hand.

Horace froze in place and called for his *zoana*. The power came at once for a change. With it pulsing in his veins, he listened but heard nothing. Alyra lowered her hand, and he whispered, "I'm sorry."

"I heard you."

She didn't turn around, but she didn't leave either. He took that for a good sign. "I've been lost since you left. You were right. I didn't realize how Byleth was manipulating me. That doesn't justify pulling away from you, but—"

She looked back at him. Tears gathered in her eyes, threatening to spill. "I pulled away, too. Because I was afraid things were getting too serious. I didn't think I could handle our relationship and my mission at the same time."

"No. I should have trusted you more."

She smiled through the tears. "Maybe trust is something we both need to work on."

He took her hand. "I want to start over. I can't change what's been done, but I can do better."

"Me too. But first things first. We need to get to the central cavern of this labyrinth."

Horace nodded, still holding her hand. The passageway split into two branches twenty paces from where they stood. "Lead the way."

Alyra tugged him toward the left-hand passage. "I think it's this way."

Horace followed along, glancing from one branch to the other. "You think?"

"I was only down here once, and I didn't come this way. Don't you know which way you came?"

"I wasn't exactly in my right mind at the time."

"It's fine," she said. "We'll find it."

The left-hand branch sloped downward as it curved gently. They passed occasional glowing runes in the ceiling. Each time they encountered one, an itch ran down the back of Horace's neck, so he knew they had some connection to the *zoana*, but other than that he had no clue what they did or how they worked. The tunnel got increasingly warm the farther it descended. He started sweating again. The air became thick with an odor like rotten eggs, making it difficult to breathe. But Alyra didn't complain, so Horace kept quiet.

The tunnel split again. This time Alyra chose the right-hand passage, and Horace started to wonder if she was choosing at random. He didn't ask, though. He was anxious enough without the thought of wandering lost in these catacombs until they succumbed to thirst and starvation. *We'll probably roast to death before that happens.*

Alyra stopped in the middle of the tunnel. "Did you h—?"

Horace stumbled back as she shoved him. "What are you doing?"

A spinning piece of metal flew past his head, almost making him jump. He turned to see four figures in long gray robes rushing in from behind them. Disentangling himself from Alyra, Horace put himself between her and the attackers. The magic coursed through his body like rivers of fire and ice. He sought to tear a few pieces of rock from the wall and launch them at the Gray Robes, but instead the entire wall and half the ceiling came down in an avalanche, covering the men under a pile of rubble. Shocked by what he'd done, and even more shocked that the power continued to rush from him, ripping out more and more of the bedrock surrounding the passageway, Horace clamped down on the *zoana*. With some resistance, the power ceased.

Horace coughed and blinked against the particles of flying dust as Alyra pulled him away.

"You've got to be more careful," she said as they moved around the bend. "You could have collapsed the entire passage with us in it."

He shook his head between bouts of coughing. When he could finally speak, he told her, "I didn't mean for that to happen. The power . . . it got away from me somehow."

She paused to let him catch his breath. "Does that happen a lot?"

"Sometimes, but not like this. I couldn't stop it, like someone else was controlling the magic. It's all. . . ." He put a hand to his chest, unable to describe the thrilling terror that had come over him. The power felt raw and untamed pouring out of him. Almost as if it had been . . . *reflecting my anger. That's what I felt when I unleashed it on those men. Rage. I wanted them dead and I didn't care how. What had Mulcibar said about the power? That it could affect our actions? Take control?*

Once the thought got into his head, he couldn't dislodge it. What if he became a slave to the power? He needed it. There was no chance he could do what had to be done without it. Yet, it terrified him at the same time.

Alyra must have sensed some of what he was thinking because she placed a hand on his arm. "You can do this, Horace. I'm here with you."

Taking hold of her hand again, he pointed down the tunnel, the only way they could go now.

Twenty minutes later an orange glow emerged from down the tunnel, which had continued to descend into the earth as they walked for what seemed like miles. One look at Alyra revealed that she felt the same way he did. They were both exhausted. Their clothes were drenched in sweat, their hair hung limp. The air had become more acrid and foul with every step they took. The tunnel walls, whenever one of them made the mistake of brushing against them, were as hot as a griddle over an open flame.

As they followed the passage around the latest bend, Alyra quickened her pace, and he speeded up to stay with her. When they reached the tunnel's end, they both stopped.

Intense heat blasted from the opening, making the air shimmer and twist. The tunnel mouth opened into a massive cavern. A network of metal scaffolding climbed the walls. The floor was a lake of molten rock, glowing cherry-red and giving off clouds of steam. An island of stone rose from the center, crowned by a strange lattice of metal beams that reminded him of the interior frame of a tower, but the girders jutted out at odd angles and came back together in ways that made no sense. Green sparks showered from the upper portion of the machine with hissing crackles.

Power hummed in the chamber, causing a vibration that ran through the stone walls and floor. Horace glanced up to find the ceiling, but it was lost in a curtain of smoke and shadows. He saw something else, however, that rooted him to the spot. Seven colossal statues carved from the living rock of the cavern's walls. Their stern visages filled him with dread.

He recalled something from his reading and knew what these must be. "Seven are the lords of Absu. . . ."

"What did you say?" Alyra asked.

"It's something I read in a book that Mulcibar was studying before he disappeared. It talked about the seven lords of Absu. That's what the Akeshians call their underworld, right? Then there was something about chaos and the gates of death. Do you think Lord Astaptah worships these things?"

Alyra shook her head. "I've heard rumors—whispers, really—of a secret cult in the city, but I never gave them much credence. Until now. Horace, if you're right and Lord Astaptah is in league with such dark powers, then he's even more dangerous than I imagined. We have to get out of here."

"Not until we finish what we came for." He took a step toward the rock island. "Is that it over there?"

"Yes. The queen called it a storm engine."

"Perhaps we can cripple it somehow, and then the court can depose Astaptah."

"Perhaps . . ."

"All right. Let's get it over with."

The stream swirled around their feet as they approached the bridge. Horace pulled at the collar of his robe. His throat was on fire from breathing the scalding-hot air. The heat of the floor penetrated his shoes, like walking on burning sand. He paused at the foot of the bridge, unsure if he could trust it. A faint vibration ran through the stone underfoot, and a low buzzing noise emanated from the other side.

"Stay back," he said. "I'm going to try from here."

Alyra squeezed his hand before stepping behind him. Horace took a deep breath and regretted it as his lungs cried out. Coughing into his sleeve, he studied the machine towering before him. He didn't have a clue how to attack the thing, so he went with his first instinct. This machine was made of metal, so the dominion of earth and stone seemed appropriate. He called upon the Kishargal dominion and sent it down into the floor. Concentrating on the machine, he wasn't prepared when the *zoana* recoiled.

Horace's legs gave out as his power rushed back through him. All his thoughts vanished in a gray haze. His vision dimmed. He felt himself hit the ground, but only faintly, as if he were remembering an old fall. Then something was pulling on him, dragging him across the rough stone. Dull pain jarred his nerves, but it didn't come alive until someone slapped him. Blinking, he opened his eyes.

Alyra held his head in her lap. The skin on the backs of his calves and feet was on fire, almost literally. He looked down to see his sandals were blackened at the heels.

"What happened?" she asked. "I almost didn't get you before you slid into the magma."

He put the discomfort aside like he'd done on Lord Astaptah's table and focused. "I don't know. It has some kind of protection. Help me up."

He tried not to groan as Alyra pulled him to his feet. He felt tattered and worn-out like an old shop rag. Eyeing the machine, he reconsidered his strategy. Obviously, the ground around the island was warded, but what about the air?

Horace summoned the Imuvar dominion. The scents and textures of sweat and burnt leather and molten stone filled his head. Drawing upon the power, he crafted a cudgel out of hardened air. He packed it together, layer upon layer. Although he couldn't see it, in his mind's eye it grew to the size of small tree. When it held as much power as he could summon, he drove the giant-sized club toward the machine like a battering ram.

The power recoiled back on him again as his attack was halted ten feet from the machine as if it had run into the side of a mountain. He gritted his teeth and held on as the pain erupted in his chest and radiated outward like fingers of fire under his skin. His air-cudgel shattered into a thousand gusty fragments that spun around the cavern, whipping at his robe and hair before they vanished.

The room spun in swift circles while Alyra propped him up. Swallowing the nausea that tried to creep up his throat, Horace took deep breaths through his mouth. How was he going to destroy something that repelled magic?

"Horace," Alyra whispered, her grip tightening around his upper arm.

He squinted through the steam and the dim glow of the magma. Shadows moved at the base of the machine. A chill ran through him as a dark figure stepped out into the light.

Alyra hated herself for it, but she couldn't help letting go of Horace and taking a step back as Lord Astaptah appeared. From the shadows surrounding the storm engine he emerged like a serpent from its lair. This was her worst nightmare. Her mission—her *true* objective—lay right before her, but it may as well have been on the other side of the world.

"I am quite impressed." Lord Astaptah stepped toward the bridge spanning the magma moat. "You are quite resourceful, Horace."

Alyra retreated another step. With numb, sweat-slicked fingers she reached for her hidden dagger, fumbling with the hilt that felt suddenly unfamiliar. Her hands shook as fear overwhelmed her, filling her with its venom, stealing away her will to act. She wanted to turn and run, but only the knowledge that it was a futile gesture kept her from giving in to the urge. There was no place to hide now.

Lord Astaptah lifted a hand, his sleeve falling away to reveal slender fingers as he threw something. It was too small for Alyra to see. A round stone perhaps. A heartbeat later, a firestorm rose from the pool of molten stone. Flames flashed around her, their greedy tongues searing her skin. She covered her face as she sunk to her knees, trying to draw herself into a ball against the awful heat. She couldn't hear anything over the roar of the fires. Through slitted lids she watched.

Her heart went out to Horace as he bent before the fiery onslaught. This had never been his fight, yet he'd taken it up. Because of her. A twinge of guilt unraveled inside her. Had she used him? *No, he made his choice freely. And I have to honor that. Somehow.*

Horace made a chopping gesture with both hands, and the firestorm flew upward, up to the ceiling where it banished the shadows dwelling there. For a couple seconds she could make out the details in the faces of the seven statues. The features carved into that black stone were misshapen, as if the artist had been trying to convey something pushing through the flesh of his subjects. Then the fires vanished, plunging the upper half of the cavern into darkness once more.

Horace and Lord Astaptah faced each other from opposite ends of the bridge. Horace shot multiple blasts of icy water at the vizier, who deflected them with a sweep of his arm and unleashed some kind of counterattack. She couldn't see it, but Horace reacted like he'd been slammed in the face with a shovel. He sent something invisible back. It didn't seem to bother Lord Astaptah, but a long furrow was ripped along the length of the stone bridge.

Back and forth the battle with unseen energies waged. Shielded by Horace, Alyra wasn't targeted by any of the attacks. *What can I do to help? If I get too close to Lord Astaptah, he'll fry me to a crisp. And I don't have anything that can reach him from here. So what's left?*

A piece of rock fell from the ceiling. It crashed into the pool of magma, sending burning droplets flying in all directions. In the momentary illumination caused by the splash, she spotted something she hadn't noticed her last time down here. A second bridge on the other side of the island, directly behind the machine. *Don't think about it! Just move!*

Swallowing her fear, she hurried along the causeway running around the edge of the chamber. The footing was treacherous, but she tried not to think about what would happen if she made a wrong step. More chunks of rock fell from above. Lucky for her, none of them hit close enough to splash her, but she noticed with no little unease that the entire magma pond was roiling from the disturbances. If its surface rose just a couple feet, it would roast them all.

When she reached the foot of the far bridge, she started across, heedless now of the danger. She had no idea whether Horace could win against Lord Astaptah. And though she didn't want to contemplate the consequences of his losing, she had to press on as if that was the foregone conclusion. Whatever happened to her, or them, the mission needed to be completed. Otherwise, all this was for nothing.

On the other side of the bridge were scattered several long metal boxes, each connected to the machine by thick copper cables. Alyra didn't have any idea what they were for, but they emitted a droning buzz, so she kept clear as she snuck toward the metal construction. The girders at the base of the machine were sunk into the living stone. Up close, she noticed that a few of them were slightly blackened with soot from some older fire. The structure appeared sound, though. *Too sound. What in the name of heaven am I going to do to this thing?*

After sneaking a glance at the vizier's back, and seeing him fully engaged with Horace, Alyra slipped around to the front of the machine. More metal boxes were here, but these had panels on the front with dials and switches. One was covered in glass-faced gauges. Alyra looked over the controls, trying to figure out which ones would shut the machine down, hopefully for good. But nothing was labeled and none of it made any sense. She reached for a switch at random and hissed as a painful jolt of electricity ran up her fingers. Shaking her injured hand, she held out the other. Slowly. Her fingertips started to tingle a couple inches from the board. It was warded with sorcery.

Then she remembered her secret weapon.

Alyra drew her dagger. The *zoahadin* blade gleamed in the harsh yellow light from the gauges. There wasn't time for experimenting. She stabbed it into the control board. The metal point met with a slight resistance, but it pushed through, and the electrical field vanished with a slight vibration that lifted the hairs on her arms.

She grabbed two switches at random and flipped them in the opposite directions. Immediately, a high-pitched whine blasted over her head, followed by a loud crackling sound. She flipped another pair of switches and turned all the dials as far as they would go. The machine shuddered with a fervor that sent jagged vibrations into the ground. In the empty space at the center of the matrix of metal struts, a milky green mist was forming. Was that a good thing or not?

Alyra froze in place as Lord Astaptah turned around. His yellow eyes stabbed at her. He gestured as she reached for another row of switches. A pain passed through her like nothing she'd ever felt before. Every inch of her skin erupted in invisible fire. She fought to grab the control panel, but she was falling, unable to control her legs anymore. Hitting the rocky ground hurt less than she expected, but her thoughts were fuzzy. She had trouble seeing, too, as the shadows from the ceiling reached down to catch her in their cold embrace.

Horace took a deep breath as Lord Astaptah turned away. The dark presence had returned, latching onto his mind like a leech. Struggling to control his own actions, he felt shredded inside from the *zoana* rushing back and forth through the fibers of his body. Frayed as if the power had scrubbed away some adhering material with its mystical transfusions. Every joint throbbed. Even his scalp hurt. It was the void. The presence was somehow tied to him through it, and he had no idea how to shed it.

He saw Alyra at the foot of the machine, messing with the metal boxes. What was she doing?

Astaptah gestured, and Alyra fell to the rocky floor in obvious agony. Horace went cold all over. The magic rose up inside him like a geyser, out of his control. Fire spewed from his hands. Dry, hot wind howled around the island as the bedrock foundation shuddered. Horace was hurled back against the cavern wall, his eyes squeezed shut against the firestorm. He didn't know what to do. Astaptah was too strong. His own control was too weak. He almost wished for the dark presence to take control so he didn't have to be responsible for this catastrophe.

A booming shriek erupted from the storm machine. The mold-green nebula at the center of the construction pulsed like a beating heart, and the cacophonic scream rose higher with each throb. Horace covered his ears. Then he felt a cool pulse against his leg. He reached down into his robe's inner pocket and felt the smooth surface of Mulcibar's orb. It throbbed against his scarred palm. He could feel the power inside it but didn't know how to unlock it. Or what would happen if he did. *It doesn't matter. We have to stop the machine.*

A tremor ran through the floor as he pulled on his *zoana*. The power responded hesitantly. Or was that him? Fear lodged in his gut, making him second-guess every action. It whispered that he and Alyra were going to die in these catacombs. Fighting back those thoughts, he channeled a tiny flow of power into the orb. It quivered in his hand as it grew warmer, like a dying ember breathed back to life. The crimson lights under its surface swirled faster. "Alyra!" he yelled as loud as he could. "Run!"

Ruby-red flames erupted from the orb. Horace hissed in anticipation, but it didn't burn him. The lights inside the sphere spun around like fireflies caught up in a whirlwind.

He threw it high over the moat, aiming for Astaptah, hoping to at least distract the vizier long enough for Alyra to get to safety. He spotted her sprinting across the island, but strangely she was running right at him. He tensed as she reached the edge of the isle and leapt, straight through the firestorm with a long knife in her hand. The flames parted to let her pass unharmed.

She landed on the narrow shelf, and he wrapped both arms around her. A heartbeat later, before he could even give her a smile, the island exploded.

A flood of light and roaring thunder filled the cavern. Horace tried to shield Alyra with his body, but his legs gave out, dragging them both to the ground as the cavern was washed in a sea of ghoulish vapor.

Alyra looked up once the detonation had subsided, and Horace had just enough strength to turn his head. The island was covered in a wreckage of charred, twisted girders. He stared at the spot where Astaptah had stood just moments before, unable to believe it. The vizier was gone. Buried alive.

He flinched when a chunk of black stone as large as a dog struck the ledge only a few feet from where they lay. The impact sent vibrations running up his spine as the stone ricocheted into the moat, throwing globs of molten rock into the air.

Alyra pulled out of his grasp. "What are you waiting for? We have to get out of here!"

He tried to get up, but his limbs were like jelly. He couldn't even climb to his knees. "I can't."

He was about to insist that Alyra go without him when she hooked her arms under him and heaved. She dragged him to the foot of the metal ramp leading up to the upper catwalks. More pieces of black stone rained down. Horace tried summoning a shield above them, but his *zoana* was dry. Empty. He couldn't even feel his *qa*.

Alyra hauled him up the ramp by the arm until Horace managed to walk on his own. His lungs were burning by the time they reached the top level. He wanted nothing more than to stop and catch his breath, but Alyra pulled him onward. He had time for a quick glance over the side.

The bottom of the cavern was awash in flame. The central isle had crumbled into several pieces, all of them slowly sinking into the lava. There was no sign of Lord Astaptah anywhere. Not that he expected any. Nothing could survive in that inferno.

Then Alyra hauled him into the darkness of a tunnel mouth.

STORM AND STEEL

Jirom and Three Moons got back to the abandoned brothel. Crawling out of the secret door into the kitchen, Jirom reached back to help his friend out. They were both covered in dust and bits of gravel.

"You doing all right?"

The warlock's scalp had stopped bleeding, but head wounds could be tricky.

"I'm too old for this kind of stuff," Three Moons muttered as he stood up. "By the desert, Sarge. We make a fine pair, don't we?"

"Outnumbered and outsmarted," Jirom replied. "Just like old times. You going to be able to keep up?"

Three Moons squinted out of the side of his eye. "I'll do my best, but no promises. If things get hairy . . ."

"Right. We'll meet in Hell."

He'd been tempted to follow Horace in his crusade to destroy the storm-making machine, but with every passing moment he'd been eaten up with concern for his men. Especially Emanon. Watching how Alyra threw herself at Horace, their bodies pressing together as if they hadn't seen each other in years, had made him wished he and Emanon could meld that easily. Anyway, he wasn't interested in visiting the palace without an army at his back.

Out on the street, they ran into a mob of citizens. While the storm raged overhead, people rushed in every direction, patricians and plebeians all mixed together in a mutual flight for survival. But Jirom doubted most of them would find it. The city was no doubt surrounded by the Nisusi legions, the gates locked up tight or under contention. No one was getting out of this alive without a plan.

Standing amid the swarming crowd, Jirom tried to determine the best way to go. There was a loud susurrus coming from the southern end of the city. That probably meant fighting. If he knew Emanon—and he did—that's where the rebel leader would be, right in the thick of it. *Gods-damned fool of a man. Why couldn't I have picked a quiet one, like a scribe or a physician?*

With a heavy feeling in his chest, he set off in that direction. They navigated the tangle of avenues, entering a neighborhood where tall tenements crowded together along narrow streets. They didn't see any citizens outside. The entire ward seemed deserted. Then something dropped out of the sky, almost hitting Jirom in the head. Glass shattered on the street, fragments flying everywhere. He searched the rooftops but saw no one. Gesturing to Three Moons, he continued on at a quick jog.

They reached an inner gate closing off the street. Beyond it, about a quarter-mile away, Jirom could see a colossal gatehouse, larger than some castles. By the sounds, the besiegers had broken through the outer gates and were entering the city. If that was the case, he and Three Moons might soon find themselves facing a horde of bloodthirsty soldiers. Which way had Emanon gone?

"Head east," Three Moons said. "That's where the replacement barracks are."

Having no better idea, Jirom hustled in that direction. He didn't need Three Moons to tell him this was a dangerous idea that would likely get them killed. Two men running through a warzone. It was pure madness, though not much crazier than what Horace and Alyra were doing. Jirom respected Horace, but his decision to go after Lord Astaptah and his storm machine smacked more of fatalism than true courage. Jirom had seen it before. When saddled with overwhelming responsibility, some men collapsed under the weight and sought out the most convenient exit. In those circumstances, death could seem like the easiest answer.

That's what he feared was gnawing at Emanon. His lover had taken on the onus of the entire rebellion—the freedom of thousands of people. Jirom had already seen the cracks in Emanon's steely demeanor. It was only a matter of time before those cracks became too large to hide.

Three Moons swore out loud, and Jirom looked ahead to see a barricade blocking the avenue. Made up of upended wagons, timbers, and pieces of furniture, it presented a sizable obstacle. He didn't see any soldiers manning the barricade, which struck him as odd, as it made a superior defensive position. The buildings on either side were shuttered up tight, with no signs of occupants inside. Jirom waved Three Moons to stay put as he approached on slow steps.

The ambush was timed perfectly.

STORM AND STEEL

Javelins flew as a dozen Queen's Guards soldiers popped up behind the barricade. But not at Jirom and Three Moons. The missiles flew over their heads. Jirom almost swallowed his tongue when he saw the phalanx of enemies advancing behind them, shields locked and pikes extended like the quills of an armored hedgehog. The javelins deflected from the oncoming company's shields and armor. Yet, a heartbeat later, a vicious barrage of arrows fired from the tops of the buildings on both sides.

Jirom hesitated, not sure which way to run. Then Three Moons staggered with an arrow stuck through the palm of his right hand. Blood spurted from the wound while the warlock looked down in shock. Jirom tore off his under-tunic and wrapped it around Three Moons' hand to staunch the bleeding. Thunder crackled overhead.

Three Moons' face was paler than was natural. "Hell of a day we're having, eh?"

Jirom picked up his axe and dragged Three Moons to an open door to the right of the barricade. Inside was the first floor of somebody's home. Small rooms with a couple pieces of furniture. A staircase to the second story. Jirom slammed the door shut behind them and looked for another way out, but neither of the two back bedrooms had doors or even windows. Sounds of fighting crept in from the street. Screams and shouts, and the din of clashing steel. Heavy footsteps marching in formation.

Seeing no other choice, Jirom led his comrade upstairs. The second floor was laid out much like the first, except there was a small exterior balcony in place of a front door. Jirom took a moment to peer out a window. Down in the street, the pikemen had reached the barricade, which they were trying to dismantle under fire. Their shields were raised against the arrows and javelins that continued to pummel them.

Jirom continued all the way up to the fifth and final floor. Just like the apartments below, there was no exit. "This isn't good," he mumbled to himself as he came out from the back.

Three Moons stood by one of the windows, looking across the street.

"Any ideas?" Jirom came over to stand beside him. From here they had a good view of the archers on the opposite building, firing down at the Nisusi. "Hold on a minute."

He glanced up at the ceiling. There had to be a way up to the roof, and from there they might be able to cross past the barricade. He found a trapdoor in the larger back room, a slab of wood painted to match the ceiling. Calling to Three Moons, he pulled it open to reveal a square of masses of leaden clouds overhead. He lifted himself up and peeked out. A squad of archers lined the northern side of the roof ten paces away, sheaves of arrows at their feet. They fired with mechanical precision: load, draw, shoot. Over and over.

As Jirom reached down and pulled Three Moons up through the trap, one of the archers happened to glance back. He gave a shout as he turned, aiming his bow at them. Jirom jumped up, but he was too far away to rush the soldier before he fired, and there was no chance the archer could miss at such close range. As the soldier pulled his bowstring to full tension, Jirom leapt to the side with some half-formed plan that if he drew the fire, Three Moons might still escape. He waited for the arrow's impact as he skidded on his shoulder and rolled, but there was nothing.

He came to his feet in time to see the last of the archers falling backward off the ledge, arms wheeling as he fell.

Three Moons sat beside the trapdoor, leaning back on one elbow. His injured hand rested in his lap. Blood oozed through the makeshift bandage.

Jirom helped him sit upright. He needed more than a field dressing. "Can you walk?"

"Help me up."

When Jirom heaved him to his feet, Three Moons tried to take a step and swooned. He would have collapsed if Jirom didn't catch him.

"Come on, old man. I got you."

"I can do it! Put me down!"

Despite the objections, Jirom hoisted the warlock over his shoulder. For the first time, he took a moment to look around and get his bearings. The row of tenements extended in an unbroken line for another three hundred paces before they stopped at the edge of an open space, possibly a square. Beyond that was a long, low building that might be the barracks, and then the man-made water channel that ran from the river all the way through the city to a reservoir at the northern end.

STORM AND STEEL

From up here he also had a good view of the southern half of the city. Small units of Nisusi invaders were spreading out through the flooding streets, but the main body of the enemy was still stalled in the River Quarter.

He set off eastward with Three Moons slung over his shoulder, complaining every step of the way. The neighboring tenement abutted directly to the building they were on, and crossing was as easy as stepping up the height of a cubit. The roof of the next building sloped down toward the rear, and Jirom took his time traversing the wet slate tiles.

Every so often he peered over the side of the roof. The fighting continued behind the barricade, though most of the pikemen had stormed the buildings on either side of the street. Those left behind formed a small turtle, using their shields to protect themselves while they worked at dismantling the barrier. Jirom hoped to be long gone before they succeeded.

After climbing down to the third apartment building and crossing its roof, Jirom found himself looking down at a wide plaza. The rectangular court was half underwater. In the center stood the long building he took for the barracks, standing by itself. A squad of soldiers stood outside the door, sheltered from the storm by a short awning. There was no sign of Emanon or the rebels.

Three Moons smacked him on the top of the head. "You can put me down now, Sergeant."

Jirom set him down gently. Three Moons held onto his arm for a moment until he regained his balance. He still looked like he'd been to Hell and back, but the warlock was a tough old bird. *He'll probably outlive us all.*

"I don't see anyone from our band."

Jirom nodded, still gazing around. They could try going back the way they'd come, but then they ran the risk of encountering more soldiers—either the Erugashi or the invaders, and it didn't matter which. Both sides would likely attack first and worry about their allegiance later.

"Something's going on over there."

Jirom followed the direction of Three Moons' finger to a column of black smoke against the hazy skyline, rising from a location roughly halfway between them and the city's eastern wall. "It looks like something's on fire, but I can't tell what it is from here. Must be pretty big to stay burning in this rain."

"Isn't that the Slave Quarter?"

Of course. It made sense. Where else would Emanon go? "I've got a bad feeling about this."

"Yeah? Join the company, Sarge. Now, are we going to go check it out or just sit up here while the city burns around us?"

Jirom grunted as he looked around the roof for a trapdoor. He found a skylight instead, which opened above a cistern. A pool rippled ten feet below, though he couldn't tell how deep it was. Sheathing his sword, he sat down and levered his legs over the edge. He took a deep breath and then let go.

The water was only a couple feet deep, but that cushioned his fall enough that he didn't break his ankles. He clambered out into a room not much larger than the cistern. The walls were painted sky-blue. As he went to the only doorway, he listened for signs of battle, but everything was quiet.

Three Moons landed with a loud splash but also managed not to injure himself. Dripping wet, they made their way through an apartment that was somewhat nicer than the ones they'd seen in the previous tenement. Judging by the toys left on the floor and a washtub filled with laundry, the occupants had left in a hurry.

They found a set of stairs descending through the building. On the second floor, Jirom had paused to wait for Three Moons when he heard a sound, like a whisper. He stalked through the living area to the back rooms. A short hallway with three doorways covered by bead curtains led to the rear of the apartment. Standing still, he listened. Seconds passed, and then a tiny voice spoke, too low for him to make out the words. Jirom swept aside the middle curtain with his axe and froze as he spied four people huddled behind an overturned bed. A man, a woman, and two young girls. The man rushed to place himself between Jirom and his family. He had a thick black beard and wore a long homespun tunic. He appeared to be unarmed.

Holding up an open palm in a sign of peace, Jirom backed away and let the curtain fall. Then he headed back to the stairs.

Three Moons saw him coming. "Something wrong?"

"No, let's just keep moving."

The first floor was vacant, or at least Jirom didn't hear anyone and he didn't bother to search. He just wanted to be out of these apartments and on his way as fast as possible. Three Moons moved slower than before, breathing heavily as he came down the last flight of stairs.

"You need a rest?" Jirom asked.

"Go fuck . . . yourself. With all due . . . respect."

Naturally.

The front door had been barricaded with two chairs and a wooden table. Jirom cleared away the furniture and opened the door a couple inches. Peering out, he saw an empty street. Sounds of fighting echoed from the west.

"Wait here," he said and then dashed across the street.

He reached an alley on the other side without incident. Even better, a quick glance down the alleyway revealed that it ran for a few blocks in the right direction. He turned to signal for Three Moons to follow, only to find the warlock already halfway across, shambling along like a drunken indigent. Swearing to several different gods about wizards who refused to follow orders, Jirom gathered Three Moons inside the alley.

"You're starting to become a real pain in my ass, old man."

Three Moons took the time between gasps for air to crack a smile. "Then I must be doing my job. Have you come up with a plan yet?"

"A plan for what? Finding Emanon and getting the hell out of this madhouse of a city? That's about the long and short of it."

"Sounds good to me. But there might be a problem."

"You mean besides the two armies slugging it out all around us and the fact that our commander is off on some idiotic crusade in the middle of this nightmare? Something tells me you're about to make me very upset."

"Not my fault, Sarge. But I thought you should know there's a hurricane of shit about to fall on this city. My joints are acting up like it's the middle of winter, and that's never a good sign. I don't know if I've ever felt anything like this, and you know we've both been through some serious ass-fuckery in our lifetimes. Er, no offense intended."

Jirom just looked at Three Moons and shook his head in resignation. "All right, so what can we do about it?"

"You and me? Probably nothing."

"Then stop worrying about it. Our immediate concern is finding the rest of the crew. Can you make it? And don't give me any of that tough-as-iron bullshit. Can I count on you?"

Three Moons met his glance and held it. Then he gave a small nod. "Right up until my last breath. And maybe a wee bit more if Death ain't in a hurry to claim this worn-out soul."

Jirom started down the alley but made sure not to get too far ahead of his companion. He kept his eyes moving, up and down, side to side, seeking threats from any direction. His ears told him the fighting was falling behind them, but he didn't let that lull him into carelessness.

They came to a bridge crossing the water channel. Shocked to see it was empty of people, especially soldiers, Jirom led Three Moons over it at a quick hustle. The buildings got taller and older on the far side as they entered into the Slave Quarter. Every city in Akeshia had such an area where the flesh merchants stored and sold their goods. Slavery was an important industry throughout the empire. Some of the wealthiest non-*zoanii* were slavers or the descendants of slaver ancestors.

The bridge-street led to an intersection of two wide avenues. The four buildings on the corners were all imposing structures built of charcoal-gray marble. The outsides were decorated with statues of sphinxes and other beasts. One look around confirmed that the violence had not reached this section of the city. Jirom saw a pair of men in expensive robes talking in a doorway on the other side of the intersection; four collared bodyguards with shields and swords stood in the rain nearby.

Jirom squinted at the sky from the safety of the alley. The column of smoke came from somewhere on the other side of these buildings. He looked both ways to make sure no one else was coming, then he pulled Three Moons along by the sleeve. They walked side by side toward the broad avenue heading north. Jirom kept his strides slow and measured, like a slave out doing his master's bidding. As they passed the large buildings, he glanced at the robed men in the doorway out of the corner of his eye. The slavers turned to look in their direction but then went back to their conversation.

Jirom let out the breath he'd been holding when they got to the corner.

STORM AND STEEL

He was tempted to approach the slave bodyguards to see if he could convince them to join the uprising, but he wanted to get to Emanon as soon as possible. On top of what Three Moon had said about the hammer getting ready to drop on this city, he had his own misgivings.

They hurried two blocks northward and finally reached the maze of stockades and pens where slaves were kept for market. Jirom remembered little from the last time he had been here. Covering as much ground as the Grand Arena, the stockades were built like a small city unto themselves. Narrow streets separated rows of corrals. There were some buildings, too; mainly trade offices and accommodations for the caravan workers.

The smoke rose from the center of the stockades where a wooden building—three or four stories tall—was on fire. A small crowd of armed men surrounded the blaze. Not soldiers, they looked more like private guardsmen. Jirom was about to pass by when he spotted movement on the rooftop. A cluster of people. They were throwing things down at the crowd. It looked like stones. *No, roof tiles. Gods below, I think that's Emanon.*

Three Moons asked, "What's the matter?"

Jirom could guess what had happened. Emanon came here to free the slaves held captive and found trouble instead. Now they were pinned on a burning building with nowhere to go. A roar echoed across the stockades as gouts of fire burst from a pair of windows on the second floor. The flames were climbing.

"The problem is we're going to have to go—"

Jirom staggered as the ground moved under his feet. Holding out his arms for balance, he latched onto Three Moons, and they both stumbled into the side of a slave cage. A sound, deep and terrible like two giant boulders grinding together, filled the air. Then it was gone, and the earth came to rest once more.

"What was that?"

Three Moons was staring down at the ground. "It's started."

CHAPTER TWENTY-FOUR

The palace shuddered with each tremor. Artwork fell to the floor in clatters of bronze and fired clay. Large cracks appeared in the frescoes as the plaster split. A marble bust of a broad-shouldered man with a long beard and a funny cap rocked off its pedestal and shattered on the floor as Horace ran past. He flinched at the crunch of shattering statuary.

He and Alyra emerged into the Grand Atrium, but they didn't stop. The cavernous chamber was empty. Harsh wind shrieked through the open skylight. Dark clouds roiled overhead, and the moist smell of rain whipped through the atrium. The feeling of dread only intensified when they reached the front doors.

Rain, warm and oily with ash, met them at the threshold. From here Horace could see that the River Gate was gone. Instead, a massive gap breached the southern ramparts. Explosions flared along the battlements, and two great flying ships—each of them three times the size of the queen's aerial barge—sailed above the defenders. Siege weapons fired back and forth between the wall and ships, inflicting monstrous damage on both sides. The fighting on the ground had pushed into the city as the invading troops poured through the gap.

"We should try to find Jirom," Alyra said.

Horace nodded, not really listening. He was still trying to formulate what he should do. The flying ships dropped another barrage of incendiaries on the wall. With the queen gone, who was leading the city's defense? Even when Byleth had still been alive, the prospects for surviving this attack had seemed remote. Without her, he didn't see how Erugash stood a chance.

A stroke of lightning stabbed the sky. A dozen or so jagged bolts branched off from the main trunk, arcing down just outside the city. Horace held his breath, and a second later the thunder boomed around them, rocking the palace compound. Ornamental trees bent at the impact, and a cloud of dust and ash formed over the city's southern quarters. People ran through the streets. Entire families tried to flee the impending destruction.

"Horace?!"

He turned to Alyra. "One of us needs to find him."

"One of us? No, you're not going anywhere without me!"

He took her hands. "I need to help them. We can't allow Erugash to fall."

He didn't say what he truly feared, that if the Nisusi took over the city, the Sun Cult's influence would soon follow.

He prepared himself for an argument as her eyebrows came together. Then she shocked him by nodding. "I know, but we need to work together. We're a team, remember?"

"We are. And I can't handle it all by myself."

A wry expression crossed her face. "Who is this? You *look* like Horace, but you're making too much sense."

"Please listen. I need you to find Jirom and help him get his people out. I'll meet you after this attack is met."

The worried look returned in her expression. Brows pulled together, lips turned down in a slight frown. "What are you going to do?"

"I don't know yet, but I'll think of something."

She looked like she wanted to punch him. "I'll get everyone to the escape route. You'll be there, right?"

He nodded. Then she surprised him again by planting a quick kiss on his lips. She held it for a moment that seemed to last for minutes. "Be careful," she whispered before hurrying away.

She ran across the drenched stone walkway to the palace's outer gates. He looked to the sky. The storm clouds worried him. Lord Astaptah's machine was destroyed, and yet the tempest blowing over the city showed no sign of abating. And there was the matter of his power. He hadn't told Alyra, but he still couldn't feel anything inside where the *zoana* had been. Mulcibar had warned him it was possible for a *zoanii* to burn out, to push too hard and lose the power forever. If that's what had happened, then he was truly just an ordinary man again. *Then make a good show if it. Every minute I stall them gives Alyra and Jirom a better chance to get out alive.*

Leaning into the driving rain, he descended to the courtyard. He was heading toward the compound's gate when a loud pop sounded from the west.

A shiver ran down his backbone that had nothing to do with the wind chill. Someone was using magic nearby. A great deal of magic. He quickened his steps, hopping over the broad puddles covering the walkway.

The heavy bronze valves of the western gate were closed shut. Stairs on either side rose to small watchtowers flanking the gateway. Seeing no one, Horace banged hard on the bronze panel to be heard over the incessant crackle of thunder. After a second banging, the door at the top of the stairs to the left-hand tower opened and a soldier peered out. He shielded his eyes against the rain. With a nod to Horace, he called inside, and the gate opened.

A row of guardsmen stood out front. It didn't appear that they'd seen any fighting yet, but they were clearly prepared for action. The officer, with six silver slashes down his breastplate, spotted Horace, and his men parted for him to pass.

"Your Lordship," the officer said. "You should have an escort if you intend to leave the palace."

"No, Captain. I'm commanding you to leave your post. Go to the River Quarter and help the militia. If we can't push them back now, the city is lost."

The officer looked back at the palace behind them, and then nodded sharply. "*Ai, Belum.* We'll fight to the last man. My honor on that."

As the guardsmen hustled south toward the fighting, Horace started off to the west, following the lure of *zoana*. The Great Plaza stretched before him. Beyond it were more public squares along the avenue, all the way to the city walls like a string of pearls. The magical disturbance was coming from directly ahead. Horace walked to meet it.

The government buildings and the citadels of the nobility surrounding the Great Plaza loomed before him, rising in tiers of stone and brick. Their irregular rooftops jabbed the gray sky like rows of broken teeth. He imagined the people inside, cowering from the enemy and storm. *Not in this part of the city. Most of these people,* zoanii *and other important personages, have probably already fled to estates outside the city. No doubt the Nisusi have orders to leave them alone, in any case. It's only the soldiers and the commoners who are truly at risk.*

A loud clap echoed from a nearby alley, which was the only warning Horace received before a large shape bolted from the shadows. He barely got out of the way before a portly man riding on an onager barreled past him. The wild ass brayed ferociously at Horace as it clopped down the avenue in the direction of the palace.

Repressing the curse he wanted to toss at the rider's back for startling him, Horace turned back on his original course. Yet before he took another step, several bolts of ghastly green lightning shot across the sky. In the sudden flash of light, figures appeared down the avenue. A mass of soldiers fought at the entrance to the next plaza. As the thunder faded, the sounds of battle took over.

Horace hesitated before plunging ahead, thoughts of the debacle at Sekhatun still fresh in his mind. *This is what you decided, to help the people of this city. So help them, damn you!*

The back of his neck itched as the beacon of magical energy flared again. A heartbeat later, bright orange light flickered from the plaza, and a hot wind rushed down the street, flowing over him. Whispering a brief prayer, he moved toward the fight.

Lying on his belly, Jirom peered over the edge of the roof. Twenty paces away and two floors up, Emanon and his fighters stood atop the burning tabularium. A cloud of smoke hung over the area, driving back the Akeshian soldiery surrounding the place. Jirom didn't want to imagine what it was like for the poor souls trapped on the roof. Seeing what he'd wanted to see, he crawled back from the ledge.

"Well?" Three Moons asked, sitting cross-legged behind him. The bloody bandage around his hand had crusted over. Grime filled the cracks in his face.

He and Three Moons had crossed the stockades of the Slave Quarter, getting as close as they could without being spotted. It had been the sorcerer's idea to break into an adjacent vacant building for a better vantage. The situation didn't look good. "The bottom two floors are engulfed. There's no way in through the ground. But if we could . . ."

"If we could what? Grow wings and fly up to your buddies?"

"Or I could just toss your scrawny ass up there."

Three Moons winked at him. "Well, maybe I have a better idea. I think I know how we can get those men down in one piece, but I'll need a few things."

"I'm ready to try anything. What do you need?"

"Some blood, to start."

Jirom stared at him, not sure if the warlock was being serious. "How much blood?"

"Just a dram or two. Nothing a big strapping man like you would miss."

"Why can't you use your own?"

"Nah. Too old. The spirits like young blood, full of vitality."

Spirits? Suddenly, Jirom wasn't so keen on the idea. "Let's think of something else. We could find some ropes and rig a line between—"

"Don't be a baby." Three Moons took out a small knife and a little brass dish from his satchel. "Give me your hand and hold it over this bowl."

Jirom hesitated. He'd been raised with a healthy fear of the spirit world and wasn't sure he wanted to meddle with it. But his pride forced him to put out his hand, fist clenched. Three Moons slashed the blade along the heel of his palm. Blood welled up from the cut and dripped into the dish. When the bottom of the vessel was filled, Three Moons handed Jirom a strip of mostly clean cloth from his bag. "Now move away and stay quiet. I need to concentrate."

Three Moons took a flask from his bag, uncapped the top, and took a long drink.

"Is that part of the ritual?" Jirom asked as he wrapped his hand.

The warlock poured a bit of the contents into the dish and mixed it into the blood with his finger. "Not exactly, but it can't hurt."

Three Moons bent over the concoction and began whispering something. Even back when they'd served together, he had never been sure how much of Three Moons' powers was real. He'd seen many men, some of them violent killers, treat the old witch-doctor with a reverence that bordered on the divine. But then again, he'd also seen Three Moons dead drunk in a pool of his own sick on more than one occasion, too.

He was expecting something momentous, like a thundering voice from the sky or a pillar of flame, but there was nothing. Then the hairs on the back of his neck stood up. The blood slowly drained from the bowl as if sipped up by a host of invisible lips.

"Well?" Jirom asked, looking around. His skin crawled as if he were the object of unseen eyes.

Three Moons bent down lower until his face was only inches above the lid. Then he nodded. "They'll help us as much as they can."

"What's that supposed to mean?"

"The psychic atmosphere of this city is choked with the hegemony of the Akeshian cults. The lesser spirits of the land have been weakened over centuries of neglect, like saplings that wither beneath the shade of the taller trees. They'll do what they can, but we can't expect too much."

Jirom shook his head, not wanting to hear any more about spirits and cults. "Just get to how they're going to help us."

"Just watch and be ready to move."

Three Moons went over to the edge of the roof. Jirom worried that a soldier below would spot him and lob a spear in their direction, but the Akeshians appeared to have their hands full with the conflagration, which was spreading faster than before. The flames had reached the third and final floor. Jirom squinted through the haze wafting from the fire, trying to find Emanon on the roof above, but the smoke was too thick. *Come on, you fucking spirits. Do something before those men get roasted alive.*

"What are they waiting for?"

Three Moons had his eyes closed again. Then something snapped within the burning building, and his eyes shot open. "Back!" he yelled. "Get back!"

Jirom jumped away from the edge as the near side of the records house sagged like someone had cut its supports. The building leaned toward Jirom and Three Moons' position with a shuddering creak. Shouts echoed below. Jirom saw what was going to happen and grabbed the warlock by the arm, looking for a safe place to land. Yet there was nothing but hard clay street below. The collapsing structure collided with their building at the moment they leapt.

They landed on the sloped roof of a shed. Jirom held onto Three Moons to take the brunt of the impact but lost his balance when they hit. They slid down the roof, over the edge, and dropped to the street. The warlock fell on Jirom's chest, driving the air from his lungs and almost killing him.

Jirom didn't move for a few seconds as his pains slowly faded. He looked over to where the other man lay on his back with his eyes closed, breathing deeply through his mouth. "You dead?"

"Not yet," Three Moons answered. "But I'm coming around to the idea."

"What in the desert did your spirits do?"

"They couldn't put out the fire, so they did the next best thing. They helped it along, but only on one side. When the supports weakened enough . . ."

Jirom got to his feet. Smoldering timber and plaster had spilled across the roof as the tabularium crashed into the building they had just vacated. Not waiting for Three Moons, he climbed back onto the shed for a better look. A sooty face appeared over the side of the roof, peering down at him. A weight lifted from Jirom's chest as he looked up at his lover. "What were you thinking, getting yourself trapped on top of that building?"

"I wasn't," Emanon said.

More rebels appeared behind him, all of them singed and covered in ash. Jirom was amazed to see so many had survived the fall. It was a miracle. *We'll have to say a prayer to Three Moons' spirit friends. That is, if we get out of this alive.*

Jirom explained what Three Moons had done. Or as much of it as he understood.

Emanon levered his legs over the side and dropped down beside him. "It's a good thing you brought him along. Between you and me, I'd rather see every wizard buried up to their eyebrows. But I have to admit they can be damned useful!"

"I'm not arguing. Come on. The besiegers have broken in through the south gate and are heading to the palace."

"Just a minute. We've got help coming."

"What are you talking about? What help?"

Emanon cocked his head and gestured northward. "Here they come. Right on time."

A square of heavy infantry marched into the slave pens. It was the Bronze

Blades, and behind them followed a mob of people. The crowd didn't have armor or even decent weapons, but they surged behind the mercenaries like a pack of wild dogs.

Emanon grabbed Jirom and gave him a long kiss. Then he said, "I found some new friends while you were gone with your boyfriend."

"So I see. Alyra has a way out of Erugash if we can get there in time."

"Or we could stay." A familiar look twinkled in Emanon's eyes. "We could make our stand here and see how it plays out."

Jirom studied the crowd of fighters assembling around the plaza. "No. You've brought the rebellion back from the dead. Now we have a duty to protect these people."

"Aye. Regroup and come back at the head of a real army. All right. Let's go before this city swallows us in its death throes."

Emanon strode away, shouting orders and asserting some discipline over the mob of newly freed slaves. Jirom went after Three Moons and found him talking to the tall lieutenant of the Bronze Blades, Paranas.

"Ovar didn't make it," the warlock said as Jirom joined them.

"It was an honorable death," Paranas said.

Jirom nodded to the mercenary. "So you have command of the Blades?"

"For the time being. We'll hold a vote for a new captain after this situation is resolved."

"Understood. Send out teams to scout for a safe route to the Garden Quarter. It's in the northwest corner of the city."

The lieutenant left to find his scouts, and Jirom turned to Three Moons. "You ready for one more march?"

"To walk into the jaws of death once more? Sure, Sarge. I'll be right behind you."

Smiling, Jirom went to help Emanon organize the mess. They got underway faster than he anticipated. Half the surviving mercenaries marched out front to clear a path. The other half followed as a rearguard in case trouble decided to chase them. The civilians marched in the center. Jirom estimated there had to be at least a thousand people. Men, women, and children. Old and young. They assembled in a long, shambling snake of humanity.

Somehow their group emerged from the Slave Quarter without incident. In fact, the streets were deserted, though a distant roaring din could be heard in brief snatches. They found another bridge over the canal and crossed it. The scouts led them northwest. Jirom's worst fear was being trapped between the two sides. His fighters were too beaten and worn-out for another extended battle.

Some of the slaves were having a difficult time keeping up, but the healthy people helped their injured brethren along, propping them up with a shoulder and even carrying them when they couldn't run anymore. Jirom waved them along while watching for signs of pursuit.

After several blocks, they came within sight of the palace, spearing above the cityscape. Jirom was about to call for a brief halt for everyone to catch their breath when a mercenary scout ran back from the front of the column. "Captain Emanon is calling for you, sir. We've got a problem."

Of course. Why would I think otherwise?

He jogged through the mass of slaves and rebels until he found Emanon speaking with Lieutenant Paranas. "What's the holdup? Why are we stopping?"

"There's a battle going on west of our position," Paranas said. "Several companies from both the local militia and invading forces."

Jirom looked to Emanon with a bad feeling in his gut. "You're not thinking of hitting them both."

"No, of course not. That would be . . . insane, right? Fine, fine. But we'll have to go around them."

Jirom was about to reply when a scream erupted behind them. One of the freed slaves, a young man with a shaved head, collapsed with a javelin through his back. A company of Akeshian soldiers emerged from a blockhouse, plunging into the column's middle. By their colors, they were part of the queen's own royal guard. *What are they doing all the way out here? And why are they after us?*

Jirom started toward the fray. When Three Moons moved to join him, he waved him away. Then he turned back to Emanon. "You and Three Moons get the slaves out of here. Make for the race track and find Alyra."

Emanon ran with him, shouting back at Three Moons. "You and Paranas take them! We'll stay with the rearguard!"

"Go with the others, Em!" Jirom growled.

"Not on your life. I'm staying with you."

"Then I guess we're both staying."

His lover grinned back at him. "Perfect. It'll be just like old times."

"We don't have any old times yet."

"Then we'd better get to it, because we don't have much time left."

Emanon wasn't wrong. The Akeshians flung more javelins as they cleaved through the slaves and rebels. The mercenaries of the rearguard had advanced to engage the enemy. Hurtled missiles reverberated off shields and cuirass as both sides marched toward each other.

Jirom reached the fighting just as the two sides clashed. He swung in an overhand chop that glanced off an Akeshian helmet and buried his axe in the soldier's shoulder. As that one collapsed, the soldier behind him stepped up, stabbing with a short sword. Jirom wrenched his weapon free and knocked the iron blade aside. More enemy soldiers were pouring in from a side street. Soon they outnumbered the mercenary troop. *This is insanity. We fought so hard and so long just to end it like this?*

The frustration ignited inside him. He was tired of losing men—his brothers. Even though he understood it was an inevitable fact of warfare, that those who dedicated their lives to battle were fated to feel its wrath, it ate at him anyway. If he was going to die today, he would sell his life as dearly as possible and float to Hell on a river of Akeshian blood. "Up!" he shouted. "Up and attack!"

He pushed through the Akeshian battle line. He could sense Emanon behind him, guarding his back, and loved the man more than ever. Sounds erupted from his throat as he hacked at the enemy, guttural growls dredged up from the depths of his rage. There was no technique to his attacks, just blind ferocity. Something bit into his right side where he'd been wounded at Omikur. Jirom chopped through the arm holding the sword that had stabbed him and kept moving.

Then Emanon was beside him, slashing at the enemy with a fury Jirom had never seen in his lover before. Emanon was usually a patient warrior, waiting for his foe to make a crucial mistake, but now he hacked and chopped like he was possessed by a god of war. Together they chewed through the

Akeshian formation. Each time one of them struck down a soldier, the other pushed into the gap, cleaving deeper and deeper into the ranks. Jirom heard grunts and the crash of arms behind him, and assumed the rebels had followed him into the melee. For a moment he regretted that, part of him wishing they had fled and lived to fight another day, but then an incredible rush of pride came over him. He took a moment after felling an Akeshian swordsman to lift his clenched fist and give a loud bellow. He was beyond words now. The sentiment behind the shout was primal. *I am here! Follow me into the gates of hell!*

Bodies piled around them, and the clay street became slick with blood, but there seemed to be no end to the enemy. Behind him and Emanon, the rebel fighters and some of the slaves were exploiting the seam they'd created.

Jirom redoubled his attacks, swinging with every ounce of strength behind his blows. Then, just as an inkling of hope entered his thoughts, the ground shook. Soldiers collided with each other, knocking their brethren to the ground. Jirom grabbed Emanon's shoulder to keep them both from falling down. An Akeshian stumbled toward him, and Jirom dropped him with an axe butt to the face.

The tremor lasted longer than before. Cracks opened across the street and continued up the walls of the nearby buildings. Plaster and pieces of broken brickwork showered the troops on both sides.

As Jirom raised his axe to renew his assault, Emanon pointed. He looked, and his blood cooled in his veins. A woman had appeared behind the Akeshians. There was nothing imposing about her—slight build, a little shorter than average, wearing no visible weapons, but her white silken dress marked her as a member of the upper caste. A *zoanii*.

Suddenly, Jirom was sorry he had sent Three Moons off. He waved for Emanon to retreat. "Get everyone back!"

Emanon looked back and gave the same gesture to the rebels behind them. "Fall back!"

Jirom parried a thrust, deflecting the blow toward an Akeshian soldier on his right who was preparing to split his skull. "No! You go too! I'll hold the line."

"Fuck that!" Emanon blocked a sword swooping toward his head and kicked its wielder in the groin. "I'm staying!"

STORM AND STEEL

With a growl, Jirom jumped in Emanon's direction. "Get your ass——!"

He nearly bit off his tongue as Emanon tackled him. They hit the street hard, with Jirom's head bouncing off the pavement. A second later, an explosion like shattering glass burst above them. A blistering cold washed over the battle, followed by sharp pains slicing into the exposed skin of his face, scalp, and down his left arm. The cuts came from thousands of ice crystals raining down on them, followed by a front of extreme cold. The explosion had the same effect on the Akeshians, too. Frost coated the soldiers' armor and made the street slippery. One soldier yelled as he peeled his sword from his hand and a layer of skin came with it.

In the midst of the chaos, Jirom moved to get up, but Emanon lay slack on top of him, his eyes closed. "Em! Get up!"

But there was no response. Jirom peered over Emanon's shoulder and wished he hadn't. The back of his lover's leather cuirass was shredded, the flesh underneath mangled and torn, exposing white muscle in places. The blood poured off him in streams.

Jirom rolled Emanon off him as gently as possible. He bellowed for help, knowing it would do no good. They were in this alone. A soldier slipped nearby and almost kicked Emanon's head. Jirom shoved him hard, and the man fell back.

Then Lieutenant Paranas appeared beside them. He gave Jirom a quick nod as he and his men formed a tight knot in the middle of the Akeshian formation. After a few furious seconds, the enemy fell back.

The *zoanii* woman had stopped at the rear of the Akeshian unit. Both her arms were upraised as if she were petitioning the heavens. Her lips moved as she stared straight ahead, though her voice was too soft to be heard.

Jirom shouted to Paranas, "Stay with Emanon!"

Then he clambered over several dead bodies to grab a fallen javelin. Yanking it free of its former owner's grasp, Jirom plunged though the melee with the axe in one hand, the throwing spear in the other. Two soldiers moved to block his way. Jirom feinted left and rammed his shoulder into the shield of the soldier to his right, shoving the man back several steps. Before he could regain his stance, Jirom's axe struck the crest of his helmet with a ringing blow. A stab with the javelin sent the left-hand soldier staggering back, clutching a hand to his bloody breastplate.

The *zoanii* had lowered both hands in front of her chest, palms facing each other a handbreadth apart. A ball of bluish light formed between her hands. Jirom spun away from a sword aimed at his face, lifted the javelin, and threw. And cursed as the missile soared over the sorceress's head.

An Akeshian infantryman stabbed at him from the side, and Jirom barely evaded the attack by twisting almost completely around. His axe batted the shortsword away. Bitten by a sudden inspiration, he pivoted on his heel and released the handle.

The sorceress's smile faltered as she looked down at the axe head buried in her chest. Jirom was moving as she fell to her knees. Standing over her, he wrenched the axe loose and slashed, opening her throat nearly to the spine. Then he stood over the body and planted his axe in her skull to make sure she was good and dead.

Breathing deeply, he turned to face the enemy.

The Akeshians were assembling a new shield wall. Jirom smiled. He was ready to die here and now if that's what the gods had decided. *Come on, you assholes. Let's have some fun.*

He took a step toward their lines but halted as a cry broke out.

"For Emanon!" Lieutenant Paranas waved his sword over his head.

The mercenary infantry fell in around him, crossbows loaded and aimed. Their first volley dropped half of the enemy's front line. The second flight routed them.

Once the street cleared, Jirom ran over to Emanon, who was awake and watching the action with weary eyes. "You're like an old dog. Tough as cowhide and damned hard to kill."

Emanon scowled and then winced as something pained him. His face was unusually pale. "I'm glad to see you, too."

"Make some kind of litter so we can carry him!" Jirom ordered.

"Do you have to yell so loud?" Emanon tried to prop himself up on an elbow before he gave up and settled back down on the ground. "It's not fair. Getting old. No one tells you how your body just quits on you."

"That might have something to do with the *sukka* that wizard made out of your back."

Emanon lifted an eyebrow. "What's *sukka*?"

As Jirom explained that it was a food his people made from pounded antelope meat mixed with the animal's blood and a few local herbs, he looked down the street. The sounds of fighting still lingered in the distance. He couldn't tell if they sounded closer than before or farther away.

The mercenaries devised a crude travois from a blanket and two spears. Jirom lifted Emanon onto it and picked up the front handles himself, not trusting anyone else to do it. A merc took the rear grips, and together they lifted Emanon off the street. Lieutenant Paranas sent a squad ahead to screen for trouble, and the small troupe set off.

Jirom tried not to let his anxiety show, but every few steps his gaze dropped back to this man he loved more than he could put into words, and the pallor of Emanon's features pierced through him. *You better make it, you old goat. After all this, you better damned well make it, or I'll come down to the under-world and beat you silly.*

As they ran, Jirom felt a cool hand on his arm. Emanon smiled his wolfish grin as he held on. "This is traveling in style. So much more relaxing than walking. . . ."

The screams of men and horses resounded from the brick faces of the buildings lining the street, filling the air with a harsh discordance that resonated deep within his chest, where it reverberated and intensified, feeding upon itself until Ismail thought the tumult would never end.

The storm continued unabated across the sky, plunging the city into pre-mature night. But rather than subduing the violence, the waning daylight inflamed it, as if every man and woman could sense the inevitability of death stalking their footsteps and it drove them to ferocity.

After being rescued from the fire by Lieutenant Jirom and his old warlock friend, the rebels and mercs, reinforced by the newly liberated slaves, had set out to escape this madhouse. They'd left the Slave Quarter and crossed a waterway into a nicer section of the city. Everything was eerily silent, as if all the people had just vanished.

Stuck in the rearguard, Ismail had been lamenting his poor luck and blaming a large pantheon of gods and goddess for his plight, when a battalion of Akeshian soldiers found them. The two sides engaged without hesitation. Unlike the slaver guards, the Akeshian legionnaires held firm against the merc infantry.

Positioned on the right flank of the formation away from the action, Ismail was trying to figure out a way to attack the enemy from a different angle when Jirom ran past him, whirling a big axe like he meant to cleave through the entire imperial army single-handedly. Captain Emanon was fast on his heels wearing a scary grin. *They might be mad, but I'm sure glad they're on my side.*

Ismail kept his eyes on the side streets and rooftops, ready for any more surprises as his force slowly marched into the jaws of the Akeshian war machine.

"Some party, eh?" Yadz shouted in his ear.

Ismail glared at him, but the nasty look was lost on the man. The rest of their squad was grouped up behind them, a mixture of swordsmen, spearmen, and Red Ox, who held an Akeshian horn-bow he'd found. Every time the man fumbled putting an arrow to the bowstring, Ismail expected to be shot. *Could be a blessing, putting me out of my misery.*

"Sergeant!" a loud voice shouted at him from the company's center.

For a moment, it sounded to Ismail like Captain Ovar's voice. Then he saw Lieutenant Paranas motioning him forward. "Get your squad up front! We have to stop the bleeding!"

Ismail beckoned for his men to stay close as he led them toward the front line. By the time they arrived, Jirom had engaged the enemy. No one could stand before him and that deadly axe. Bit by bit, the center of the Akeshian line collapsed. Jirom waded into the enemy ranks as if he were scything through a field of wheat. Watching as one Akeshian soldier after another fell to the terrible axe, something boiled inside Ismail, fighting to get free. He opened his mouth and out sprung a terrific cry. "Aieeeee!"

It was formless and guttural, but none of his men needed a translation. As one body, they surged forward, and Ismail pushed through the exhausted ranks of the mercenary force. Then he was faced with a wall of Akeshian shields. Jirom was still wreaking havoc ten paces ahead of him, so he charged into the enemy line. For the next several minutes he was too busy trying to stay alive to worry about the larger battle.

The legionnaires fought with a discipline he found at first to be lacking in passion, giving him and his ferocious squad mates an edge. But, as time passed, the cohesion and restraint of their enemy began to take its toll. Yadz fell back with a deep puncture to his shoulder, and Ismail felt the pressure mounting. Sweat rolled down his face and neck, and he'd lost sight of Lieutenant Jirom again. He tried to push deeper into the Akeshian ranks, but it was like trying to cut into a stone wall. A tall shield smashed into him. He caught the blow on his own shield, but the force of it knocked the breath from his lungs. His vision got hazy for a couple seconds until he recovered. By that time, legionnaires pressed in on three sides of him. A cold chill ran through Ismail even as he gulped for the hot, humid air.

So many times he had thought about what it would feel like to die. Oddly, it wasn't as terrifying as he had imagined. A strange tranquility settled over him as he plied his demilance to keep the enemy at bay.

Without warning, something exploded above the street, and a wave of freezing cold swept down over everything. Ismail huddled under his shield and clenched his teeth to keep from yelling as pain sliced through the hand holding the grip. A sheet of frost formed across the bronze as bitter-cold air stole the heat from his lungs. All the combatants—Akeshians, rebel, and mercenary—stopped fighting as the icy blast scoured their ranks. Many fell where they stood.

Ismail swayed on shaky legs as he tried to understand what was happening. Then a platoon of mercenary reinforcements arrived.

"Sergeant."

Ismail turned to find Lieutenant Jirom striding up to him, holding the front of a litter. He was spattered in blood from head to shins. His eyes were bloodshot as if he'd been drinking hard all day. There was something about his gaze that made Ismail nervous, as if this man could turn on him at any moment. Then he noticed Captain Emanon was the man in the litter.

"Fall back with your men," Jirom ordered.

"But we've got them now, sir. If we keep pushing—"

The lieutenant shook his head. The fierce intensity in his eyes diminished, though Ismail could still see it lurking behind the mask of command. "It won't last," Jirom said. "In a minute or two, those soldiers are going to be coming back this way looking for blood."

"But the mercenaries . . ."

Ismail closed his mouth as he recalled the tenement building explosion in Sekhatun. Of course, they knew what they were doing. *Sacrificing themselves for the rest of us.*

Then he realized he had stopped thinking of them as sellswords. As strangers. Somehow, over the course of the past couple weeks, they had become his comrades. *Brothers-in-arms. That's what they call each other. Now I understand. They aren't dying for a cause or for money. They're dying for each other.*

The Akeshian shield wall was re-forming two blocks away. More militiamen poured in from the east to swell their ranks. Any minute they would start advancing again, and this time Ismail doubted the mercs could hold them off. And if the Akeshians got past them, they would chase down the fleeing slaves and massacre them.

As Lieutenant Jirom carried their captain away, Ismail made up his mind. "Shields up!" he called to his weary fighters.

They looked at him as if he were insane. *Maybe I am.*

He returned each look with a firm nod and was amazed as they drew themselves up and returned his nod. Each man lifted his shield.

"Fall back!" Jirom shouted to them.

Ismail lifted his lance in a brief salute and then led the way. The entire squad fell in behind him, charging straight at the enemy. They raced past the mercenary rearguard. The ice on the street made for slippery purchase, but he kept his balance. The rain felt good on his face. Leading with his lance, he aimed for the middle of the hastily assembling Akeshian line.

His initial charge nearly bowled over the first legionnaire in his path. As the soldier staggered back, Ismail thrust his lance. The point dug into the gap between his foe's breastplate and armored skirt to embed in the layer of chain mail underneath. As he tried to wrench the weapon free, something pinched his right knee. All the strength ran out of that leg, and he dropped to the ground. He looked down to see a spear piercing through his knee joint, blood spurting everywhere. *So strange, it doesn't really hurt that bad.*

The spear withdrew and another jabbed down to stab him in the stomach. He had lost his lance in the forest of legs surrounding him. A war-hammer rebounded off his shield and left a dull, distant ache in his forearm. His head felt like it was stuffed with rocks. That image struck him as hilarious, but instead of a laugh, a gout of blood spilled from his mouth. The pain was growing, but he could bear it. He looked back, straining his neck.

The sky was black now. Lieutenant Paranas and his mercenaries were watching, their faces strained and taut. Ismail tried to smile so they would see. *It's a good thing, brothers. The rebellion goes on.*

Peira, remember me.

Inch by inch, his vision of the world turned dark.

The stench of smoke and burning flesh carried on the wind as Alyra reached the street just north of the palace compound. Horace's estate perched amid the other manor houses.

Armed men stood at every gate along the block, even if it was just the household staff holding garden implements and antique pikes. The neighborhood was troubled. *They should be. This city is on the edge of disaster, whether it be conquest by the outside or civil war. Noble blood will stain these streets before long.*

Alyra got out of the way of a white carriage laden with baggage, driven by a pair of burly manservants. The black horses in the traces snorted as they trotted past. She tried to peer inside the vehicle's windows, but the shades were pulled low. Where did they think they could go? Perhaps they thought to bribe the gate wardens to let them out. But where to then? Like as not, they would run straight into the arms of the invaders. If they were wealthy enough, she supposed, they might go free. Or be ransomed. Or perhaps their captors would slap them in chains, to be sold off as booty. *Still, perhaps they risk no more than those choosing to stay here in the imaginary safety of their fine houses.*

When she reached the manor, Alyra found the gates shut and a group of twenty or so people standing outside. More of Horace's admirers. Though soaking wet and bedraggled from the storm, they were singing and chanting with a plaintive tone as if they expected Horace to suddenly appear and protect them.

Harxes, the house steward, was in the courtyard beyond the bars, with staff in hand and a pair of guards. As Alyra made her way through the crowd, she ran into Mezim. Horace's secretary looked as if he had barely survived a traumatic event. His clothing was torn and dripping wet, though he still held his leather satchel tight under one arm.

Alyra suddenly realized she didn't know much about him outside of his official capacity. Did he have a family? "Master Mezim," she said. "Why aren't you at home?"

"Forgive me, my lady. I didn't know what else to do. The First—Lord Horace may be gone, but I believe he would want me here, assisting his loved ones."

"Horace is alive, Mezim."

The relief that filled his face at those words touched her heart. Nearby adherents looked at her with shock. Alyra leaned closer to Mezim and whispered, "We're leaving the city."

He nodded with gusto. "Please, I would accompany you and the master, if you'll have me."

"Of course. Come along. Make way please!"

Mezim helped her push past the people. When the steward saw them approaching, he lifted his staff as if to warn them off, but then he squinted. "Mistress Alyra? Pardon me, my lady! I did not expect to see you here. What are you doing out in the streets alone at a time like this? Haven't you heard? We're being invaded!"

Harxes produced a ring of keys and unlocked the gate. Alyra took his hand. "Thank you. I've come to make sure everyone is safe."

"Of course, mistress. We're all locked up tight here. Anyone tries to loot this house will be in for a nasty surprise!"

"No."

Harxes's bushy eyebrows lifted. "No, mistress?"

She didn't have time to explain everything. "All of you, guards and servants, must come with me. Right now."

"Come? Wherever to, my lady?"

"Never mind the questions for now. Gather everyone. Pack a change of clothing and plenty of food and water, as much as you can carry. Leave everything else."

The steward looked dubious. "I'm not sure I can—"

"Master Harxes, listen to me. The River Gate is falling as we speak. Soon, thousands of enemy soldiers may be marching through these streets. You don't have enough men to hold this position, so either you come with me, or everyone here dies. Do you understand?"

The steward stared at her for a long moment. Then he nodded. "Yes, yes. Of course. Everyone, listen up! Spread the word. Everyone must pack a bag with food and clothing."

"And plenty of water," Alyra reminded him.

"And lots of water! We're leaving with Mistress Alyra. Come, come! Get moving!"

Once the steward was convinced, he became a model of efficiency. Soon the entire household, including Mezim, was rushing about with sacks and sloshing gourds. Alyra went up to the solarium. After a quick look around, she rolled up Horace's meditation rug and tied it with a leather thong that would double as a carrying strap. Then she saw the three gigantic books on his desk. She could tell he'd been reading them, and there were even several pages of notation. *What are you trying to figure out, Horace?*

Grabbing the notes, she yelled down for Harxes to send three people upstairs to fetch the books. Then she stopped by her old room.

It looked the same as when she had left. She dug out some clothes and an extra pair of worn sandals, and wrapped them up in a blanket that she tied off with another thong and slung over her shoulder. She was on her way out when she stopped at the vanity table. The wooden carving Horace had given her still rested there. Delving down into the catacombs under the palace, she'd been consumed with finding him and bringing him back to safety. That was love, wasn't it? For better or worse, their lives were inextricably entwined. She tucked it into the belt of her tunic and rushed out.

Most the staff was gathered in the main atrium, including Dharma, who held a small boy who couldn't have been more than two in her arms and a girl a couple years older clinging to her legs. *This is going to be hard on the young ones, but what choice do we have?*

Harxes tried to maintain order, but everyone was asking questions and arguing about what they should do. Alyra wanted to slink out quietly, but she had given the order. Now she was responsible for them. "Everyone, listen!"

No one looked to her. Instead, everyone continued to clamor at the steward. Harxes stamped his staff on the floor, but the noise only added to the chaos and started the young boy crying against Dharma's shoulder. Alyra gathered herself and shouted, "Listen!"

Her face grew warm as everyone turned to her. "Please. The city is under attack, and we have to leave before it falls."

Her announcement produced a chorus of worried questions, but she lifted both arms to quiet them. "We don't have time to talk about it. I know a way out. A safe way. I'm going there now and I urge everyone to come with me."

"Listen to her," Harxes said. "Lady Alyra will watch over us."

Unsure how she felt about being addressed as "Lady" Alyra, she nonetheless moved through the crowd to the door. Dharma touched her lightly on the shoulder and gave her a smile as she passed. Alyra returned the gesture with a squeeze of the hand. "All right. I need everyone to form a line. Single file. Captain Gurita and his men will walk on either side of us."

She nodded to the guard captain, and he answered with a firm nod. "We're not going to run," she continued. "Just stay together and remain calm. Is everyone ready?"

They surprised her by lining up quietly. The guards stood ready. *I can't believe I'm going to attempt this. I hope someone is watching over us.*

At a look from her, Harxes opened the front door. A gust of humid wind rushed into the house. Rain pounded the walkway outside. Alyra marched out into the storm with the train of servants and former slaves in tow.

Two dozen eyes watched their arrival from beyond the fence.

CHAPTER TWENTY-FIVE

Heavy drops of rain pelted Horace as he trudged toward the plaza. The ground shook as bright flashes of light filled the street at the end of the block where two armies were locked in vicious battle. Broiling flames washed over the soldiers, decimating both sides. Their screams, thankfully, were short-lived. A building on the far side of the plaza collapsed as if a giant invisible foot had come down from the storming heavens to stomp it into a pile of debris. Then Horace saw the robes.

Bright crimson, they stood out in the mob like a tongue of living flame. The man wearing them was tall, or perhaps he only seemed so because of the fiery nimbus that surrounded him. His bare scalp was covered in the red tattoos favored by the Sun Cult's priests, with a large sun imprinted on his forehead like a third, glowing eye.

Horace reached for his power, but his *qa* refused to open. Frustration beat down on him. He had come to help, but he was useless. Powerless. Just a man. *But I've accomplished so much. Does it all end here? What's my problem?*

He looked deep inside himself, and what he found was fear. It filled him to the core, infecting his every thought and action. And he knew the reason why.

In his mind he went back to the roof of the Sun Temple. The bodies of dead sorcerers lay around him, their flesh ruined by the powers he had invoked. He was on his back, fighting for his life. He remembered the pain as Rimesh's dagger pierced his shoulder, the warm flow of his own blood. He relived the sickening terror of what it meant to take a life. It seized his heart and squeezed, robbing the strength from his limbs. In that moment, as the menarch drove the knife down to finish him, Horace hadn't been able to tell which was worse. Dying or killing.

That feeling had haunted him since that night, always lying beneath the surface of his thoughts like a crocodile waiting to strike. It had crippled his ability to use the *zoana*, so afraid his power might kill again. Yet, as he looked out into the plaza where people were fighting and dying, his fears seemed insignificant compared to the raw terror infecting this city. He thought of the pit under the old Sun Temple where he'd been interred to rot, and the cultists who had left Lord Mulcibar's corpse in the street. Then he thought of the queen, hounded at every turn by these zealots who hid behind the aegis of their gods. Like a mythical beast, every time he struck down one pillar of this cult, more sprouted up to confound him.

Horace clenched his fists as the rage trickled through him. If he did nothing, how many innocents would suffer? How much misery would result from his lack of conviction? *I can't let that happen.*

He lifted his right hand, open palm facing the sky, and called upon the power again. For a long moment it refused him, but he was no longer content to wait. He wrenched open the gateway inside him and wrested the *zoana* within.

The power was sluggish at first. He could sympathize. His legs trembled just from standing. His shoulders and back were one solid mass of aches, and all his joints were on fire. Pushing those troubles behind him, he took a deep breath and held it. For a moment, he thought it odd that he was going to try to stop this man—even kill him, if he must—without knowing anything about him. Not even his name. Yet the red robe said everything he needed to know. Whatever happened, he needed to stop this threat now, before it spread to the rest of the city.

He wove his first attack.

The Order sorcerer didn't hesitate. He reached out as if offering his hand in greeting, and instead a crack appeared in the scorched pavement in front of him. The crack ran straight toward Horace, growing wider the farther it extended with a tremendous roar as the clay split and separated. Flames erupted from the crevice, bright gold like molten lava. Horace fell back on a ground that was rapidly falling away beneath him. The extruding fires made him think of the icy power nestled in his right hand. Fire and ice. He slapped that hand palm down on the street at the end of the crack as he rolled to the side. The *zoana* burst from his hand for the brief moment it made contact, then he was rolling away.

Horace got back to his knees beside an overturned fruit cart, braced to leap away again if the crack continued toward him. Yet the splitting of the pavement had stopped, capped by a knot of blue ice. He glanced down the street. The sorcerer strode through the piles of smoking carcasses toward him.

Horace seized hold of his power and sent it out in two separate attacks. The first was a burst of raw fire aimed directly at his foe. Much as he expected, the sorcerer walked right through it without so much as scorching his crimson robes. Then Horace brought in his second attack from above. He used the Mordab dominion to collect as much of the falling rain as he could hold and funneled it directly into the street. The water fell in a startling cloudburst, overflowing the gutters instantly and filling the street within seconds. Then he added a flow of Imuvar, and suddenly everything froze.

The sorcerer jerked to a halt as he was encased in ice.

Breathing hard, Horace lowered his hands. He'd done it. He'd faced his fear and won.

The fighting had moved to other streets, leaving behind scores of bodies. Horace was preparing himself to follow it when a vise of living stone closed around his middle and picked him up. He glimpsed a massive shape approaching from the south. It had a head, two arms, and two legs, but that's where the resemblance to a human being ended. The knot of fear returned in his belly.

A *kurgarru.*

Before he could react, he was hurtled through the air like a doll. He struck something hard, cracking the back of his head, and then everything went dark.

So this is what it means to possess the holy power.

The ground trembled beneath them with every stride, the wet clay cracking as their heavy feet trod upon its face. Their sandals had fallen away, ripped to shreds by their stony heels until only tatters of the leather thongs remained, trailing behind them in the puddles. Abdiel/Mebishnu paused to take a deep breath. As the moist air filled their lungs, which expanded slowly as if made of lead, they looked ahead.

The fall from the sky-ship should have killed them both. It would have, had Mebishnu not used his last instant of life to weave a final enchantment. He'd gasped as the power of Kishargal entered him, a seemingly endless well-spring of power and light suffusing every fiber of his body. His master's dying gesture. As it had turned out, he survived.

They both had, though Abdiel was less sure how he had been saved. He was inside Mebishnu's body, too. A silent passenger. His last memory of his own body was as he fell, certain that death awaited him when he struck the ground. Then suddenly he stopped falling to hang in midair like a puppet on its strings. And yet he could see his body lying on the street below, horribly broken. Then his vision flickered, everything too dark to see.

When his sight had returned, he was in this new body, joined with Mebishnu. He saw what Mebishnu saw, heard what he heard. When this body took a step, he felt the vibrations run up through their legs. He could not explain it, nor did he care to. If this was a dream, he was content to remain asleep forever.

They were transformed. Mebishnu's flesh had turned to living stone. Huge, cumbersome, and indestructible. In another time and place, Abdiel might have been struck with the wonder of this feat, but there was no time for wonder. They burned with fury, and only one thing would quench the awful fire consuming their brain. The destruction of this city.

They started toward the queen's palace, their great arms swinging back and forth with every stride, torso creaking as the hard flesh rippled. The storm continued to crash over the city. Lightning flashed in jagged forks. Rain fell in sheets that washed mounds of garbage and the occasional dead body down the overflowing gutters. None of it concerned them any longer. They could weather anything the tempest hurled down. At last, they had become the perfect weapon of their god. They had become death.

A troop of Erugashi soldiers approached from the north. As the soldiers stuttered to a halt of mass confusion, Mebishnu and Abdiel unleashed their wrath. Euphoria flooded their hardened veins as the *zoana* shot forth. Bright ropes of Girru sizzled in the rain to wrap around entire squads of soldiers. They melted armor and seared away flesh in bloody rivers.

When a file of soldiers charged them, Abdiel/Mebishnu met them with open arms. Their huge, stony hands tore through mail, crumpled shields, and ripped off limbs. When the soldiers tried to flee, they chased them down and crushed their bodies underfoot. Screams filled the plaza with a beautiful music.

As they continued their rampage, spots of light flashed down the street before them. Abdiel/Mebishnu quickened their pace. They saw Brother Opiru in a plaza. A moment of elation filled them to see their brother-priest, but it was cruelly stolen away as Opiru was encased in a tomb of ice. Their eyes turned to the enemy who had done this. A lone *zoanii* standing between them and their righteous vengeance.

Abdiel/Mebishnu reached out with their power and seized the man in a fist of stone ripped from the ground. With a flick of contempt, they tossed the *zoanii* aside. He collided with the wall of a building and fell to the flooded street, unmoving.

They held onto the *zoana* for a few moments more just to feel the energy running through the hardened clay beneath their feet more keenly. Then they started off again, down the boulevard that led to their final goal.

"Are you certain this is the right way?"

Rain pounded the narrow avenue cutting through the Garden Quarter, filling the gutters with murky brown water. Alyra waved at Harxes, who stood a dozen paces behind her with the rest of the household staff, to be quiet. Their trek through the city had been tense up to this point, as sounds of fighting and the storm put everyone on edge, but so far they hadn't encountered any real danger. Until now, possibly.

She was leading a group of more than forty people, as many of those who'd been chanting outside Horace's home had accepted her invitation to join them. It hadn't been part of her plan, but she couldn't just leave them there.

STORM AND STEEL

When they'd finally found the street that would take them to the escape route, Alyra spotted a group of soldiers outside a gated manor house a few blocks down. The soldiers had pushed through the gate before she'd gotten a good look at them. Were they part of the Erugash militia or Nisusi invaders?

She took a few more steps down the avenue, staying clear of the gutter. The homes here were large, each enclosed within its own yard, most of them walled from the outside. They had decorative frames and deep stone gables. Elaborate scrollwork ran up the corners and across the overhanging cornices, depicting harvest designs such as grapevines and fishnets. This section of the city was home to the well-to-do citizens, those who had wealth but not the benefit of a noble title. As such, it attracted syndicate merchants, dealers in rare goods, and successful artisans. There was a reputable collegium nearby where many of these families sent their children. Alyra didn't know who lived at the manor down the street, or why the soldiers were there, but she didn't like the look of it. She was devising an alternate route in her head when Harxes called to her again.

"My lady! I don't think we should tarry here. We're all getting very wet."

She glowered back at him. She didn't intend to be cruel, but the look made Harxes take a step back. Alyra sighed and brushed the rain-soaked hair from her eyes. He was right; they needed to get moving. The longer they stayed in the city, the better chance trouble would find them. She took another look at the open gate. She thought she heard voices, but it was hard to be sure over the storm. She might have tried her luck alone, but she couldn't risk the lives of her charges.

Finally, she hurried back to the group. "We have to find a different way around."

Questions came at her, asking why. Alyra shook her head at them. "No time for arguing. We'll go north and try another approach."

"We're getting close to the wall," Captain Gurita said in a low grumble.

"The Stone Gate, my lady!" Harxes said, referring to the city's northern-most entry. "Perhaps we could—"

She cut him off. "It will be blocked by the enemy. Or, if not blocked, at least watched. It's too risky."

When no one commented, she started up the next street. Three blocks to the north, they discovered a public garden she'd forgotten even existed. The gates were open and unguarded, so Alyra took her people inside. The high fence and rows of fruit trees allowed them to move unimpeded. It was surreal to hurry past the tiers of beautiful flowers, so carefully maintained and manicured, their fragrances filling the moist air, while people were fighting and dying less than a mile away.

When they exited the gardens, Alyra went out first alone. The street was clear in all directions. One block to the south was an intersection. A dappled brown-and-white horse lay dead in the middle of the junction. A draft beast, she assumed by the heavy yoke around its neck. Probably part of a wagon team. It had been cut free of its traces and left to lie where it died. Water pooled around the dead animal. Through the gaps between the large houses before her, she could see sections of the old racing stadium.

Alyra waved to the others, and they filed out, all of them soaked to the skin. The children were shivering despite the humid warmth of the day. Forcing herself to smile, she led them down to the intersection. From there it would be only a short walk to the track. The homes along this street looked vacant, without lights in the windows or signs of occupants within. *Everyone is probably hiding, hoping the danger passes them by.*

Part of her wished she had chosen that option. She could be back at Horace's manor, locked up tight and waiting it out. But she'd heard too many stories about enemy occupations over the years. The Akeshian legionnaire was the backbone of the empire, the epitome of modern military perfection, and yet no force was so feared in all the world because of the terrible cruelties they were known to inflict on the peoples they conquered. Alyra didn't want to experience that firsthand.

When she reached the intersection, Alyra peeked down the avenue running east-west in both directions. There was some movement down the eastern way, but it was far off. Most importantly, the path to the stadium appeared empty.

Motioning for her followers to keep up, she rushed down the avenue. The stadium rose before them. A centerpiece of Erugashi sport when chariot racing was popular, before gladiatorial games came into fashion, its former glory was still evident in the grandeur of its size and design. The high outer walls were battlemented in the ancient style with stone eagles set along the edge. Once they were inside, Alyra hoped they would be safe until Horace arrived. *He'd better be here soon. I don't know how long we can wait.*

She was just about to step onto the brown brick causeway surrounding the stadium when a tremor ran through the wet pavement under her feet. It was more shocking than fearsome. Some pieces of stonework fell from the outer face of the stadium, adding to the detritus of broken brick and overgrown weeds lining its walls, and a flock of black birds flew from the upper levels with a chorus of shrieking caws.

It ended after a few seconds. Alyra waited a moment for her stomach to regain its equilibrium. Then she turned to wave the others forward. As she raised her hand, another quake rumbled through the earth, this one stronger and more sustained. She reached out, but there was nothing to catch her as she stumbled, all sense of balance lost. Many of the household staff fell as well, except for Harxes, who clung to his staff to remain upright, and Dharma, who clung to him, with her children hugged close with one arm.

Alyra was getting back up when she glimpsed movement beyond her people. A mass of soldiers, two or three score, approached from the other side of the intersection. Alyra's heart pounded hard as she saw the crimson and gold colors of their uniforms. Nisusi legionnaires.

"Move!" she yelled.

The sight of the advancing soldiers spurred the people to running. The household guards came in behind to cover their flight. She breathed a little easier when everyone reached the stadium grounds before the soldiers had even crossed the intersection, but her relief died quickly. What would they do now? All she could think of was to get the people inside.

"Go! Go!" She pointed to the nearest gateway. Thankfully, it was not secured by doors or bars, just an open, dark tunnel leading into the vast structure. *Please let it not be blocked inside.*

As the people streamed past her, she watched the enemy soldiers. The rain spattered off their tall oval shields and the planes of their armor. She wracked her brain for an idea. Even if she got the people into the underground tunnels, the soldiers would eventually run them down. She needed a ploy or a distraction, but she was out of tricks. *Now would be a great time for you to arrive, Horace.*

She was standing on the gateway's threshold as the last of the staff entered past her. The guards took up positions around the entrance.

"Go ahead, my lady," Captain Gurita said, pointing into the tunnel with his sword. "You tend to them, and we'll hold the gate."

"No."

"My lady—"

Alyra stopped him with a raised hand. "One moment, Captain. Harxes!"

The steward hustled back to her. "Yes! The way is clear. But where are we to go from here?"

"Listen carefully."

As she started giving him instructions on how to find the escape route, Harxes shook his head. "Your Ladyship, why are you telling me this? You lead the way, and we'll follow."

"No, I'm staying with the guards. We'll buy you the time to get out of the city."

"No!" both Harxes and the captain said at the same time.

"Both of you listen to me! We're doing this my way. Harxes, go inside and help the others find the tunnel. Captain, I'll need a weapon. Not a sword. A spear will do better, I think."

She didn't give the steward a chance to continue his argument but shooed him back inside the tunnel. He didn't understand. She couldn't let these men die out here alone. This was her mission. She would see it through to the end.

The Akeshian soldiers were a short bowshot away now. Their front rank had locked shields with pikes extended. Looking at the row of glittering steel points made Alyra feel sick, but she took her place among the defenders. The guards looked nervous, their faces slick with rain. Alyra wanted to say something to boost their spirits, but it would only be empty words. Each guardsman made some private gesture as he prepared for what was to come, whether it was a whispered prayer or touching his heart and forehead in silent genuflection. All except for the captain, who merely stood in the center of their line, his gaze on the approaching enemy.

"How long can we hold them?" she asked.

Gurita leaned over and spat on the bricks at their feet. Wiping off his chin, he replied, "Long enough."

The Akeshians launched a volley of javelins from their back ranks. Most of the missiles flew too high. Alyra ducked, though none of them came close to hitting her.

"Steady, lads," Captain Gurita said. "Make them come to us if they want to tangle."

Alyra grasped her spear with both hands. The rain made the shaft slippery. Suddenly, she needed to pee, of all things. She couldn't help herself from cringing as bestial war cries broke out in the street. She could see the eyes of the enemy under the ridged visors of their helmets.

The enemy increased their pace to a double-time march, pikes lowered. They were only fifty paces away when a hail of darts and short spears rained down on their formation from behind. The Nisusi advance ground to a halt as commands rang out and the soldiers turned to meet this new threat.

Alyra got up on her toes to try to see what was happening, but she didn't have the height. "What's going on?"

"I can't quite say," Captain Gurita said. "But it looks like we've got some help coming."

She didn't want to believe it, didn't want to get up her hopes only to have them dashed, but it appeared as if another force had come to their aid. The Nisusi ranks were struggling to turn around in the narrow space of the avenue. Fighting exploded on their flank as a small band of men plunged from the mouth of a side street, and Alyra finally allowed herself to smile. "These are friends, Captain. We need to help them."

Captain Gurita nodded. "Lads, form up on me."

Alyra fell in as the guards formed a triangle with their captain at the lead. Gurita lifted his blade, and they all let loose a bellowing shout. As one unit, they charged at the enemy.

She focused on the captain's back as she ran. The distance between the two sides seemed to take forever to cross as her breaths came fast and shallow. Then a screeching clang filled the air. It took her a moment to realize they had encountered the enemy. The captain's sword rose and fell, making an awful clank with each downswing like he was beating a metal drum. Alyra blinked, and suddenly Gurita was several paces ahead of her.

The guards pushed forward to keep up with their commander, but when Alyra hurried ahead a Nisusi appeared before her. His eyes were hard as flint as he stabbed at her with a shortsword. As she'd been taught back in Nemedia, Alyra pushed the point of her foe's attack to the side with the shaft of her weapon and responded with a forward thrust. The spear jumped in her hand as it connected. The head struck his shoulder without penetrating, but her attack spun him halfway around. One of the household guards opened a deep gash across the soldier's throat. Alyra stepped over the dying man and kept moving.

Twice more she found herself facing an enemy, and both times she fended them off. The second time her counterthrust found a gap in a soldier's armor in his armpit and stabbed deep, crippling him for the others to finish off. The momentary victory filled her with conflicting feelings of hope and sorrow, but there wasn't time to dwell on it.

Sooner than she expected, the fighting ended. She leaned on her spear, gulping down air as fast as her lungs could work and feeling like she'd been running for hours. Blood coated the street and mixed with the water in the gutters. Bodies lay everywhere, giving off a horrible stink that lodged itself in the back of her throat.

Then a familiar face approached her. Jirom was covered in cuts and scratches. "You made it," she said.

"Sorry we're late. I had to pull Emanon's nuts out of a fire."

A litter came up carrying the rebel captain. "Don't listen to him," Emanon said. "I had everything well in hand."

"Are you all right?" Alyra asked.

"I'll be fine. Just tired of all this walking and thought I'd take a break. Are we ready to go?"

"Where's Horace?" Jirom asked.

"I'm not sure," Alyra answered. "We ran into some trouble, too, and split up. But I was hoping he'd be here by now."

Jirom looked back toward the palace. "I'll find him. Where did you last see him?"

"Jirom . . . ," Emanon said in a low whisper.

"No," Alyra said. "We can't afford to lose anyone. We have to leave and hope that he catches up."

Jirom looked her in the eyes, surprising her with the depth of his caring. "Are you sure?"

"Yes. Now get everyone inside the stadium."

They worked together to get the wounded fighters into the tunnel. As the darkness closed around her, reminding Alyra of the catacombs under the palace, she hoped Horace was on his way.

His head ached like it was about to split open as Horace staggered down the empty street. The air reeked of ozone and death, a mélange that followed him with every step along with the terrible pain.

He had awoken in a pile of rubble, hurting all over and not sure how he had gotten there. Something had hit him like a kick to the face. Sounds of fighting echoed through the streets, but the plaza had been empty when he came to—except for the numerous dead—and he'd decided it was time to get out of the city. He couldn't stop what was happening here. It had been a fool's errand from the start. He didn't know how many Nisusi had gotten inside the walls, but he was spent. Even if he could think of trying to grasp the *zoana* without flinching, he was tired of fighting. *I've played my role in this disaster. So be it. I'll make my peace with that.*

As he stumbled past scorched and broken buildings, he thought of Alyra. If hope could be trusted, she was already gone from the city. Yet he knew her better than that. She would wait for him, no matter what the danger to herself. He turned north, past shuttered windows and dark empty doorways, following the vague map of the city in his head. He knew the old chariot track was in the northwest quadrant, but he'd never been there in person, so he was relying on Alyra's directions, which he only half-remembered. The sounds of battle grew fainter as he put more distance between himself and the plaza.

The storm made it more difficult to find his bearings. The streets were flooding as gutters overflowed. He could only imagine how much damage would ensue if the Typhon broke free of its embankments.

Horace passed by a park, its tall trees bending to the wind behind stone walls. Just as he got to the end of the greensward, the ground shook. He staggered into the wall as sharp slivers of pain radiated through his chest. He closed his eyes and waited.

When the tremor was over, the pain abated. He pushed off from the wall. Around the corner to the west he spotted a gigantic stone structure above the rooftops of gated manor houses. Gaps showed along the upper edge of the building where bits had fallen away, and the entire outer shell was marred by cracks and creeping vines. This had to be the place.

As he hurried toward the stadium, he crossed another wide avenue where stands of cypress and cedar trees separated the huge houses. The rush of the wind through their branches distracted him for a moment as he listened to the sounds of the storm. Then another quake jarred the street out from under his feet. He fell hard and landed on his elbow. This tremor lasted longer than the first, spanning several seconds before the ground quieted.

Horace's insides were churning as he climbed to his knees. He had to force his arms and legs to move, inch by inch, until he was back on his feet. He was close now. He couldn't give up.

He managed to travel the rest of the block without falling on his face. As he passed beyond the last house and its bulwark of secluding trees, the stadium emerged before him again. A row of broken columns surrounded the lowest tier, their bases eroded down to dingy yellow nubs. Then he saw the dozens of bodies. Mostly Nisusi soldiers, judging by their armor, but among them were men and women with no uniform. A couple wore iron collars.

Jirom's rebels.

Horace found the entry to the stadium. A man in a bronze breastplate lay at the threshold, still holding his spear. Horace couldn't help from looking down at the man's face, and wished he hadn't. It was one of his house guards.

STORM AND STEEL

Horace struggled to remember the man's name, but couldn't come up with it. *Damn me, I never made the effort to know his name or anything about him. He was a stranger who died here.*

Horace glanced around. Why was this man here?

He was about to enter the tunnel leading into the stadium when icy claws scraped down his backbone, filling him with dread. Seconds later, a massive explosion ignited somewhere to the south, but still inside the city.

He flinched as a fireball rocketed from the city center. Trailing smoke, it arced across the leaden sky before falling back to earth. Horace imagined that burning missile was heading straight for him, but it landed several blocks to the east. The impact caused the ground to tremble for a third time, and he feared this episode would never end. Trees bent over sideways, their boles cracked in half, limbs flying away. Stones ground against each other along the stadium wall, expanding the network of cracks and fissures that nature had begun. The uppermost tier sagged outward above his head.

With a desperate lunge, Horace dove into the tunnel. Masonry crashed behind him, throwing stones and gravel after him.

Coughing and spitting out grit, he picked himself up. The rockslide had plunged him into darkness. He staggered down the tunnel with his hands out in front of him. His feet encountered small pieces of what felt like rock or debris, but not enough to impede him.

About forty feet later, he emerged into the rain again. What little light came down from the gloomy sky showed him the inside of the stadium. Tiers of stone seats rose all around him, reminding him of the Grand Arena, although longer and narrower. Most of the track had collapsed to reveal a complex of chambers underneath. Only the long stone island around which the chariots had once raced remained, rising from the ruins like the prow of a great ship.

Horace looked around, suppressing his wonder as he tried to find some sign that Alyra had been here. He knew her escape route was inside the stadium, but nothing more than that. *I hope she didn't try to go back to the house.*

He started making his way down to what remained of the track floor when someone called his name. It echoed eerily through the massive stadium. Alyra waved from a dark tunnel mouth on the other side. A weight lifted from his chest as he hurried along the walkway at the bottom of the stands. She met him halfway with a look of relief that echoed what he was feeling.

"You had us worried," she said.

"Things got ugly." He glanced around the stadium. They appeared to be alone. "Us?"

"Jirom and his crew showed up just before you. Also, I had to go back to the house to pick up some things." He felt himself start to frown, and she hurried on. "Well, I couldn't leave them there alone. It wasn't safe."

"The staff?"

"And a few others."

He put a hand on her shoulder and squeezed. Touching her sent electric currents up his arm. "You did the right thing. So where are they?"

"I sent them along. In case you haven't realized, the city is falling apart."

Seeing the concern on her face, Horace realized one of the things he loved most about her was that endless compassion for others. It was heartwarming, and a little frightening at the same time. What did the world ever do to deserve such sympathy?

Alyra led him to the far tunnel where the floor sloped down sharply into the darkness. "Be careful," she said. "Some of these bricks are loose."

Side by side, they descended into the depths, and Horace tried not to think about what might happen if another tremor struck while they were underground.

Twenty minutes later, he finally began to breathe a little easier. They emerged from a brush-choked opening so narrow they had to turn sideways to squeeze through it one at a time. The roots of an ancient olive tree perched above partially obscured the exit.

They were in a long ravine. The red stone walls rose above the uneven floor. Rain puddles filled the depressions and made the walls appear as if they were dripping blood.

Behind them, the tops of the city walls could be seen above the rim of the ravine. Thunder continued to roll amid the black clouds above, but he hadn't seen any lightning since his battle. He hoped people were finding other ways out, but he had a sick feeling in his stomach that they had left thousands to die. *So what do we do now?*

STORM AND STEEL

A call echoed down the canyon. Horace clenched his teeth as he tried to reach for his *zoana*. Sharp pains erupted inside him like the burning ache of an over-worked muscle. Yet the power came, easing the pain as it flowed through him.

But the man stepping out from behind a boulder fifty feet down the ravine floor appeared to be alone. Alyra waved as if she knew him, and the man waved back as he trotted up to them. He was short and thin with golden skin and quick, dark eyes.

"You're Seng, right?" Alyra asked.

"I am. Lieutenant Jirom told me to wait for you. The rest have moved on."

Alyra took Horace's hand and pulled him along. Amused, and a little excited, he followed along. She glanced over and caught him staring. "What?"

"Nothing. I was just . . . I was thinking I'm very lucky to know you. That's all. This is the second time you've saved my life."

"Third. But who's counting?"

The ravine snaked across the landscape for about a quarter mile before it ended at a drainage ditch between two farms. They tracked through fields of wheat and barley and waist-high squash vines growing out of the dark soil. The storm's intensity lessened the farther they got from the city. After half a mile, the sky cleared, and they were inflicted with nothing more than a driz-zling rain as the afternoon dwindled into twilight.

They left the fields to enter a flat, barren stretch of ground. The plains north of the city were broken with defiles and natural arroyos. Horace tried to remember what lay beyond them but soon gave up. He simply didn't care. Whatever lay before them, it was better than the fate that awaited Erugash. He couldn't see the city any longer, but he felt the power pulsing at its heart.

Seng led them along a narrow path, down a rocky path into another canyon. A mass of people were below, standing or sitting on the stony ground. Hundreds of them.

Horace stopped in his tracks. "All these people! Where did they all—?"

"The slave pits," Alyra answered. "The rebels freed them on their way out."

"There's so many. . . ."

"I'm only sorry we left so many behind."

Jirom and his friend, Emanon, waited at the bottom of the trail. Emanon was wrapped in bandages and looked a little pale, but otherwise he seemed in good spirits.

Jirom clapped Horace on the side of the neck. "I'm glad to see you made it."

"Why does everyone keep saying that?"

Alyra winked. "Well, you do have a penchant for getting yourself in trouble."

Horace gestured to the people camped out along the floor of the canyon. "It looks like you brought your own private army."

"We'll need them," Emanon muttered.

Jirom glanced back at the refugees. "Most of them left with only the clothes on their backs. We'll need food and shelter, a source of fresh water."

"Don't forget weapons," Emanon said. "Shields and helmets, and something more protective than old rags."

"We should keep moving. We're not safe here."

"To where?" Alyra asked.

"This band won't last a minute if we're caught out in the open by a regiment of cavalry," Emanon countered.

"We'll travel at night," Jirom said. "And use the terrain to con—"

"Gentlemen!" Alyra shouted. Faces looked over to see the commotion. "Where do you intend to take these people?"

"Into the desert," Emanon answered.

Jirom gave the other man a glance that looked as if he wanted to argue but said nothing.

"Fine," Horace said. "Choose wherever you want, but get them moving."

Jirom and Emanon exchanged a long glance and then left. Horace was faintly surprised they didn't dispute him. After all, he was the outsider here. *Again.*

Alyra pulled him toward the people. Everyone turned to watch them, which made him nervous. Some smiled, but most wore concerned expressions. Children chased each other and laughed, and no one had the energy, or the cruelty, to tell them to stop.

Horace kept his eyes down, feeling the need to withdraw into himself. So many things were spinning around inside his skull, but mostly he felt alone, even surrounded by all these people. He felt like a piece of him was missing, and not even holding Alyra's hand could completely alleviate his anxiety. He wished for a drink. Spirits or wine. Hell, even beer would've been nice.

He was thinking about his thirst when a voice called out to him. "Mezim?"

His secretary pushed through the crowd to meet him and Alyra. His clothes were in tatters, but he still had his leather satchel in his hands. "It's good to see you, sir."

"I'm glad you escaped."

"That's entirely thanks to Mistress Alyra." Mezim ducked his head as he said her name. "She rescued us all. In any case, I was wondering . . . well, hoping, actually . . . that you might still have need of my services."

"I'm not First Sword anymore, Mezim. In fact, I'm nothing."

There was something cleansing in those words. *I'm not a lord or an official envoy. I'm just me.*

"Of course, sir. But you'll still have need of someone to do things for you. I can cook or clean, and I'm handy with a needle and thread, too."

Horace put a hand on the man's shoulder. "We'll find something to keep you busy."

The look of relief that crossed Mezim's face was almost comical. Bowing, the small man fell in behind them, clutching his satchel tight.

Gurita and three of his house guards approached. Every one of them bore wounds, though nothing too serious. They drew up in a line before him and Alyra. "Permission to escort you, sir," the captain said.

Horace smiled. "Like I was just trying to tell Mezim, I don't need servants, Gurita. But it would be nice to have friends."

"As you say, sir." Gurita motioned, and the guards fell in behind Mezim.

Horace sighed, but Alyra squeezed his wrist. "They need to return to the routine," she whispered.

As he considered that, Horace allowed Alyra to lead him down the canyon floor. Jirom and Emanon were herding the people northward, but the mob moved at a snail's pace.

While they waited, Alyra found a small niche in the canyon wall that was out of the wind. Horace sighed as he rested his back against the hard wall. "I miss my mansion."

"I could really use a bath," Alyra said. "And perhaps a glass of wine."

They looked at each other, and both burst out laughing, which drew sharp looks of alarm from the nearby refugees.

When the laughter faded, he said, "I'm just glad it's over."

"It's not." All mirth was stripped from her voice.

His sigh came from a place deep inside. "I suppose it isn't."

They gazed up at the stars emerging though the blanket of clouds above the canyon bluffs. A cool wind whistled through the canyon. He saw Alyra shiver and moved over to offer her a warm shoulder to lean against, and she didn't move away. *That's a start.*

A young girl brought over a broad leaf holding two small squashes. Horace thanked her and took them. As he and Alyra ate together, he was reminded of the first time he saw her, when she had been a slave in the palace. *And I was something between a captive and a guest. It feels like a lifetime ago. Now everything feels different.*

He recalled the way he'd felt about her on the night of the *Tammuris* as they escaped the Sun Temple, with the rain and the wind beating down on them. He felt the same way now, but also different. Deeper. Even though they'd been apart, he felt like he was finally seeing the real woman beneath the mysterious exterior.

"What do you see in our future?" he asked.

Her gaze remained on the heavens. "The storm is lifting, but more tempests lay ahead. Someone will rise up to take the reins in Erugash. That's how power works. You defeat one tyrant, only to find that you've helped another take her place."

"You make it sound hopeless."

"Not hopeless, just . . . difficult. Much will depend on what Emanon can make of these people. Not everyone is born to fight."

"Maybe we need fewer fighters and more thinkers?"

"Maybe."

She rested her head on his shoulder, and together they watched the stars swim across the sky in silence.

STORM AND STEEL

Jirom watched the crowd filing down the rocky path. A cool wind was blowing down from the north. A pair of mercenaries stood higher up on a canyon ridge, crossbows in hand.

"So what do you think?" Emanon asked from beside him.

About what? Our chances of getting these people anywhere they can settle down without losing most or all of them? No, you don't want to know what I think about that, my love.

"I think we were damned lucky," he finally replied.

Emanon snorted. "Luck doesn't play any part in it. We've got the best damned fighters in the empire. With all these new recruits, we can plan a proper campaign. So what's the plan?"

Jirom shook his head, too exhausted to laugh. "Why are you asking me? You're in charge of this outfit."

"I've been thinking about that. When I was up on that burning roof, I worried about the cause and what would happen to it. Then I realized something. You've been the real leader of this rebellion ever since I found you in that iron box."

"You've taken too many hits to the head, Em. These men love you like a father. It's you they follow."

"Nah, Jirom. I'm just the face of the movement. You're the one they rally behind when the fighting is fiercest. You're who they look to when everything turns to shit. There's no use denying it."

"So what are you saying? You're stepping down?"

"That's up to you. If you're ready to take the reins . . ."

"I don't want the job. I'm content just being one of the grunts."

Emanon laughed, and it turned into a cough. He hacked into his fist for a few seconds before it cleared up. "That's fine. I'll stay on as captain. But this is your unit, Jirom. The gods know I've made enough mistakes. From now on, we'll do it your way."

"We'll see," Jirom said, almost to himself.

The near-death experience may have shaken up Emanon, but Jirom didn't believe for a moment that his lover would turn over the leadership role as easily as that. Emanon lived for the cause. It was more important to him than anything. *More important than me, though he'll never admit it.*

Being in command was never something he'd wanted, even before when soldiering had been his profession. Following had felt so natural, so easy. Yet, as he gazed ahead to the end of the canyon where the trail rose to meet the dusty plain, he found himself planning the next stage of their escape. *Enough time for planning later. Let's just focus on surviving the night.*

Jirom looked over, and Emanon looked back, both of them smiling. And a wellspring of contentment filled his heart. For this moment, despite everything they had suffered, despite all the friends and comrades they had lost, he was happy.

EPILOGUE

The catacombs beneath the royal palace quaked from tectonic disturbances deep inside the earth. Power, pure and raw like a spike to the brain, surrounded him. It filled him up to the point of breaking, making every nerve dance and scream, forcing every sinew and muscle to constrict as they reattached to the bones. The pain was exquisite in its simplicity as it forced him to devote every ounce of concentration to just one thing. Survival.

Up through the molten rock he was pushed by a thousand grasping hands until he broke the surface. The air caressed his ruined flesh like the kiss of a barbed whip. With fingers locked into bony claws, he crawled onto the shore and lay on his back in absolute darkness for many minutes. Then, slowly, the tissues of his eyes congealed until a faint shimmer entered his brain. It gradually resolved into the burnt orange glow of the chamber.

The storm engine.

He turned his head, feeling the liquefied flesh thickening across his face, to gaze at the island. Beyond the shattered remains of the effigies of the Dark Lords, now fallen and half-submerged, nothing more than a pile of twisted metal and wire remained.

Voices whispered inside his skull—compelling him, admonishing him, blaming him, praising him, instructing him. He looked up to the five graven images still looming above, their features swathed in shadow and smoke. He basked in their unholy radiance, so much closer now to this world. *Ancient Ones, you brought me back. What lesson shall I take from this?*

The cavern shuddered, and chunks of rock fell from the walls to splash into the pool. Droplets of magma sizzled on the stone beside him. A reminder, then, that all was not forgiven.

With agonizing slowness, he began the long climb to his feet while the catacombs continued to quiver, the bones of the earth grinding beneath him. He did not fear being buried alive, for his masters would not permit it. Not yet. His destiny still lay before him, only half-completed.

STORM AND STEEL

The sounds of hesitant footsteps buzzed in his ears like annoying insects. His servants appeared and gazed upon him with timid eyes. Only a handful left, not even a dozen. Astaptah grasped the nearest henchman by his throat. Uriom's life energy flowed into him, hastening the rejuvenation process. As the youth's withered husk dropped to the floor, he considered draining another but restrained himself.

Two of his servants aided him out of the cavern, up through the winding tunnels to the surface. The great iron door opened at his touch, and another quake struck as they entered into the lower depths of the palace. While he'd been submerged in the blood of the earth, he had felt the thrum of power unleashed on the surface. He had to see the damage for himself.

The floor of the Grand Atrium was littered with rubble and flora stripped from the botanical display. The outer doors were ajar enough for a man to pass through, but his servants threw them open wide and revealed a sight of devastation such as he had only seen in his deepest dreams. A haze of smoke hung over the city, hastening the advent of night. Fires flickered in different quarters, their flames showing ruined, blackened buildings in stark relief. He couldn't see the battle being waged, but he sensed that blood was being spilled. The ineffable finality of death clung to the air.

They ripped the palace's outer gates from their hinges with their stony hands and threw them over their shoulder to crash in the street behind them. No sentries stood in their way as they strode into the compound. Mebishnu/Abdiel's eyes never wavered from the apex of the queen's palace.

The great dome at the summit was shrouded in mist and rain, though the steady barrage of lightning reflected off the golden surface in a thousand twinkling points.

Their strength had only increased on the trip through the city as they learned to work together. Abdiel had discovered that, although Mebishnu retained ulti-mate control of this body, he could assist with the motor functions to a certain extent. When they grabbed something, he clenched their fingers for a tighter grip. When they marched, he lengthened their stride. He had never felt so powerful. It was euphoric, like drinking nectar from the heavens.

They were halfway to the palace proper when they spotted a figure coming out the main entrance. The person looked tiny between the winged statues flanking the entryway. He was definitely a man, bone-thin, and wrapped in a gray mantle, but there was something wrong with his skin. It was sooty black as if he'd been burned in a great fire. He looked down at them with deep-set yellow eyes. *Is this the foreign sorcerer?*

They marched forward. Abdiel clenched their mighty hands into fists to smash and crush, and allowed Mebishnu to control the *zoana* that surged inside them. Now they would finally deliver their retribution for the temple that had been destroyed, for the Order brothers slain and desecrated, for the insults done to the name of their most perfect Lord.

A cold wind washed over them, its chill penetrating through the stony armor of their flesh. A stench floated on that breeze, like a rotting carcass left lying in the hot sun.

Mebishnu began the action that sent them running on long, lumbering strides, and Abdiel tried to focus on keeping them from tripping over their own feet. Yet he felt the power stirring inside them, building up like a miniature sun inside their chest. It both excited and frightened him, but he had faith in his master. *Almost there! Another dozen paces and we'll smash this pitiful creature aside. Then we'll enter the palace as the rightful conquerors!*

They almost laughed when the man in gray lifted a blackened hand. Why didn't he flee for his life? Was he demented? A fool? They saw deeper into his eyes now, glowing like pools of molten copper. There was no fear there. Abdiel's confidence began to waver, but it was too late now. They had reached the short flight of steps that led up to the palace portico. Their *zoana* surged.

Then, without warning, the power left them.

They stumbled halfway up the stairs as the strength poured out of them. Their limbs were suddenly too heavy to lift, and so they hunched on the steps with barely enough vitality left to lift their head. The fire that had surged inside them was gone, snuffed out in an instant.

STORM AND STEEL

The burned man stood above them at the top of the stairs. Abdiel/Mebishnu tried to climb, but they had nothing left. Abdiel felt his master reaching for the *zoana*, but it was gone. Beyond their grasp like a delicious meal behind glass.

Their adversary looked different now. Sturdier. His skin wasn't as charred as it had been a minute ago. Perhaps it was just seeing him up-close, but they didn't believe so. *No, he's changing before our eyes. Getting stronger, even as we weaken.*

Breathing was becoming more difficult with each passing heartbeat because they lacked the strength to move their lungs. Black spots appeared in the air. They strained to rise up, one last time for the glory of the Sun Lord, and strike down this evil menace. Their sluggish muscles creaked but refused to move. *We are betrayed by the very power that saved our lives. Amur, aid your servants!*

A stab of pain blossomed in the pit of their stomach. There was no source, no attack to cause it, and yet the pain remained. They clenched their rock-hard tooth ridges to keep from groaning. *We won't let you see the pain, demon! Die! I wish you a thousand deaths! May your spirit be rent by every fiend in Absu. I spit on your family's name and the ashes of all your ancestors. Die and die again!*

Another ripple of agony burst in their chest, moving upward through their vitals as if drawn by a lodestone. Heat like nothing they had ever felt rushed up their throat, and flecks of orange ichor dripped from their mouth, sizzling where it landed on the wet steps. With a grunt, they collapsed and slid down the stairs to the broken pavestones below. The rain poured in their eyes, its coolness a blessing against the awful heat expanding inside their chest.

The foreigner was hale above them now, his flesh a deep rich bronze with no trace of burns or scars. An emerald corona hovered about his head as if he were wreathed in lightning.

Hatred rose up inside them, deeper and blacker than their hatred of the night. *How did we fail? Holy Lord, where did we go wrong? We are your most faithful servants . . . Master . . . Oh, my son. My son.*

With a shuddering moan, they closed their eyes against the rising tide of pain and darkness.

Astaptah's gaze dropped to the huge, ungainly thing lumbering toward the palace. Its flesh resembled jagged stone in hues of gray and black, as if it had pried itself loose from ancient bedrock.

The *kurgarru* made a noise like two massive boulders grinding together as it approached with ground-shaking strides. When it reached the steps, it swung both arms as if to smash him between its massive fists. Astaptah held out his hands, palms down. The rush of eldritch power flowed out of him, and the *kurgarru* fell to its knees, causing the stairs to quake with its impact.

Astaptah saw inside the elemental, saw its stony heart slow as the Shinar burrowed within. Then it slid to the ground and lay still.

Astaptah looked past the dead thing, which was now shrinking and twisting into a semblance of two men, side by side in death. His gaze raked the city's skyline. *The dawn of a new empire arrives. It all begins with a single seed.*

Thunder crackled across the sky. Astaptah closed his eyes as it rolled on and on, growing louder with every beat of his heart. The afterimages of emerald lightning danced behind his eyelids, and with each strike a spot of darkness blossomed within the city, spreading outward like a drop of black ink in a glass of water. The circles of darkness grew, converging as they expanded. Everywhere they touched, life was extinguished. Snuffed out in an instant. And with each death, Astaptah felt his power increase. He held onto it until the blots of darkness filled every corner of Erugash, until every life remaining within the walls had been consumed. Then he released it in an intoxicating rush of raw chaos.

For several minutes, there was only silence. The thunder abated, the winds died down, as if the entire world was holding its breath. Then came movement. Slow, almost lethargic movement, yet it was inexorable. Figures appeared in the street, staggering toward the palace. Astaptah opened his eyes at last to see his army. Their vacant faces turned to him. All the people of Erugash and every invading soldier, united together in undeath.

The crowd sighed when he raised his hands. Their hunger was a palpable thing. *Soon you shall feed. What I have begun, I shall finish. The old barriers are falling. The time of the sky gods is at an end. It is time for a new age. An age of chaos.*

Lightning slashed the sky once again as he sent his followers out to begin their voracious conquest. Overhead, storm clouds reached out to span the firmament.

HERE ENDS THE SECOND PART OF
THE BOOK OF THE BLACK EARTH.

ABOUT THE AUTHOR

Jon Sprunk is the author of *Blood and Iron* (The Book of the Black Earth, Part One) and the Shadow Saga—*Shadow's Son, Shadow's Lure,* and *Shadow's Master*—which has been published in seven languages worldwide. An avid adventurer in his spare time, he lives in central Pennsylvania with his family.

Author photo by Jenny Sprunk

Author website:
www.jonsprunk.com

Social media:
Facebook: JonSprunkAuthor
Twitter: @JonSprunk